ENIGMATIC DESCENT
GASTONS GORGE

JASON POKOPEC

TATE PUBLISHING
AND ENTERPRISES, LLC

Published by Tate Publishing & Enterprises, LLC
127 E. Trade Center Terrace | Mustang, Oklahoma 73064 USA
1.888.361.9473 | www.tatepublishing.com

Tate Publishing is committed to excellence in the publishing industry. The company reflects the philosophy established by the founders, based on Psalm 68:11,
"The Lord gave the word and great was the company of those who published it."

Book design copyright © 2015 by Tate Publishing, LLC. All rights reserved.
Cover design by Samson Lim
Interior design by Jomar Ouano

Published in the United States of America

ISBN: 978-1-68207-221-9
Fiction / Action & Adventure
15.09.18

ENIGMATIC DESCENT

To my brother, Jeffrey "Vinny" Pokopec, who passed away on July 13, 2008. You are missed and loved by many

ACKNOWLEDGMENTS

I would like to thank Kevin Liston for all of his time spent help-ing edit this book. Special thanks to my mother, Barbara, for all you have done throughout my life. A very special thanks to my wife, Billie, for going through this with me and my daughter, Monica, for all of your great ideas.

PROLOGUE

September 28, 1994

Through windswept leaves the little blonde-haired girl skips past a row of scarlet oaks and breaks into a sprint along the road's edge, putting more distance between them. Thirty yards behind, her brother walks along the blacktop with his head in the clouds, lost in his own little world as usual. Taking advantage of the boy's absentmindedness, she hurries past the intersection of Beanery Hill and Barrow Street and sprints toward an ominous structure towering above a row of ailing pine trees lining the front yard. She dashes across the wet street, glances over her shoulder, and sighs in relief.

He is nowhere in sight.

Despite mild panic fluttering through her gut, she races toward the ghostly building thinking it would be the best place to hide and watch the boy act like a fool. Golden locks sway across her pale blue eyes as she squeezes through the pine trees, ducks around the corner, and stops dead in her tracks on a moss-ridden concrete slab that looks like it might have once been a fancy sidewalk. Feeling confident, she kneels on the ground and takes a quick peek around the corner of the building, eager to see the daunted expression on her brother's face.

High above, charcoal clouds eclipse a luminescent autumn sun, casting long black shadows across the landscape.

Moments ago, her gargantuan shadow danced across the aged gray stone as if a fabled champion guarded her courage. Now, as her silhouette shimmers across the dying brown weeds and stretches into the skeletal forest, a disquieting fear of being alone sends shivers along the small of her back. A deep need to abandon the hiding place arises; however, she feels obligated to stick it out a while longer. As a soft breeze blows chilly air on her face, she appreciates the light blue windbreaker her brother Ethan convinced her to wear.

In the oak trees across the street, a raven caws a discordant tune.

Her heart races as her brother appears around the corner. He kicks soggy leaves across the mud-streaked pavement like a slapstick comedian in desperate need of a laugh. A lackadaisical grin rolls across his lips as he glances toward the scarlet oaks, stumbles into a small embankment, and falls flat on his face in the squishy mud.

Running a finger through her hair, she chuckles.

With an outstretched hand, he pushes up off the ground, wipes the wet leaves from his faded blue jeans, and scrutinizes the street with two humiliated eyes. After a deep breath, he wipes mud from his sneakers and limps toward a steaming storm ditch at the bottom of the hill with a comedic scowl stretching his face. With both hands cupped around his eyes, he glares at the pines that obscure his view.

A feeling of sudden remorse chases away her soft laughter.

Across from a yellow metal gate on the corner of Beanery Hill, he kicks loose gravel into the sewer with both hands jammed deep in his pockets. "Lauren," he shouts with a look of skepticism in his soft blue eyes.

Absorbed in his apprehension, she clings to the stone like a spider toying with its prey and watches his every move. Deep down, she wants to step out and end his misery, but a mischievous part of her desires the satisfaction of seeing the panic twisting his face into amusing shapes. Though a touch of shame overcomes her, an unfamiliar need to watch his frustration escalate prevails. With a feeling of insecurity, she continues to endure the childish game of hide-and-go-seek that her brother does not realize he is a participant in.

Across the street, his panic escalates.

She leaps to her feet and sneaks to the opposite side of the building for a less obvious vantage point to keep an eye on the nervous boy. With a tinge of satisfaction, she watches as he paces back and forth between the sewer ditch and the yellow gate.

"Come on, Lauren, come on out! This ain't funny."

Despite the guilt she feels for tricking her older brother, she watches as he abandons the street and walks sluggishly up the steep hill as the neighborhood dogs woof their displeasure. Though she feels sympathetic, she has no control over the soft laughter that tickles her throat.

"Come on out, Lauren," he shouts again. "I know you can hear me." His eyes shift back and forth between the neighboring yards and then focus on the building she takes cover behind. "Get your rear end out here right now," he screams. After a few minutes of indecision, he descends the hill and stops to the right of the gate near a dirt road that zigzags toward the railroad yard. His eyes dissect the woods behind her as an irritated frown twists his mouth into a humorous shape.

She dislikes putting him through this cruel game; however, he has no choice but to give her his full attention for once. Her heart beats faster and faster as he seems to grow more anxious with every failed response to his panic-stricken pleas. She derives a plan—simple yet ingenious. Enjoy the game a few more minutes and then spring out and scare the pants off him.

"Come on, Lauren," the boy shouts, "this really isn't funny anymore."

Covering her mouth, she fights back laughter.

His eyes abandon the darkening woods, scrutinize the building she hides behind a few drawn-out seconds, and then shift back along the dirt path toward the railroad yard. Rubbing his palms nervously, he kicks the ground, scattering pebbles through the high brown weeds beyond the yellow gate, and then he disappears behind the trees along the trail.

Feeling an eerie sense of fright, she inches closer to the edge of the building, crouches down on one knee, and stares through the branches hoping to catch a glimpse of his bright red shirt. No luck; he's nowhere to be seen, and she suddenly feels alone. She gets up off the ground with intentions of running back around the corner but stumbles on a jagged piece of wood embedded in the waterlogged yard. Humiliated, she crawls up off the ground, brushes the mud from her clothes, and scurries back along the side of the building. With an amplified pulse pounding through her temples, she surveys the dreary landscape but sees no sign of Ethan. In her mind's eye, she imagines him rummaging through box cars, thinking she might be hiding somewhere in a dark corner of a deserted passenger train. *Not in a gazillion years,* she thinks. The thought of the discarded train cars that house the murderous vagrants Ethan warned her about leave her skin chilled to the bone. Unable to shake the image of a knife-wielding hobo wanting to hurt her, she decides to end the game and let both of them off the hook.

A branch snaps from behind.

The morbid thoughts of murderous vagrants depart from her mind. She whirls around, expecting to see a condescending smile on her brother's face. Instead, a hulking figure cloaked in doleful black robes towers above her. Unlike her indecisive brother, something evil has no trouble discovering her hiding place.

Birds scatter from branches in the woods behind her.

She tries to scream, but as she stares at the horrified expression reflecting through the thing's dismal red eyes, no sound seeps from her mouth. Swooping down with a dark leathery hand, it shrieks, stinging her eardrums and shattering her hope. She staggers back, scrapes her fingers against the coarse stone, and feels confused as her head squishes into the muddy earth. Paralyzed by fear, she stares into its eyes for what seems like hours and hours and feels pure terror as it reaches for her. She attempts one last cry for help as it clutches the front of her jacket with two large powerful hands, drags her through the squishy black mud and stinging wet grass, and jerks her into the building. She fights but is overpowered with ease. Her fingernails dig into rotted wood and hold an agonizing second before the wood is brutally ripped from her hand. The last thing she sees as it carries her into darkness is Ethan leaning against the dull yellow gate with a bewildered expression on his face and frantically yelling out her name.

PART I

DESCENT INTO DARKNESS

1

October 29, 2003

Until a deadly car crash shattered his world early in the winter of 1998, Ryan Laville looked forward to a brilliant future with the girl of his dreams. He planned on making her his wife, but that was a long time ago. Back in those days, he lived a carefree and happy life filled with high hopes and endless possibilities. That was five years ago; now Ryan took solace on back trails in remote wilderness. He enjoyed backpacking, and like everything else these days, he preferred doing it alone.

A few hours before the sun rose into the darkening New York sky, he gathered a few items from his parent's home and slid behind the wheel of his dinged-up tan Ford Pinto with no destination in mind. He crossed the narrow bridge spanning the Red River, instinctively turned left, and drove for the interstate as the small town of Raging Gap grew smaller and smaller in the rearview mirror.

He planned to never set eyes again upon the town he once loved.

After years of wallowing in self-pity, he deserted the town that once considered him a football hero and drove away in search of a fresh start. The town of Raging Gap left many memories—both good and bad—but over the last several years, the bad outweighed the good by a wide margin. With an attempt to leave behind the guilt he felt surrounding his girlfriend's death, he drove southeast across New York, through the scenic Adirondack Mountains, and into the keystone state. Several hours later, he arrived at Falls River, an isolated town deep in the hills of Southwestern Pennsylvania. He parked at the far end of a vacant lot next to an unfamiliar trail that carved its way through infinite wilderness, grabbed his backpack from the trunk, and walked to a large sign erected at the base of the trail. He stood a minute and read the sign out loud. "Greater Allegheny Passageway," he whispered. He smiled, thinking it was as good a place as any to separate himself from the cold hard world that has become his reality.

With only the familiar guilt to keep him company, he hiked along the trail, admiring the beautiful scenic landscape that only the hand of a marvelous God could create. He sat for a while on a bench and watched a dozen or so kayakers manipulate the rough waters of the river until they disappeared around a bend far in the distance. After the kayakers were gone, he sat a few minutes longer and felt envious of the freedom the men must have felt floating with the currents of the river. With no sense of time or direction, he followed the trail and passed over a long wooden bridge that spanned the river. He walked backward until the bridge was no longer in his sight. Later, he came across a campground with aged, decrepit huts that looked as if they had once been marvelous and thought about the camping trips his father used to take him on years ago. A few miles past the old campgrounds, he deserted the main path and trampled through the wet brown leaves, jagged underbrush, and broken tree branches with a smile of freedom on his face. Though completely lost in acres of strange woodlands, he felt alive for the first time in almost five years.

Leaves crunched from behind, and the sound of a hollow twig snapping echoed through the forest.

Spooked by the sudden noise, he spun around to investigate the disturbance. Instantly terror melted away his newfound feeling of serenity. Warm blood drained from his racing heart, leaving his body cold and his mind on the verge of lunacy.

Twenty feet in the distance, a large, manlike figure draped in a long black hooded robe broke through the shrubbery toward him. He tried to run, but two wobbly legs rendered his body useless. He screamed as the thing's evil crimson eyes blinked behind its malevolent hood. As it closed the distance, Ryan was reminded of a sunset he once admired after playing a game on the road. That night, while his teammates celebrated victory, he wandered upon a deserted hillside with a breathtaking view of the town below. As the sun crept toward the far horizon, the sky turned a mysterious shade of ebony blue in the starless and cloud-free night. The breathtaking scene left him feeling magical, like a supreme being overseeing a new world. The next day, he described the mysterious sunset to Molly as an enigmatic descent. The robes covering the hulking figure bearing down on him were the same color as that sky.

In seconds, it closed the gap.

Ryan screamed.

His legs felt as if they were submerged in quicksand.

Birds scattered from the tree branches above, leaving behind a dangerous silence.

Unable to move, he watched in horror as it pounced upon him like a wildcat on a hapless field mouse. At that moment, he felt pure terror. As its hot, rancid breath stung his nostrils, several powerful blows pummeled the side of his face. Overcome with dizziness, he struggled to hold on. He tried to take a deep breath, but a leathery, muscled backhand sent burning agony into his cheek and bit deep into the bone.

Specks of floating silver filled his vision.

Like a deflating balloon, warm air rushed through his lungs, and strength deserted his muscular frame. Gritting through the pain, he collapsed to the ground, and his head slammed against a tree stump hardened by the chilled autumn air. Struggling to hold on to reality, he tried to squirm backward, but two powerful hands seized his ankles and jerked him forward through the soggy brush.

He screamed again.

As bulbous white clouds drifted across a swirling gray sky above, he slipped from the conscious world.

As usual, Molly filled his dreams.

2

Leaning against a faded yellow gate, Ethan Wysong stared at the massive stone structure he knew was responsible for nine long years of vivid nightmares and regretful memories. Though no one took him seriously, he had always felt the place was somehow connected with his sister's disappearance. Only Devon Whitfield, a lunatic with beady black eyes and a bald pastel scalp, agreed with him. In fact, it was his old roommate and only friend at the Peaceful Lady Mental Institution who convinced him to return to Gastons Gorge and search for the truth of what happened that day.

Consumed with guilt, he glanced away, not wanting to gaze upon the dismal building a second longer. Instead, he watched dirty rainwater flood the shallow grooves in the dirt and flow like a miniature stream toward the old railroad yard where he played as a kid.

A faint smile crossed his lips as memories of a better time teased his mind.

He remembered hanging around the old boxcars along the unused tracks. One warm summer afternoon, Ethan and his friends found a passenger car stocked full of thin, mildewed, and rotting mattresses. After piling them high off the ground, they spent hours diving from the rusted roofs of the broken-down train cars onto the springy cushions. It was innocent fun, and no one got hurt. At the end of each day they would stash them in a gutted passenger car and skulk toward home looking forward to tomorrow. They played on the mattresses a few dozen times that summer until one day when they heaved the rusty doors open and they were gone. He missed those innocent days spent with boyhood friends. The biggest dilemma back then was thinking of new and exciting things to do with the guys.

As the memory dissolved, he glanced across the road and felt the smile depart his lips. At the bottom of the big hill, a sun-bleached street sign reminded him that life could be cruel. As he read the name of the street silently, his thoughts returned to Lauren.

Hard to believe it's been nine years.

"What happened to you?" he whispered, once again glaring at the building. "I know I'm right. You're still alive somewhere, and I'm gonna find you."

Devon's raspy voice echoed through his head. *They never found her. If she was dead, they would have found something. I'm right, and you know it. Go back there, find the truth, and find her.*

With tears blurring his vision, he climbed down from the chilled metal railing, splashed through a shallow puddle, and took two steps toward Barrow Street intending to head home for another evening spent obsessing over his sister's disappearance. Filled with the usual regret, he glanced at the heavens, searched for signs of a higher being, and wondered why this happened. High above, radiant streaks of purple and silver merged into smoldering orange vapor casting dark shadows across the land. Beyond that, the sun dipped deeper into the horizon, nearly restoring his faith in God. As he stood in awe watching nature begin her nightly ritual, Ethan felt at peace with the world.

A dog's raucous barks disrupted his thoughts.

Instantly the feeling of peacefulness dissolved.

Startled, he whirled backward and reached for the steel railing. Where the road disappeared around a corner, a German shepherd stood its ground with an intimidating stare. With sweating palms, he gripped the top of the gate and hoped the dog would pass by without a confrontation or retreat the way it came.

Instead, it stood with both ears pointed to the brilliant sky and scrutinized him with a look of uncertainty in its big brown eyes. Thinking the dog may attack, Ethan scaled to the top rung, slid a trembling left leg over the upper rail and scooted to the edge with both hands clamped around the bar below him.

The dog growled as if it wanted to attack but decided to wait him out instead. Only a couple of seconds ticked by, but it felt like an eternity. Tension swelled deep in his gut as chills rippled underneath his skin. If he ran, the dog might attack, despite its tail tucked between two hind legs. Seeming content with the distance between them, the Shepherd glanced backward along the road.

He grinned at a sudden realization.

The dog wasn't alone. It was obviously waiting for somebody. Relief swept through his shuddering frame, easing his panic to a mild buzz. A confrontation seemed unlikely, or at least he hoped so.

After another raucous bark, the dog glimpsed over its rigid body as a girl rounded the corner and moseyed along the path toward the main street. She seemed unaware that a stranger was watching her every move.

His eyes widened, and drums pounded deep in his chest.

Long strawberry blonde curls swayed below her shoulders and dangled across her back. On her head, a worn blue baseball cap accentuated a complexion fit for a goddess. She wore faded blue jeans and a burgundy sweat shirt with the words Red Raiders etched across the front in cracked white letters. She looked no older than in the early twenties, no younger than in the late teens. She was tall, slender, and gorgeous.

She walked nonchalantly along the road past the dog, appearing to be absorbed in deep personal thought.

As she drew within a few feet, his head buzzed from the mesmerizing beauty sparkling deep in her eyes. They were a stunning shade of green that reminded him of an elegant actress he once saw in an old black-and-white movie from another era. The actresses' name escaped him, but like the girl walking gracefully along the path, her beauty was forever etched into his memory.

"Come on, Sage," she mumbled. "We don't have much daylight."

Left with a numbing knot in his gut, he grinned as a look of shock widened her thick, red lips.

Her feet came to a dead stop as her eyes met his.

3

Caught off-guard, Josie McShay came to a stop a few inches in front of a wildly handsome young man with shoulder-length black hair and warm, soft blue eyes stretched out on the top rung of the old railroad gate to her right. Quickly, he sat upright, waved a sluggish hand, and threw his leg over the railing with a humiliated expression on his face. He seemed nervous, and that stirred waves in her imagination.

"Howdy," he said.

Sage glanced up, barked twice at the boy as if voicing his disapproval of his master talking to a strange man. As usual, Sage made her feel secure. She mulled over the idea of walking on by without returning his pleasantries but found herself standing in the middle of the road with a perplexed look on her face. Nudging Sage with her foot, she smiled as he abandoned his guarded position and walked slowly toward a bulky maple tree to the left of the gate.

"Sorry about my dog," she said, feeling the smile diminishing on her face. "He usually doesn't act like that."

The boy shrugged, and the grin disappeared from his handsome face.

"It's just that he's a little bit protective of me is all."

"No apology necessary," he said and climbed down from the top railing. He seemed more relaxed than he was a few seconds earlier. "My name's Ethan Wysong."

"I'm Josie, and my overprotective companion here is Sage."

"It's a pleasure to meet you both."

"Are you from here? I mean, are you from Gastons Gorge?"

"Once upon a time I was," he said. "Why, do I look familiar?"

"No, but your last name rings a bell."

With a faint smile, he shrugged.

She felt the tension slip away. Her initial awkwardness faltered as the conversation wore on. Feeling more and more comfortable, she giggled and pointed to the ivy-plagued structure across the graveled road. "So tell me something, Ethan Wysong. Why in the world are you hanging out down here across from that awful place?"

"No reason. I Guess I just had a touch of cabin fever, and this is where the yellow brick road led me."

For a moment, she thought she might have said something wrong. His face tightened at the mention of the building, but it relaxed a few seconds later.

He stood in silence and stared at the building as if mesmerized by a powerful wizard's spell.

Josie turned to look. "You know what they say about that place?"

"Nope, I don't have any idea what you locals say about that place. I'm not from here, remember?"

"They say it's supposed to be haunted."

"Really, who says that?"

She chuckled. "Only almost every person in this town."

"Well what do you think?"

"I guess I never really gave it much thought," she said, beginning to dread the direction the conversation was taking. "I can see how people might get that idea. It is pretty big, ugly, and scary-looking."

The smile returned to his face. "Yeah, I'd say it looks like a ghost or two might have rattled some chains deep inside."

Despite knowing this boy only a few short minutes, she liked him. It was something about his smile that made him seem trustworthy. The longer they talked, the more comfortable she felt. Usually she was a person of few words, but for some reason, he inspired her to ramble on. For the first time in a very long while, she felt at ease in the presence of another human being. As if Sage could read her thoughts, he plopped down in a dry patch of soft grass under the skeletal maple. After a low whimper, he dropped his head on the ground and closed his eyes. He looked as comfortable as she felt.

"Actually, that place kind of creeps me out."

"I hear you," he said. "I wouldn't go in there for a million bucks."

"Me either," she said and glimpsed at the once grand hotel.

He sounded genuine, like he knew something about the place she didn't. She remembered hearing stories when she was younger, but they meant nothing to her. It was just that one place in town with a metaphorical black cloud hovering high above it.

Sage raised his head and growled, interrupting their conversion.

Falling backward, Ethan flinched and banged his elbow off the metal railing. He reached back with a wide-eyed grimace and massaged his arm.

With the hair on his back pointing at the sky, Sage jumped to all fours and glared in the direction of the old building with his teeth bared in what she perceived as anger. His deep, guttural barking chilled her bones, and thousands of short brown hairs rose across the dogs back. Birds scattered from the trees lining the backyard, confirming something wasn't right.

Unaware of what had her normally gentle animal in a frenzy, she grabbed Ethan's jacket sleeve with a trembling hand, dug her heels into the loose dirt, and spun around to see what had Sage agitated. Her jaw dropped in disbelief. Dashing through knee-high grass stretching across the backyard, a hulking figure fully clad in black dragged what looked to be a man around the corner of the building. Unsure if what she saw was real or a figment of her imagination, she spun backward and stared at Ethan. An eerie look of fear and confusion on his face proved her eyes witnessed the truth.

Sage stood a few seconds with his teeth bared and then sprinted through the yard and disappeared around the corner.

With a horror-stricken look in his eyes, Ethan jumped off the railing and chased after Sage, squishing through soggy brown grass and high weeds. Running with graceful agility, the boy followed the dog around the corner, leaving her alone on the road with both hands clutching her trembling hips.

4

As his muscles worked feverishly to keep pace with the dog, Ethan dared a peek over his shoulder and nearly collided with the cold stone wall of the old hotel. The terrified expression on Josie's face painted a clear picture.

She saw it too.

Guided by the sounds of infuriated growls and nails violently scratching against wood, he skidded through the slippery grass and hurried around the corner, leaving the petrified girl behind to eat his dust.

Sage stood on two hind legs, gouging his black nails into an aged wooden door.

A weathered door was the only thing between him and his deepest fear. Fighting an urgent need to get far away from the building, he rushed forward as the dog clawed and scratched at the splintering wood with reckless abandon. With uneasy nerves, he nudged the dog aside and landed a mud-soaked boot into the bottom of the surprisingly sturdy door. Jagged fragments tore away as it fractured with an energetic crack. After a second forceful kick, more splintered wooden shards whistled through the air, creating a gaping void almost wide enough to wiggle through.

Sage dashed past him and jumped between the shattered boards. The dog disappeared into the one place he had never dared to venture into.

After taking a deep breath, he worked the sharp wooden fragments away from the opening and wiggled inside, gaining courage from the animated barking echoing from within. He felt oddly invigorated. Maybe it was the shock of what he and Josie just witnessed or Lauren's memory guiding his actions. Either way, leftover adrenaline from demolishing the doorway gushed through his pounding heart.

Fading daylight filtered through the cracks, casting golden rays of dying sunlight through the spacious room. Against the back wall, a stairwell descending into the black depths filled his vision, and a familiar brown tail vanished into darkness. Fear rushed through him like a giant sea swell. With a feeling of uncertainty, he glared at the gruesome stairwell and dreaded the thought of giving chase.

"Sage," he shouted and dropped to one knee.

From the darkness below, Sage answered his call with a braying bark.

No way in heaven are you going down there.

A splintered club lying on the dusty ground shattered his paralytic state. He climbed from one knee, sprinted across the room, and grabbed the crude weapon with an unsteady hand. With the club perched on his shoulder, he tiptoed downstairs one creaky step at a time and prayed each wooden plank was sturdy enough to hold his weight. He squinted, barely penetrating the darkness. His heart boomed deep inside a winded chest, rendering his balance somewhat shaky. Suddenly, his fear heightened as a disheartening creak penetrated his ears. An image of tumbling down the wooden planks and breaking every bone in his body came to life in his overactive imagination. He cringed as both feet abandoned the flimsy wooden stairs and squished into dusty concrete. Sage's barks echoed through the blackness guiding his way. He shivered, fighting a deep chill in the small of his back. He stood in the darkness underneath the inspiration for every nightmare he had suffered the past nine years drenched in a cold sweat. Despite his panicky terror, he took a step forward and imagined a terrified nine-year-old little girl screaming out for her brother's help.

"Sage," he shouted and continued forward.

From a chilled corridor, a heavy dose of ageless decay drifted into his face. Cold tears stung his eyes and left him gasping for air as another shiver spread through his bones. Feeling edgy, he rubbed two sweating palms together and listened for any sign of Sage. Instead, a low heartbeat echoed through his temples.

Calm down, you idiot. You can do this.

He felt at a disadvantage cowering in an unfamiliar basement with his hand submerged deep in ageless spiderwebs and God knows what else. Several seconds later, after what seemed like an internal struggle for courage, he took another deep breath of the dirty thick air and continued forward on two trembling legs, desperate to find a doorway or anything that led to the dog. His stomach churned with disgust as something with soft spongy legs crawled along his arm and slithered through his fingers.

From somewhere in the darkness, Sage barked violently, and then an earsplitting shriek echoed around him.

He yanked his hand from the wall and sent the creepy crawler spiraling into the blackness beyond. Squeezing hard on the club, he walked across the floor, enduring a tight knot wrenching his stomach. With the taste of decay strong in his mouth, he squeezed harder on the coarse wooden handle and followed the sound of claws scratching against concrete. The dog's deep snarling and barking served as a guide, but his presence did much more. Josie's German shepherd gave him the courage to move forward. Sage gave him the strength to tuck the fear deep inside. Whether or not they'd be able to rescue the unfortunate person being dragged through this underground crypt was yet to be determined, but if not for the courageous Shepherd, he felt certain the stranger would suffer a horrible fate.

Uncomfortable silence drifted through the hallway.

Sweat tickled his scruffy cheek as his foot stumbled over something squishy on the floor. Without thinking, he grabbed the wall and felt disgust as his fingers slithered through more of the sticky webs. Thinking of Lauren, he staggered forward a few feet to a narrow hallway and stopped dead in his tracks. He stood as still as possible as chills once again cast doubt on the little bit of courage he was clinging onto.

A strident bark boomed out through the darkness.

Like dew under a hot sun, his bravery rose from a troubled soul and evaporated into the atmosphere. Deep down, he wanted to get out of this place and leave both the dog and the unknown man to their own fates. Never once did he claim to be heroic. Years ago he proved that when Lauren disappeared. He didn't save her all those years ago. How did he expect to save a complete stranger now? Terror throbbed through his heart stronger than before, yet his legs marched forward.

Yeah, maybe I did let Lauren down. That was a long time ago, and things have changed. I'm not a scared little kid anymore.

An image of Lauren's youthful face flashed through his mind. Maybe he didn't save her years ago, but he'd be dragged through a bed of scorching coals before abandoning Sage and the helpless stranger now. No way could their lives be sacrificed because of his inability to face a haunted past. Unwilling to live with another burden, he moved with an unknown swiftness through the dark basement. If he gave into this fear now, no mental institution on God's green earth would be able to restore his fractured mind again.

Biting his lip, he let go of the wall and hurried through the doorway toward Sage. In the distance, muffled noises ricocheted off the walls. Survival instinct took over. He squeezed the club with both hands, raised it high in the air, and rushed toward the shadowy shapes twisting deeper in the corridor.

5

Josie had no choice but follow them.

A broken door stood between her and the inside of the building. Her heart raced as she wiggled inside. She felt simultaneously energized and on the verge of uncontrollable tears of terror. A few minutes ago, she felt giddy, like a schoolgirl with an innocent crush on a handsome boy in class. Now, standing inside this ghostly room full of rubble and filth, she felt cold and abandoned. She wanted to scream but didn't dare.

Splintered wood and shattered glass littered the floor. Though dozens of broken bottles were scattered haphazardly about the room, she thought the majority of glass was from the empty windows residing high in the walls. She suspected local kids more than likely used the building as a place to party over the years, though the thought of hanging out in such a atrocious building made her cringe with disgust.

Being careful not to step on the littered debris, she maneuvered through the gigantic room looking and listening for signs of the boy and Sage. Though the sun had already begun its nightly ritual outside, a dim light filtered through the glassless windows. However, that would soon change, and Josie dreaded the thought of being stuck in such an awful place when the darkness crept in. Pushing the thought aside, she noticed a rotted wooden stairway rising up along the east wall to an unstable platform twenty feet above. The stairway was in shambles and unusable. The remaining wood looked flimsy and aged. Even the wooden platform looked wrecked and incapable of holding the slightest weight. What few pillars remained were disintegrating and a few drops of dust away from collapsing to the floor. She walked to a door on the far side of the room and pushed it with a forceful shove. The door squealed on three rusty hinges. Beyond, a hallway ran sixty feet through a cluttered hallway to what looked like a dead end. Thick silvery dust polluted the floor, and ageless cobwebs drooped from a low wooden ceiling.

Ethan and Sage were nowhere to be seen or heard.

Disregarding the hallway, she glimpsed a stairway across the room. From what she could tell, the stairs leading down to a dark basement looked intact and usable. After coughing on a mouthful of the thick dust, she hurried to the stairs, dropped to her knees, and wished for a brighter view of the basement below. Unfortunately, only impenetrable blackness filled her vision.

She had one option.

She wanted to laugh at the glum situation but was too terrified of making even the slightest noise. After all, being scared to the point of insanity is not something to be taken lightly.

Don't be an idiot, Josie. Go get help!

Ignoring the voice of reason shouting orders inside her head, she glanced back over her shoulder at the door leading outside and then tiptoed down the first couple of steps. Her hands trembled as thoughts of never seeing the light of day again disturbed her panicky mind. She doubted anyone would believe her current predicament. In fact, she barely believed it herself even as it was happening. Coming to a halt on the fourth step, she squinted into the darkness, desperately hoping to hear anything that proved Ethan and Sage were waiting for her down there.

"Ethan," she shouted as her foot made contact with the next step below. "Are you down there?"

Silence plagued her ears.

A mouthful of chattering teeth overpowered the sound of a hammering heart. "Ethan, if you're down there, please say something—anything!"

Wood creaked as her weight shifted onto the next plank. She never realized the sound of squealing doors and creaking wood could be so hair-raising until right then and there. The drawn-out creaks left her feeling like a six-year-old kid instead of an eighteen-year-old woman. She expected a ghost to rise from the darkness and float along the stairwell, rattling rusty chains and moaning the word *boo*. Despite an urgent need to find Ethan and Sage, she stood still and decided to wait until someone answered her before taking another step into the cellar.

"Can anyone hear me?" she screamed and crouched lower on the step in need of a better view below. "Somebody, please answer me."

Her pleas went unrequited.

Against better judgment, she crept down a few more steps and felt sweat dampen her hair. She was three quarters of the way down and about to shout out one last time when a shrill bark ricocheted through the basement halls and escaped up through the stairwell.

Sage, thank God.

His barks sounded far away, but at least she knew they were down there.

Holding her breath, she stood as still as possible, hoping for a repeat of the familiar noise. After a few seconds of silence, she heard her own raspy breathing instead. Despite nerves hammering her foot against the plank, she squatted on the bottom step and hoped for the best. An image of a serial killer chopping away at some moronic character in a low-budget horror movie with a bloody machete flashed through her mind.

Not wanting to be the next victim, Josie swallowed her pride and scurried back to the top of the stairs.

6

Dark shadows shimmered across a dusty floor and danced along the walls around him. They were difficult to make out because of the darkness and the constant vertigo clouding both his thoughts and vision. Despite the pain throbbing through both temples, Ryan heard what he thought sounded like a dog's bark echoing through the narrow corridor he found himself laying in.

He squinted hard but still saw only unidentifiable shadowy shapes.

The barking ceased, and deep growling replaced it. Seconds later, something brushed up against his leg, and a heavy weight landed on his chest, knocking the wind from his lungs. The weight shifted, and something that felt reptilian rubbed against his face. Then a massive shadow jumped toward the other end of the corridor. A dog yelped in pain, and then the dizziness grew too intense to overcome. Feeling confused and disoriented, he closed his eyes and slipped again into unconsciousness.

7

Squinting into the darkness, Ethan walked cautiously through the corridor toward the shadowy forms with the club held high in the air and ready to swing at the enigmatic figure engaged with Sage. His heart raced with a mixture of terror and excitement as he crept to within ten feet of the quarrel.

A bloodcurdling wail echoed through the dark hallway and stopped Ethan in his tracks.

Seconds later, Sage yelped in agony, and the sound of sharp claws scraped against concrete. He shivered and prayed the horrible sound was the product of his overactive imagination. Lowering the club, he crouched inside a narrow doorway, anticipating a repeat of what he heard seconds earlier.

Instead, Sage barked with a rage he had never heard before.

Sharp wooden fragments littered the floor just inside the entrance. Perhaps years ago when the hotel was considered grand, a finely crafted door covered the morose entryway. An image of the formidable figure dressed in black scampering across the dust covered floor and shattering the door with a bone-breaking kick flashed through his mind. He pushed the thought aside and treaded deeper into the narrow corridor. Five feet in the distance, a monstrous shadow shimmered along the opposite side of the floor. A familiar chill raced through his shaking frame, and the hairs on his arms rose toward the ceiling. Squinting harder into the dark, he lifted the club over his head and rushed forward with intentions of dislodging the strange creature's hooded face from its shoulders. As he squeezed the weapon and felt splintery wood piercing the palms of his hands, adrenaline pumped blistering blood through his veins.

Quick as a lightning flash through an ominous southern sky, the shadow melded into the darkness, leaving behind a faint swirling trail as it scurried out of sight.

"Sage, come here, boy."

Sage slid through the hallway and skidded into the wall with a soft yelp. He staggered backward, rolled forward, jumped to his feet, leapt through the air, and disappeared into the shimmering black as though he was never there. A second later, a maddening cry echoed off of the walls, and heavy footfalls scampered deeper down the hallway.

Despite his shaking legs, he chased after Sage and swung the club high, hoping to avoid hitting the dog.

A dull thud penetrated the blackness, followed by a low bark. The German shepherd trotted through the passage, jumped at his chest, and licked his cheek with a wet, slimy tongue. Panting heavily, Sage barked and then trotted back down the hallway. Moments later, the Shepherd came back into sight, pulling the unconscious man with his teeth. In awe, Ethan grabbed the stranger's shirt collar and yanked with every muscle in his back. The man's clothes were soaking wet, and his skin felt chilled to the bone. Aided by Sage, he pulled the man along the corridor, through the cobweb-infested doorway, until arriving back in the large room with the stairs.

At the top of the cellar steps, a shadowy form knelt on the platform.

"Is that you up there, Josie," he shouted and gently eased the man to the floor.

"Yeah," Josie shouted. "What in the world is going on down there?"

Sage barked with enthusiasm.

"Honestly," he said, "I don't know, but this dog is crazy nuts. He chased whatever that thing is away and probably saved this dude's life."

"That's really nice, but can we please get out of this place. It gives me the willies."

He glanced at the man on the ground. "Yeah, sounds good to me," he said, trying to catch his breath. "But first, you're gonna have to come down here and help me get him up the steps."

She crept toward the bottom step with a look of skepticism on her slender face.

As each plank creaked under her feet, he chuckled.

"What's so funny?"

"Nothing," he said and pointed at the strange man on the floor. "Does this guy look familiar to you?"

Running her fingers across her dog's back, she squinted. "No, I've never seen him before in my life."

"Think we can get him up the steps?"

"He looks pretty heavy," she said. "I bet he goes well over two hundred pounds."

"We have to try. I don't know about you, but I wanna get out of this place as soon as possible."

"Me too."

"You grab his legs. I'm gonna try and hold him under the shoulders. Let me go first so you don't have to go up the stairs backwards."

Josie stood silently and stared at the unconscious man.

He wondered if she was sure about whether or not she had seen him before. "You ready?" he said and slid his hands under the man's back.

She nodded.

"Grab his legs," he said, straining under the heavy weight.

With doubt in her eyes, she grabbed both feet and followed.

Despite a few bumps and insignificant bruises, they reached the top of the stairs without doing anymore damage to the stranger. On the platform, they lowered him to the floor. Ethan reached for his knees and took a few deep breaths. He needed a few minutes to regain his composure.

Sage stood on the top step and looked intently into the cellar as if guarding them from whatever evil might still be lurking below.

"How far do you live from here?"

"Twenty minutes. Fifteen if I hurry."

Still feeling edgy, he climbed from his knees. "Here's what I want you do," he said, staring back and forth between the dark room and the stairs. "Get to your house as quick as possible, grab your car, and get your rear end back here."

Her mouth opened as if to protest, but she only stared with a look of confusion on her dirt-streaked face.

"You do have a car?"

"Of course I do," she said with her eyes fixated on him. "Well, actually, it's an Explorer."

"That's better yet."

"While I'm gone, what are you going to do?"

"Drag him outside and stay behind the building so nobody sees us. I have a feeling that someone might get the wrong idea if they see us dragging an unconscious human being around the building and across the street."

She batted her eyes and looked even more confused than before. She was hard to read. Though she was the most beautiful girl he has ever laid eyes upon, the expression on her face made him feel inadequate. He sensed she didn't approve of his plan.

"I'll run as fast as I can, but I really hate that you're staying here all alone." She glared at the staircase as if expecting to see the robed figure emerge over the top step at any second. "Remember, there's something freakish and vile down there."

He looked at her with a confident smile. He was still a little freaked out, but she didn't need to know.

"Be careful, okay?"

"I always am."

She kissed his cheek, raced to the door, and slipped out of the building toward Barrow Street with the dog a few steps behind. As if contemplating staying behind, Sage glanced back, tilted his head to the left, and then disappeared into the night.

Despite being alone and vulnerable, he felt a smile curl his lips.

Having had a few classes on first aid and minor medical symptoms during his time in the many mental institutions he called home, Ethan believed the stranger was simply knocked out cold. He obviously took a nasty lump to the head, but he seemed otherwise unharmed. Fortunately, his shallow breath warmed the back of Ethan's hand.

"You're one lucky son of a gun."

Feeling a little lucky himself, he pulled the man out of the building into the open air and laid him gently on the squishy wet grass. Autumn was nearing its end; stars sparkled high above between dark globs of swirling grey cotton. On occasion, a bright yellow crescent slithered out from behind the fast-floating clouds. A slight wind tossed crumbled leaves through the dreary yard, chilling his blood and bones. Branches ruffled deep in the darkened woods as an owl's strident screech rang out through the darkness.

Lauren's memory weighed heavy on his mind.

He glanced at the stranger. "Maybe that thing carried Lauren in there too," he said. "Maybe she really is still alive."

He thought this man was probably just in the wrong place at the wrong time, but if he knew or saw anything that could help unravel the mystery, Ethan intended to find out. Thinking of his sister made him feel anxious, and a sudden need to be far away from this wicked place overcame him. He had had enough of being afraid, at least for today. The thought of running home and leaving this unfortunate man all alone entered his mind, but if that creature decided to retrace its steps and come searching for its lost prize, it would have easy pickings. He couldn't have that on his conscience. He swallowed his fear and thought about the gorgeous red-haired girl who he hoped would return soon.

Abandoning the stranger meant never seeing her again.

Sometime later, as he obsessed over Lauren, headlights danced across the barren oaks that lined the backyard and then disappeared through the branches. Seconds later, a car door slammed, followed by footfalls crunching through crispy leaves. Josie and Sage appeared around the corner.

"Thank god," he said and exhaled a mouthful of silver breath into the crisp air.

"Glad to see you too."

"Come on, let's get this over with," he said and rose to his feet. "I'm tired of this place."

As a strong gust of air whistled through the branches behind them, they lifted the man off the ground, followed Sage around the corner, and stumbled through soggy grass toward the Explorer parked next to the yellow gate. With two exhausted arms, Ethan heaved the stranger from the gravel and eased him into the backseat beside Sage. Seconds later, he crawled into the passenger seat and felt relieved as the vehicle backed onto Barrow Street and maneuvered along the blacktop. As she accelerated into a bend past a row of scarlet oaks, he glimpsed back over the seat and took a deep breath. Fifty feet in the distance, the hotel towered above the menacing pines.

He relaxed as the oaks obstructed his view.

"Where are we going?"

"My house."

With a look of shock, she eased her foot off the gas. "Really," she said, "I was thinking more along the lines of the hospital in Crayton."

"That's not an option, Josie. We can't take him there."

"Why not?"

"What are we gonna say, Josie? That we found this guy lying unconscious in the basement of the one and only condemned building in this town? You know, the same one we just so happened to be trespassing in and, not to mention, were stupid enough to do it after dark."

"That sounds all right to me."

"No one would believe a word of it," he said and ran his fingers across the back of her hand. "They'd think we were up to no good. Seriously, they might even think we did something to him. I don't know where you're from, but in my world, people always think the worst of other people."

In silence, she stared.

"People would be doubtful. Besides, I'd like to talk to him and see if he knows anything.

"Knows anything! What are you talking about?"

"I'd like to know what that thing is."

She squeezed hard on his hand. "He could be seriously hurt."

"He's not."

"How do you know, Ethan?"

"Trust me," he said, jerking free of her grip. "I just know."

"When he wakes up, we're going to do what he wants."

Feeling slightly irritated, he broke eye contact.

"Agreed," she said, raising her voice.

"Yeah, all right. When he comes to we will do whatever he says."

He pointed to a house on the left. "Go up the driveway and park behind the truck."

Obediently, she drove along the paved driveway, parked behind a dark green Toyota Tacoma, and killed the engine. He sat silently in the dark a few moments until Josie opened the door, and an annoying bell rang throughout the inside of the vehicle. After a five-minute struggle, they had the stranger up the stairs and inside the house.

PART II

GUIDED BY FATE

8

In the far end of the parking lot on the left side of the stadium, she waits behind the wheel of a navy-blue Chevy Cavalier and stares into the side view mirror with a haunted expression on her face. She appears lost in deep thought. He hurries across the snow covered concrete, admiring her beauty, wanting nothing more than to wrap his arms around her slender body and kiss her deeply. Ryan had love in his heart for many things: his mother and father, his aunts and uncles and cousins, the camaraderie of playing football for the high school, all animals big and small, and a few of his teammates that he went to battle with over the past few years. But more than anything, he loved Molly. He loved everything about her: the angelic smile on her perfect face when he made her blush, the unfashionable clothes that only she could make look stylish, the melodic sound of her voice when she sang along with the radio, and the way her light-blue eyes turned a darker shade of sapphire when the summer sun shimmered against her face. Ryan loved Molly, and from the moment he first saw her sitting under an elm tree twirling her finger through her hair at his friend's uncle's farm, he wanted to spend an eternity with her.

Despite the school's strict policy of players riding home on the team bus, he made plans with Molly to drive back to Raging Gap together. Luckily, he convinced Coach O'Malley to let him slide. After all, they just won the championship, and he was voted the most valuable player.

He opens the passenger door, slides inside, and is delighted to feel the warm air blowing gently through the heater vents.

After a long passionate kiss, she shifts the car in gear, maneuvers out of the parking lot, and drives in the direction of the interstate.

"Want me to drive?" he says as she pushes down on the pedal and swings the car onto the town's main street. "The snow is coming down harder than expected, and it's making the road pretty slippery."

She takes his hand and smiles. "Not a chance, babe. You got to be the big hero in the game, and you honestly believe there's a chance that you're going to rip glory from my grasp."

Despite the cold air blustering outside, he feels warm. As usual, being close to Molly makes the world feel right.

"Relax, hero. Once we get to the interstate, you can drive."

"Nah, don't worry about it. You're doing fine, babe. Just take it easy on these roads 'cause the snow is really starting to come down."

Focusing on the road, she maneuvers the car through Albany's main street, speeds past a city limits sign and drives nearly twenty miles until they see a sign for the interstate. After assuring him she could handle the slick highway conditions, she exits the main street and yields at the bottom of the ramp before hitting the gas and merging with a small convoy of multicolored cars traveling along the interstate.

With a buzzing head, he grabs her leg and wiggles his fingers along the inside of her upper thigh. Her foot pushes harder on the gas pedal as his fingers continue exploring her body. Distracted by his passionate touch, Molly sighs, slides the seat back, and swerves across the yellow line at well over seventy miles an hour.

Suddenly, he feels the tires slide across ice. Feeling tension tighten the muscles in her leg, he jerks his hand away and stares in horror through the frosted windshield at a six-foot barrier dividing the highway.

Twisting the wheel violently, she stomps the brake to the floor and screams as metal screeches and sparks against the concrete barrier. The car slides backward through the ice, skids across the passing lane, slams into a guardrail, squeals sideways through the snow down a twenty-foot hillside, and comes to a dead stop at the base of a wide tree. On impact, his seatbelt rips along the seam, tearing up the middle with a sickening ripping sound. His head crashes against the windshield, knocking common sense from his thoughts. Seconds later, the trees beyond the shattered windshield spin out of control, and blackness rushes through his head, putting an abrupt end to his pain.

Sometime later, his eyes open as sirens wail from every direction. They sound close, but his head throbs so badly his judgment can't be trusted. He's not sure where he is as the loud wails of the constant siren amplify the worst headache he's ever experienced. Through wooziness, he prays to God for the sirens to quit wailing before his brain explodes into a thousand pieces of crimson sludge.

Seconds later, they oblige.

He awoke on a strange bed, confused and afraid. He was dreaming about that night again. Though it happened five years ago, the dream seemed as real now as the day it happened.

The nightmare always felt real.

Though strident wailing no longer tormented his ears, dull pain still lingered in his head. Though he lay on an unfamiliar bed in an unfamiliar room, he felt at peace. For the time being, the ghost of Molly took a hiatus from his memory.

He closed his eyes, and seconds later, he slept.

Sometime later, sunlight seeped through closed venetian blinds, casting soft yellow light throughout the room. He was in a bedroom with two dressers, an open closet centered in the wall to his right, and a large king-sized mattress that felt like heaven on his sore bones. He felt confused and trapped in a never-ending nightmare. He must have been dreaming again. Something strange happened in the woods. Without a doubt, he knew something bad happened in the wilderness, but he was fuzzy about the details.

Someone attacked me.

In the corner of the room near the door, a dark-haired man stared at Ryan with skepticism in his eyes. He was young, maybe in his early twenties, half an inch shy of six feet, one hundred sixty pounds, and skinny with a scruffy goatee and light blue eyes. He held something in his hand, but Ryan couldn't make out what it was.

Molly's memory disappeared, but guilt still plagued his heart.

That night, while he slept in a hospital bed, she slept eternally on a concrete slab in the morgue two stories underneath his room. As usual, he dreamt of the night she died. Though it happened a long time ago, it seemed like yesterday. Now he was someplace strange. Though he couldn't remember any details of yesterday's exploration, he felt certain that someone attacked him in the woods. His head pounded too hard to focus on anything except the here and now.

What happened out there? Where am I, and how did I end up here?

He remembered waking on a hard dusty floor in a long dark hallway after the attack in the woods. Perhaps he only dreamt about it, but he remembered seeing long twisting shadows battling each other on a wall and along a floor. One of the shadows growled and barked like an infuriated dog, and then he remembered dreaming of Molly's demise. A tear dripped from the corner of his eye and rolled along his face.

He glanced at the man standing by the door. If he had ever seen this guy before, he couldn't remember where or when, but their paths had obviously crossed. Not intending to act irrational, he decided to play it cool. Thinking the stranger was unaware that he was awake, he let out a soft groan. Ryan was anxious to speak with this man and hoped to unravel the mystery.

The man approached the bed with a glass of water in his trembling hand. He appeared nervous, which left Ryan feeling insecure. He wondered if this man might be responsible for the attack in the woods and the painful thumps pounding through his head. If so, he intended to get to the bottom of it one way or another.

The man sat the glass on a nightstand beside the bed, smiled half-heartedly, and took a step back while rubbing his hands together nervously.

The guy looked guilty of something.

"What happened to me?" Ryan said and tried to think of a justifiable reason for someone to keep him a hostage. Nothing came to mind, but the world was a crazy place populated by some really sick monsters. *You never know*, he thought, recalling his mother telling him that the only monsters in this world are people. *People are motivated by greed and lust, especially in this day and age.*

"My name is Ethan," the boy said glancing back and forth between Ryan and the glass of water sitting on the nightstand. "You're in my house, and you've been out cold for quite some time."

The boy's voice sounded calm.

Ryan felt more relaxed with each word the nervous guy spoke. The last thing he remembered was hiking through mountains and getting somewhat lost in the woods. After getting attacked by something big and ugly, he remembered having a bizarre dream involving long stretched-out shadows and an enraged dog. He wasn't completely sure if it was a dream or if it actually happened. The only thing he knew to be certain was waking up in this room a few minutes ago after dreaming of the dead girl he loved more than life itself.

He felt frustrated and wanted to scream.

"Do you remember anything about what happened to you?"

Ignoring him, Ryan massaged a monstrous knot on the top of his head in hopes of dulling the pain. "Why exactly am I in your house?"

Ethan picked up the glass from the nightstand. "You must be thirsty," he said and extended the glass toward Ryan. "Like I said, you've been unconscious pretty much since I found you last night."

Though he wanted nothing more than a wet swallow of the water, he motioned the glass away. If this stranger was responsible for his current condition, drinking the water might not be the smartest idea.

The only monsters are people, his mother's voice whispered in his head.

The boy grinned. He wore a bewildered expression that screamed discomfort.

Ryan wanted to laugh but managed to hide his emotions.

Suddenly, he looked surprised. "No! I didn't—"

"No, you didn't what, hit me over the head out in the woods?"

"No, dude," he said. "We didn't hurt you. We rescued you from…well…I'm not sure from what, but to be truthfully honest, I didn't really get a good look at it."

"The last thing I remember was hiking through the mountains." He glimpsed at Ethan's hand with a craving for the glass of water. "I was kind of lost for a while. I was out in those woods for the better part of a day, and someone came out of the thickets and attacked me but I didn't see his face."

"Seriously," Ethan said, sounding a bit too disappointed. "You didn't see anything at all?"

"One minute I was being attacked in the woods. The next minute I'm waking up in a room I've never seen before and talking to you, who, coincidently, I have never met before."

"Sorry, I just thought you might remember something or anything about what happened out there."

Despite the possibility that Ethan might be a psychopath, Ryan doubted his plans included anything menacing like poisoning a glass of water. His throat was as dry as a desert on a 120-degree day and sore from dehydration. At this point, he decided it didn't matter. Regardless of the consequences, he really wanted a drink. He pointed to the nightstand. "Does your offer still stand?"

"Of course, dude."

He gulped it down in two swallows. "Thanks," he said and handed Ethan the empty glass.

"No problem," Ethan said through a giggle. "I bet you're probably hungry too."

"Actually I'm starving. The only thing I've eaten over the last few days is dry and tasteless beef jerky."

"Yum, now that sounds scrumptious."

He tried to sit up, but nausea forced him back to the mattress. His legs felt as deflated as two leaking hot air balloons. Every muscle in his body felt inflamed as he struggled to sit up.

"Take it easy for a while," Ethan said. "I'll go get us some grub. Is fast, greasy food cool with you?"

"Sure."

"We look roughly the same size. I'll get you some clothes, a towel, and a washcloth. You can take a shower while I'm gone or whenever you feel like it."

Relaxing on the bed, his dizziness diminished to a slow buzz. Through the buzz, he rehashed the memories of yesterday's misadventure through the woods. He was happy to be here and not have gone astray in the mountain wilderness though he had no clue where here was. He would eventually have to get off of the bed, but a few more minutes resting on the soft mattress sounded like a great plan. He stretched his arms. "Sounds good to me," he said through an elongated yawn. "Normally I'm more of a shower person, but a nice, hot bone-soaking bath sounds pretty much like heaven right now. I think that might be just what I need."

"Take your time, dude. I'll be back in a few minutes with some clean clothes and another glass of cold water."

After Ethan departed, Ryan laid on the bed and thought of Molly. Why did she have to die? He would have gladly traded places with her if he could, but, unfortunately, it was beyond his control. Though he wasn't the most religious person ever to walk the earth, his faith in God was strong compared to a lot of other people he knew. He believed God had a basic plan for everybody. His was to continue living while she died young. Unfortunately, it seems like God takes the good ones early. Though Molly's memory haunted his thoughts on an everyday basis, he had to find a way to live with the guilt and move on with his life.

God, I loved you.

"She loved me too," he whispered.

After Ethan returned with some clothes and another glass of water, he crawled off the bed and felt the spinning in his head subside almost immediately. He drank the second glass much slower than the first, but it tasted every bit as good. Minutes later, as a door slammed somewhere in the house, he hobbled to the bathroom and soaked in a tub of steaming hot water for what seemed like an eternity.

9

The inharmonious sound of a ringing telephone woke him from a deep sleep.

Shawn Preston opened his eyes and stared at the alarm clock on the nightstand. It was still a few minutes before seven o'clock. He wasn't expected at work until noon; so much for a relaxing morning in bed.

"Hello," he grumbled into the receiver.

"Shawn," the deep baritone voice on the opposite end said.

Though several years have passed since last hearing the monster's voice, Shawn recognized it immediately. This was the phone call he had been dreading for the past five years.

"Yeah, this is Shawn."

"This is Gregory Stephens," said the deep voice on the other end. "Someone's been meddling in our business, and you're needed at home as soon as possible. How soon can you get back here?"

"Give me two days."

"See you then," the voice said and then hung up.

Shawn dropped the cordless on the nightstand, sat up, stretched his arms toward the ceiling, and crawled out of bed before making the short walk to the doorway and flipping on the light switch.

For a long time he had been wondering if another call would ever come. He had been dreading it ever since the last time he was forced to return to the town he grew up in. For the first time in over five years, Shawn had to go back to Gastons Gorge, which meant atrocious acts of brutality committed against anyone who managed to stumble into his former hometown's best kept secret. He knew the threats Gregory Stephens told him all those years ago were one hundred percent true, so he intended to return home and protect their secret without hesitation.

He left the bedroom and made his way along the hallway before opening the bathroom door.

He didn't want to help them, but he had no other choice. He always did his duty even though the consequences meant long nights of gut-wrenching guilt that would eventually suck the life from his bones. The penalty for disobedience was far too steep to do anything but agree to do whatever they asked. He flicked the switch on the inside wall and hurried to the sink as the overhead fluorescent bulbs flickered a few seconds and then painted the room in soft yellow light. Shawn loved his father with all his heart and would do anything to protect him from the evil associated with his hometown. Yes, he would help Gregory Stephens, even if it meant hurting blameless people. Though never proud of his actions, he had no intentions of watching his father suffer a slow and agonizing death.

After a quick shave and shower, he turned off the lights and left the bathroom wrapped in a dark brown bath towel. He had to get ready for the long drive back to Pennsylvania.

With a heavy heart, he thought about his father, Steven Preston. One day he would be gone from this world. That day, Shawn would be free, although, he suspected they would try and silence him. Why not? Once his father slipped from the living, they would have no one to dangle in front of his face. They would have nothing to keep him from revealing their secret to the world. After that, there would be no worrying of ramifications against anyone he loved. As painful as losing his father to a natural death would be, it would hurt a lot less than the horrendous pain they would inflict upon him. On nights when finding sleep proved difficult, which is a little more often than he'd like these days, he would think about the day of his father's passing. That day, he planned to exact revenge against Gregory Stephens and the dark creatures he followed. His vengeance wouldn't be sweet, and it would not eradicate every vile act those things launched against the people of Gastons Gorge, but it would guarantee they never harmed anyone from that town or anywhere else ever again, and it would give him peace of mind.

Nearly a year ago, a contact that Shawn helped get out of some serious legal issues managed to get his hands on an explosive device constructed from wires and a few sticks of dynamite. To repay the debt, his contact handed it over without question. Shawn kept it hidden away in an isolated cabin he owned located about an hour south of the Upper Peninsula. Despite the dangers of getting caught or setting it off during the journey, he planned on bringing the explosive back to Gastons Gorge in case Gregory and his minions forced his hand.

He dressed and made a few phone calls, and within ten minutes, he had the week off of work. After yanking a dusty suitcase out of the closet, he packed it with a week's worth of clothes, cigarettes, and enough cash to make the journey. The drive from Wisconsin would take two days because he had no intentions of driving straight through. Obligation would take him back home, but he was in no hurry to get there. They expected him in two days, and that's when he would arrive.

10

Though still a bit sore from the strange events of yesterday, he felt re-energized after soaking in a bathtub full of hot water for what seemed like an hour. He dressed quickly and left the steaming hot room feeling a lot less pain than he did after waking up on a strange bed. He was impressed with the way Ethan tried to make him feel comfortable in his home. Old-fashioned hospitality, clean clothes that were a few sizes too small, and a charming, yet eccentric, personality made Ryan feel a little less awkward. The kid seemed decent enough; however, Ryan sensed he was hiding something.

He shut the bathroom door, and a after brief journey through Ethan's living room, he stumbled into a kitchen. A large oval table centered the small rectangular room. Four wobbly chairs were equally spaced evenly around the cherry wood table. He walked across the floor, pulled out a chair, and took a seat. Although he felt strange being alone in the home of a stranger, he thought it was better than being lost in miles of secluded wilderness.

A clock hanging on the wall above a stainless steel sink ticked out of rhythm. He sat with both elbows on the table and stared at the long black plastic hand and waited for his host to return. Silently, he counted each drawn-out second.

The low rumble of an engine approached the house 1,327 ticks later.

Grimacing through minor pain cramping his leg, he hobbled to the window and watched a green Tacoma drive slowly up the driveway and disappear under a carport. Seconds later, a car door slammed, and heavy footsteps pounded against concrete. From the basement, a door banged shut, and Ryan hurried back to the empty chair and scooted closer to the table. The footsteps grew heavier, and then a door to his right flew open and thudded against the wall. With a crazy smile on his face, Ethan appeared through the kitchen archway carrying two large white bags and a cardboard holder with three glasses of orange juice.

Ryan heard his stomach grumble.

Ethan dropped the bags and the juice on the table, hurried to the refrigerator, and pulled a bottle of ketchup from the inside shelf. After a quick stop at a drawer, he dropped three forks on the table.

"These things aren't the healthiest meals in the world, but man, do they taste like hunks of heaven in a Styrofoam box."

Ryan laughed and opened one of the containers as the delightful scent of eggs and sausage filtered through his nostrils. "You must be really hungry," he said as Ethan pulled two more containers from the bag and sat them on the table in front of the bag.

"Heck yeah I'm hungry. Rescuing dudes in distress really works up a hearty appetite."

"I'll say, but there are only two of us."

He blushed. "Oh yeah, I wasn't alone last night," he said and grabbed a set of bright red salt-and-pepper shakers from the countertop. He slid them across the table. "Josie and Sage are on their way over. They helped out a little last night too."

"Oh."

Ethan tossed a fork across the table and watched it bounce off Ryan's arm. "I hate those stupid plastic spork thingamajigs they like to put into the bag. They're a pain in the rump and way too easy to break."

A vibrating growl rumbled through his stomach. More than anything at that moment, he wanted to feast. Not wanting to offend his host, Ryan stared at the sausage and eggs and felt the saliva wash over his taste buds like a wonderful tidal wave as the heavenly aroma filtered through the kitchen.

Ethan smiled and pointed at the food. "Don't wait for me, dude. Eat up already. After what you went through last night, you're more than entitled."

With a nod, he swallowed the food like a dog eating a marshmallow—noisily and with barely any chewing. He inhaled the pancakes without maple syrup, swallowed the sausage and eggs in less than three bites, and sucked down all of his orange juice before Ethan was able to look away.

"Dang, dude," he said and slid another container across the table. "You're hungrier than I thought."

Shaking his head, he swallowed a mouthful of egg and stared at Ethan.

"Just eat it, dude."

"Nah, I can't eat yours. You've been more than generous already."

"I wasn't planning on eating it anyway."

"Really, are you sure, man?"

"Yeah, I'm a hundred percent positive. I think you can use it a lot more than I can." A genuine smile drifted across his face. "Besides, you got to eat some grub to get your strength back."

"Thanks a bunch, man. I really appreciate it."

When Josie and Sage arrived a few minutes after ten o'clock, he chuckled as introductions were made. Instead of a person, which Ethan led him to believe, Sage turned out to be a medium-sized German shepherd with a bright blue collar fastened loosely around his neck. As the dog trotted to the far corner and flopped down on the linoleum, Ryan watched Josie walk across the room and sit down between them. She was as pleasant as Ethan. She was mildly attractive and overly polite. He waited patiently while she finished eating her food. Although he was anxious to hear about last night's escapade, he thought a few more minutes while she ate a quick breakfast seemed more than fair.

After Josie finished, Ethan swept a moist rag across the table. "We were hanging out across from this old and half-ruined hotel yesterday around early evening," he said and grinned at Josie. "Some kind of enormous creature dressed in what looked like a long black trench coat with an oversized hood pulled you across the yard and into the building."

"It looked more like a hooded robe," Josie said in an enthusiastic tone.

"Regardless of what that thing had on its disgusting body, it yanked you inside that place. It's a good thing we saw you too, or I don't think you'd be enjoying this fine breakfast. Fortunately, Sage managed to fight it off long enough for us to get you out of there."

His mouth opened in surprise. "Really? That really happened? Are you serious?"

Ethan frowned with a dubious expression on his face. "You really don't remember anything?"

"Nope, I just remember being ambushed in the woods by someone."

"So what are you going to do now?" Josie asked.

"Not sure exactly. I guess I should probably figure out where my car is and head home."

She smiled. "So where is home?"

"Upstate New York," he said. "Do either of you have any clue where the town of Falls River is?"

"Falls River, is that in New York, dude?"

"No, It's somewhere around here."

"I'm just messing with you. I've heard of it but I'm not real sure how to—"

"It's about twenty miles away," Josie interrupted. "You have to follow Gorge Creek through the mountain road to the end and then make a left. From there you just follow that road until you come to Falls River. Sounds confusing, but it's actually easy to get to."

"What's going on in Falls River?" Ethan asked with a befuddled grimace on his face.

"That's where I parked my Pinto."

"Pinto," they said simultaneously.

Ignoring them, Ryan said, "I followed an atlas to find the place, but I doubt I can find my way back without it. It seems like forever since I abandoned my ride and ran off into those woods."

"So if you are from New York," she said. "What made you want to go hiking around here?"

"It's a long story."

"Well, dude, maybe we can hear all about it later."

In appreciation, he nodded.

"But seriously, you were lost out there in some crazy wilderness." Looking at Josie, Ethan chuckled. "Those woods are filled with lions, tigers, and bears. Oh my!"

Josie smiled. "He's a bit on the nutty side, but he's right." She stared at him. "There's some dangerous wildlife out there. Those woods are home to bear and wild dogs. I've heard rumors of mountain lion too, although I've never actually met anyone who's seen one. Not to mention hunting season is right around the corner. I'm not certain how things are where you come from, but around here, we have a lot of crazy deep-seated maniacs tramping around those woods this time of the year looking for any excuse to shoot something."

"Funny, but not far from the truth," Ethan said. "She forgot to mention those maniacs are also usually plastered out of their gourds."

Laughter filled the kitchen.

After a few minutes, their laughter faded. A somber mood swept through him as he thought of his adventures the past few days. He took a deep breath and wondered about the creature that carried him into the building that Ethan and Josie spoke about.

"So where in New York are you from?"

"It's just a dinky little town a few miles from the Canadian border. You probably never heard of it."

"Does it have a name?" she asked.

"Yeah, Raging Gap."

"You're right, I've never heard of it."

"Me either," Ethan said. "But then I wasn't being overly nosy like some people."

With hands folded on the table, she grinned and batted her eyes at Ethan.

He winced hurtfully but managed an innocent smile.

"Anyway," she said turning from Ethan, "do you feel all right?"

"Yeah, I feel decent enough. My head doesn't hurt all that much anymore, but I'm achy all over, especially my legs and my feet."

Ethan cleared his throat. A dismal smirk replaced his usual happy-go-lucky grin. "I guess our next move is exploring the hotel."

"Next move? Are you crazy?"

Ethan pushed away from the table and walked across the room to the window. He stared outside a few moments before turning back to face them. "I don't know what exactly you saw, Josie, and I'm not going to stand here and pretend that I got a really good look at that thing, but I can tell you both"—his face crinkled as a frown formed on his lips—"that thing wasn't a man. It was something else—something stronger and darker."

She scowled. "You're right. I didn't get a good look at it either, but how can you say with definite certainty that it wasn't human? It had to have been a man. What else could it have been?"

Ryan wished he could remember anything that might help shed some light on the situation, but his mind was blocking the memory. He felt insignificant as they tried to figure out the event that linked their fates the previous evening.

"It was Sage's reaction," he said. "His behavior toward whatever that thing was."

"What do you mean reaction?"

"I don't think your dog would have responded to a person the way he did to that thing. I know I only just met you yesterday, but that dog has a friendly way about it."

"Even friendly animals are aggressive if they're protecting the ones they love."

"I agree. Dogs do protect the ones they love, but it was the way he acted that makes me wonder. His demeanor was sort of creepy. It chilled my blood, Josie."

"He was agitated, but I think he was just being protective is all."

"Then why did he chase after that thing?"

"Gee, let me think, to save Ryan!"

"Maybe," Ethan said with uncertainty in his voice. "Seriously, Josie, none of us ever met Ryan until that moment, and I don't think Sage would have ran off like that and risk danger to rescue someone he never met before."

Ryan knew there was more to it. The peculiar feeling he had earlier about Ethan hiding something resurfaced. For now, he would keep his opinions tucked away, at least until he understood more of what happened. "Seriously, you guys only met yesterday?"

"Honestly, dude, only a few minutes before we saw whatever that thing was drag you into the basement."

"Really, the way the two of you act with each other, I just assumed you were a couple."

Josie blushed and turned to look at Ethan. "Honest, we just met."

"But we make a pretty good team," he said returning her stare.

"Sorry guys, I didn't mean to embarrass you."

For a few seconds, they stared into each other's eyes as if they were the only two people in the room. He could see something special going on between them, but he had a hard time believing they only met a few hours ago. Though they had different ideas about what happened last night, they seemed to click. Feeling like a third wheel, he slid off the chair, knelt beside Sage, and gently stroked his back.

Sage lifted his head and wagged his tail.

"I need to pick up a few things at the store," Ethan said. "Do either of you have anything in mind that we can whip up for dinner? I pretty much live on fast food, sour cream and onion potato chips, and candy bars."

"I'll go with you," she said and rose from her chair. "A woman's touch at the supermarket is always appreciated."

"Dude, you feel like getting some fresh air?"

Ryan nodded. "If you don't mind, I'll just hang here and take it easy. My head still hurts a bit."

"Hey, as they say in Mexico, my house aye your house."

Ryan laughed and continued to pet Sage.

After Ethan, Josie, and Sage left for the grocery store, he tossed the empty containers and plastic glasses in the garbage can beside the refrigerator, hobbled into the living room, and fell backward into a black reclining love seat. He hoped to clear his head. After a few minutes of channel surfing, he came across an old rerun of a black-and-white sitcom his father used to watch. He sat the remote on the arm of the chair and leaned back. Five minutes later, he snored like a bear with a belly full of food.

11

The deep-blue Explorer rolled along the outskirts of town, turned right onto the highway, and headed for the market in Crayton Village. The shops sat just off the main highway. Josie turned left at the stoplight and followed the two-lane access road to a large parking lot. After a quick survey of the spacious lot, she pulled into a vacant space a dozen aisles back from the main entrance.

With his window cracked a couple of inches, Ethan slid out of the seat, locked the door, and followed Josie through the pothole-ridden lot, leaving Sage behind to guard the vehicle. For a Tuesday afternoon, the grocery store appeared overly crowded. He wondered where the numerous people driving along the highway and walking up and down the grocery store aisles worked. He never paid attention to how many people busied the town on a weekday afternoon until just this moment.

Inside, Josie broke left and grabbed a shopping cart, momentarily disappeared from his sight. As he stood in the entranceway waiting, a weird feeling stirred in his gut. He couldn't shake the feeling of being watched. Despite the numerous strangers tossing their items in their wobbly carts, he saw no one acting suspiciously. Disregarding the feeling, he dismissed it as paranoia and chased after Josie, who pushed a green-and-silver cart through a fruit and vegetable aisle in the front of the store. Over the next half hour, they hurried through every aisle searching for ingredients for tonight's meal. Despite the thousands of items the supermarket carried, they had a difficult time deciding what to buy. Ethan wondered if everyone had as hard a time as he and Josie about dinnertime decisions. On occasion, as they abandoned one aisle for another, the eerie feeling of being watched returned. After looking around and seeing nothing unusual, the feeling would fade, and they continued with their search.

Sixty-two dollars and seventy-three cents later, they loaded two bags of groceries into Josie's Explorer and listened to Sage barking from the backseat.

On the way home, much to his surprise, she drove past his driveway and sped toward the bottom of Barrow Street. Despite knowing the destination, he kept his mouth shut and dreaded the sight at the bottom of the hill. The last thing he wanted was an argument over his views on what happened yesterday. If Josie knew about his past, maybe her opinion would change.

Perhaps, later on, he would tell her the tragic story that is his life.

They drove by the old hotel in awkward silence.

Despite a nervous feeling fluttering through his stomach, he stared at the pine trees as the Explorer turned around at the end of a dead-end street. Seconds later, she drifted the vehicle onto the dirt road across the street and eased the gearshift into park. He sat quietly listening to the low hum of an idling engine and focused on the intimidating structure with thoughts of yesterday heavy on his mind. On the surface, it was nothing more than a crumbling building that should have been demolished years ago; however, a menacing creature lurked somewhere in the dark corridors waiting for another opportunity to pull unsuspecting people from this town inside.

Do you really want to go back in there? You can forget everything and get on with your life.

He glanced at Josie.

Maybe she can be part of your future.

His head buzzed with confusion. Deep down he felt consumed with guilt that ate away at his heart like a flesh eating virus. Until he found the courage to go back inside that place and face a haunted past, he could never move forward.

She deserves better than you.

Curiosity alone would not provide enough motivation to overcome his selfish fears. For him, searching for Lauren would be the key to a complete future. Maybe he was dead wrong about everything, but the obsession he developed years earlier grew more intense since meeting Josie and Ryan. In the awkward silence, he wondered what crazy thoughts tortured Josie's mind. Did she have demons in her closet? As he wondered what the future might hold, the engine rumbled to life, and the Explorer rolled up the road.

Minutes later, he hurried through the front door carrying a bag of groceries. Josie followed with another bag, and Sage trotted a few feet behind, panting heavy and wagging his tail as usual.

Inside the house, he smiled at Josie and pointed toward the living room.

Ryan snored loudly on the love seat, drowning out the sound of the television.

"Let him sleep awhile," she said.

Being as quiet as possible, they put the groceries away and then crept along the hall to Ethan's bedroom. He flopped on the bed and watched as she snuggled against him. Sage found a spot on the floor and closed his eyes. As they lay on the bed holding onto each other, he wanted to kiss her lips and feel the warmth of her body against his. Instead, he wiggled closer and inhaled her sweet intoxicating breath. Somehow it seemed natural. He thought kissing her might ruin the weird chemistry they seemed to share. After a few minutes, he felt her shallow breath on his neck as she fell asleep in his arms.

Not long after, while lost in deep thoughts of murderous monsters, long dark corridors, and a sister he missed with all of his heart, he drifted into to a wonderful sleep filled with heavenly dreams of Josie McShay.

12

Alyssa Thorpe swung the light blue Grand Am into the parking space outside of her apartment building and hopped out of the car. Feeling uncharacteristically foolish, she unlocked the front door and hurried inside out of the chilly air.

She lived a hermit's lifestyle.

Alyssa did almost everything alone. She lived in an apartment on the outskirts of town and attended classes at the local university. When not sitting at home with a book in her hand, she was at Gastons Gorge public library researching for a class project or studying for an exam. Except for the occasional date on a Saturday evening, which happened rarely these days, she kept to herself. To Alyssa, getting an education was the most important thing in life. Other people distracted her from that goal. After twelve grueling years of near-perfect grades through elementary and high school, her future was beginning to take shape, and secondary needs for companionship couldn't jeopardize what she worked so hard to achieve. When other girls her age were on dates with their boyfriends or socializing with their girlfriends, she worked her brain to the brink of exhaustion to achieve the highest grades possible.

Unfortunately, because of what happened at the store, studying was the last thing on her mind. The young man at Crayton Market looked strangely familiar. Without a doubt, she'd seen him before. As the hours rolled along, the obsession ate at her to point of near madness. She first noticed him standing inside the sliding doors. He looked twenty years old at the most. While trying to keep out of the boy's sight, she hurried past the aisle and ducked around the corner hoping that no one noticed her strange behavior. She jogged through the next aisle over from where he and a girl pushed their cart, trying to circle around for a closer look. As she peeked around the corner past a shelf full of potato chips and chocolate snacks, he walked down the opposite side with a red-haired girl. Unfortunately, she could only see the back of their heads. After they disappeared around the corner, she gave chase at a safe distance.

Sometime later, she ducked behind a magazine rack as the girl pushed the cart into a checkout lane a few feet away. The girl looked familiar as well. She was thin with strawberry blond curly hair. Though not a hundred percent certain, she thought they might have gone to the same school.

At one point, she thought he spotted her, but as he turned toward the girl and began laughing, she ducked behind a book rack and breathed a sigh of relief. His eyes intrigued her. At some point in the past, she'd seen that same beautiful color.

Who are you, and where have I seen you?

She grabbed her keys from the pocket of her jeans, hung her jacket on the coat rack, and fell backward onto the sofa. Grabbing the remote, she tried to recreate a mental image of the boy's face. As the television flickered on, shattering the silence, it suddenly became clear. "No freaking way," she shouted as her keys slipped through her fingers and clanked onto the floor. The last time they were together, she was nine years old, and he was twelve.

The man at the grocery store was borderline skeletal. Though his face aged quite a few years, he was without a doubt the kid she knew a long time ago. He was quite a few inches taller with slightly darker hair and scruffy facial hair that gave him an appealing look, but he mirrored Lauren's brother. Remembering the look on his face at the checkout line, Alyssa was positive he was Ethan Wysong, her best friend's big brother. Eight years ago, after his mother's suicide, he disappeared from Gastons Gorge, and she never saw him again, until today.

She jumped from the couch and grabbed the keys from the floor.

Why the heck did you come back here, Ethan Wysong? What are you up to?

She planned to find out.

13

Ryan swallowed down a plate of spaghetti that Ethan whipped up while he and Josie slept. The food tasted like heaven on a ceramic dish. In fact, Ryan couldn't remember the last time a plate of pasta tasted so good. Much to his surprise, the scrawny boy proved handy in the kitchen. After dinner, they cleared the table and retired to the living room. Yesterday's weird confrontation left all three of them feeling mentally exhausted. They needed to rest. Despite Josie barking orders about medical treatment and emergency room visits, he agreed with Ethan and voted against it. When pushed on the matter, he told her the hospital might help but agreed with Ethan about answering questions they had no answers for.

He took a deep breath and glanced at Ethan. "Earlier today you asked about our next move."

"Yeah, I can't shake this curiosity about whatever that thing is."

"I didn't think much about it at the time. Honestly, I thought you were sort of nuts asking a question like that, but I've been thinking about it, and I think you might be right."

Curious expressions hung from both their faces.

He wanted them to understand how he felt; after all, they saved him from certain death, so why would they doubt his curiosity about what might be happening. Besides, it seemed Ethan was as curious as he was.

"Josie, you asked me why I came here."

She grinned. "Yeah, but—"

"I could have chosen anywhere in the country to go hiking." Exhilaration pumped through his heart. "Seriously, I could have gone anywhere in the world. I've always wanted to go to Europe or Australia or New Zealand, but I hopped in my car, and for whatever reason, I found the two of you. Well actually you guys found me, thank God."

"And?" Ethan said.

"I was supposed to meet you guys. I think our paths are interconnected somehow. I think the way the two of you were from the same town and didn't meet until yesterday, only moments before I was nearly…" He looked up at the black television screen and sighed. "Something mysterious is at work in this town, and we're right in the middle of it."

Josie scooted to the edge of the cushion. "That's just crazy talk," she said with wide open eyes. "I don't believe in fate and destiny and all that supernatural mumbo jumbo."

Ethan smiled. "Then explain exactly why all of this is happening."

"We're responsible for the decisions we make in our lives, and we pay for the ramifications of those actions regardless of whether or not we do them on purpose. I don't mean to offend you, Ryan, but I find what you're saying a little hard to swallow. The thought of being jerked along in life as if we are just mere puppets on some higher power's strings really irritates the crap out of me."

"I don't know, Josie, but think about—"

"Think about what?" she said interrupting Ethan.

"I've never met you before in my life, and then all of a sudden yesterday afternoon when I was scoping that place out, you and Sage come bee bopping up the trail, and you know the rest of the story."

With her head on her hands, she glared at Ethan.

Ryan interrupted, "You see, he gets what I'm saying."

She looked at him and frowned. "Oh, I get what you're saying too, but I have a hard time believing the three of us were destined to hook up."

Feeling a bit insecure, he glanced away. He felt something, but how could he expect her to understand.

"Listen, guys, I dunno what's going on either," Ethan said, "but I do know this. If Josie and Sage wouldn't have come along yesterday, we wouldn't be having this conversation right now."

"Probably not," he agreed.

"I hope you don't take this the wrong way, but if Sage wouldn't have chased that thing into the basement, I really don't think I would have had the guts to go in there after you."

Grinning, he nodded. "No need to apologize." He understood Ethan's dilemma. The boy's inadequacy left him feeling slightly uncomfortable. If the shoe was on the other foot, would he have had the courage to go in after Ethan? He couldn't honestly answer that question.

"My point is this," Ethan said. "Sage gave me the courage to chase after you. If I had been alone, well, dude, you'd be up the proverbial creek without the proverbial paddle, if you're picking up what I'm putting down."

Ryan nodded in agreement.

"You said that you were scoping out that place," Josie said. "Why in God's green earth would anyone want to do that?"

His eyes darted to Josie, "Yeah, I did say that, didn't I?"

"Why?"

Color drained from his face. Ryan thought he looked like a criminal caught red-handed as Josie drilled him on what definitely was a mistake he let slip out. Afraid of offending them, he managed to keep from laughing, but swirls of burgundy flushed the boy's face, making it harder to refrain.

Rubbing two sweaty palms together, Ethan slid off the sofa. "I need to use the bathroom," he stammered and went down the hallway.

14

Irritably preoccupied with thoughts of the boy, Alyssa switched off the television and walked to the kitchen, hoping a few hours of studying would chase the memory of Ethan Wysong from her mind. She opened a criminal law textbook, wanting to forget about the day, and began reading an article about fingerprint technology. After finding it impossible to concentrate on the article, she slammed the book shut in frustration.

She glanced at the microwave and smiled with delight. The library was open until eight. It was only a few minutes past six. The quiet atmosphere made it easier to concentrate. Besides, she needed some fresh air. She grabbed her jacket, slid it over the long sleeved shirt she wore, and trotted back into the kitchen. After gathering her keys from a small wicker basket on the counter beside the microwave, she pulled the door shut, locked it, and hurried through the lot to her car.

A chilly gust of wind tousled her hair as she slammed the door shut.

Light rain beaded off the frosted windshield as the engine rumbled to life. As cold air whistled through the vents, the windshield wipers squished back and forth along the smeared glass. Minutes later, her chilled blood began to warm as melted frost trickled down the windshield. She put the car in reverse and backed out of her parking space.

The Grand Am pulled in the library parking lot five minutes after leaving the apartment. Except for a muddy station wagon belonging to one of the librarians, the graveled lot sat empty. She locked the door and walked along Barrow Street to the library. Farther down the road, three young boys kicked a red ball through shallow puddles. Eyeing the kids with mild envy, she hurried along the sidewalk, enduring a nippy breeze whipping through the main street. Ten feet ahead, the library's main entrance sat under a darkened roof.

In the distance, a dark haired boy misjudged the ball and nearly tumbled to the wet pavement. Grinning with embarrassment, he chased it along the street where it stopped a few feet from where she walked along the sidewalk. She smiled as the boy retrieved the ball with a trembling gloved hand and then raced back along the street to his friends. As innocent laughter filtered through the dim street, she pulled open the heavy glass door and stepped inside out of the drizzle.

15

After losing his composure a few minutes earlier, Ethan studied his reflection in the bathroom mirror. He was nervous and a little ashamed to tell them the truth about Lauren and his mother's suicide. If Ryan and Josie were going to risk their lives trying to figure out the bizarre circumstances surrounding his sister's disappearance, there could be no secrets between them. Ecstatic to have made a couple of new friends, he abandoned the bathroom and stepped into the hallway.

He gathered his jacket from the hall closet and walked into the living room. They sat across from each other in silence, glancing up as he entered the room. Sage rested beside the love seat a few inches from Josie's feet, snoring like he had nothing to worry about. He envied the dog.

Devon Whitfield was right; destiny called upon him to find Lauren. The courage he needed to delve deeper into the mystery depended on their help. He stood a minute watching his friends with the realization that he could not embark on this journey alone. Like Ryan, he couldn't shake the feeling that some unseen force had brought them together. Though they only met yesterday, an unspoken bond had formed between them. He was desperate, and Josie was wrong. If rehashing the memories of that horrible year would give them an understanding of why he needed to get back into the cellar, then so be it. First, he needed to clear his head.

He cleared his throat. "I'll back in a bit."

"Where you going?" Josie asked and jumped to her feet. Sage picked his head up from the floor and looked curiously at the girl.

"I need to clear my head. Believe it or not, the cold air helps."

"Feel like having some company?"

Smiling, he nodded.

"Come on, Sage," she said and hurried to the kitchen.

"Well, dude, you feel like a walk."

Ryan shook his head. "Nah, I'm still a little sore."

"And miss out on the guided tour?" Josie shouted from the kitchen.

He smiled as Ryan chuckled.

With Sage leading the way, they played follow-the-leader down the steps, walked briskly along the driveway, and hurried past Josie's Explorer. Spherical charcoal clouds raced across a monstrous sky, adding to his already dismal mood. Grey darkness lingered in every direction. A chilly breeze howled across the knee-high grass, swaying the branches of the tall pines lining the front yard and the bulky chestnut trees behind the house. He shivered and grabbed her hand as drizzle dampened their clothes. The cold alone was bearable, but chilly air in cahoots with the distant memory of the creature in black combined to produce a spine-chilling effect that lingered a boding evil. After shedding the feeling of unknown forces conspiring against them, he led them to the bottom of the driveway and stared at the menacing rooftop silhouetted in the distance.

"Which way?" Ethan asked, already knowing the answer.

"Go left," she said. "The further away we are from there the better."

They walked the streets through the dimly lit town of Gastons Gorge, saying nothing more than a few words to each other. Only a few people populated the streets. They saw a few kids playing on the sidewalk and an old man staggering down a dark street; his destination was as unknown to them as theirs was to him. He looked cold but walked like a man that didn't have any particular place to go. Ethan found himself wondering what skeletons the old man might have in his closet as they continued along the dim streets. They walked a while in the bitter drizzle in silence. As usual, Sage led the way, sniffing the sidewalk like a bloodhound hot on a trail of a wanted criminal. He led them downtown and along Mountain View Road and finally back toward his house. By the time they cut through a shadowy alley to avoid a stroll past the hotel, the time was shortly after eight o'clock, but it seemed later due to the overcast sky. The howling wind sounded like a pack of wild dogs hunting for food. The treetops shook violently from the forceful wind whistling through the branches. Dangling leaves broke free from their stems and spiraled to the ground below. Shivering from the cold, he walked hand in hand with Josie and dreaded the thought of tonight's conversation.

For the better part of the last eight years, he felt alone. He had relatively few friends that were made up of inmates and counselors at the numerous institutions he frequented. Yesterday afternoon, he encountered Josie and Ryan, and everything changed. The time had come to lay it all out there and see what happened. Maybe they would agree to help him with the burden that rested solely on his shoulders for almost half of his life.

At the end of the alley, they made a right onto Barrow Street and headed for home. Although he looked forward to getting in out of the cold, he dreaded what would come after. As usual, the cold air invigorated his state of mind. The time had come to tell them about Lauren and his mother.

Josie stopped dead on the street a few inches from the driveway and pointed at his house.

Startled, he squeezed tighter onto her hand and squinted through the yard.

Silhouetted in darkness, a form crouched on the muddy ground below his bedroom window. It peeked through the blinds into his room. Like the thing dragging Ryan through the grass last night, it wore a doleful black hooded robe.

Sage growled and broke toward the house with his tail pointed to the sky.

With catlike agility, the figure spun backward, glared at Sage a quick second, tore off through the yard, and jumped the high fence separating the property line in one stride. Sage galloped with speed, but the thing's head start was too great to for the dog to overcome.

It ran through the neighboring yard and disappeared behind a row of pines.

On two shivering legs, he squeezed tighter on to Josie's hand and pulled her up the driveway as Sage dug at earth under the fence and barked aggressively at the dying grass in the shadowy yard.

"Come on, boy," Josie shouted.

After one last threatening bark, he leaped backward, landed on four paws and sprinted through the slushy mud, joining them on the front porch. Panting heavily, he chased Josie through the door and into the hallway.

After staring at the swaying pine trees hoping that the creature stayed out of sight, Ethan followed them inside, slammed and locked the door, and stood a minute clutching his knees.

16

In regards to Ethan the trip to the library was a waste of time.

She searched the computer diligently for recent articles about Ethan Wysong. There was no new information. Only old tidbits she already read a thousand times before appeared on the screen. There were articles about his life in Gastons Gorge, but no recent photographs were attached to any of them. However, upon digging up a few old high school yearbooks, she learned the identity of his girlfriend. She graduated from Gorge High last spring—the same year as Alyssa. Her name was Josie McShay. The girl in the photograph was a lot bigger than the girl in the grocery store, but she was positive they were one in the same.

Jesus, she must have lost a hundred pounds.

After pouring through real estate information, she learned the Wysong's house was left to Ethan. As a kid, she spend more nights in that house than she could remember, but after Lauren's death, she never stepped foot into it again, not even to say goodbye. After Mrs. Wysong committed suicide in one of the bedrooms, Alyssa grew to fear the house.

Memories of regret filled her mind. For the first time in years, she cried over Lauren's death. It had been a long time since she dwelt on such things, and now, standing alone in the library, Alyssa wished Ethan had never came back to Gastons Gorge. His return stirred up too many unpleasant memories. She was nine and forced to suffer with the death of her best friend. Ever since the day of her friend's funeral, she avoided making new friendships. Life was easier that way.

After wiping the tears from her cheeks with the back of her hand, she zipped up her jacket, hurried through the library door, and jogged to her car. With Lauren's memory fresh on her mind, she wondered if investigating Ethan was the right thing to do. She fired the engine, backed out of the lot, and followed Barrow Street from the library toward the back end of town to a tan house she had hoped to never see again. After zipping past the driveway, she pulled off the road and killed the engine. Two vehicles sat in the driveway: a green Toyota Tacoma and a deep blue Ford Explorer.

She couldn't breathe.

Her throat tightened. She had a hard time concentrating on the task at hand. Being this close to the house made her stomach flutter with nerves. Inside her head, an energetic voice ordered her to start the vehicle and drive far away from this place. Succumbing to the voice of reason, she fired the engine, swung onto the road, and drove until hundreds of yards separated her and that awful house. She wanted to forget about stumbling upon him earlier this afternoon and to push Lauren's memory aside for good.

Instead, Laurens youthful face flashed through her mind.

She slammed the brakes and skidded a dozen feet on the wet pavement. To her left, the old hotels shadow danced across the landscape under a depressing moon. Her heart pounded as cold sweat chilled her trembling hands. Looking away, she swung the vehicle around, stomped hard on the gas pedal, and sped back toward Lauren's house.

Dating back to its origins, the hotel has played a sinister role in numerous mysterious deaths and disappearances occurring in Gastons Gorge, including Lauren's. Despite rumors that Ethan might have been somehow involved in his sister's disappearance, she could never shake the feeling that the building was somehow connected. After all, Lauren Wysong wasn't the only person to last be seen near the building before vanishing into thin air.

Remorse replaced her terror.

As the hotel vanished in the rearview, she felt warmer blood chase the chill from her skin and bones. Glancing from the mirror, she drifted to the side of the road and parked in plain sight of his house and felt relieved to be away from that place. With the heater cranked on high, she sat a few feet beyond the driveway contemplating what to do next. She considered walking up the graveled driveway and pounding on the door demanding to know why he came back home but decided that might not be the best course of action.

He wouldn't remember you anyway. Even he did, how would he react?

Maybe tomorrow her confidence would rise. She would approach him and demand to know why he was back in town. He might not have a clue who she was, but she would never forget his face again.

As she pulled away, she thought about tomorrow's course of action.

In the rearview mirror, a large man dressed in a long black trench coat stood on an embankment and stared through a dark yard at the Wysong's house. Ignoring an urge to slam on the breaks, she drove home thinking Ethan probably had a right to know someone was spying on his house.

They wouldn't believe you anyway.

17

It's now or never, Ethan thought while sitting a glass of water on the coffee table beside the love seat. After a deep breath, he struggled to find a good place to start. After deciding there was no good place to begin, he smiled at Josie and twirled his finger through his hair. "Do you remember when we met yesterday and I told you my name? You said it sounded familiar."

"Yeah, and it still hasn't come to me."

"You've probably heard my name quite a few times in your life," he said, "but you would have been just a kid. You would have been maybe eight or nine years old. You probably heard it from your parents or maybe even overheard it on the news."

She shook her head.

"I lived in this house until I was almost thirteen. The worst thing that ever happened to me occurred a year earlier when I was still too young to know better." He closed his eyes, took a deep breath, and then continued. "The worst thing in my life happened late that September almost nine years ago."

With a sympathetic grin, she took his hand and gently stroked his fingers.

"I had a little sister. She was almost three years younger than me. Her name was Lauren," he said thinking it was strange saying her name out loud.

Enthralling expressions formed on their faces. He had their full attention, which made him feel strangely comfortable. It was hard to talk about her to anyone but Devon Whitfield, but they needed to hear it.

Sipping a glass of water, he closed his eyes. "Her name was Lauren." After a deep breath, he continued. "It was a Saturday afternoon. The day was warm considering how late into September it was, and she wanted to go outside and play. She had just turned nine, and I was a few weeks shy of twelve, so you could probably guess that I wasn't all that thrilled about spending my Saturday afternoon hanging out with my kid sister. My mom worked all day as a nurse's assistant in the hospital over in Crayton, and she took night classes at the university trying to get a nursing degree at night. More than anything, she hated being told what to do by the more educated nurses."

Aware they were watching him, he opened his eyes.

"She cleaned waste and vomit all day and put up with arrogant nurses who thought they knew everything because of a piece of paper given out by some college. She really, really, hated taking orders from them. She thought her talents would be better served helping people instead of cleaning up after them. My mom seemed to be in a bad mood a lot back then, but she really did try her best not to take it out on us kids; sometimes she did, and sometimes she didn't. I never begrudged her for it. I loved my mom. Between the long hours at the hospital and her schooling, I was given the responsibility of being the caretaker for Lauren. During those days, my mom's life was difficult, and she expected me to help her take care of our family, and I let her down."

Yeah right, let her down. Because of you, she's dead.

"My mom was working the afternoon shift at the hospital that day, and Lauren didn't want to spend the day inside the house. I wanted to stay in and play one of those old video games that seemed pretty cool at the time. I think it was called *Toejam* and something."

"Earl," Ryan said, "the bigger guy's name was Earl. I think he was a giant hotdog."

"Anyway, we got dressed for the weather after Lauren told me she wanted to go for a walk around the neighborhood. That sounded like a decent idea to me too. I thought we might bump into a few of my friends. So we left the house and walked along Barrow Street toward that place. Lauren was out in front, and since she stayed on the sidewalk, I let her get ahead of me. I was distracted by the events of the day. I could think of a thousand other things that would be better than hanging out with my sister. I was desperate and hoping to come across my friends playing combat, which is actually nothing more than a glorified game of hide-and-seek with teams."

"We used to play a game like that," Ryan said. "We called it team freeze tag."

"I wasn't allowed to leave the yard long enough to play," Josie said with a subtle smirk. "Besides, I didn't have any friends to play with. My parents always made sure of that."

Sensing her discomfort, he squeezed her fingers.

"It was warm for the time of the year, but it was still a little chilly. Lauren wore a blue jacket. Let's just say she stood out in a crowd."

He took a long swig of water and continued before losing his nerve.

"We walked along Barrow Street with Lauren a stone's throw out in front of me. I could see her in the distance. I know I should have run to catch up to her, but my mind was somewhere else. I cared about myself. I didn't think it was fair for my mother to dump Lauren on me. I was only eleven years old, and most kids that age are somewhat selfish, especially when it comes to wasting your time taking care of your sister."

The room was silent as they waited for him to continue.

"She was a good ways ahead of me. I saw her there, but when she ran past the corner near the end of the street, she vanished. That was the last time I saw her."

"Jesus," Ryan said.

Ethan nodded. "I searched everywhere. It was so weird. I mean, how someone could be there one minute and not the next, I don't get it."

Though he tried to fight emotion, he felt the tears drip from his eyes.

"I searched every single inch of this town except for inside that place because I never thought she would go near there. Never in a million years did I think she would have gone inside that place."

"You don't think she actually did?" Josie said.

"I should have looked there, but I was scared."

His eyes began to itch from the tears.

"I searched the neighborhood thoroughly, from the hotel to my house. That's where I called my mom at work. She was home in less than ten minutes, and within a few hours my house was swarming with police. The town had four officers back in those days, and they spent the next two days searching for my sister. I remember it like it was yesterday. Search parties spent days checking the areas along the railroad yard and the creek."

"Did they find anything?" Ryan asked.

"They searched everywhere they thought Lauren might have wandered off to. Search parties made their way past the railroad yard and walked along Gorge Creek until it emptied into the Youghiogheny River. They even drug the river and came up empty. The same with the forests surrounding town. Crews looked for days in those woods, and again they didn't find any trace of my sister anywhere. Fliers were posted all over the area. There was even a cash reward for anyone who had information. After a few days, no one came forward, and my mother went on television offering the same reward. However, like everything else they tried, nobody had any information."

He paused and glanced over their faces. They hung on his every word.

"They claimed to have searched the hotel as well. According to the police, there was no trace of her there either."

Ryan cleared his throat. "Did they ever find anything?"

"Not a clue."

"Wow," Josie said, wiping tears on her sleeve. "That must have been tough to deal with."

"It got even tougher when some people in town got it in their heads that maybe I did something to her. Can you believe that? They actually thought that I did something to my little sister. For a few weeks following Lauren's disappearance, I was the main suspect, and it wasn't until federal agents determined I didn't have the necessary means to hurt her and then dump her body where no one would ever find her that the law eased off me."

More tears fell from the corner of Josie's eyes and trickled down the side of her face.

"I can't imagine," Ryan said.

"Even though I was proven innocent, some people were still skeptical. They thought the cops were wrong. My life here wasn't very easy after that. People looked down on me, and I just couldn't cope with it."

"I never heard anything about you from my parents," Josie said, "but, like I told you guys, they were very protective. However, I do remember hearing about a little girl about my age that disappeared when I was a kid."

"They imposed a curfew for a few months afterwards," Ethan said. "Kids had to be off the streets and in their houses before dark."

Ryan's eyes were wide open. "That would stink big time."

"I spent the next year in Gastons Gorge, but it wasn't the same place that I loved. I was treated different in school by both the kids and the teachers. Needless to say, I got into quite a few fights that year, and I always took the brunt of the punishment. Once you get a reputation, it sticks."

"How'd you get through it?" Ryan said.

"One day at a time," he said, managing a smile.

"I don't understand how people can get their kicks tormenting other people," Josie said, dampening her sleeve with more tears. "Especially kids, they can be so cruel sometimes."

"By the end of the school year, I missed more days than I can remember. After a while, the school gave up on me. I mostly played video games and gained weight. I lost every bit of initiative that I ever had in life. I felt sorry for myself when I should have been trying to ease my mom's pain. Can you imagine what losing a kid must have felt like? Back then, I was too selfish worrying about my own grief and guilt to see what she was going through."

"You were just a kid," Ryan said.

"Yeah," Josie agreed, "A kid can't be expected to deal with a situation like that. I don't think most adults could handle it."

"Maybe, but that woman had her nine-year-old little girl snatched from her without a reason, and half the people in this godforsaken town blamed her son. I should have done something to help her deal with the pain."

"Did she blame you?" Josie asked.

"To tell you the truth," he said, "I think she wasn't sure what to believe. Can you imagine losing one kid and someone putting an idea in your head that maybe it was your other kid that did it? I don't really know what she believed."

She glanced away, "I'm so sorry."

Ethan cleared his throat. "We didn't really talk. I think we said maybe ten words to each other after Lauren disappeared. I don't know how she felt about me. I think it didn't matter to her if I did something to Lauren or not because in her eyes, I was responsible anyway. She was in my care when it happened. I don't think she ever forgave me or herself. She made it one year after Lauren went missing. It was almost one year to the day when I found her. She lived as long as possible with her demons and then overdosed on a bottle of sleeping pills. I found her after she didn't come out of her room for two days. She did that sometimes, liked to stay in her room for days at a time, but she eventually came out to eat or get something to drink or go to the bathroom. This time she never came out, and I had something new to feel guilty about."

"You must have lost it," said Ryan.

"After that, I belonged to the state of Pennsylvania. I was twelve when my mom killed herself, and by the time I turned eighteen, I lived in six different mental institutions and over a dozen foster homes. Over the next couple of years, I worked odd jobs here and there and along with the rent from this house, I managed to save enough money to move back here. An uncle watched the house after my mom died and had been renting it out for me ever since. He called me a few months ago and asked if I was planning on selling the place. At first, I thought I would be better off staying as far away from Gastons Gorge as I possibly could. I figured that would be the best thing for me. I was afraid to come back, but then I kept thinking about her. I thought I could move back here and find the courage to finally go inside that horrible place. Ever since Lauren vanished, I just felt that that place had something to do with her disappearance."

"You said the cops searched it." Ryan said.

"They did," he said, "but I think that there may be more to it than that. Like I said, I thought the place was somehow responsible, but until yesterday, when I watched that thing dragging you through the yard, I was never completely sure. Now I know it's true."

Silence filled the room.

Josie whispered, "Maybe we did all meet for a reason."

"Then you'll help me?"

"Count me in," Ryan said. "I owe you two that much for saving my sorry self."

Josie nodded but remained silent.

18

He stood beside Ethan on the front porch and watched Josie back down the driveway and then drive along Barrow Street toward downtown. After her vehicle disappeared over a slight grade, she was gone, and his new friend looked troubled.

"We saw it earlier after our walk," Ethan whispered and watched his silvery breath cut through the thick cold air.

"Huh, saw what?"

"That thing, or creature, or whatever the crap it is," he said while glancing around the yard. "Josie and I saw it when we came back from walking. It was nosing around outside my bedroom window."

"Why didn't you say something earlier?"

He hesitated. "Because of Josie," Ethan said and then looked at him with a skeptical glimmer in his eyes. "She saw it too, but I don't think she wanted to believe it was the same thing that pulled you inside that place. She seemed to think it was just some pervert up to no good. So I played it off as that to ease her mind, but I'm telling you, Ryan, I know what it was."

"Seriously, man, are you sure?"

"Yeah, dude, I'm positive. I think a random pervert hanging outside of my house and staring through my window after what happened yesterday might be just a little too coincidental."

"You sure Josie's isn't right?" he asked. "How do you know for sure?"

"Dude, the thing in the window was there because we spoiled whatever plan it had for you last night. I'm telling you, it wasn't some pervert hoping to catch me dancing around my room in my skivvies."

His heart dropped as Ethan words spoke the truth. He wanted Josie's theory to be right. The thought of that thing lurking around Ethan's house made him nervous. "Do you by any chance happen to have a flashlight?"

Ethan nodded.

"Good," he said. "Go grab it, and let's go have a look."

Ethan disappeared through the front door and returned a few minutes later dressed in a dark blue jacket and holding a long black flashlight in his right hand. In silence, Ryan followed him down the steps and around the corner of the house to the window.

Ethan shone the light toward the ground.

Under the window, pressed into the moist earth, two large bootprints collected rainwater.

Ethan swept the light across the yard.

Behind them, chestnut trees swayed against a brisk breeze, adding to his paranoia. "Come on," he said and hurried back around the house. After sprinting up the steps two at a time, he raced across the porch, followed Ethan through the door, and engaged the deadbolt. A few minutes later, they had every door and window in the house shut tight and locked.

"Josie's right," he said. "Those bootprints out there were made by a man. They are definitely human."

Ethan looked skeptical. "I'm telling you, dude, that thing that Sage fought to save you from was definitely not a man."

"Either way, somebody's keeping tabs on us."

"I say we sleep on the couches tonight with one eye open at all times."

"No doubt. That sounds like a good idea to me."

After gathering blankets and pillows from the bedrooms, Ethan plopped down on the recliner and offered him the couch.

Ryan felt strangely exhilarated but couldn't shake the morbid sensation rolling back and forth through his gut. *With any luck we won't be murdered in our sleep,* he thought as he stared at the ceiling and imagined the creature in black dragging him through a dark corridor.

"Thank you."

"For what?" Ethan whispered.

"For coming in there after me."

"Thank Sage, he saved you. I just helped."

"Then thanks for helping. I owe you and Josie's dog my life."

"You don't know that for sure. Maybe you would have figured out a way to save yourself."

"I shudder to think what might have happened to me down there in the darkness if you three didn't come along."

"You're welcome, dude."

His mind drifted to the person that stood outside the window earlier. "What do we have for weapons?"

"Nothing much, but I can go get a few things in the morning."

"Good deal," he said and then shut his eyes.

As the strange hooded figure finally drifted from his thoughts, he fell asleep and dreamed about Molly.

19

Slumped down in the seat behind the steering wheel, Alyssa stared through the dirt-streaked windshield and watched for movement of any kind inside the house. Although her car was parked a few hundred feet away and a dozen trees stretched across the front yard, she had a great view of the front door. The green truck sat under the carport, but not much else happened since Ethan parked about an hour earlier and carried two plastic bags inside the house. Though she had no idea what he was up to, her curiosity grew more intense with every passing second.

As her desire to know his business heightened, she struggled with an urge to abandon her car, run full steam up the driveway, and pound on the door demanding to know his intentions. Instead, she listened to an old compact disc as the time ticked slowly by. The singer bellowed out something about really needing a raincoat when an Explorer turned into the driveway and pulled behind the truck. Josie McShay and a German shepherd exited the vehicle and disappeared from sight.

What's with those two?

At first, she thought he might be selling the house and she was interested in buying it, but their relationship appeared to run deeper. There was something between them. Ethan Wysong and Josie McShay had no business knowing each other, but for some reason, they seemed thick as thieves.

Deciding to stay put and wait them out, she turned the radio up and thought about the person who watched the house last night.

Maybe she wasn't the only one interested in his homecoming, or maybe the man last night just stopped for a breather on his evening walk, and her paranoid mind perceived it as something more sinister.

Yeah right. He was up to something mischievous, and you know it.

Twenty minutes later, as the singer on the radio bellowed out the word *shame* over and over again, Ethan, Josie, and another man followed the dog along the driveway and hopped inside the girl's vehicle. They backed out of the driveway and turned left. A few seconds later, after they were out of sight, she drove along the road and saw them parked a hundred feet in the distance. Across from the hotel, Ethan and Josie climbed out of the vehicle and followed the dog across Barrow Street. The stranger, a muscular man with light brown hair, stood alone on the road and eyeballed the neighborhood. His wide-eyed expression heightened Alyssa's interest. He seemed nervous. After a few seconds, he turned around and chased after the others with a long black flashlight clutched in his hand. A faded backpack strapped across his shoulder bounced against his back with every lumbered footfall. With the Shepherd ten feet out in front and sniffing the ground, they followed the dirt path toward the old rail yard and disappeared behind a line of trees. The big man glimpsed over his shoulder seconds before vanishing around the corner.

Feeling gullible, she chuckled.

She fired the engine and stared at the trail. *God, sometimes you're an idiot,* she thought and pumped the gas pedal. It appeared her suspicions were wrong about their intentions. As she drove past the dirt path, she glanced to her right and spotted them walking through the high weeds toward the rear of the hotel.

She turned the car around in a driveway.

20

In the daylight, the room seemed less threatening.

Ryan stood in what he thought was once the main lobby between Josie and Ethan and crinkled his nose in disgust. A faint scent of musty decay drifted through his nostrils. Faded ivy and crumbled black moss clung to the deteriorated brick. The room looked and smelled disgusting.

Beside him, Josie coughed. "I didn't notice the stink of this place last night."

"Yeah, I didn't either," Ethan said.

Ryan pointed at the debris. "I think this place has seen its better days."

"No doubt, dude. Like a hundred million years ago."

In front of them, ruined steps rose to a broken upper balcony. Dirty water dripped from a hole in the ceiling, splashed onto a busted wooden handrail, trickled down the blackened stone, and disappeared under the broken glass and splintered wood strewn about the floor. Though the structure was in ruins now, he thought the staircase must have looked extravagant in its heyday. Feeling curious, he took a step closer to the once-grand architecture and studied his surroundings. Behind the ruined staircase, rotted wooden horses blocked a deteriorated elevator shaft. It appeared all valuable metals were gutted and carried out years ago. Only a black void filled with floating dust and musty air remained.

"Watch yourselves a minute," Ryan said and turned on the flashlight.

Ethan and Josie stood beside Sage a few feet away.

A beam of light sliced through floating dust and pierced the blackness. Broken chunks of concrete littered the floor below. For a split second, red beady eyes glared up at him and then scurried out of sight so quick he wondered if they were ever there or just a figment of his imagination. Taking a step backward, he glanced at the wall to the left of the elevator shaft. A set of rusted doors caught his attention. Not waiting for the others, he maneuvered across the room trying to avoid the cluttered junk and kicked the doors hard. Dust exploded from the top as the heavy doors banged against the wall behind it with a hollow thud.

"Guys, check this out," he said as dust settled on his hair.

Ethan and Josie hurried to his side.

Obscured in dust and thick clumpy spiderwebs, four broken doors lined each side of a long hallway.

"What do you guys think?" he said as he swept the beam through the hallway. "Let's check out these rooms first. I'm not too thrilled about going downstairs until we see what's up here first."

"Do we have time?" Josie said.

"I don't know," said Ryan, walking through the open doors. "I know I'd feel better if I knew what was above us when we're exploring the darker parts of this creepy place." He killed the light and led the way along the passage.

Thick and wet spiderwebs clung from the corners of the wall and along the ceiling. Gaps of light filtered down through the roof, filling the hallway with soft shadowy light. At the first room, Ryan stopped, ran his fingers across the broken wood, and gave them a curious grin.

Sage trotted past Ethan and Josie and stood beside him as if waiting for a command.

Ryan pointed. "You search this room, and I'll search that one. Josie, you wait here and keep your eyes peeled for anything unusual."

"No way!" she shouted, "I've seen enough horror flicks to know that splitting up is a good way to get hurt or worse."

"Amen to that, sister," Ethan said.

"Okay then," Ryan said. "Let's stay together."

He pushed the door halfway open with his boot and followed Sage into the room.

Except for shattered glass, busted concrete, broken hunks of wood, and scattered animal droppings, the room appeared empty. What looked to be a bathroom was built into the back wall. A large filthy bathtub sat along the back of the room, infested with black mold and dark green stagnant water. Nothing else sparked his interest.

They spent a few minutes searching each room on the ground floor. Except for the occasional skeletal remains of rats and birds stuck to the floor, every room appeared nearly identical.

21

At first, she thought about calling the town constable, but what would she tell him? She sat in the car and wondered why anyone would go inside such a depressing place. In the past, on several occasions, she drove down Beanery Hill and hit the gas without as much as a second glance. Though she was weary of the old structure, for the first time, she seriously considered breaking into the historic landmark. Over the years, townspeople fought successfully to protect its cold and lonely walls from demolition, though she had no idea why. Feeling uncertain what to do, she absorbed its awe-inspiring gothic atmosphere and understood why local children steered clear of its walls.

They should have knocked this place to the ground years ago.

Her mind flashed backward to a few years after Lauren vanished. After eavesdropping on a weird conversation her parents were engaged in regarding other mysterious disappearances near the hotel, she scoured library computers and newspaper archives for other strange occurrences and was baffled by her findings.

This place has numerous skeletons in its closets.

She killed the engine and abandoned the sanctity of her Grand Am. After a difficult stroll through the knee-high brown grass and crumbled leaves, she stood behind a row of pine trees with her hands buried in two deep pockets and stared at the ominous view in disbelief of her situation. Gathering courage, she hurried around the corner looking for an entrance. Embedded into the muddy soil, four sets of differently shaped footprints guided her to a busted door at the rear of the building. Feeling conspicuous, she glanced over her shoulder and then wiggled between broken pieces of wood and stepped inside.

Buzzing with fear and excitement, she surveyed the room, looking for signs of Ethan and his trespassing friends. She felt like a detective hot on the trail of an ageless mystery, scrutinizing scattered footprints strewn about the dusty floor. For the time being, their whereabouts remained unknown.

Unnatural silence tickled her nerves.

High above, grand architecture captured her breath. Lost in the mystique of what was a place where high-class people came to marvel in the exquisiteness of this once-fancy hotel, she temporarily forgot her current predicament. For a second, she imagined herself a wealthy wife parading through sparkling halls with her prestigious husband on her arm.

From behind a rusted door, muffled voices vanquished the daydream. Jittery panic pumped nervous blood to her steadily beating heart. Glancing backward, she entertained the idea of running back through the door and forgetting all about Ethan and his gang of misfit meddlers.

A vision of Lauren's face flickered through her mind, and a single tear dripped down her cheek. She owed it to her best friend to investigate her brother's intentions, regardless of personal danger. Deep down, despite different opinions from the local media all those years ago, she always believed his innocence. Now, while searching the area for someplace to hide, uncertainty slipped into her mind.

From behind the door, the voices grew louder.

Panicking, she surveyed the large room for someplace to hide. Straight ahead, steps descended into darkness. Lacking the nerve to hide in the basement, she scurried past the broken glass and ducked behind a large counter to the left of the heavy doors.

22

As the door flung open and bounced gently off the wall behind it, Sage barked vigorously and sprinted toward a large counter on the far side of the main room. Josie reached for his collar but only swept at empty air as a wide-eyed girl popped up from behind the counter.

Ethan's heart sank as she waved her arms in the air.

Surprise filled her deep brown eyes. Dust glistened through her short jet-black hair as she stepped out into a widening beam of sunlight that broke through an opening in the ceiling high above. Dressed in tight blue jeans and a red bulky sweater, she stepped backward with her eyes fixated on Sage.

Josie crept up behind the barking canine and grabbed his collar. "Easy, boy," she said and pulled him away from the girl.

Her eyes darted from Sage and focused on him. Her flawless face twisted with a strange grin as she stepped closer to his group. The strangely accusing smirk on her face left him feeling nervous, and a touch of guilt fluttered through his stomach. Though she looked a few years younger than he did, Ethan found her wildly attractive, yet somehow familiar. Her eyes remained focused on only him.

The grin vanished from her face, but the accusing look remained. "What are you doing in here?"

"Well, we were just…," Ethan started to say but his nerves and a sense of paranoia kept him from finishing his words. Though the questioned was asked to all three of them, he couldn't shake the feeling that her words were meant for his ears only.

"What business is it of yours, and what are you doing in here?" Josie said, stroking the back of her dog's neck in an attempt to calm him.

Ryan took a step forward and stood beside Josie. "Are you following us?"

She broke eye contact with Ethan and glanced back at Sage. He took a deep breath and hoped the girl didn't notice his nervousness. At some point in his life he had seen this girl before but couldn't remember from where. As she stood a few feet in front of him, he closed his eyes a quick second and tried to remember.

"What are you doing here?" she said again and lowered her arms to her side. "This place is private property owned by this town's historical society, and unless you have permission, you are not allowed to be inside this place."

"Not that it's any of your business," Ryan said, "but we're just checking the place out. Kind of doing some exploring of sorts, I guess you could say."

"I don't believe you. Why would anyone want to go poking around in a place like this?"

"Well like it or not, sister, that's the bottom line." Ethan said, struggling to fight off a grin. He couldn't shake the feeling of knowing this woman. Maybe she looked like someone at one of the mental institutions or in one of the many towns he called home while in foster care. He couldn't place her, but he knew for certain that they've met before.

Ryan stepped forward. "I met my friend here a few months back at a retreat, and he was telling me about an old haunted hotel in the town he grew up in, so here we are, knee-deep in ghost poop."

With skepticism, she stared at Ryan.

"It's sort of a hobby of mine," Ryan said.

"You're a bunch of liars."

He couldn't take it any longer. "I know you from somewhere," he said. "From where, I can't remember, but we know each other, don't we?"

Her eyes darted from Ryan and scrutinized him with frigid fascination. He wanted to look away from her accusing stare but managed to stay focused on her eyes instead. For some reason, he couldn't fathom why this girl made him nervous.

"You're right, Ethan Wysong. You do know me."

"Who are you?"

"Her name's Alyssa," Josie said. "I don't know your last name, but we went to the same school. We were in a few classes together, but you probably don't remember."

Upon hearing her name, he stumbled forward and nearly tripped over his own feet. Stunned and speechless, he gawked at the girl standing in front of him and felt guilt wash through his entire body. She was a lot younger the last time they saw each other. In those days she was a timid little girl. Now she was a beautiful woman with an obvious attitude. Alyssa Thorpe, his little sister's best friend, was drop-dead gorgeous. She stood five foot five, weighed around 120 pounds, with flawless white teeth and a body most guys would empty their bank accounts for.

"Your name's Josie," she said with a condescending smirk on her face. "That's right, I remember you."

In awe, Ethan shut his eyes and visualized Lauren's childhood friend as she had been all those years ago. The woman standing in front of him was really Alyssa Thorpe. His sister's best friend who spent many nights at his house when she was just a little girl was this grown woman. "Oh my god, you're little Lyssa Thorpe," he said and took a step closer to her. "I can't believe you're standing there all grown-up looking as awesome as you do."

She smiled, and warm blood painted her cheeks red.

He wanted to reach out and touch her cheek but thought better of it. Getting whacked across the face in front of Ryan and Josie was an embarrassing occurrence he wanted to avoid.

Now that he knew who she was, how could he not have made the connection? Though all grown up, she looked almost identical to that little kid he knew nine years earlier.

"Lyssa and Lauren were best friends as kids," he said, struggling to control his emotions. "Anyways, this is my friend Ryan, and you apparently already know Josie."

Ignoring the introductions, Ryan said, "So why are you spying on us?"

"I just want to know what you three are doing in here."

"Are you following us?" Josie said, seeming slightly annoyed.

"I saw the three of you break in here, and I thought seriously about calling the cops, but something urged me to find out the reason first. So please, tell me what you are doing in this place."

"I doubt you'd believe us if we told you," Ethan said.

"Try me."

He cleared his throat. "Two days ago, I—"

Josie interrupted. "Are you sure about this?"

Ignoring her, he explained their situation down to every last detail, including how he thought this place had something to do with Lauren's disappearance and their paths crossing being tied into it.

She stared at him for what felt like a hundred years with a bewildered expression on her face.

With regret, he glanced at Ryan and Josie. If she didn't believe him, she would call the cops, and once again, he would look like a monster to the people of this town.

Seconds later, her grin disappeared. "I'm coming with you."

"Really? You actually believe me?" he said with a realization that he should shut his mouth. "I don't think I would believe that story if I didn't see that thing with my own two eyes."

Ryan sighed. "Hush up, Ethan."

"It's fine," Alyssa said. "As crazy as your story sounds, I really do believe you. I always believed you. Never in a million years did I think you would have hurt her. I'm so sorry for Lauren, and I'm sorry for your mother and for everything you had to endure over the years. I loved you back then as if you were my own brother, and I still feel the same way. I miss her so much, Ethan, and I want to help you."

"I miss her too, and I welcome your help," he said with tears dripping from his eyes. "What do you guys think?"

"Fine by me," Ryan said. "Glad to have you with us."

"The more the merrier," Josie said.

"Then it's settled," he said. "But we need to hurry because we only a few hours before the sun goes down, and honestly, I don't want to be in here once that happens. This may sound crazier than I am, but we don't have a clue what that thing is, and I'm not ruling out the possibility of a vampire."

Ryan chuckled. "Really, man, a bloodsucking vampire?" He clapped the back of Ethan's shoulder. "Come on, man, are you serious? You said yourself that it was still daytime when you guys rescued me."

"Besides," Josie said, "Vampires don't exist."

Josie and Ryan giggled simultaneously like immature children having their first schoolyard crush.

Alyssa's expression hardened.

Their laughter faded, and a comfortable silence drifted through the room.

"What's that look for?" Ethan asked.

"Last night I saw a man covered from head to toe in all black standing on the road and staring at your house."

"Say what, dude."

"He was a few feet off the road, squatting on the edge of the lawn. I guess I just thought he was from the neighborhood. I thought maybe he was just out for a midnight stroll or something."

He glanced at Josie and gave her a crooked smile.

"Was it definitely a man?" Ryan asked.

"I think so, but it was dark, and I didn't really get a look at his face."

"Regardless," Ethan said." We really need to get going."

"Listen," Alyssa said and glanced back and forth between the members of the group. "This place has a bit of a history."

"What do you mean by history?" Ryan said.

"Have any of you guys ever thoroughly researched this place?" she said. "Maybe checked newspaper articles involving strange happenings in Gastons Gorge and stuff like that?"

His eyes dropped to the floor. "Yeah, a little, but I never found anything."

"Well I have and I think you're right about a lot of things."

He stood speechless, staring at Alyssa.

"I've found quite a few interesting tidbits of information linking this place to some crazy stuff that's happened in this town over the years."

His skin tingled, and the hair rose on his arms.

Though obsessed with this building, he never thought about digging into the hotel's history. He felt stupid but realized Ryan and Josie had the same dopey expressions stamped on their faces. He wanted to learn more before descending into the basement in search of Ryan's abductor.

"Let's postpone this until tomorrow morning."

"Are you sure?" Ryan and Josie said simultaneously.

"He's sure," Alyssa said with her eyes once again focused on him. "I need to tell you guys everything, and then we can come up with a decent plan."

"Let's go back to my house and figure out what to do next."

Josie turned and walked toward the door leading outside. "Sounds good to me. Let's get out of here."

"I'm with her," Ryan said and followed Josie out into the daylight.

Like a loyal soldier, Sage disappeared through the opening after his master.

"Thank you for believing in me," Ethan said and wrapped his arms around Alyssa. He held her briefly and then kissed her cheek and felt a sense of relief he had not felt in many years. "Come on, sister, let's catch up with the others."

Alyssa smiled and followed him outside.

PART III

DEEP UNDER EARTH

23

She sat on the couch, holding on tight to the envelope she's looked at over a hundred times before. Inside, she had a half a dozen photocopied articles she thought these people might be interested in. Over the years, through countless hours of research and time spent on library computers, she managed to find dozens of news articles connecting the old hotel to the many strange occurrences taking place in this town over the past century; however, she thought the ones inside the envelope were the most important. For the first time, Alyssa felt comfortable enough to share the information with strangers. Despite the fact that these people will more than likely believe every word she was going to say, she still felt a little uneasy as their eyes focused on her.

The glass of cold water Ethan handed her helped steady her nerves.

She took a sip, sat the glass back on the table, and looked over her audience. Ethan sat on the love seat with Josie while Sage lay between them on the floor and enjoyed a belly rub from Josie's foot. Beside her on the larger sofa, Ryan sat with his hands on his knees and stared at her with big brown eyes that she felt lost in. Despite their eagerness to hear her morbid news, her lingering apprehension did not falter.

After all of these years, she thought the house looked somehow different than it had before but it had the same feel. She missed Lauren more than ever. "Evil surrounds that place," she said. "Bad things have been happening there since the Deep Earth Mining Company first built it back in the late 1800s."

"Evil," Ryan said." How can a building be evil?"

"Come on, dude, let her talk."

"Oh yeah, I'm sorry, Alyssa."

"For a small percent of their paychecks," she continued, "the mine workers were allowed to live in the basement. They slept on cots during the workweek and traveled home to their families on their days off. Back then, miners would sometimes spend weeks in the mine shafts before seeing the light of day. The workers had to enter and exit the building through a side door on the first floor. The big shots didn't want dirty workers interacting with the guests. The hotel thrived for many years but had to shut down to the public sometime in the 1930s. After the big franchise hotels sprang up throughout the area, people could rent rooms for cheaper rates. The mining company managed to keep the place open for another ten years or so, but eventually they had no choice but to shut it down."

"How did they survive for another ten years?" Ryan asked.

"I don't really know," she said and took another sip. "There was talk of a sale to the railroad, but nothing ever came of it."

"That would have made sense," Ethan said "The railroad could have used the place for a number of reasons."

"Anyway," she said. "The first incident happened back in 1899." She pulled a small stack of papers from the envelope, grabbed the top page, and handed it to Ryan. "Here, read it out loud."

Ryan grabbed the paper and looked it over.

The bodies of Joseph Pulaski of Cobblers Ridge and Jeremiah Hutch of Wampum were discovered early last week at the Deep Earth Hotel by coworker Greg Swayzer. Swayzer told local police he awoke early as usual to take a hot bath before heading off to work when he noticed two of his friends covered in blood. Swayzer alerted hotel staff immediately after making the horrible discovery.

After an initial investigation from the local authorities proved to be inconclusive, federal agents arrived from Washington with hopes of uncovering evidence leading to the arrest of the person who committed such a brutal act. Swayzer, who was the first person on the scene, along with the other mine workers who lived in the hotel's basement during the workweek, told police they heard or saw nothing unusual during the night and couldn't think of any reason why someone would want to do such a thing.

Upon further investigation the authorities concluded Greg Swayzer murdered Pulaski and Hutch in their sleep after information surfaced that the three parties were involved in an altercation involving Swayzer stealing company property. Swayzer told police they had a minor argument regarding a few tools, but that was hardly a reason to commit murder.

Swayzer maintains his innocence at the county jail where he will be arraigned in front of Judge William Shaw sometime in early January. Swayzer said the unusual thing about what happened was the amount of blood splattered along the bottom of the wall. He said it didn't look natural, and eventually he would be proven innocent of this crime.

Police are certain they got their man, though Swayzer continues to declare his innocence. The facts are solid, and the evidence points to Mr. Swayzer. The rest will be left up to a judge and jury one of the investigating officers was heard saying.

"He rode the lightning a few years later," Alyssa said, "and maintained his innocence until the day he died."

No one said a word.

"This one's from 1943," she said, sliding it to Ethan. "You'll find this one particularly interesting."

Gastons Gorge resident Wilma Stottlemeyer mysteriously disappeared while walking her dog last Thursday. She was last seen walking along Barrow Street with her Irish setter around two o'clock in the afternoon by a neighborhood resident. Miss

Stottlemeyer took long walks with her dog every afternoon, one resident told local police as they continue to investigate the whereabouts of the woman.

Search parties scoured the woods surrounding Gastons Gorge, and after finding no trace of Miss Stottlemeyer, professionals were brought in to drag Gorge Creek and the Youghiogheny River. After two days of intense dragging, police found nothing.

The search continued three more days before the chief of police called it off. He said the people of Gastons Gorge rose up and answered their call to duty. The people of this town took time away from their lives to help with the search, and after more than a week, it is clear Miss Stottlemeyer is somewhere other than Gastons Gorge.

"A few months later," Alyssa said, "they put up a pretty big reward, but no one ever came forward."

Ethan shook his head in disgust. "It's almost the same thing that happened to Lauren, except fifty years earlier."

"There's more," Alyssa said and handed another page to Ethan. "This one's from 1952."

A Maryland man was found dead in the woods across from the railroad tracks in Gastons Gorge. Employees of the railroad found the body of Michael Tremble III of Flintstone, Maryland, early Friday morning as they cleared loose debris from the railroad tracks.

Jonathon Sparks told police that while gathering branches and garbage, he saw a patch of something orange in the woods. Sparks and fellow workers searched the area and discovered a body on the ground. They quickly contacted the Gastons Gorge Police Department, who arrived on the scene shortly after.

Detective Samuel T. Grayson stated that after an investigation, it was discovered Michael Tremble III was in Gastons Gorge with Scott Blake, a resident of Big Bear in Maryland. Friends of the victim claim the two men planned a hunting trip near the town of Gastons Gorge and were out scouting the area for deer. A common friend of both Tremble and Blake told police the two men had been best friends since grade school.

Detective Grayson stated that foul play couldn't be ruled out at the present time. "Two men go out on a hunting trip, and one ends up dead. I've seen this song-and-dance before. You tell me what happened," Grayson said and slammed the front door of the police station.

The county coroner ruled Tremble took blunt force trauma to the back of the head and was killed instantly. Police are looking for any information leading to the whereabouts of Scott Blake. He is considered dangerous, and anyone coming in contact with him should call the Gastons Gorge Police Department immediately.

"Scott Blake was never found," Alyssa said, handing Ethan another article.

Josie snatched the page from his hand. "Let me read this one."

Ethan leaned back and sighed mildly.

"July 13, 1967," she said.

While playing in the woods near the old mining hotel, three local girls were attacked. According to thirteen-year-old Jennifer Anthony, the assailant appeared to be in his early forties. Anthony told police she and her friends were playing in the woods behind the hotel when a strange man appeared from nowhere. She said he hit her over the head after coming out of a clearing in the woods. Upon gaining consciousness, Ms. Anthony ran home and alerted her parents, who then contacted the local authorities.

After several days of meticulous searching for eleven-year-old Colleen Flanagan and twelve-year-old Jessica Harper proved uneventful, police postponed the manhunt until new evidence arose leading to the two girls or their assailant. Family and friends are asking anyone with information to please contact the Gastons Gorge Police Department with the details.

Ms. Anthony described the man as being in his late thirties to early forties, with medium brown hair and a scruffy beard. He is approximately six foot tall, weighing between 180 and 200 pounds.

"The girls were never found," Alyssa said. "Their families offered a reward and even hired private investigators. Both girls would be about fifty years old today."

"What happened to the other girl?" asked Josie.

"Still lives in Gastons Gorge with her husband." Alyssa said and pulled another page from the pile. "This one's from the summer of 1978."

"That's interesting," Ethan said.

Ryan reached for the paper. "Want me to read it?"

"Sure, go ahead."

Three local juveniles were reported missing after not returning home Wednesday evening. The boys set out to do some hiking along one of the many trails located in the mountains northeast of Gastons Gorge. George Boynton, the father of one of the juveniles, worried when his son never came home for dinner. He told police that boys sometimes try to stretch their time as long as possible, but when those woods darken, it's easy to get lost.

Johnny Boynton, Zachary Fitzgerald, and William Carver of Gastons Gorge disappeared in the wilderness on Wednesday afternoon. Search parties checked the woods in a thirty-mile radius throughout Thursday and Friday but came up empty. Police chief Samuel T. Grayson told reporters that they have to keep searching the woods diligently because it's easy to become disoriented and confused in miles of nothing but acres and acres of wilderness.

Shawn Preston told police he began to feel ill shortly after they hit the trail. He made it as far as the dirt road just past the Deep Earth Hotel before suffering a stomachache and turned for home. The last time he saw them, they continued along the dirt road that led to the trails. "It's a tragedy when things of this magnitude occur to people you know, but all we can do is try to help our boy deal with the current circumstance, and keep those boys and their parents in our prayers while we continue to look for them," Steve Preston told the Journal *when asked about his son.*

The juvenile was taken into police custody for questioning Saturday morning and held until late that afternoon. Local police chief Grayson said the Preston boy was in no shape or form involved in those boys' disappearances. He hoped the boy could give them additional information that might help track the boys.

A reward of $5000 will be awarded to anyone who can produce information leading to their whereabouts. They were last seen a mile east of the Deep Earth Hotel.

"Despite thousands of dollars the families spent on rewards and special investigators, the boys were never seen again. The police investigation continued on a small-scale level for the next three months before the case was closed."

"What happened to the other kid?" Ryan asked.

"He moved away, but Tommy Carver, the younger brother of one of the missing boys, still lives here."

Ethan grinned. "Maybe we should talk to him and see if he knows anything."

"And Jennifer Anthony," Ryan said.

"Yeah, we should talk to her too," Ethan said.

"This is the last one," Alyssa said, handing it to Ethan, "it's from 1989."

Ethan took the article and looked it over a quick second before reading it out loud.

Workers discover mutilated bodies inside an empty boxcar. Upon opening a boxcar, railroad employee Nathan Ballston was horrified to discover three people drenched in blood. Ballston immediately radioed for coworkers to alert the police.

Police officers arrived on the scene shortly after the call and discovered one of the three still alive. Jacob Stern was taken by ambulance to Crayton Memorial Hospital and treated for his injuries.

Police determined that foul play existed. Charlotte Riggs and Bobby Dean were stabbed multiple times. Stern was taken into custody and charged with the murders.

Twenty-two-year-old Jacob Stern of Gastons Gorge followed the young couple through the railroad yard and watched as they entered into an empty boxcar. He surprised the couple with a serrated pipe and stabbed them repeatedly. After murdering the couple, Stern turned the pipe unsuccessfully on himself.

Stern told police he and the victims were together in the boxcar when the door suddenly opened, and a strange figure dressed in black appeared with the murder weapon. Stern said the hooded figure attacked his friends before stabbing him in the stomach and then jumped from the train car and disappeared into the woods.

"After a long trial," Alyssa said, "he was convicted and sentenced to life in prison."

Ryan glanced at Ethan. "His description sounds a lot like yours."

"Yeah, I think that proves my point."

Josie glanced at her, "How far away is the prison?"

"He's not there anymore," Alyssa said.

"So what happened to him?"

"After a few years of rambling on about hooded monsters killing people, he was transferred to the nuthouse up in Somerset County."

Josie's eyes widened. "That's pretty close to here."

"Think they'd let us talk to him?" said Ryan.

"Well, dude, I'd say it's worth a try."

24

A few hours after Alyssa shared her news articles, Josie sat across the street from the Bissell house but hesitated to leave her vehicle. She struggled to choose the words to initiate a conversation of this magnitude. *You don't just walk up and say, "Hello, Jennifer, how are you? Oh, and by the way, could you possibly tell me about the time when you were thirteen, and some mysterious homicidal maniac stormed through the woods and killed your friends?"* Deciding to be mannerly and lie, she slid out from behind the seat and walked up the lengthy flight of stairs and rang the doorbell.

The porch gave her the creeps.

The usual knickknacks and paraphernalia people use to show off their homes to passersby traveling along the road were absent. The Victorian had a cold, empty quality to match the dismal sky hanging above it. A faded sun hid from view and painted the town a dreary shade of gray. A chill ran along her spine as she waited for someone to answer the door. A gusty wind swept through her hair as she rang the doorbell a second time. Her nerve faltered as she stood alone on a porch that she passed by hundreds of times on numerous walks. Though she never noticed it before, this house was downright spooky. Ready to cut her losses and run back to the Explorer where Sage waited in the passenger seat, she heard faint footfalls shuffle toward the door. Not wanting to look suspicious, she stood her ground as the front door opened slowly with a sharp squeaking clatter. A thin middle-aged man with short auburn hair and a handlebar mustache of the same color poked his head around the half-opened door.

"Can I help you with something, miss?"

Though he looked vaguely familiar, she couldn't place him. "I'm looking for Jennifer Bissell," she said, feeling uncomfortable. "Does she live here?"

A faint yet friendly smile slid across his thin lips.

She shivered.

His expression looked like some brilliant reflection traversed his mind. He resembled an evil genius hatching a malevolent plan to gain world dominance. Despite his weird expression, he seemed reasonably charming.

"That would be my wife you wish to speak to," he said and eased back inside the doorway. "Let me go fetch her. She's baking treats in the kitchen."

"Thank you."

Soft footfalls faded along the hall.

She felt cold and alone.

The thought of discussing the circumstances surrounding the hotel with a stranger, combined with a howling gust of air swirling dead leaves up and down the street, left her missing the others, especially Ethan. Questioning this woman about the mysterious circumstances surrounding her childhood friends being abducted near that building was a task she wished was designated for Alyssa or Ryan.

Suck it up, girl. You volunteered for this.

Seconds later, familiar footsteps shuffled toward the door.

She stepped back toward the porch stairs as the door eased open, and the redheaded man stood in the doorway. Frigid air blew through the entrance, leaving her skin decorated in goose bumps.

"My name's Kelly Bissell," he said. "Welcome to my humble home."

"I'm Josie, and thanks."

He waved her forward. "Come in," he said, holding the door, "and follow me."

She followed him along a hallway, past a narrow staircase, and into a large kitchen. A lanky woman stood at a counter with a bright red mitt covering her hand and a matching apron around her slender waist. Hazy heat poured through the opening as she pulled a tray of cookies from the oven and placed it on the countertop.

A heavenly aroma of sweet chocolate drifted through the kitchen.

For an older woman, Josie thought she was pretty. A bright yellow ribbon sat atop her graying red hair that hung halfway down her back. A gentle smile crinkled her thinning lips as Josie entered the room behind the woman's husband.

"Hello there, young lady," she said. "My husband says you wish to discuss something with me."

"Yes, ma'am. I do."

Standing inside the doorway, Josie had no idea how to begin a conversation about a tribulation this woman probably had not thought about in years. She had to think of something quick, or coming here would be a waste of time. Not wanting to sound foolish, she said the first thing that popped into her mind. "Was your name Jennifer Anthony?"

The woman smiled, revealing a mouthful of snow-white teeth. "It was," she said, stripping off the oven mitt and flinging it on the counter beside the tray. "I haven't gone by the name Anthony in a very long time."

"This is Josie," Kelly said.

"Nice to meet you, dear," she said and walked to the kitchen table, gesturing for Josie to have a seat. "How can I help you?"

She pulled a chair out from the table and took a seat. "I'm a student at the university," she said hoping to sound sincere. "I'm doing a research paper on possible local paranormal buildings, like haunted houses and stuff like that throughout our area. My project is the old hotel at the bottom of Beanery Hill."

"And how can I be of any help to you, dear?"

She took a deep breath and swallowed hard. A vision of being screamed at by an old lady with a tray of hot cookies flashed through her mind. She imagined the older woman hurling chocolate chip treats through the kitchen after being accused of something sinister involving her past. "This may sound kind of strange, but I found these articles about people disappearing near that place. One of those articles led me here to you."

She grinned, shuffled backward to the counter, grabbed a cool tray and sat it on the table. "Cookie?" she said.

Smiling, Josie took a cookie from the tray. "I don't mean to rehash bad memories, but I'd really like to hear about what happened when you were a little girl. I'd especially like to hear about your missing friends."

After pulling a chair out from the table, Jennifer sat down across from her.

Kelly stood near the counter twirling a thin finger through his mustache.

Josie regretted her decision to come and talk to the woman.

It's been over two years since she last enjoyed the sweet taste of chocolate. She wanted to swallow it in one gulp but fought the urge and nibbled on the corner instead. For most people, eating sweets was a pleasure. For her, after shedding over a hundred pounds the past few years with grueling exercise and strict dieting, chocolate was a reminder of a time she would rather forget.

"Well then," the woman said and glanced at her husband. "Let's relive that dreadful day."

"You can call me Josie if you like."

"When I was just a young girl, Josie, back in the sixties, two of my girlfriends and I were playing in the woods not far from where I lived." She bit into half her cookie, chewed a few seconds, and swallowed it down. "Would you mind heating the teapot?"

she said to her husband. "Cookies always taste better with a hot cup of tea."

"Don't mind at all," he said and walked around the table toward the stove. Glancing away, he twisted the knob until a blue flame rose an inch from the stove, grabbed the teakettle from the burner, walked to the sink, and began filling the kettle.

"Thank you, my love."

Smiling, he sat the pot on the burner. "The usual?" he said, opening the cupboard and pulling out a small box of teabags.

"That'll do fine."

"How about you, Josie? Would you like a cup of hot tea?"

"I'm ok, but thank you for—"

"It's really no trouble, and my Kelly don't mind waiting on a pretty young lassie like you."

"Oh, okay then," she said, feeling suddenly uncomfortable. "Okay, Kelly. You can make mine the same as you make your wife's."

With a nod, he walked slowly to the refrigerator and pulled out a jug of milk.

"We played in the woods behind the hotel," Jennifer said as tears began sweltering in her light green eyes. "They were my best friends, and we were inseparable. We loved each other like sisters at least we thought so."

Grabbing a napkin from the holder, Jennifer wiped her eyes.

"Back in the sixties, things were different than they are today. At least I thought so until the day I lost my best friends. We were in the woods and far out of view of our folks. Not to make you think less of our folks, but like I say, in the sixties parents could afford to let their children play by themselves without having to worry. That was the day that mothers and fathers throughout Gastons Gorge began thinking differently."

The teapot screamed, and Josie jumped backward, nearly falling out of the chair. For the next half minute, she watched Kelly fill two cups with boiling water, prepare the tea, and sit a steaming cup of liquid in front of each of them. Relieved to watch his every move, she breathed easy and stirred the steaming milky liquid.

"We were playing with our dolls in a clearing in the woods when we heard a strange rustling noise. It sounded like someone was stomping on branches along the ground. It was a frightening sound. I'll never forget it as long as I live." She looked at Kelly."

"It's ok, dear," he said. "You don't have to—"

"A man broke through the weeds and ran at us before we could react. He whacked me across the head, and that was the last thing I remembered until I woke up alone with dried blood in my hair. I remember feeling ashamed to be grateful as I sat on the ground crying. Even after I realized my friends were gone, I was happy the man didn't take me."

"You were a little girl," she said. "Anyone in your position would have felt the same way."

"You're right," Jennifer said through muffled tears. "I was just a kid, but it still bothers me how I felt that day. I remember the look on his face like I saw him yesterday. He wore a long, dirty brown coat that matched his dirty brown eyes. Those eyes of evil bore into my soul and have never left. That day, I gazed upon real evil, and I don't ever want to feel that way again."

"You didn't see which direction he came from?"

"Just from the woods is all I could tell."

"Did he come at you from the direction of the hotel?"

"No, I think he came from the railroad side of the woods, but I really can't be sure."

Though the woman's story sounded believable, she thought it felt rehearsed as if she had told it over and over again until every detail was perfect. Despite her earlier paranoia of Kelly poisoning her cup of tea no longer being an issue, she felt certain the woman was withholding information. Hoping to detect a flaw in the woman's story, Josie maintained eye contact with her as she rambled.

"They never found him, but I pray every night that I will one day learn the truth of what happened that day. I mean, what kind of person could steal two little girls from their families? I can't imagine what kind of monster would do that."

I don't have to imagine what kind of monster would do that.

"I'm sorry about this," she said, pushing the thought aside, "but I need to ask you one last question if you don't mind."

Kelly handed his wife a napkin.

Wiping her eyes, Jennifer took a long sip from the steaming tea and stared at Josie with a disheartening expression on her face.

25

Ethan banged on the door of the two-story, white split-level house that belonged to Tommy Carver. The cold wood stung his knuckles.

"I'm coming," a voice shouted from behind the door.

Not wanting to appear overanxious, he took a step backward.

A blond-haired man opened the door and stared at him with wide, curious eyes. "Can I help you?"

"I'd like to speak with Tommy Carver."

"That's me," he said, with an uncaring monotonous tone in his voice. "Whatever you're selling I'm not buying."

He raised his hands in the air in protest. "I'm not selling anything." Feeling suddenly embarrassed, he considered running off the porch, hopping back inside his truck, and leaving Tom Carver standing on the porch wondering who the crazy man was. He fought the urge and waited for Tommy's reaction.

"If you're not trying to sell me anything," he said. "Then what do you want?"

"My name's Ethan, and I'd like to talk to you about your brother, William."

A curious sneer formed on his face. "My brother died a long time ago, buddy, and honestly, I really don't feel like discussing it with a total stranger, so just get your scrawny self off my porch and don't come back."

Thinking Tommy might take a swing, Ethan took another step back. "When I was a kid, my little sister disappeared, and I never saw her again."

Like a schizophrenic chameleon, Tommy's expression changed again. This time, curiosity replaced his unsympathetic look. He eased the door open and backed away, allowing Ethan a view of a disheveled sun porch. "Come in," he said and stepped aside.

Pulling the door shut, he walked inside and wiped his feet, hoping not to track dirt on the floor.

"What did you say your name is again?"

"Ethan."

"She disappeared almost ten years ago?"

"Close, it was nine years a few weeks ago."

"Well, kid, I guess we have something in common." He opened another door and waved him through. "Come on inside where it's warm."

Instantly, warm air chased the chill from his bones. He followed Tommy through the hall and into a large, cluttered living room. The house was warmer than he was used to, but for the time being, he didn't mind.

"Have a seat, kid. I'll be right back."

He sat on a burgundy love seat and felt instantly uncomfortable. Waiting for Tommy to return, he eyeballed the junk in the living room. An ancient floor model television that must have weighed over a hundred pounds gathered dust along the wall in front of the sofa. On top of the antique television, black-and-white photographs sat uneven between stacks of mildewed textbooks. Moldy boxes stuffed with faded newspapers lined the opposite wall on a shelf that looked like it had seen its better days years ago. While lost in his search of the cluttered room, he barely heard footsteps approaching from the hall.

Tommy walked into the room with a bottle of beer in each hand. After handing one to Ethan, he plopped down on an equally old and worn couch across from the love seat.

"I remember seeing your face in the newspapers back then. Of course, you look a lot different, but I remember."

"Yeah, well the newspapers have a way of printing things that aren't true," he said, recalling his reputation being trashed on an everyday basis. "Once they finally figured out they had printed lies about me, they didn't give a good hoot because making things right doesn't sell their stupid newspapers."

"Hey, kid, take it easy, I'm not trying to bum you out talking about the newspapers, besides, anybody who knows how to pay attention to detail could see you were not involved with any of that crap."

"What do you mean?"

"Like I told you, I read about you. You were a just a frightened kid who made an unfortunate mistake of letting your guard down. The police in this town like to close their cases as soon as they can, regardless of the truth."

"Trust me, they tried really hard to find any evidence against me," he said. "They wanted something that would put me away for her disappearance. I'm thankful they couldn't fabricate anything that would stick, or I'd still be stuck in a prison cell."

"The cops around here aren't smart enough to tell the difference between fact and fiction. They care about one thing only, solving their cases by any means necessary regardless of the truth."

"Dude, that sucks."

"Well, kid, life can be one bitterly cold ride sometimes," Tommy said in the same monotonous tone he spoke in earlier. "So what do you want to know about my brother?"

"According to the articles I've read, your brother and three of his buddies went out exploring those trails, and only one of them came back home."

"That's the official story," he said and rolled his eyes as if he didn't agree. "Seriously though, kids who spent their entire lives playing in those woods don't just get lost out of the blue. It's a bunch of horse manure, kid, and a little tough to swallow if you want my opinion."

"So what do you think happened?"

"To be honest with you, pal," he said with a touch of anger in his voice, "I'm not sure what happened out in those woods that day, but that story just doesn't sit right with me."

"Why don't you believe it?"

"Honestly, I don't believe that kid's lame story."

"That kid who got sick and went home?"

"That's right, Shawn Preston. I remember him when I was just a boy. He spent a lot of time at my house with Billy. He had a way about him. Shawn was one of those kids that everybody wanted to pal around with." Tommy swallowed a mouthful of beer and reached for a pack of cigarettes on the stand beside his couch. After a few drawn-out drags, he stared across the room with a blank expression on his face and continued. "The thing that no one else seemed to get was the Preston boy had a complete personality change after my brother and his friends went missing. I guess people noticed he acted different, but I don't think they have any idea why."

"So what do you think?"

"I talked to him a few times afterward, and I'm telling you, kid, he was hiding something. I heard it in his voice. I don't know what he knows or what part he played in the disappearances. All I can say for sure is that Shawn Preston played a role in the whole stinking mess."

"Did you tell anyone?"

"Yeah right, who'd believe me?" he said and chugged half a bottle of beer. "According to most people around here, I'm just a drunken idiot."

Feeling anxious, Ethan took a sip of his bottle.

"Why am I'm telling you? I think it's because we have experienced a bit of the same hardships in our lives because of this town."

"Agreed," Ethan said and thought of his friends. Josie, Ryan, and Alyssa believed something weird was happening around that hotel, but they never experienced the loss he and Tommy endured or the ridicule.

"So tell me, kid, why are you really here?"

"I already told you—"

"Cut the bull crap, buddy," he said, raising his voice. "I know you're not here to ask a few idiotic questions about my brother that you can read in any newspaper archive in any library in this county."

"All right, dude, take it easy. I'm here to find out what you know about that hotel. There's something weird going on with that place."

With wide eyes, Tommy jumped of the couch and ran out of the room.

As footsteps faded through the hall, he considered getting up and tearing out of there, but curiosity compelled him to stay. Afraid he struck a nerve, he inched to the edge of the couch and guzzled the rest of his beer. Despite the weird behavior of Tommy Carver, he had to know what had him so excited, even if it meant an awkward altercation with a much bigger man who looked like he knew how to fight.

26

The drive to the mental institution on the outskirts of the city of Somerset took a little less than an hour. They stood outside in a dismal parking lot staring at the entrance to a massive gothic structure, hoping to speak with one of the institution's more famous residents. Jacob Stern came to Wayward Home in the fall of 1993, where he would spend the rest of his life under close psychiatric care. Ryan had no idea if the man was allowed visitors, but he intended to find out.

Dead leaves swirled under his feet and danced across the parking lot past a grove of maples showing of their barren branches. Brown grass covered the once-beautiful lawn surrounding the massive structure. A near full moon played hide-and-seek with monstrous black clouds that raced across a gray sky overhead. In the distance, unseen big rigs rambled along the wet interstate asphalt.

Holding on to a chilled metal railing, he led Alyssa along the steps that lead to the front door. They hurried inside to escape the cold air. A clean-shaven man in his early twenties sat at a large desk working a crossword puzzle. He glanced up, tossed the newspaper on the counter, and frowned as they hurried across the lobby.

"Hello," Ryan said, feeling conspicuous. "We're here to visit one of your patients."

"Visiting hours ended hours ago."

Alyssa stepped around him and smiled. "We were thinking maybe you'd let us have a word with Jacob Stern?"

"Not tonight, but come back tomorrow morning with the proper documentation," he said and grabbed the newspaper from the desk. "You can visit anytime between the hours of nine and three."

"Thanks anyway," Alyssa said with a disappointing frown on her face.

With an uninterested grin on his thin face, he lowered his eyes and went back to work on the crossword.

Feeling disappointed and a little angry, Ryan walked back through the parking lot and slipped inside the passenger side door. After a few seconds of sitting in the dark, Alyssa pulled open the door and hopped inside beside him with a blank look in her eyes. They drove back to Gastons Gorge with unclear ideas on what they intended to do to gain access to Jacob Stern. It was a decision they would have to make with Ethan and Josie.

27

Josie stared at Jennifer and continued to have a guilty feeling linger in her stomach. Despite their need for answers, she felt genuinely bad for grilling this woman. She couldn't help but think that if it weren't for the straightforward inquiries she directed at the woman, Jennifer would be alone in her kitchen with Kelly enjoying freshly baked chocolate chip cookies and sipping hot tea and not rehashing memories of the horrible day that took place years earlier.

She twirled a finger through her hair and stared. "Did you notice anything weird about the man who took your friends?"

Jennifer wiped her mouth with a crinkled napkin, dropped it onto the table, and motioned to her husband for another. After a few seconds of an uncomfortable silence, she took a cookie from the plate and chewed it slowly. "What do you mean weird?"

"Did you see where he took them?"

"No, I already told you that he hit me from behind," she said, seeming irritated by the question. "Like I said before, I don't remember anything after he hit me."

Earlier, she sensed dishonesty in Jennifer's voice. Now, she knew the woman was outright lying. In the article, she gave the police an accurate description of her assailant; she said he was over six feet tall with a scruffy beard and weighed around two hundred pounds. She gave the police a detailed description of the man, yet she sat across from her and couldn't remember which direction her attacker came from or which direction he fled.

Josie smiled but wanted to shake the truth from this woman. "I'm not trying to interrogate you, Mrs. Bissell."

"I know you're not."

"The interesting thing is that I've found a few eerie facts tying that place to some really strange things occurring throughout this town's history."

"You don't say."

"Over the years, several people have disappeared near that place and were never seen or heard from again. Other times, dead bodies were discovered while their killers vanished into thin air. Sometimes there are witnesses and sometimes not, but one common element always comes into play."

Jennifer swallowed a mouthful of cookie and continued to stare.

"Do you know what that commonplace is?"

"The old hotel," Kelly said, handing a napkin to his wife.

"That's right," she said, hoping to sound excited. "Every time something out of the ordinary goes down in this town, that hotel looms in the background like a bad omen."

"You think what happened to me is linked to that place?"

"I don't know for sure. I was kind of hoping you might be able shed some light on the situation."

"I'm sorry," she said, sliding her chair away from the table, "I told you everything I know, and that hotel has nothing to do with what happened to me."

Taking the hint, Josie gave her a smile and climbed to her feet. "Again," she said, feeling like she blew a great opportunity to find out valuable information. "I'm sorry for rehashing these memories you'd probably rather have forgotten."

"No worries, my dear," she said and escorted Josie through the hallway to the front door. "I've had a few hardships in my life, but the good Lord has allowed me to have a second chance at it, and I make the best of my life."

Josie stepped onto the porch. "Again, Mrs. Bissell, I really am sorry."

"I never had the opportunity to go to college myself, but I know it can make life complicated at times for you youngsters. I wish you the best of luck, missy."

"You have a good night, ma'am," she said and then turned toward her vehicle.

"You do the same."

Afraid to glance back, she opened the door, jumped inside, and fired up the engine. Relieved to be out of their house, she drove slowly along the deserted street and watched Jennifer Bissell in the rearview mirror watching her drive along the dark street.

28

Not knowing what to expect, Ethan balled his fist nervously as heavy footsteps descended the stairs and shuffled through the hallway. Tommy appeared in the doorway with a crazy look in his eye. He held a dark object in his right hand. Whatever he carried, Ethan thought it must be something important. If Tommy went through the trouble of going after it in the middle of their conversation, it must mean something to him. Though curious, he leaned back and waited for Tommy to break the silence.

"What about the hotel?" he said as if nothing strange had just happened. Gasping hard for breath after climbing up and down the stairs, Tommy fell backward on to the burgundy couch with a strange grimace of excitement on his face.

"Do you think it's possible some kind of monster might be living inside?"

Tommy's eyes widened.

"Like something evil that snatches people from this town."

He stared a few seconds as if distracted. "What are you getting at, kid?"

"There's something living in that place! I think it took my sister and maybe took your brother as well."

"Come on, kid, are you serious? You really think a monster took your sister?"

"I know it sounds nuts, dude, but yeah. That's exactly what I think happened."

"Listen, kid. I pay attention. Over the years, there have been multiple murders, suicides, and disappearances going on in this town. Do you know what I noticed?"

He shrugged.

"There's one thing rarely looked upon but is involved in every single bad occurrence. Sometimes, it's the center of the crime, while in other times, it lurks in the shadows without anyone but me taking notice."

"The hotel."

"That's right, there's something about that place that attracts bad things, kid." Tommy glanced down at his hand and then looked at Ethan. "I've managed to sneak inside on a few occasions, but honestly, that place really scares the crap out of me."

"Welcome to the club."

"Listen," Tommy said. "I'm not afraid of the dark or the boogeyman, but being inside there freaked me out."

"Maybe you should be afraid of the boogeyman."

Ignoring his remark, Tommy took a long drink of beer, swished it in his mouth, and slid further back into the love seat. "About five years ago I found this." Tommy opened his hand and tossed a black object at Ethan.

Caught off-guard, he lunged forward and caught it in midflight. In the palm of his hand, a piece of damp, velvety cloth sat neatly folded on both ends. A unique smell of mildew drifted through his nostrils. Running a finger across the soft material, he grimaced, guessing years of lying around in such a horrendous place was responsible for the musty stench.

"Go ahead, unwrap it."

"Oh, sorry, dude," he said, feeling embarrassed by the momentary lack of concentration and unfolded the material. In the center, a large decaying tooth grabbed his attention. Perhaps he was right after all. Maybe they were dealing with a vampire or the boogeyman. "What in the world is that thing?" he said, completely flabbergasted as he examined the tooth.

"How's that for weird," Tommy said, sounding proud of his bizarre discovery.

"What is it?"

"You tell me."

"Looks like a tooth from a big dog." He decided to withhold the notion of dealing with a vampire.

"Your guess is as good as mine. All I know is that I found it down there lying near a wall in one of the old storage rooms. I have no idea what kind of freaky animal it came from."

"Maybe I know."

With wide-open eyes, Tommy slid to the edge of his seat.

"I saw something drag a man into the building a few days back."

"Sincerely?"

"Yeah, seriously, it was freaking huge. Whatever it was, it was dressed in all black with a hood covering its head like those dead people in that old flick where that guy was the last man on earth—"

"Omega man."

"Yeah, that's it, the Omega man," he said, surprised Tommy knew the name of the movie that he has never actually watched from beginning to end but seen at least a dozen times on late night television. "A few days ago, I met this girl and her dog. We were just standing there talking across from the hotel when her dog started acting nuts. Oh, by the way, his name's Sage. Anyway, Sage started barking and growling like he had rabies or his bone had been stolen or something. That's when I saw it, and the girl saw it too. Whatever that thing is, we watched it drag a man through the backyard and inside through the back entrance."

Tommy sat wide-eyed, staring with enthusiasm as he explained the events of the other day. As strange and implausible as his tale sounded, he thought Tommy Carver believed every word of it.

"Wow! Really, kid?"

"My friends Josie and Ryan think it was a person, but now that I saw your tooth, I wonder."

"You think she's still alive?"

"I honestly do. I've thought that since the day she disappeared."

"I've always been skeptical about the circumstances surrounding my brother's disappearance, but I never in my life thought he might still be alive."

"I'm not saying he is, but—"

"Count me in," Tommy interrupted. "If there's a chance Billy is still alive, I need to help find him. Or at least settle the score with whatever took him and those other boys."

"We're meeting at my house," he said and gulped down the rest of his beer. "Won't you come and help us think up a plan or something?"

After agreeing to come to his house in a few hours, Tommy led him to the door and promised to see him shortly. He felt confident. He expected the visit to be different. On the drive here, he envisioned being forced off the man's porch by threats of violence or harsh words and a sermon about minding his own business or even advice on how to deal with the loss of a loved one, but he never thought that their little group of four would add a fifth member.

29

With a queasy stomach, Jennifer slammed the front door and hurried through the hall to the kitchen where Kelly was waiting at the table. He wore a bewildered frown as she sat back down on the chair and sipped her cup of lukewarm tea. With a grimace, she finished the tea and stared at her husband.

"What are we going to do?" he asked.

"What's expected of us?"

"We're going to make a phone call," he said with uncertainty in his hazel eyes. "The thought of calling that man makes my blood curl."

"We have no choice."

He looked away with disgust in his eyes.

She stared at her husband a few seconds with regret filling her heart. She dreaded picking up the phone, but their future and the future of their children and grandchildren depended on it. Their kids were grown and living in other parts of the country, but she believed wholeheartedly that Gregory Stephens would track them down and make good on a promise he made her a long time ago.

"It's that girl or our family," she said and stared at the telephone. "We have to protect our kids."

"I don't think she knows anything."

"She knows something. I'm sure of it."

"And we don't know if she's alone or if other people are involved."

Tears dripped down her face. "If we don't call and they find out—"

"Then I'll make the call," Kelly interrupted and slid off the chair. He walked slowly to the counter. A few seconds later, he picked up the phone and dialed the number.

Looking disturbed, he nodded a few times but never said a word.

Frowning, he dropped the phone on the receiver and looked at her with grief-stricken eyes. "He'll be by tomorrow," he said. "Apparently, he's already here in town."

"Then he already knows."

"It seems that way."

"See, honey? We did the smart thing."

"Come on, sweetie," he said and took her hand. "Let's go to bed. We'll both need our strength for tomorrow."

She tossed and turned and thought about Gregory Stephens for the first time in years. Except for the monstrous things that kidnapped her friends, she despised him more than anyone else. The thought of that monster being in Gastons Gorge left her feeling repulsed.

He is a despicable man, but despicable things have to be done to protect the kids, even if it means people will be killed.

More than anything, she wished they never went into that building that day, but regrettably for all involved, they did. In order to protect her family, she and Kelly had to help silence the pretty redhead and anyone else unfortunate enough to have stumbled into this mess.

She closed her eyes and thought of her children.

30

Shawn slammed the door, dropped his suitcase on the floor, and eyed the king-sized bed on the far side of the small room. He drove most of the day and wanted a few hours of sleep before finishing the drive into Pennsylvania. He was a few miles east of Columbus, almost four hours from Gastons Gorge. Sure, he could finish the drive and sleep in his car in front of the Bissell's house, but he was in no hurry to go back, especially after receiving a second phone call a little more than an hour ago.

The call disturbed him.

A few hours ago, a girl showed up at the Bissell's asking questions about strange occurrences near the old hotel. She had to be silenced. He despised helping Gregory Stephens, but what choice did he have? In the morning, that despicable man wanted him to meet at the Bissell's, and he planned on being there.

Not bothering to turn on the light, he fell onto the mattress and laid on his back staring at the ceiling. Comforted by the darkness, he closed his eyes and thought about his life. He had a great career as a detective in a small community in Wisconsin that could be jeopardized by refusing to protect those monsters. Evil has called Gastons Gorge home for as long as he could remember. Years ago, he fled with hopes of never hearing from that evil again, yet here he was in a hotel room in Ohio waiting to make the drive back.

He opened his eyes, picked up the phone, and dialed the operator.

"Front desk," said a monotone voice.

"I need a wake-up call for three," he said and hung up the phone.

After a quick glimpse at a dusty clock on the stand, he closed his eyes. A few minutes later, he slept.

31

Alyssa arrived back at Ethan's a few minutes past nine. Ethan leaned against the counter while Josie and a hefty man in his early thirties with messy dirty blond hair and pale blue eyes sat across from one another at the table. Sage snored quietly on the floor under the window. She glanced at the stranger with curiosity as Ryan followed her into the kitchen and took a seat on an empty chair.

"You guys hungry?" Ethan said.

"I can eat," she said.

Ryan stared at the table and shrugged. "Me too, I'm always hungry, but where's the food?"

"I ordered a few pizzas from some place called campus pizza. Josie said it's the best in the state."

She nodded at Josie. "Actually, it might just be the best in the world."

Laughing, Ethan disappeared through the hall and returned a few seconds later with a black cushioned chair on wheels. He rolled it to the table and squeezed in between her and the newcomer. "Guys, meet Tommy, he wants to help us," Ethan said. "As you know, his brother disappeared just like Lauren did."

"Hi, Tommy," Ryan said.

"This is Ryan."

Tommy waved. "It's nice to meet you."

"And this is Alyssa," Ethan said, pointing at her. "She and my sister were best friends before the incident."

"I think we've met before," she said. "I've lived here all my life too, so I guess we may have probably seen one another throughout town over the years."

Tommy chuckled. "Actually, I was at your house a few times. I worked with your dad at the power company for a couple of years. How's he doing?"

"He's retired and driving my mom nuts in the process."

They talked as if they were lifelong friends reminiscing about days gone by as they ate pizza and drank orange soda. No one mentioned the hotel or the hulking figure in black. After dinner, they cleaned the kitchen and then gathered around the table.

"They wouldn't let us see Jacob Stern."

"Yeah, what a wasted trip," Ryan agreed.

"So you guys went to Somerset," Tommy said and slid his chair closer to the table. "I went up there a few years back."

"Really?" Ryan said with his voice full of excitement. "Did he say anything interesting that might help?"

"Not really," Tommy said with an apologetic shrug. "He blabbed about being innocent and some dark man that he claimed murdered his friends."

"Sounds familiar," said Ethan, staring wide-eyed at Tommy. "Maybe the dark man he spoke about is the thing Josie and I saw."

"More than likely," Tommy agreed.

"We know that some crazy things have been going on in the general area of that building," Ryan said and wiped his hands on a greasy napkin. "We also know that over the years a few of the people involved have claimed to have seen a large person or thing dressed in black."

Ethan nodded. "And we're sure it lives somewhere around or inside that place."

"I know one thing for sure," said Tommy with a disheartening look in his eyes. "Shawn Preston was different after my brother's disappearance. He was a cold and distant person afterward, but before, he could light up a room."

She glanced at Tommy and smiled. "Traumatic experiences can change anyone's outlook on life."

"No, darling, he didn't change like that. Listen, I know you guys don't really know me all that well, but I'm telling you, after the incident, that kid became something completely different. There was motivation behind his actions."

"What do you mean?" Josie asked.

"He seemed somehow less human, almost like something controlled his emotions. I went to talk to him about my brother, Bill, a few years after the incident, and he threatened me. Said I need to quit asking questions about the missing boys and I should forget about it altogether unless I wanted more bad stuff happening to my family."

"So what did you do?" Ryan asked.

"I did what any frightened teenage boy would do under the same circumstances. I got the crap away from there. He scared me when I was a kid, and to be honest, he still does."

Ethan looked at Tommy. "I thought I remember Alyssa say he was a cop in Wisconsin?"

A lackluster grin formed on Tommy's face. "Yeah, I guess he's done pretty well for himself."

She could hear the bitterness in his voice as the room fell uncomfortably silent. All eyes focused on Tommy as he rubbed his palms nervously and looked away.

"It doesn't matter anyway," he finally said. "He lives in Wisconsin, and I doubt he's in any real hurry to come back home."

"Not meaning to change the subject," Ethan said and smiled at Josie. "Did you have any luck with the Bissell woman?"

"Not really, we talked about her friends a little, and she seemed genuinely distraught by what happened to them. I think she feels guilty because she lived and they didn't."

"Anything else?" he said.

"No, I think she was just another victim."

"Do you believe everything she told you?"

"Honestly, I think she's fibbing about something, but she really sounded sincere. Maybe she was just a little surprised by my visit."

"Either way," Ryan said, "we didn't learn anything from her, and if she was holding back on Josie, she was just lying to some college kid investigating a haunted building for a research paper."

Josie smiled. "What do we do now?"

"Stick to the plan," Ryan said. "Get up early and go exploring."

"Sounds good," Ethan said. "Something's going on in this town, and we need to figure out what it is." He closed his eyes as if in deep thought. "Let's do this for Lauren and Bill and all the other nameless faces who suffered over the years."

Alyssa chuckled. "And what if we do find something dangerous down there in the dark?"

Sage lifted his head, glanced around, lowered his gaze, and fell back asleep.

"Does anyone have some firepower?" she asked. "If that thing's as big as you say it is, Ethan, I think we could use something that might actually hurt it."

"Really, you think we'll need guns?" Josie said, sounding surprised.

She snickered at the girl's gullibility. "I don't really know, Josie, but obviously we all think we might be dealing with something that might not be human." She glanced at Ethan. "You saw it drag Ryan into the hotel?"

"Yeah, and I'm telling you guys, it was definitely not a person."

She glanced back at Josie. "You didn't really get a good look at it, but you're sure it happened. Am I right?"

"I didn't see what Ethan saw, but I sure saw the way my dog reacted, and I helped get Ryan out of there."

Ignoring her rant, she glanced at Tommy. "You've told us that you went down there a few times alone, and despite being afraid, somehow you found the courage to go far enough to find a tooth and a torn piece of fabric."

Tommy nodded.

"And, Ryan, you don't remember being knocked for a loop or drug along by anything or anyone, but I can see you believe something happened, and if it wasn't for these two, you wouldn't be here right now."

"That about sums it up."

"Except for me," she said. "Everyone has encountered something that proves at the very least there is something dangerous prowling around near or inside that place that could probably rip our heads off. I'm just not convinced that five unarmed people can hurt it!" Her intent wasn't to scold them as though they were kindergarteners in need of a reality check, but something had to be said for everyone to realize the severity of the situation. They acted as if they were going on a harmless field trip to the zoo to see exotic animals trapped in sealed cages. Maybe she did overreact and they wouldn't encounter anything but a few rats and roaches, but if they stumbled upon something deadly, she wanted to be protected.

"I got a couple of rifles," Tommy said. "Do any of you guys know how to shoot?"

Ryan's hand soared into the air. "I used to hunt with my uncle when I was a kid. I imagine I can still shoot."

Pretending his finger was gun, Ethan squeezed the trigger and shot Ryan with an imaginary bullet. "That's great, dude, 'cause I've never shot anything in my whole stinking life. Except for clay pigeons when I was a kid, but they don't fight back."

"Let's just hope you can shoot real targets as well as you shot clay pigeons," Alyssa said, giving Ethan her best "I'm trying to be as serious as I possibly can" look. "It won't make a difference if that thing is ten feet tall or not, you can send it straight back to the devil that created it."

Josie chuckled and glanced at Ethan. "Unless that thing turns out to be a bloodsucking vampire, then we'll need wooden stakes, holy water, and a big old silver crucifix."

Despite a pleading glance from Ethan, Alyssa joined Josie and Ryan in a bout of laughter.

Tommy shrugged. "What in the world is so funny?"

"Ethan is under the impression that we may be dealing with a vampire," Ryan said through abundant bouts of laughter.

"Black robes and a sharp fang," Tommy said uneasily. "It don't seem so farfetched to me."

Their laughter faded.

She felt certain that vampires didn't exist, but until a few days ago, she doubted the existence of black-robed figures dragging people into deserted buildings.

"So it's settled," Josie said. "Tommy and Ryan handle the guns, and the rest of us carry flashlights and food." She eased her chair away from the table and rose to her feet.

Ethan stood beside her. "Where are you going?"

"Home. I need to get some clothes for tomorrow. I don't care to be tramping around down there in my Sunday best."

"Are you coming back?"

"Of course, I'll be back in twenty minutes, give or take a few."

"Mind if I tag along?" Alyssa asked Josie. "I wouldn't mind stopping by my apartment and grabbing a change of clothes. Honestly, I don't really want to spend the night alone either."

"How about you, Tommy?" Ethan said. "You feel the need to crash here tonight as well?"

"Nah, but I'll be here first thing in the morning. We should go early and give ourselves more than enough time."

32

Ryan stood with Ethan at the kitchen window and watched the Explorer's headlights disappeared around a bend. They stared at each other a few brief seconds before Ryan broke the silence.

"What do you think?"

"It's funny, really. For nearly half my life, I've wanted nothing more than to figure out what happened to Lauren. Now that we're going in there tomorrow, I'm not so sure I really want to."

"We don't have to go," he said and patted his friend's shoulder.

"Yes, we do."

"Yeah, I know we do."

"Dude, let's go inside."

33

Rubbing the sleep from his eyes, Shawn opened the driver's door and surveyed the shadowy parking lot, fighting a slight ache in the back of his head. *You're just tired is all,* he thought shivering as a chilly breeze whipped off the interstate and blew threw his hair. *Once you get some coffee in you, the pain will go away.* He tossed his bag on the passenger seat, slammed the door, took one last look at the dreary hotel, hopped behind the wheel, and fired the engine.

Minutes later, as warm air defrosted the windshield, he glanced at the clock radio.

It was 3:07.

Still groggy from a lack of sleep, he stopped for a glazed pastry and a stale coffee at the convenient store on the same street as the hotel. After a quick fill-up of gas, he drove along I-70 east a few miles per hour over the speed limit. The early morning drive from the gas station in Ohio to Gastons Gorge took less than four hours because the usual heavy traffic of the interstate was surprisingly nonexistent.

Dreading the familiar sights that would soon plague his vision, he veered right, decelerated along the exit ramp, turned left onto Route 201, and drove through an old steel town toward the town of his youth.

Nerves tightened inside his stomach.

Turn this car around. Forget Gregory Stephens, and forget them.

Because of Gregory Stephens's threats that he wholeheartedly believed, turning his back on the vile things prowling around his home town meant jeopardizing his way of life. Next to his father's safety, being a police officer was the most precious thing in the world to him. To protect his lifestyle, he would keep his mouth shut and help protect their secret. He hated it, but he had no choice.

He thought about his friends.

Most nights, he lay in bed, staring at the ceiling, unable to sleep because his conscience had a hard time grasping the reality of that afternoon. On more than one occasion, he thought about coming clean and exposing their secret, but if he tried to tell someone of their dark intensions, they would have locked him up in a rubber room and thrown away the key. Besides, they warned him all those years ago to never ever utter a word, or they would torture and kill his family and friends.

He believed them.

Guilt pumped through his heart as memories of that day flooded his mind. As a scared teenager all those years ago, he believed they spoke the truth. As a man forced to fight on the side of evil, he feared for his father's life.

Reality chased the memory from his mind.

With a heavy heart, he sat idling at a red light. A large green sign spelled Gastons Gorge in faded white letters. Longing for the small city of Moose Jaw, he grinned and gathered speed through the intersection as the light turned a dull green. With a knot in his gut, he accelerated along the winding stretch of road and entered the dreary town of his youth. Evil in the form of Gregory Stephens waited for him at the Bissell's house.

Deep inside, he knew this was more than likely his last trip home. Steven Preston was all he had left in this world, and his time was growing shorter by the day. "After that," he whispered, "all bets are off."

He was an only child, born to Steven and Elisabeth Preston in 1965. His mother suffered a massive heart attack in the winter of 1999 and died instantly in their home before the ambulance had pulled out of the hospital parking lot. By design, he didn't get married nor have children. The idea of having a family seemed cruel—more puppets to dangle in front of his face. He knew after the death of his mother, if anything ever happened to his father, he would wipe out every last one of them, even if it meant his own demise. Until that day, he intended to do what they demanded.

A dreary yellow sun emerged from a monochrome sky as he bounced across the railroad tracks and turned left onto Barrow Street. A few locals staggered along the street as he ascended a small hill, turned right onto Second Street, and followed the road up a slight grade until it leveled off in a quiet neighborhood. He turned left onto High Street and parked across from the Bissell's house. With no desire to mingle, he eased the seat back, took a deep breath, and closed his eyes.

As he slipped into a deep sleep, memories of that day haunted his dreams.

He walks beside Bill Carver, his best friend in the world, excited about the possibility of adventure. As usual, Zach follows behind Johnny, the unspoken leader of their gang of four. He picks a chunk of gravel off the road and hurls it at a stop sign. Johnny laughs as the rock misses the sign by a mile and disappears into the woods with a clank. Zach shrugs and grabs another piece of gravel as dull grey concretes turns into a narrow muddy trail winding its way through wilderness.

After what feels like miles of tramping through squishy terrain, Johnny signals for a break.

Breathing heavy, he takes a seat on a wet boulder a few feet off the path.

Bill slides off his backpack, tosses it on the boulder, smiles, and zips open the front flap. "Here," he says and pulls out a silver thermos. "It's probably not all that cold, but there's plenty enough for everyone."

After a long swallow, he hands it back to Bill and sighs.

Grinning, Johnny stands above the boulder with an outstretched hand. "Don't drink too much," he says and takes the thermos from Bill's fingers. "We should save some for later just in case." He takes a sip, swishes it through his mouth, spits, and tosses it to Zach.

Minutes later, after one last swallow, Bill tucks the thermos into his pack and slides the zipper shut.

"Anything to munch on in there?" Zach asks.

"Peanut butter sandwiches and a bag of oatmeal cookies my ma baked for us last night."

"Yuck." Zach mumbles and wrinkles his nose. "Oatmeal makes me want to puke."

Ignoring his remarks, Bill slides the pack over his shoulders, tightens the front, and takes two steps toward the path when sounds of branches crackling and leaves crunching stop him dead in his tracks.

Johnny's eyes widen with surprise. "What the heck was that?"

"I don't know," Bill says, "but it sounded huge."

He jumps from the boulder and points at a large skeletal oak. "Whatever it is, it sounded like it ran through there."

"It's probably just an animal or something," Zach says. "Come on, guys, let's get going so we can get some real exploring in before we run out of daylight."

Branches crack and pop through the forest on the opposite side of the muddy path.

With fear in his eyes, Bill inches closer to the boulder, squints through the trees, and points a trembling finger at a patch of shuddering underbrush. "There it is again."

"Who's out there?" Johnny shouts. "We can hear you tramping about."

"Show yourself," Zach says and moves closer to the path, inching farther from the group.

"Maybe you should get back here," Shawn says with a bad feeling in his stomach.

"Screw that," Zach said and takes another long stride along the path. "Like I already told you guys, it's just some stupid animal."

From behind, Johnny screams.

Startled, he whirls, stumbles on a busted branch, but grabs the boulder in time to keep from tumbling into the wet leaves. Breath abandons his lungs as a hulking figure draped in tattered black robes gallops between two ash trees. Unable to breath, he stares in horror as a second figure steps out from behind a tree and rushes them. Despite an urge to run, his feet feel cemented into the ground.

Zach screams from behind.

Beside him, Johnny drops to his knees and dissolves into thick slushy water with tears dripping down his face. He points as the second figure seizes a handful of Zach's light brown hair, heaves his writhing body high in the air, and smashes his face into the stagnant earth. With a maddening shriek, the thing kicks Zach aside and charges Johnny.

Shielding his eyes, Johnny screams.

Sickened by heavy footsteps splashing around him, Shawn throws up his oatmeal cookie, drenching his shirt with warm, digested water. He wants to look away, but radiant crimson eyes under its hood hold his gaze. He whimpers as a heavy backhand knocks the wind from Johnny's chest and shoves him into the dirt with a sickening squish. Wheezing for air, Johnny lifts his head and looks at Shawn with black tears streaking his face.

Shawn reaches, trying to grab Johnny's fingers, but he is too far away.

Johnny lunges forward and misses his hand by a foot. He climbs to his knees and reaches out with a flicker of hope in his eyes, but a blow across the back of his head knocks his face back into the ground. His eyes slip shut.

"Shawn, run," Bill screams and flings the backpack at Johnny's attacker. Shaking like a loose gutter in a Texas wind, Bill turns and scampers toward the woods on the left side of the path. Glancing back, he wears an expression of disbelief as the other creature blocks his escape. Looking confused, he stops on the path and stares at Shawn as it crashes into his back, knocking the wind from his lungs and the agility from his

legs. After another shriek, it shoves him into an oak tree. Bill screams and tumbles into a patch of brown grass under the tree.

They turn simultaneously and rush him.

Shawn takes one last look into their soulless eyes and is knocked into darkness.

With a dizzy head, he wakes in a shadowy room, shivering on a cold hard floor. A tall red-haired man with callous icy blue eyes towers above him with two muscular arms crossed over an equally massive chest. Upon seeing Shawn stir, the man grins, drops onto one knee, and leans forward and breathes a mouthful of stale tobacco into Shawn's face.

"Your friends are ours now."

Overcome with fear, he blinks back tears.

"Listen, son," he says, scratching his bearded chin. "Here's how this is going to play out. You'll do exactly what I say or suffer the consequences that befall your family. Trust me on this, kid. We know who you are and where you live. If you fail to do what I say, we'll hunt you down and kill everyone you care about or ever will care about.

The hair on the back of his neck rises as tears drip from his eyes.

The man balls his fist and holds it inches from Shawn's face. "You started feeling sick in the woods and decided to go home. Though disappointed, your buddies bid you goodbye but continued on anyway."

"Where are my friends?"

"You should be more concerned with yourself," he says, unclenching his colossal hand and slaps Shawn's face gingerly. "Wait until people start asking questions, and then say what I told you. Do you understand, boy?"

Shaking and shivering, Shawn nods.

"When the time comes, we'll summon you." The man seizes his hand, stands up, and jerks him from the ground with the force of ten heavy mules. "Now get your little butt out of here, but remember,"—with a demonic grin, he slides his hand sideways across his throat—"cross us, and we'll torture your parents while you watch."

After a nod of understanding, he runs through a door and squints as bright sunlight shoots pain through his eyes. He runs fast through waist-high weeds and comes to a dead stop on the far side of a dirt path. Still shivering, he glances back over his shoulder and sees the hotel towering above a row of thirty-foot pine trees.

34

After eating a delicious breakfast of crunchy bacon and scrambled eggs, Ryan slid out of his chair, enjoying the feeling of a full stomach. Today is the best he has felt since first arriving in Pennsylvania. He walked through the kitchen to the closet in the hallway and grabbed his jacket from a hanger in the back. He slid the lightweight jacket across his arms and yanked it over his chest. Feeling strangely excited, he grabbed his backpack from the shelf, hurried back through the kitchen archway, and strolled by as eight sets of inquisitive eyes watched his every move. Ignoring them, he opened the refrigerator door.

Shaking her head, Alyssa smiled. "What exactly are you doing?"

"I'm preparing for the worst," he said, dropping to one knee and tossing eight bottles of water into the backpack. "Just in case."

"In case what?"

"In case of whatever," he said, doing his best not to raise his voice. "I have two bags of beef jerky, a first aid kit, and water just in case we might need them."

Tommy slid from the table and climbed to his feet. "Good idea," he said and exited the kitchen through the hallway. He appeared a few seconds later with a small camouflage pack, two rifles, and four boxes of bullets. "Toss the ammo in there," he said and handed Ryan the boxes of ammunition. "That saves us the trouble of packing them around, and besides, they don't fit in mine."

"Anybody else got anything?" he said and placed the box of ammunition between the water and beef jerky.

Ethan and Alyssa shook their heads.

"I'm good," Josie said.

After zipping the bag, he couldn't take his eyes off the two rifles in Tommy's hands. "Which one is mine?" he asked, feeling more excited than he did earlier. For reasons he could not explain, Ryan wanted to get this show on the road. Despite the possibility of getting his head knocked off by some kind of humungous monster in the very near future, he couldn't wait to embark on this journey.

"This one's my favorite," Tommy said. "It's a Remington mountain rifle I bought a few years back. This baby is forty-two and a half inches with a twenty-two-inch barrel. It don't look it, but it weighs less than seven pounds."

"Sweet," Ethan said. "Is that good?"

Smiling, Tommy raised the other rifle in his left hand, "Now this beauty is also a Remington," he said. "She's just short of forty inches with a twenty-inch barrel. Don't worry, Ryan, she packs quite a punch."

"Good deal," he said and grabbed the smaller rifle from Tommy's left hand.

35

Ethan couldn't have been happier when Ryan volunteered to carry one of the rifles. He didn't want the responsibility, so he was more than happy when they gave him a flashlight instead. His chest pounded harder and harder as Tommy led the plunge into the basement, pointing the long steel barrel through the damp, musty air as each wobbly plank squeaked under his weight. Being careful not to bump into the bigger man, he stayed two steps behind, angling the beam of light toward the bottom of the stairwell, half expecting a big black monster to be glaring up at him. Behind him, Ethan heard the sound of chattering teeth as Josie inched down the steps with her fingers clenched around the belt loop in his jeans. The flashlight dangling in her hand pointed south, and no light glowed from its bulb in an attempt to conserve the batteries for later. Further back, claws clicked and scraped against wood as Sage descended the stairs a few feet in front of Alyssa. Behind her, looking anxious to shoot anything that moved, Ryan backed cautiously down the stairs.

Splintered chunks of wood and scattered beer cans littered the dusty concrete floor. Depressed into inch-thick dust, large footprints trailed off through the large room and into the corridor.

Motioning for the others, Tommy dropped to his knee and poked at the ground with the tip of the rifle. "They look pretty fresh."

"And pretty freaking huge," said Josie.

Alyssa pointed toward the far hallway. "Look, guys! It looks like something was pulled through there."

Steadying the light on the footprints, Ethan winked at Ryan.

"I guess we all know who carved that path," Ryan said with an insecure grimace tightening his face.

"I followed Sage through here the other night," Ethan said with a smile directed toward Ryan. "Thank God too. If it weren't for that crazy dog, you'd have never had made it out of here."

Ryan glanced away.

"That thing pulled him across the floor and through those doors." He pointed to the wrecked doorway on the far end of the basement wall. "It wasn't too far past there where Sage fought it off and pulled Ryan towards me."

Tommy glanced up. "Did you see it?"

"Nope," he said, shining the flashlight along the hallway. "It was hard to see anything in the dark. Not to mention, I was scared out of my wits. Like I already said, if it wasn't for Sage, I wouldn't have continued."

"Something tells me you would have," Josie said and clapped him gently across the back.

"I don't know, maybe."

The cellar looked less threatening cast in the flashlight's beam. Though it was only a few days ago, he remembered the paralyzing terror he felt while searching for Ryan and Sage as if it happened an hour earlier. Not sure if it was a lighted cellar or the company of four other people and a gutsy canine, but he felt less intimidated as he watched the light ricochet off the walls where Sage pulled Ryan from the clutches of evil. Even the gooey cobwebs clinging on the walls seemed to lose their eerie quality.

"There's not much too look at in here," Ryan said with a strange look in his eyes. "I expected something more."

"I wonder where all this wood came from," said Josie as she walked toward the scattered piles of wood with her flashlight now casting a soft yellow light. "There's a ton of this stuff lying around."

The club he found upstairs in the main room the other day must have come from the pile below Josie's feet. For all he knew, that weapon could be smack in the middle of the woodpile. He couldn't remember what he did with it after helping Sage assist Ryan. "Didn't they set cots up for the mine workers and hotel staff in the main room of the basement?" he said, still thinking of the wooden stick he had held onto so tightly a few days ago. "This stuff is probably what's left of those cots. It's more than likely been here since they closed the place."

"Yeah, more than likely," Tommy agreed.

"Look at all these webs, I bet there are some big, nasty spiders or worse in this place," Alyssa said and inched a step closer to Ryan. "Just the thought of squirmy things that bite gives me the willies."

"I think spiders are the least of our worries," Ethan said.

"Maybe, but I don't want those things anywhere near me."

Josie made a disgusted face. "Me either."

"Spiders or no spiders, I think we've wasted enough time in this room," Ryan said. "Let's get going before we lose our nerve."

"I hear you, dude," he said and reached down and grabbed a bulky piece of wood from the pile. "This stinking place is downright nasty."

A wide grin rolled across Ryan's face. "What's the wooden stake for?"

He waved the club through the air like a valiant swordsman. "I don't have a gun like you and Tommy. This may come in handy if anything jumps out at us."

"Maybe you were expecting a vampire?" Josie said through a soft chuckle.

"Yeah," Ryan said and broke out into laughter. "You could run your little stick through its heart and save the day."

"You just keep joking about it," he said, trying not to reveal the halfhearted smile on his face. "We don't have a clue as to what that thing is that knocked you for a loop the other day. If it comes at us, I want to have something to protect myself with."

"You convinced me," Josie said and picked up a long and skinny piece of wood from the pile. "Too bad we didn't bring some holy water and a big old stinky clove of garlic."

"Seriously, we don't know what that thing is. I doubt very much that it is a bloodsucking vampire with a hidden coffin stashed down here in the dark somewhere, but I think if we keep an open mind, we'll be able to deal with it more easily."

"You're right, I'm sorry."

"Apology accepted."

"Now that that argument is settled," Tommy said and started to walk deeper into the hallway, "let's get moving."

36

A loud bang woke Shawn from his nightmare.

Still shaking from the dream, he saw the redhead with the burly auburn beard standing beside a burgundy Silverado. He glanced at Shawn, walked slowly along the edge of the road, and tapped the glass with a long meaty finger. The man he thought looked like the lumberjack in the old paper towel commercials was Gregory Stephens. After a quick glimpse into his ice-cold eyes, Shawn looked away as mild nausea spun through his head. Just the sight of the man left him feeling repulsed, and the fact that he had a lot in common with the monsters made it seem worse. Gregory Stephens was the mastermind who protected a wicked secret that has been hidden away from the people of this town for nearly a century. Just like Shawn, Gregory grew up in Gastons Gorge and was forced at an early age to keep their secrets. Despite their similarities, Shawn harbored deep hatred toward the man. Shawn has been forced to commit some atrocious acts over the years in order to protect his family, but Gregory Stephens killed for the pleasure of it.

Shawn opened the door and forced him a few steps back.

"Glad to see you made it on time," he said and extended a muscular hand.

With reluctance, Shawn shook his hand and smiled. Sickened by the man's touch, he followed him across the road, along the sidewalk, and onto the Bissell's porch, where Jennifer and Kelly waited for them. Despite a few horrific orders the older couple were forced to obey, he liked and respected them. Like him, they did what had to be done to protect the ones they loved.

Seconds later, he sat across from Kelly and listened to Jennifer explaining about the young girl who visited their house yesterday evening.

"Was she believable?" Gregory asked in a deep, unemotional voice Shawn found bone-chilling.

Kelly slammed his palm against the tabletop. "She called you, didn't she?" he said. "We always do."

"Good thing you did," he said and glared at Kelly with malevolent eyes. "They summoned me the day before you called."

Kelly looked away and glimpsed at his wife.

Shawn could see the fear in the man's eyes. He was smart to be afraid of Gregory—and with good reason. The monster was six foot four, two hundred and forty pounds, strong as a dozen oxen, and dangerously intelligent with a lust for violence. More importantly; he was their number 1 man.

Jennifer glared across the table and into his icy eyes, seeming unfazed by his threats. "What did they say?"

"They told me a couple of kids might have gotten a good look at one of them a few days back."

"Do they know who the kids are?" asked Shawn.

"That's why I'm here."

Biting his tongue, he glanced away. Gregory taking charge was more than fine with Shawn, but the way he went about getting his point across was appalling. Regardless of what anyone else said or did, he ridiculed and embarrassed them with bullying tactics. The man got his kicks degrading those around him.

"You said that they might have seen one of them," Jennifer said, continuing her questioning.

"Yeah, that's right."

"Then how does the girl that came here fit in?"

"We'll get to the girl in a minute, but for right now, bite your tongue, woman, and wait for me to talk," he said sarcastically.

"One of them grabbed a guy out of the woods a few days ago. It was in the process of taking him back when some kid's dog took it by surprise. The dog ambushed it, and hurt it pretty bad from what I gather. All it could do was run away and hide as the dog and another man carried the first guy out of the basement."

Shawn felt a glimmer of hope flicker through his heart.

Ever since that dreadful day in the woods, he has been a slave to things he never imagine existed and forced to do their bidding through Gregory Stephens's threats of pain and murder. Never once did he imagine they could be hurt. With their superior size and beguiling eyes, he assumed they were invincible. *If a lowly dog could hurt one bad enough to stop it from taking another person from this town. Perhaps they can be stopped for good.* For the first time since the day they took his friends, the idea of killing one suddenly seemed real, thanks to some kid's dog.

"How do we find out who they are?" asked Jennifer.

"I've had people keeping tabs on the place since they first summoned me. Yesterday, three kids snuck inside the backdoor. There were two guys and a redheaded girl with a German shepherd that fit the description."

Finally breaking eye contact with Gregory, she looked at her husband. "That girl that was here had red hair."

"They were only inside for about twenty minutes or so when a skinny girl with short boyish hair followed after them," he said and smiled coldly at Jennifer. "Not too long after she went in, they all came out and left together."

"Do you know who they are?" asked Shawn.

"Of course," he said as a condescending snicker escaped his lips. "My sources informed me who they are. The man who was attacked in the woods is a complete mystery. They couldn't find out anything about him. They seem to think he is just a passerby, someone not from around here that just so happened to be in the wrong place at the wrong time, and I agree."

Gregory's shrilling laughter made him feel small. Like everything else about the man, his odd laugh lacked human emotion. As usual, Shawn thought he seemed overly enthusiastic, as if he enjoyed other people's suffering the way some people enjoy watching football or having a picnic. Being anywhere near Gregory and this creepy little town made him feel like that same little kid who was forced to watch as those monsters took his friends from the woods.

"The red-haired girl is Josie McShay—"

"Yeah, that's what she said her name was!" Kelly said and then slumped further down in his chair after a disturbing stone-faced stare from Gregory Stephens.

"Her name is Josie McShay," he said while looking away from Kelly and addressing the group. "She's from Gastons Gorge, and the dog belongs to her. I'm not sure how she fits in with the rest of them, but obviously she needs dealt with as well."

"How old is she?" Jennifer asked.

"The other girl's name is Alyssa Thorpe," he said, ignoring her question. "Her best friend was taken a little over nine years ago. The interesting part is that the young man who helped drag the other guy from the basement is Ethan Wysong, the older brother of the missing girl."

Shawn felt nauseous listening to him talk about people as if they were nothing but cattle for his precious freaks. He closed his eyes a brief second and wished they had nothing to hold over his head. An image of his dad's face forced his eyes open.

"Right before I got here I got another phone call. It seems those troublesome little rats are at it again. Not long ago, they went back inside with another person," Gregory said and stared at him. "Someone you know quite well."

His heart raced. "Someone I know."

"Yeah, someone we've had our eye on in the past. Your friend's pain-in-the-rump little brother, Tommy Carver."

A sharp pain tore through his gut at the mention of Tommy's name. It had been a long time since Shawn talked with the kid about his brother's disappearance. About ten years back, Tommy showed up in Moose Jaw and demanded to know exactly what happened that day. Like a hundred times before, Shawn told him the same old lie, but as usual, he sensed the kid didn't believe a word of it. He had a difficult time keeping a straight face because of the guilt he carried over the kid's big brother. He had hoped to never have to look into Tommy's reproachful eyes ever again.

"So what do we do now?" Jennifer said.

"It's simple. We follow them into the hotel and slice their stinking throats."

"You're insane!" Kelly shouted. "There's no way we're going to take part in this."

Jennifer continued to stare at Gregory. "There has to be another way."

"They need to be disposed of."

Feeling disgusted, Shawn glanced at the table. Thoughts of that day once again haunted his memory. More than anything, he wanted to be one of the abducted boys instead of the one left behind. Compared to what he would have to partake in, they got off easy. At the moment, death sounded like the better fate.

Gregory rose from the chair with an enthusiastic grin stretching his face. "Oh, I almost forgot. It appears our little group of meddling rats are packing some heat."

Minutes later, they left the Bissell's and drove toward the hotel with intentions of slaughtering five human beings. Staring out the window at dismal houses and leaf-strewn streets, Shawn felt on the verge of throwing up.

He closed and eyes and prayed for Tommy and his friends.

37

Staying a few steps behind Tommy, Ethan positioned the light where the trail in the dirt came to an abrupt halt. He glanced down at Sage and felt thankful for his heroics. A knot tightened in his stomach as he tried to imagine what might have happened to Ryan if the dog hadn't intervened. He pushed the thought aside and shined the light briefly along both sides of the hallway.

"There are rooms along both walls," he said and swept the light along the walls a second time. "Ryan, Josie, and I can check this room, and Tommy and Alyssa can take Sage and search the opposite one."

Ryan tapped his shoulder. "Are you crazy?" he said while scraping the barrel of his gun through a pile of dirt on the floor. "I really think we might want to check out these rooms together."

"Dude, you're way too paranoid," he said defensively. "I'm not talking about splitting up or anything. I mean, theses two rooms are right beside each other. If anything pops out, the other group will hear the commotion and come running."

"I'm with Ryan," Tommy said. "I'm in no hurry to separate, kid. Besides, I kind of agree with the whole 'safety in numbers' philosophy."

Alyssa appeared beside him, crinkling her nose. "Didn't we come down here this early to give ourselves plenty of time to check this place out thoroughly? Sorry, Ethan, but I vote for sticking together too."

"All right already. It was just a suggestion," he said and shrugged his shoulders. "You dudes made me see just how dumb of a suggestion it was."

Tommy sniggered and disappeared into the dark room.

"Wait up," he shouted and shined the beam of light throughout the room. Except for a massive furnace covered in thick black dust that rested along the far wall, they found nothing interesting. After a thorough search uncovered nothing useful, they left the furnace room and crossed the hall to an equally large room. Small animal tracks were scattered haphazardly across the dusty floor as if a gang of rats had recently patrolled their territory. Except for thick cobwebs and scattered debris strewn along the floor, they found nothing useful among the rubbish.

Feeling his heart sink, he followed Tommy and thought about Lauren.

Farther along the corridor, large footprints came into view beside a doorway. They disappeared into another large room along the left side of the narrow passageway.

Tommy stopped and glanced at the others. "They look identical to the ones we saw earlier."

Josie pointed at the doorway. "Looks like it went through there."

"After you, hombre," he said and smiled at Tommy.

"How do you do it, kid?" Tommy said, sounding a little annoyed by his antics. "How do you keep your sense of humor in a situation like this?"

"It keeps me sane. When you've spent as much time as I have being bounced between mental institutions and foster homes, you develop a defense mechanism."

"Sorry kid, I didn't mean to—"

"Don't sweat it," he said and slapped Tommy gently on his shoulder. "Besides, I've been around guys whose defense mechanism is violence, and they're not half as interesting to be around as I am, or safe for that matter."

Looking puzzled, Tommy walked inside.

Grinning, he followed with his flashlight lighting the way. As light filtered through the large room, the smile melted from his face. A thick blackish-green substance formed a small puddle where the footprints ended.

"Ew," Alyssa said, throwing her hand over her nose. "That stuff smells and looks like slimy antifreeze from my dad's car."

Ethan chuckled. "It looks more like finger paints mixed together."

"Finger paint," Ryan said sarcastically.

"Seriously, dude, it does," he said, trying to lighten the mood. "When I was locked up in the crazy house, we were allowed to draw with finger paints because it was nontoxic. They didn't have to worry about us inmates eating it and getting sick, which I've seen done a handful of times—the eating part, not the getting sick part. Anyway, we spend a lot of time throwing the colors together, and it reminds me of that crap on the floor."

"I really don't think that stuff is finger paints," Josie said.

"Then let's hear what you think it is if you're so sure I'm wrong!" he said despite knowing the goop wasn't paint.

"I think its blood."

"Me too," Ryan said.

"Yeah," he said. "It's probably not finger paint."

"Sage did that to it!" Ryan said, "That's a good thing!"

"Good for you, Sage," he said, making an attempt not to laugh but failing miserably.

"No, you don't understand, if—"

"If the dog hurt it that easily, then maybe we're giving this thing a little more credit than it deserves," Tommy interrupted.

Ryan's eyes widened to the size of quarters. "Not only did Sage hurt it, I think he might have frightened it."

Josie swept her finger under her chin. "Then we might stand a chance against this thing."

He suddenly understood. Before this moment, the robed figure was an intimidating force that found its way deep into his subconscious where that space was reserved for the guilt surrounding Lauren's disappearance. It seemed so powerful and dangerous, like an intelligent alien life-form capable of unknown death and destruction. Its appearance alone was enough to make him think twice about joining this crazy crusade, but standing with his friends near the puddle of blood, he felt hope rise up through his throat.

"Maybe we shouldn't get ahead of ourselves," Alyssa said. "Once we become overconfident, we lose our advantage."

Tommy sighed sarcastically. "What advantage is that?"

"Our advantage is that we are careful. Our advantage is that we're scared to death, which makes us think clearly about what we need to do. If we rush in, throwing caution to the wind, then we might as well just shoot each other with those guns of yours."

"Sorry," Tommy said. "This place just makes me a little uneasy."

She grabbed his shoulder gently. "Me too, Tommy, but I just want us to be careful and not lose our fear of this thing."

Weary of the negativity, he glanced around the room as they squabbled about how to approach the situation. Except for the usual dust, debris, and thick spiderwebs that covered the top edge of the wall, the room looked deserted. After another quick look over, he returned his attention to the others. "It must have hidden in here while Sage and I dragged Ryan to safety. I think you're right, dude. It must have been afraid of Sage."

"Come on," Tommy said, scraping the blood with the toe of his boot. "You actually expect us to believe that something that big is afraid of a measly little dog." Tommy cleared his throat and glanced at Josie. "No offense, but I'm just trying to get my point across."

Josie shrugged as a chuckle vibrated her lips. "No offense taken."

He shined the light at Tommy's face and smiled. "Then why do you think it was hiding in here?"

Tommy shielded his eyes and gave Ethan a disapproving stare.

"I think you guys took that thing by surprise and it panicked," Alyssa said. "I also think that it probably won't make the same mistake the next time we happen across it. I think you need to start taking this serious."

"I feel like I'm stuck in an episode of *Scooby-Doo*," Ryan said and pointed at him and Alyssa. "Over there, we have Shaggy with his silly antics and the always practical Velma standing next to him regurgitating logic."

"Real funny," Alyssa said.

"I guess that makes us Freddie and Daphne," Ryan said and smiled at Josie.

"Come on, Scooby," he said with a chuckle. "Maybe we can find a snack in the next room." Through a grin, he winked at Sage and hurried across the hall toward the opposite room with the flashlight's beam slicing through the dark like a beacon guiding lost sailors through the ocean fog. Listening to the sounds of soft footfalls behind him, he shined the light from one side of the room to the next and grimaced in disappointment.

"This place is dull," Ryan said as he stepped through the doorway and stood beside him. "I don't know what I expected we might find, but I'm feeling a tad disappointed."

"Shine that over here a minute," Tommy said from the hallway. "I think these footprints lead past these rooms."

Satisfied that nothing sinister lurked in the shadows of the cluttered room, he swung around and aimed the beam where Tommy knelt on the floor.

Tommy stood up and wiped thick gray dust from his pants. "Look," he said and pointed straight ahead. "They keep going down the corridor."

Holding the light steady, he took a few steps toward Tommy and angled the beam along the ground. Through sparkling dust floating inside the bright beam, his eyes followed the footprints as they disappeared into darkness. Splotches of dried green blood trailed off past the last set of rooms and continued along the hall.

Tommy glanced at Josie, scratched his head, and stared into the room where they first noticed the blood. "Your dog must have got a good chunk of that thing," he said and knelt back down for a closer view. "It must have been bleeding pretty bad."

Ryan nudged past him and knelt beside Tommy. "It looks like it's thinning out a bit though."

"You're right, it does," Tommy said. "The blood leads to the end of the hall and past these rooms."

"I agree," Ryan said and pointed at a door at the end of the hall. "These rather large footprints lead through there."

Shining the beam further along the hallway, Ethan could see that both the trail of dried blood and the large footprints disappeared behind a door on the far end of the corridor. Judging by the puddle of blood in the room beside them, he assumed that that thing must have hung around until he and Sage were gone and then continued down the hall to where ever it planned on going. Thoughts of that thing lurking on the other side of the door left his skin chilled.

Tommy glanced back and forth between the four of them with an excited look in his eyes. "What do you guys think? Are you ready to find this thing and then do what we came here for?"

"Lead on, dude," he said in an attempt to sound brave.

Tommy smiled and then pointed to the door.

"You're right, Ryan, this place is pretty dull," he said and helped Ryan to his feet. "I expected a little more excitement from a century-old haunted hotel."

"What would excite you?" Josie said doing her best not to laugh. "Maybe you'd like to go toe to toe with a half a dozen of Ryan's big black monstrosities. If you're really lucky, they'll be waiting on the other side of that door just waiting to make our acquaintances."

"Well actually, miss smarty pants, I was thinking more along the lines of a fire-breathing dragon perched on top a gigantic pile of jewels and gold."

"You're weird," Alyssa said and wiggled between them. "I mean that in the best possible way."

Josie took hold of his hand and grinned. "I could do without the dragon, but the gigantic pile of treasure sounds pretty good to me."

Ryan laughed. "Seriously, Josie, what fun would it be to find a heaping pile of gold if you didn't have to battle a dragon for the right to claim it?"

"While you guys slay the dragon and plunder its loot, I'll see what's behind the door," Tommy said and walked down the hallway.

"Good plan," Alyssa said and followed Tommy.

"That chick has no sense of humor," Ryan whispered.

Ignoring him, Ethan broke free of Josie's grasp and hurried through the hall trying to steady the light a few feet in front of Tommy.

"Stay back," Tommy said and kicked the door. A few pieces of wood broke away from the frame with a hollow bang. After landing a second powerful boot, most of the remaining wood broke, revealing a small room thick with dust, spiderwebs, and chunks of broken concrete.

Maneuvering between Ryan and Josie, he swept the light through the darkness and followed Tommy into what appeared to have once been a cement stairwell leading to the main lobby above. Piles of concrete littered the small room that looked to be a dead end.

"We missed something somewhere," Tommy said irritably.

"Yep," Ethan said, feeling frustrated.

"What now?" asked Josie.

"We go and check those other rooms. This time, I'll concentrate more on what we're doing and less on being a second-rate comedian."

"I don't know what we're gonna find, but we didn't come down here to give up so easily," Tommy said and walked back along the hallway with a disgusted expression on his face.

Feeling confused, he looked around the area and listened to the sound of footsteps fading back through the hallway.

That thing brought Ryan down here for a reason. Unless Sage scared it away for good, it's more than likely still down here somewhere.

He stood alone in the stairwell and suddenly felt afraid.

He wanted to turn and run but felt as if his legs were submerged in quicksand. Foolish instinct urged him to stay and search for anything that could lead them to the creature, but fear of the boogeyman left him feeling vulnerable. Taking a step back into the hallway, he squinted through the rubbish and hoped to glimpse something interesting.

Only dusty concrete floated through the rank air.

With a sinking feeling in his gut, he overcame curiosity and backpedaled along the corridor with intentions of catching up with the others. As the flashlight cast a beam of light into the stairwell, he saw a small puddle of green blood staining the floor.

38

Gregory Stephens sat patiently in the passenger seat of the Bissell's minivan and stared out the window as they drove toward the hotel. Snuffing out troublesome meddlers always rated high on his list of entertaining things to do. More than anything, he enjoyed ripping the life from anyone threatening their existence. He doubted anyone would take the kids serious if they started yapping about hooded monsters lurking about the town, but he had no intentions of taking that chance. If anyone ever learned of this town's dark little secret, his life would be less significant.

Tired of the dreary view, he closed his eyes and envisioned his hands around the pretty little redheads' neck. Imagining the life seeping from her warm body, he smiled and hoped to make it a reality very soon. Throughout the years, a few people have accidentally stumbled across Cornelius's monsters but were disposed of with little effort. He's had to silence a couple of vagrants seeking shelter in the old building and a few runaway kids hiding out from their parents but never a group as large as theirs.

Though confident he could deal with them on his own, Gregory hoped the two idiots watching the hotel and the three morons in the van were up to the challenge. Unlike the Bissell's and the useless cop in the backseat, he served Cornelius and his wonderful creatures out of free will. Except for Cornelius and his creatures, he cared for nobody but himself. They gave his life meaning, and he intended to protect their secret no matter what consequences fell his way. Since he murdered his parents well over a half a century ago, they were the only family he had left.

He was born in the late 1800s in Gastons Gorge to Reilly and Ethel Stephens. The small town was more a village back in those days with a population just barely over five hundred people. In those days, the Deep Earth Mining Company was in its heyday. Back then, upper-class people from town and all of the surrounding areas came to wine and dine and pretend to be high society. Like most of the locals, his family dipped well below the poverty line. His dad worked as a laborer for the mining company but was never permitted to stay in the hotel. He seldom heard his dad complain, but he usually steered clear of the man. He disliked his father more than his mother. At least the old hag did things for him on occasion, but thinking back, he guessed it wouldn't have mattered if Reilly was the world's greatest father; he would have hated him anyway. For as long as he could remember, his heart has always been filled with hatred.

Listening to the steady buzz of the engine, his thoughts drifted back in time. As a child, he played at an old garbage dump he stumbled upon a few hundred yards from Gorge Creek. After weeks of spending entire days rummaging through ancient piles of squishy garbage, he realized the town had abandoned the dump years earlier. From that day forward, it became his private sanctuary. On the day of his thirteenth birthday, while enjoying some of life's greater pleasures, he met the wizard that changed his life for the better.

Annoyed by his present company, he closed his eyes and remembered the best day of his life.

"How's that feel, Fluffy?" he says and jams the sharp edge of a hollowed out pipe through its stomach again. The cat writhes and claws with an earsplitting screech, but his grip is too powerful. Watching the cat thrash about in agony eases the hatred burning deep in his soul. He sits on a makeshift bench

and smiles as the animal clings to its final seconds of life. He feels delighted as warm sunlight breaks through a gray sky and beats down upon his shoulders. Seconds later, the cat slips from the living world with a painful groan, forcing a smile on his face. He wipes the blood from the pipe with a dirty rag, throws it on the ground, rises to his feet, and scrutinizes the dump in hopes of glimpsing something else to torture.

Nothing but rubble and a few rats he doesn't feeling like catching.

Enthralled with enthusiasm, he heaves the cat high in the air by its tail, swings it like a sling, and watches it skid over the garbage heap and disappear over the far side. He chuckles and thanks himself for the wonderful birthday present. Digging his heels in the dirt, he spins around while dreading the thought of calling it a day and sees something move through the shrubbery to his left.

"Who's there?" *he shouts.*

A tall hooded man draped in long crimson robes steps out from between two towering trees and waves him forward. At first, he stands his ground, weary of the bizarre figure but feels a strange buzz deep in his brain. Feeling suddenly courageous, he takes a few drawn-out strides closer toward the figure, hoping it doesn't run into the woods before he gets a better look at it. Instead, it waves again as he approaches within a few feet.

A raspy voice fills his head. What's your name little boy?

"I'm Gregory, who are you?"

Come with me, and I'll show you.

"Where are we going?"

We're going someplace where you can torture and kill animals without having to worry about the consequences. Where we're going, you can do anything you wish. Doesn't that sound nice, Gregory?

"Sure does, but guess what?"

I don't know, tell me.

"Today's my birthday, and I'm thirteen."

How nice, but are you ready to go?

"I sure am."

Follow me.

With robes dragging through branches, it whirls around and walks into the woods.

Strangely woozy, he follows it deep into the forest until it comes to a halt in a small clearing.

Standing over six feet tall, it towers above him. With extraordinary speed, it reaches for his neck with a dark-skinned muscular hand and squeezes. He feels consciousness begin to slip away as the mysterious figure clenches his windpipe, blocking his breath. Seconds later, swirling silver specks fill his vision as he tumbles face-first into the ground.

With a pounding head, he wakes on a concrete slab surrounded by six hooded hulking forms covered from head to toe in lengthy deep black robes. Despite dark creatures with menacing red eyes towering over him, he feels safe and warm. As they spread out around him, making room for a tall dark man with pure white shoulder length hair draped in the same crimson robes as the thing from the woods, a smile stretches his childish face.

"Hello, Gregory, my name is Cornelius. I was wondering if you would like to help me with something important."

"I'd like to help you," *he half shouts and feels the beginning of an erection between his legs.*

"I been watching your town, hoping to find someone special to aid me in a little project I been working on."

He flashes a smile of understanding.

"My minions will be visiting your little village from time to time, and I need somebody I can trust to help keep others from knowing they exist. I chose you, Gregory, because I think you have what it takes to keep their existence a secret from others of your kind. Would you help us do that?

"Can you talk inside my head again? That was really neat."

If you help me, I'll do anything you want.

Gregory loves the magic voice inside his head. He wants to be friends with this man and his creatures for the rest of his life. "Heck yeah, I'd love to help you out."

For right now, you need to go home. We don't want anyone wondering where you've gotten off to.

"How long have I been here?"

Not long, but you need to go home really soon. Once there, do nothing until I summon you.

"Summon me, how cool. How long will it be before you summon me?"

Enough questions, my little friend. It is very important that we get you back to your time before someone misses you. If anyone asks where you were, tell them you fell asleep at your secret hangout.

"Sure, I can do that."

"Goodbye, my little friend," Cornelius says and mumbles strange words in a language Gregory's never heard before.

Seconds later, his eyes are too heavy to hold open. Black lights dance through his mind and numb his brain. As the strange language fades into oblivion, he feels his body rise into the air and then remembers nothing else. With the pounding still in his head, he wakes and sees the dump in the distance. Not sure what time it was or how long he was gone, he walks home along the railroad tracks to celebrate his birthday with his parents.

His eyes opened as the van's engine went silent.

39

Shawn stood in front of the pine trees and stared at the dirt road to the left of the hotel. Two men he had never seen before hurried around the corner and stopped at the edge of the grass. One of the men walked across the yard and shook Gregory's hand. He wore a dark blue sweat suit with a matching baseball cap turned backward atop his short brown hair. He looked like an ordinary man out for an early morning jog.

"That's their vehicle," he said and pointed to a dinged-up Explorer parked beside an open gate.

"Are they inside?"

"Yeah, they went in about an hour ago."

"Good. Now let's go before some nosy idiot peeks out his window and gets suspicious," he said while motioning for Shawn and the Bissells to hurry up. "They'd probably just think we were planning to go walking along the trail, but why take any unnecessary chances?" His ice-cold eyes glared at Shawn a quick second before he disappeared around the side of the building. Like obedient soldiers, the Bissells marched through the knee-high grass, following their commander into the backyard.

With a feeling of being watched, Shawn looked back across his shoulder at a deserted wet street, sighed with disgust, and squished through the swampy yard to the rear of the hotel, joining the others beside a busted door leading inside. The other man, who was a few inches shorter than his cohort, stood beside Gregory Stephens. He dressed in ragged blue jeans and a bleached stained black-and-gold sweatshirt that appeared a few sizes too big for his skinny frame. With two sunken yellow eyes making his face look unnaturally sad, he nodded at Shawn. A lengthy goatee hung from a pointed chin, accenting his long dirty blond hair that hung halfway down his back. Shawn waved halfheartedly, returning his gesture and glanced at the door.

Rubbing his beard, Gregory stared at the busted door and motioned for everyone to gather around. "I prefer no gunfire," he said. "The racket might draw unwanted attention, and I don't want that. However, if you have no choice, do whatever is necessary."

"No problem, sir," the man in the sweat suit said.

"Relax, Christopher. You're not in the military anymore," he said and shoved the door open. He wiggled halfway through and glanced back at Shawn. "I know you got a gun, Mr. Policeman. I'm guessing it's not your standard police-issued variety, and I doubt you'd care to explain why your piece was fired in your hometown."

"I don't, and it's not."

His eyes shifted to the Bissells. "I want you two to carry these," he said as the man with the goatee pulled two flashlights from a backpack and handed one to each of the Bissells. "Don't screw this up, or I'll make sure they make good on the promise I made you."

Kelly stared hard as if he had something to say but looked away instead. He reminded Shawn of a scared little kid on the playground who was afraid to stand up to the bully.

"I mean what I say."

"Don't worry, we won't let you down," Jennifer said and stepped in front of her husband. "We always do what you want."

He looked past Jennifer giving Kelly the evil eye and then slipped inside after motioning them to follow. Once everyone was inside, he pulled what was left of the door shut and turned toward the man with the goatee who was squatting on the platform above the stairs and peering into the basement.

"Did you hear something?"

"Nah, boss. I was just having a look."

Frowning, he glanced away and stepped between Shawn and Kelly Bissell. "You three ready for this?"

Shawn stepped to the side. "What choice do we have? It has to be done."

"I wish there was another way," Kelly said.

"Well, Mr. Bissell, there isn't another way, so you better just shut your mouth and do as I say or else."

"I'll do what's expected of me."

"Oh, I know you will, old man," Gregory said with a conceited grin on his hardened face. He stared a second longer and then joined the man with the neatly trimmed goatee at the top of the stairs.

Despite the big man's influence with the monsters, Shawn considered landing an uppercut across his bigger-than-average nose but decided that probably wouldn't be the smartest course of action. Instead, he winked at Kelly. For whatever reason, Gregory had always been their number 1 man, and he had no desire to invoke their wrath. At least not until after his father's passing.

"Hey, Andre," Gregory said.

"Yeah, boss?"

"Hang out up here in case one of those meddlers manages to sneak past us. If that happens, take care of them."

"Will do, boss."

He turned back toward Shawn and the Bissells. "The rest of us are going down there and putting an end this mess right now. Anyone have a problem with that?"

Shawn shook his head.

Sliding past Andre, he followed Gregory and Christopher into the basement. Deep down, he felt remorseful about the murders he would soon be forced to partake in. In the basement, he closed his eyes and silently prayed for God to forgive his sins.

I hope I can forgive myself.

40

"The blood," Ethan shouted as he stepped back into the ruined stairwell. Except for his own rasping breathing, he heard nothing but disconcerting silence. Panic spread through his muscles like a crippling disease as the flashlight slipped through his fingers and thudded against a chunk of concrete. Darkness filled every inch of space, heightening the terror chilling his bones. A hollow sound of blood pumping through his veins forced his eyes closed.

"Where are you guys," he shouted, fighting a desire to run blindly through black space. A mental picture of smacking head first into a hard wall and tripping backward over a jagged piece of concrete kept his feet planted firmly on the ground. Something scurried through the crumbled rubbish and scampered through the small room as he stood in the dark and waited for someone to respond. He prayed the creepy noises were a result of his paranoia, but as the unsettling rustle continued along the wall and through the scattered debris, tears gathered in his eyes.

Soft whimpering rose from his throat.

Sweat dripped along his face as something slithered past his feet. He thought of dropping to both knees and feeling for the flashlight when a dull beam flickered off the wall in front of him.

Gasping for breath, he glanced over his shoulder.

"Ethan," Josie said with a confused smirk on her face. "What the heck are you doing?"

As the light filtered into the area and revealed nothing but hunks of concrete, sanity returned to his mind. Struggling to regain his composure, he took a deep breath as she walked toward him.

"Josie, the blood!"

"Blood? What about blood?" she said. "Did you fall and bump your head in the dark?"

"It stops in there." He pointed at the dried splotches in the ruined stairwell.

Instantly, her confused smirk transformed to enlightenment.

"It was definitely in here. Unless it climbed the walls and got back outside, it had to have gone another way."

"Let's get the others," she said and pointed back through the hall. "They're back in there, convinced this old freezer we found is hiding some secret door."

Seeing the flashlight, he snatched it off the floor and chased Josie through the hall. As he followed her into a doorway, he saw the others searching a walk-in freezer. Though he'd only been separated for less than a few minutes, he thought it seemed like an eternity.

"Guys, the trail of blood stops in that room back there."

They whirled around to face him with surprised expressions on their faces.

"I think there might be another door in there."

"Yeah," Josie agreed. "That thing didn't just disappear into thin air."

Tommy walked toward the doorway. "We looked in there and didn't see anything."

"Obviously we didn't look good enough," Ethan said with newfound energy. "I think we need to take another quick peek."

"It can't hurt," Tommy said. "Lead the way."

After twisting the cap and relighting the beam on his flashlight, Ethan led them back into the stair room. With Josie lighting the room, they rummaged through debris but found nothing. Ethan watched as looks of frustration filled each of their faces. Ryan tossed chunks of crumbled concrete from one area of the room to another with the patience of a five-year-old child, Tommy slapped the walls looking for hidden doors, Alyssa poked at the blood with a sharp stone as if attempting to devise a master plan, and Josie traced the footprints across the floor where they ended a few feet from the far corner.

"I guess I was wrong again."

"I don't get it," Ryan said. "Where the heck did that thing get off to?"

"Hold up a minute!" Josie shouted.

In the midst of kicking a broken chunk of concrete, he spun backward. "What did you find?"

"There's something different about the floor over here," she said falling to her knees and running a finger across the rugged cement. "It looks a little different."

Followed by the others, he jogged across the room, stood behind her, and eyeballed the marks left by her fingertips. "Holy crud, guys, it looks like something carved an outline in the floor." Making room for the others, he stepped aside and knelt beside her in the rubble.

Josie's eyes opened wide. "I think we can pull it free."

Tommy and Ryan wiggled in between them and felt along the ground. After a few seconds, Alyssa grabbed the flashlight from Josie and kept the beam on the cracks. After digging their nails under the seams, they lifted the concrete slab a few inches in the air.

"Push," Tommy said and shoved his hands forward.

Along with Ryan and Josie, Ethan gripped underneath one of the edges and heaved with all his strength. He grunted as the slab slid of its niche, revealing wooden rungs leading into the darkness below.

"Unbelievable," Ryan whispered.

Giddy with hope, he swept his fingers across the top rung and watched loose dirt disappear into the darkness below. "I guess we're going down there."

"Yep, looks like it," Tommy said and handed him the rifle. "I'll go first and make sure nothing is waiting for us at the bottom."

"Be careful," Alyssa said.

Tommy crawled backward into the hole. "When I say, Josie and Alyssa can come down and help me get Sage on the ground. After that, one of you two can slide the slab back over the hole."

"Sir, yes sir," Ethan said.

"Good idea, Tommy," Ryan said, ignoring his friend's sarcasm. "I think covering our tracks is an excellent idea."

"I'll go last since Ryan's lugging that gun. I should be able to slide it over the hole. It's kinda heavy, but I can manage."

Minutes later, he watched Ryan climb to the bottom of the crude ladder and scurry to the side. After waiting a few seconds to make sure his friends were clear, he crawled inside, climbed halfway down, lowered the gun to Tommy, and jerked the lid back over the secret entrance.

41

For the better part of an hour, they rummaged around the damp basement, searching every nook and cranny for the small group of kids. Except for a wide variety of disheveled footprints scattered up and down the hallway and throughout the rooms, no proof of their being down there existed. After a methodical exploration of the last of six spacious rooms revealed nothing useful, Shawn deserted the room for the hallway, leaned against the filthy wall with a grin of satisfaction on his face, and waited for the others to finish up.

Minutes later, Gregory came through the doorway with both hands balled up into fists at his side. His face was a bright burgundy as he delivered three hefty boots to the wall to the left of the doorway and mumbled something Shawn couldn't make out. Deep down, he was enjoying watching the man act like an idiot in front of people that feared him. The best part was that he didn't have a clue as to what a complete imbecile he was making of himself.

Feeling the faint traces of a grin on his face, he glanced away.

Seconds later, after one last heavy boot to the wall, Gregory glared at Christopher with fuming eyes, whispered in his ear, and stomped back through the hall and into the large room where they entered the basement. He came to halt at the bottom of the stairwell and screamed for Andre.

"Yeah, boss," he said and scurried down the first few steps.

"Did you hear or see anything?"

"No one came up the stairs."

Gregory deserted the stairs and stormed over to the man standing between Shawn and Kelly. For a moment, Shawn thought he was going to punch him in the face. He grabbed him by the front of his sweatshirt with his face less than an inch from Christopher's head. "Are you absolutely positive they entered this building?"

"Yes, sir, we watched them go inside."

"You're positive?" he said and released his grip.

"Yeah, they definitely came inside. We called you shortly after and stayed outside the entire time until you guys showed up."

Gregory backed away and stared through the hallway as if captivated by something magical on the far side. He glared through the dark a few minutes longer and then hurried back to the stairs and took a seat on the bottom plank. With bated breath, he sat with his head cupped around his forehead as if lost in deep thought and then climbed to his feet and looked back up toward Andre. "You still up there?"

"Yeah, I'm right here, Mr. Stephens."

"I want you to stay there. If you see anyone but us coming up these stairs, I want you to separate their meddling heads from their meddling shoulders!"

"Not a problem, boss."

"Do I make myself clear, Andre?"

"Yes, sir."

Watching the scene unfold, Shawn thought the man took himself a little too seriously. Maybe he spent way too much time watching farfetched gangster movies where everyone feared the mob boss. Despite the fact that he was big, mean, and tough as nails, his fear of the man was dwindling by the second. He thought about snatching him up in front of his two goons and bringing him back to reality, but what good would it do?

"I guess they must have found the trapdoor."

"Gee, boss, what gave you that idea." Shawn said, hoping his sarcasm would further infuriate him.

The big man looked up, smiled, walked past him, and started down the dark hallway. "Let's go," he said and disappeared into the black space.

42

Ethan jumped from the last rung and stood in awe of what looked to be an old coal tunnel. Black dust hovered in the air and drifted through both beams of light as his eyes glanced over the others. For the moment, he could think of nothing to say as he scrutinized the different expressions unique to each of his friends. Like them, he guessed he looked flabbergasted. Closing his eyes, he thought of Lauren.

She must have been deathly afraid being carried through here.

Tears dripped from his eyes and gathered in the corner of his mouth. An image of Lauren screaming for help forced his eyes open. An ocean of guilt filled his heart and soul as the group gathered around him and a soft ray of light shined on his face.

"What's wrong with you?" Ryan said. "Are you crying?"

Unable to speak, he nodded.

Josie grabbed his hand and squeezed gently. "Why are you crying?"

"I'm normally not this emotional," he said, hoping the tears would stop their flow. "I can't shake the feeling that something beyond our understanding brought us together. It's like we were all meant to meet each other and figure this thing out and stop—"

"I feel the same way," Josie said and squeezed his hand tighter. "You're right, if I would have followed the bike trail home instead of taking the old path, we would have never met. Ethan, I never stray from the main trail because being anywhere near this building scares the crap out of me."

Fighting a smile, he held each of their gazes a brief moment and then smiled at Josie. "Tommy, Alyssa, and I have connections with people who disappeared. I get what motivates the three of us, but I can't figure out why you and Ryan were sucked into this mess."

"My life has been running along a miserable road for a long time," Ryan said. "I feel guilty about something that wasn't my fault. My girlfriend was killed in a car crash, and I survived. I've had to live with that for way too long. I don't know why I chose this area to go on a hiking trip, but I think it may not have been my choice."

"Misery loves company," Josie said with a smile. "Sage and I are just tagging along to make sure you guys stay out of trouble."

"You're not doing such a good job," he said and felt the feeling of guilt vanish from his heart.

"You're not funny."

They stood in a circle and gathered around each other in the dim passageway. He drew strength from each of them—especially Josie. He was scared of what might lie ahead in the narrow coal mine, but the bond he shared with his friends provided him the courage to press on. At that moment, he felt confident that they would uncover the mystery of the many disappearances and unsolved murders that have burdened his town since late last century. Like them, he had no clue as to what awaited them ahead. Later, after they complete the task that fate had obviously intended for them, he would worry about the consequences. Right or wrong, he was ready to push on through the coal mine until they found what had been eluding him for the past nine years.

"Thanks," he said.

"For what?" Ryan whispered.

He smiled and looked upon each of their faces. "For risking your lives and for not judging me."

"No, kid, thank you," Tommy said and grabbed his shoulder. "I think because of you, we might actually learn what happened to them."

"I don't mean to sound insensitive," Alyssa said, her voice laced with skepticism. "It's been nine years since Lauren was taken away, and it's been even longer for your brother, Tommy."

Ryan sighed sarcastically. "Jesus, girl. Why are you always so negative?"

"All I'm saying is that we have to prepare for every possibility."

"She's right," Josie said. "We may not like what we find. I mean, it's been a long time since they were taken."

"If we find anything at all," Alyssa said.

"They're down here somewhere. I know it sounds unreal that they could still be alive after so many years, but I'm telling you guys, they're down here. I can feel it in my bones, and we're going to find them."

"What if they're not alive?" Alyssa said. "What if you're wrong, Ethan?"

"Then we make sure that thing never hurts anybody else!"

"Amen," Tommy shouted.

"For what it's worth, I hope you're right. Lauren was my best friend, and I loved her. I pray to God we find them and bring them back home. I really mean that. I do Ethan, but I think you—"

"I know you do," Tommy said and smiled.

"Yeah, me too," Ethan said and took one last look at his friends. Though feeling mentally and physically drained, he was ready to plunge further into the unknown and discover exactly what fate had in store for them. He was ready for the challenge that lay ahead, and he prayed they were too.

"Let's go!" Tommy said and started through the tunnel.

Alyssa walked beside Tommy, lighting the dark with the flashlight he gave her before climbing down the ladder. Ryan followed a few steps behind, leaving him standing alone with Josie and Sage. With confidence, he grabbed her arm and gently spun her back toward him. Surprise filled her big beautiful green eyes as their bodies stood inches apart.

"Ethan," she said, "what are…?"

Closing his eyes, he leaned forward and kissed her mouth. Since the moment he saw her appear around that corner, he wanted to kiss her. Considering their circumstances, this could be his only chance. He had no intentions of letting the moment slip by the wayside. As he kissed her with passion, he felt her body loosen. Seconds later, her moist tongue swept across his. Thirty seconds later, he pulled gently away with a dizzy head.

"What was that for?"

"In case I never get another chance."

He gazed into her eyes a few moments longer and then turned and hurried through the tunnel. Josie walked beside him with a weird and wonderful smirk lighting her face as they caught up to the others.

"Hey, Josie."

She glanced into his eyes but said nothing.

"I know we don't really know each other that well, but I want you to know," Ethan smiled and touched her hand. "I think I love you."

She took his hand as her smile deepened.

Blushing, he looked away.

43

Gregory Stephens pulled the stone slab back over the hole and climbed into the old mining tunnel. If any one of those meddlers managed to get past him, they would have the burden of wasting valuable time pushing the heavy slab out of the way. Feeling much calmer than a few minutes ago, he took a knee and searched around the ground. "Shine some light down here," he said and noticed fresh tracks as both beams danced across the gritty soil in front of him.

Christopher took a knee beside him. "They're down there, all right."

Excitement filtered through his veins, and every ounce of anger he felt toward Preston dissolved away. Very soon, he would take great pleasure in ending their pathetic existences. Glaring at the footprints trailing deeper into the tunnel, he realized that those kids finding the secret door was a blessing in disguise.

Down here they can scream as loud as they want, and no one will ever hear them.

He turned away, hoping no one noticed the smile on his face. He would kill the dog first and make them watch just to see the terrified looks on their smug faces. As much as he enjoyed torturing dumb animals, he rarely found an opportunity to partake in his favorite childhood hobby these days. Nothing this world had to offer compared to the rush he felt when he watched the life seep from his victim's eyes. Imagining the two girl's faces, he felt the beginnings of an erection as the thought of torture and rape excited his mind. After he took care of the men, he planned to send Christopher ahead with the others and remain behind with the girls.

He glanced backward and stared at Preston.

He hated the Bissells, but at least they were afraid of him. They were weak, which made them easy to control. Preston, on the other hand, was dangerous. Gregory couldn't intimidate him like the others, but they could. They kept him loyal by threatening his old man's life. Although he's never had to actually get his hands dirty, Preston has never had the fortitude to go against them. He loved his dad too much to chance doing anything stupid. If Shawn was foolish enough to betray them, he would get the honor of torturing the old man in front of him.

Feeling suddenly powerful, he looked away from Shawn and relished the mood.

He wished Cornelius would let him strangle both Preston and the Bissell's, but there would be too many questions regarding their whereabouts. For now, he would have to endure the hatred he felt toward them and focus his rage on the meddling kids.

"They can't be too far ahead," Christopher said and rose to his feet.

Feeling his erection wither, he glared at the others. "Let them stay ahead of us for now. The farther away from town we get, the better it is for us."

"Good plan, boss."

"It is," he said. "After we kill them, the rats can feast on their bloated carcasses. They lucked out finding that door, but never in a million years will they make it through the magic portal to Cornelius's world, at least not with life left in their lungs."

"Let's just get this over with," Shawn said and glimpsed at the Bissells with a look of sorrow.

"After all they've done for you. One would think you might appreciate the importance of our current situation. If any one of those meddling little maggots manages to discover what they are and escapes this place, we'll all be in deep trouble."

"Maybe, Mr. Stephens," he said. "I just don't get my rocks off by hurting innocent kids like you do."

"You think they're innocent?" he shouted. "If they were so freaking innocent, they wouldn't be down here in the first place."

Preston stood face-to-face with him as the argument grew more heated than he had liked. Preston was pissing him off so bad he thought about shooting him in the face right there. Unfortunately, he would have to explain his off-the-handle temperament to Cornelius if he acted upon the impulse. Being allowed certain fringe benefits like snuffing the life out of meddlers is rewarding enough, but he wished they would let him get rid of people like Preston who only help his monsters out of fear and not loyalty.

"They're down here because bad things have happened to them because of your precious freaks of nature," Shawn shouted, standing on his tiptoes an inch away from Gregory's face. "They believe in what they're doing down here."

"What about you? Do you believe in what you're doing down here?"

"Believe in what," he screamed. "I'm down here because if I don't help, you and those murderous freaks will kill my dad. Where in the heck do you get off asking if I believe in what I'm doing?"

Fighting an urge to pull out his gun, he backed off, giving Preston his space. The loudmouthed lecture would be his last speech. After they deal with the meddlers, he would shoot him in the face, regardless of Cornelius's wrath. He would stand back and watch with delight as Preston lay on the dirty ground withering in pain as blood sprayed from his face like a summer sprinkler.

"No, Mr. Stephens, I don't want to do this but I have to."

He smiled and stepped backward. "That's the difference between us, Shawn. I don't get emotionally involved regarding the duties expected of me."

"That's not the only difference between you and me," Shawn said and turned away. He walked toward the open end of the tunnel and disappeared into the dark.

Feeling calm, he watched Preston go.

Cornelius wouldn't begrudge you the pleasure of giving Preston a painful death. After all, he sympathized with the meddlers.

The Bissells stood beside Christopher with fearful expressions on their faces and waited for a command like disorganized soldiers.

You can take care of them while we're down here too.

He never understood why his master recruited people like them, but today, he planned to severe their contract. His head buzzed with eagerness as the thought of shooting Shawn and Kelly and squeezing the life out of the tall scrawny woman with his bare hands would soon be a reality.

"Boss," Christopher said, sounding concerned.

"Get moving," he said sternly. "We got a long walk ahead of us."

Excited about the pain that he would soon execute, he followed a few feet behind the others. Despite the enthusiasm invigorating his mood, he wanted to be alone. He hoped Cornelius would understand why he needed to dispose of Preston and the older couple. If not, he would think of some way to gain his forgiveness. Regardless, he thought silencing Preston's sarcastic mouth would be worth his master's wrath.

No one talks to you like that without suffering the consequences. The big shot Wisconsin detective will get his real soon.

44

Tommy walked a few feet out in front, his finger gently stroking the trigger. He glanced nervously at the shadowy walls as if some nightmarish creature might jump out from a well concealed hiding place and attack him. Every third step, he glanced over his shoulder to make sure everyone still followed behind him. Like the rest of the group, he was terrified, but Ethan had a strong feeling they were in capable hands.

Recruiting Tommy proved to be a good decision.

They walked for what seemed like miles through the dusty coal tunnel until it opened into a large cavern with a small bluish-green pond tucked into the far corner. As he followed the others deeper into the cavern, a strong stench of rotten eggs tormented his nostrils. "Anyone thirsty?" he said and took a few steps closer to the water in need of a better view.

"It smells like sulfur," Alyssa said.

Tommy's face twisted in disgust. "It smells like my dog after I feed it chili."

"Thanks, Tommy," Ryan said. "That's one mental image I could have done without."

Mildly offended nobody laughed at his joke, Ethan strolled past the puddle to the far side of the room and took a seat on the black and gritty soil. Agony that had been plaguing his feet most of the long journey melted away as he stretched his legs and leaned back against the wall.

With her arms crossed over her chest, Josie shook her head in disapproval. "You're going to get filthy dirty sitting on that floor."

"Maybe, but my legs and feet hurt way too much to give a good crap right now."

"I feel your pain, brother," Ryan said, leaning his rifle against the wall. "It seems like we've been walking for a couple of hours."

"It feels like it, dude. I bet we hiked a good ten miles through that tunnel."

Ryan yawned, stretched his arms, and dropped to the ground, being careful not to bump into the rifle. He settled in, leaned against the wall, and grinned at Ethan as loose dirt dribbled down the wall and showered his hair. "It doesn't get any better than this," he said and closed his eyes, feeling unfazed by the black gritty shower.

Admiring Ryan's resilience, he covered his mouth and muffled his laughter. "How far do you think we walked?"

"Two miles, maybe three at the most, but down here it's hard to judge," he said and opened his eyes. "It feels like we've been underneath this town a really long time."

Josie stood above them with both hands on her hips and a look of uncertainty in her eyes.

Ryan chuckled. "This is why you didn't wear your Sunday best."

"You're real funny."

Scooting a few inches to the left, Ethan motioned for her to sit.

She scratched her head as if debating whether or not to dirty her tattered jeans and then wiggled in between them. "You're right, this feels like heaven," she said and reached for the ceiling with a drawn-out yawn as Sage flopped into the soil in front of them and stretched his front paws.

Seconds later, he snored quietly.

With envy, he stroked his fingers across Josie's hand and watched Tommy and Alyssa circle the area, shinning beams of light up the walls and across the ten-foot ceiling. The large room stretched nearly forty feet from one side of the wall to the other before it rounded at the far corner where the sulfuric pond collected floating ebony dust.

"Another dead end," Tommy shouted as he and Alyssa approached.

"You didn't see anything unusual?"

"Nope, just a big empty cave," Alyssa said.

"Let's take a break and have some lunch, and then we can thoroughly search around this place," Ryan said. "I'm hungry, and it feels like a year and half since we ate breakfast." He leaned forward, slid the backpack over his shoulder, and dropped it on the ground beside the rifle. After unsnapping the straps, he pulled five bottles of water from the pack and handed them to Josie one at a time. After a long, deep swallow of cold water, he pulled out the small camouflage sack with the sandwiches Tommy whipped up and tossed it on the ground.

Ethan giggled as Tommy grabbed a bottle of water from Josie and joined them on the ground.

Tommy stared. "What's so funny?"

"Is camouflage your favorite color, dude?"

"Is *dude* your favorite word?"

"No, actually it's not," Ethan managed to say between fits of laughter. "During one of my stints at the nuthouse, I found myself spending a lot of time with this one inmate named Jimmy Johansson. I liked him because of his catchy name."

"I think it's kind of goofy," Ryan said.

"Not goofy," Josie said and nudged Ryan. "It sounds like he might be Swedish or Norwegian or something like that."

"Anyway, Jimmy was a pretty decent dude. He was paranoid, which was the reason for his incarceration, but he would go the extra mile for a friend. We hung out the better part of a year before he was shipped off to another hospital. I never saw him again. I assumed he was from the West Coast because he talked like one of those surfer guys you see in the movies. Every other word out of his mouth was *dude*. It was 'Dude, do this,' and 'Dude, do that' all the time. It kind of got annoying after a while in a good way, if you know what I mean."

Giggling, they shook their heads.

"I missed the way he said it, and after a while, it just became a part of my vocabulary."

"Sorry, kid, I didn't mean to be so defensive about the camouflage thing."

"No problem. It's cool that we can tease each other. It keeps everyone's spirits up. For me, it makes this situation a lot easier to deal with."

Feeling calm, he bit into his peanut butter sandwich and closed his eyes. He swallowed, took a sip of water, and kept quiet as his friends engaged in small talk as if they were five old chums hanging out at the mall instead of roaming underneath the town chasing after a monster.

45

Jennifer squeezed her husband's hand as they marched deeper into the coal mine. Though his pulse vibrated through her sweaty fingertips, she felt alone and slightly nauseated. Murdering those kids didn't sit right with her. In the past, she and Kelly had been forced to participate in covering up for them, but it usually meant providing alibis for Gregory Stephens and the others. Until today, no one expected them to tag along and help do the dirty work.

Up ahead, Shawn kept his distance from the monster calling himself Gregory Stephens. He walked in silence beside Christopher, shattering the dusty black with the light from the flashlight he confiscated from her a while back.

Like Shawn, she hated the man's guts. Since the day he took her friends for those monsters, she despised everything he stood for. His arrogance made her want to puke. Unfortunately, he scared her way too much to ever go against his orders. For the moment, she felt at ease, knowing the madman was up ahead where she could keep an eye on him. The thought of having her back to such a maniac sent chills through her body.

Thank God for Shawn, she thought and squeezed tighter on Kelly's hand. She liked the cop but pitied him for having to deal with that evil man. To his credit, he managed to stay composed when they argued. Without him, she and Kelly might be in serious danger. Since the day they met, Gregory has despised her husband for reasons she wasn't a hundred percent certain about. She suspected he might try and kill Kelly at the first opportunity.

"How are you holding up?" Kelly whispered.

"I feel like I'm going to be sick."

"I don't like this either, my love, but we don't have a choice."

"Shut up back there," Christopher shouted.

She smiled at Kelly and continued walking.

He was right, they had no choice. Her mind raced back to the day she first encountered Gregory Stephens. That afternoon, she spent hours playing in the woods behind the hotel with Colleen and Jessica. After realizing their parents might be worried, they ran through the forest, hoping to make it home before anyone knew they were gone but emerged twenty feet from a back entrance into the hotel instead.

Tears filled her eyes as her mind took a ride back in time.

Jessica stops in the back yard and stares at the building with a strange smile on her face. "Come on," she says and runs to the door.

Grabbing Colleen by the hand, she chases after Jessica and comes to halt a few feet from the entrance.

"Let's go inside," she says with excited eyes.

"No way, there are ghosts in there."

"That's just crazy talk. I bet there are all kinds of cool things inside." Without glancing back, Jessica shoves the door open and hurries inside.

Against better judgment, she grabs Colleen's hand and follows Jessica through the door. Her friend's fingers quiver as they jog across a dusty floor and join Jessica at the top of a dingy stairwell.

Peering into the black space below, Jessica seems oblivious to her surroundings, as if some unseen entity possesses her mind. A blank expression hangs on her face as she takes a step forward.

"Jessica," she shouts. "Let's go."

Ignoring her commands, the girl takes two more steps into the impenetrable blackness.

"Please don't go down there."

Twisting back toward the two frightened little girls, she grins and disappears into the blackness.

"Jessica, get back up here!"

Afraid to let go of Colleen's hand, she falls to one knee and peers into the staircase. Cold sweat drips down her forehead as her heart pounds like a drum in a marching band.

"Come down here and see what I found," Jessica shouts through bouts of creepy laughter.

Shivering with fear, she steps back and stares wide-eyed at the door. Instinct demands she take Colleen and run as far away from the haunted building as possible. More than anything, she wants to go and get her father but dreads the thought of being punished for breaking into the one place they were warned to stay away from. Against good judgment, she descends the squeaky steps and pulls Colleen behind her.

"Jessica, please, this ain't funny. Where are you at?"

"Back here," she giggles. "Come see what I found. It's wonderful."

She squints, but her eyes can't penetrate the darkness. Beside her, Colleen whimpers as her hand clamps tighter around her fingers. Enduring the minor sting, she glances about for the other girl but sees only long stretched-out shadows dancing across the floor.

"Come over here and see what I found." Her voice sounds miles away.

Tears wet her cheeks as her legs wobble. "Please, you come over here," she says as Colleen sobs loudly beside her. "We're scared, okay? If that's what you wanted, you can stop now!"

Eerie laughter echoes across the room, sounding closer by the second. Jessica's soft giggles sound farther away than before.

"Jessica, stop that. You're scaring Colleen!"

In the distance, the girl continues to giggle.

She looks back at the lighted stairwell, swallows, and pulls Colleen across the floor toward the sound of eerie laughter. Terror ignites her heart as the darkness grows thicker around them. Tremors vibrate her fingers as Colleen's whimpering falls silent. Against her will, she heaves the trembling girl deeper into the basement toward the sound of Jessica's laughter. She is scared beyond belief, but it's too late to turn back.

Suddenly, the laughter ceases, and the room fills with mind-boggling silence.

Squinting into the dark, she stops dead in her tracks.

In front of her, soft footfalls shuffle across the floor and fall silent. She wants to turn back and run as Colleen's whimpering grows louder and louder. Though her friend stands inches away, grasping her own sweaty palm, she feels alone and misses her dad.

"Jessica," she whispers. "Please quit scaring us."

Shadows dance through the room and draw closer.

As she shivers in the dark cellar waiting for Jessica to cease her antics, she sees a shape slowly moving closer. At first, relief rushes through her as she thinks it is her friend, but as the shadow dances to within a few feet, she realizes it is too large to be Jessica.

Colleen's hand rips away from hers as something heaves her into the air. As it carried her through the darkness, Colleen's weeping diminishes, and a lonesome silence lingers in her ears. With her eyes closed tight, she prays this is only a nightmare.

As powerful hands ease her to the ground, a deep voice sends chills down her spine. "Don't be scared," it says as strange grunting noises and large feet pounding against concrete fill the dark space.

She tries to speak, but her teeth chatter too hard to concentrate.

"Do as I say, and you'll be spared."

"Where are my friends?" She finally manages to say with her eyes still closed tightly.

"Go home and tell your folks you were playing in the woods when a man came out of nowhere and took your friends. Tell them you ran away before he could get you too."

"Where are Colleen and Jessica?"

"You should really be more concerned about yourself right now."

Tears drip down her face as her mind tries to grasp what was happening to her. This strange nightmare couldn't be real.

At any moment, she would wake in her bed surrounded by her mom and dad.

"Do what I want, or everybody you love will die horrible deaths."

The last thing she wants is to leave her friends with this man who's offering her a chance at freedom, but her parents will be killed if she doesn't obey. She swallows hard and prays for forgiveness. "Don't hurt my mom and dad, and I'll do what you want."

"Convince people your friends were kidnapped by a maniac in the woods and then wait to hear from me."

"Hear from you, why?"

"When the time comes, I'll summon you. If you don't obey me, your family will suffer for your disobedience. Do you understand?"

"Yes, I understand."

With massive hands, he heaves her into the air and carries her through the darkness. She sees a dim light at the top of the stairwell. Seconds later, he sits her gently on the platform and disappears back into the basement. Glancing back, she sees a hulking man with bushy red hair disappear into the cellar. Without a second glance, she runs for the light and hurries out through the door into the bright sunlight.

Kelly nudged her side and pointed through the tunnel.

The others stood a few feet from the opening, huddled against the wall. As she and Kelly drew closer, they saw a dim light in the large room.

"Kill the lights!" Gregory whispered. "We don't want them seeing us coming."

46

Ryan felt confidence slip away as the beam of light danced across the same section of the wall for the umpteenth time.

Frowning, he looked at the girls.

Alyssa and Josie stood in the center of the room waving light through the dusty air at the walls. They reminded him of beams from a lighthouse guiding lost sailors in from the sea. He eyed the light as it shimmered along the black wall and danced across the ceiling. After searching the large area three times over the past hour, he wondered if they missed something elsewhere in the coal mine.

Ethan gave him an irritated grin and then staggered toward the girls. "Dang it!" he shouted and stopped next to Josie. "I think we need to kill one of these lights. I don't know how long those batteries last, but being stuck down here in the dark doesn't sound like my kind of entertainment."

Across the room, Tommy threw his hands up in disgust. "There's nothing here," he said and balanced the rifle against the wall. Frowning, he slid to the ground, leaned backward, and closed his eyes as if trying to unravel the mystery in his mind.

Alyssa switched off the flashlight in her hand, obviously agreeing that conserving the batteries was a good idea. "My legs hurt, I need a break," she said and lumbered across the floor. Using Tommy's shoulder as a crutch, she knelt down and took a seat beside him.

Josie shrugged and stared at Ethan.

Ethan pulled a chunk of coal from the ground and tossed it in the puddle. Seeming peculiarly fascinated, he watched as small waves rippled across the water and disappeared along the edge. Turning, he grabbed the flashlight from Josie and shined the beam across the water with the same look of disappointment on his face. "What now?" he said, sounding defeated.

Tommy opened his eyes. "I don't know, but there isn't anything in here but tainted air and black walls."

"You two sound as if you're giving up."

"What are we supposed to do? We've searched and searched and then searched some more, and we still haven't found anything."

"He's right, dude, we've hit a dead end," Ethan said. "We don't have anywhere else to look."

"So what then, we give up and go back to your house?"

Ethan threw his arms up in the air and looked away.

"That thing brought me into that basement for a reason," he said. "It has to be down in this place somewhere."

"Settle down, Ryan," Alyssa said. "Everyone's just a little tired right now."

"Josie, come on! Help me out here."

Petting Sage, she glanced at him with exhausted eyes. "I don't know what you want me to do."

"How about not giving up so easily?"

She rolled her eyes and continued to pet her dog.

Anger spread through him like a flesh-eating virus. He felt like an idiot. They led him on an exploration of a hotel that became a spelunking expedition in an abandoned mining tunnel. He didn't sign up for this adventure only to give up when they were on the verge of uncovering the truth.

This is Ethan's crusade. Why are you the only one determined to resolve it?

He sighed and gawked at Ethan. "What happened to fate brought us together, or was that just a bunch of bullcrap you used to get me to come down here?"

"He didn't make you come down here," Josie said glancing up from Sage. "You came on your own."

"No, Josie, he did make me come down here."

"Dude, nobody forced you to help us, so take it easy."

"You did!" he said and pointed at Ethan.

"How did I force you?"

"You and Josie saved my hide. You rescued me from something that shouldn't exist, some kind of horrible monster that you only see in low-budget horror flicks. But it does exist because it took your little sister away from you. How could I say no to that after you saved my butt from that thing?"

Ethan stood quietly with a flabbergasted look on his face.

Despite the anger boiling inside his chest, Ryan wanted to laugh.

Josie rose to her feet and glared at him as if she had something to say but looked away instead.

"You," he said and pointed at Tommy. "It deprived you of a life with your brother, and now you would just leave this place and forget all about him."

Tommy lifted his head and stared blankly.

He was unsure where the words were coming from as he continued to lay a guilt trip on these people. Normally despising being at the center of attention, he felt a slight sense of satisfaction as dejected expressions hung from each of their faces.

Ladies and gentlemen, Ryan the pathetic loser has the floor.

"You too, Alyssa," he said, aware of the irritated glare in her eyes. "You have a part in all this too. His sister was your best friend, and obviously you never got over it or you wouldn't have shoved those articles in our faces. Despite your skeptical attitude, you wanted to come down here and search for her as much as he did."

Alyssa looked away.

He took a step toward Josie and smiled. "You said you don't know why fate has you here, but I do know." He reached for her hand as he moved closer. "You did something you wouldn't normally do. You stopped and struck up a conversation with a stranger long enough for Sage to be where fate wanted him to be. Don't you see, by saving my life, that amazing dog of yours got the ball rolling?"

Except for Alyssa, they scrutinized him with guilt-ridden eyes.

"If you guys want to call it a day, I'm all for it. Just give me one of those flashlights, because I'm going back through that tunnel, and then I'm heading home to tell my parents that I understand Molly died. And I can get on with my life, even if it means living without her." After taking one last look at their somber faces, he glanced toward the opening with intentions of walking back through the coal mine alone. Feeling deceived, he hurried toward the tunnel as Sage lifted his head and began a low steady growl while staring at the large opening. Trusting the dog's instinct, he stopped a few feet from the opening and backpedaled toward the others as Sage jumped from the dirt with his tail pointed at the ceiling, looking ready to attack. "Get your dog," he said and hurried for the rifle he left against the wall.

"Did you see something?" Ethan said.

"No, but Sage obviously does."

Tommy reached for his rifle and crawled from the dirt. With a look of enthusiasm, he grabbed the Remington and swung the barrel at the opening. "Who's there?" he said and yanked Alyssa from the ground with his free hand.

Ethan stepped in front of Josie and arched the flashlight upward, casting dim light on the entrance. Shadows disappeared along the walls like soul-possessing demons vanquished by a holy priest.

"Step out and show yourself," Tommy shouted.

Sage fought to break free of Josie's grasp but couldn't wiggle free of her clenched fingers.

"Ryan, get your butt over here," Tommy said and stared at the girls. "We're going to walk slowly toward the tunnel. Stay behind me and Ryan at all times. Ethan, keep that light on that opening so we can see if anything decides to jump out."

Ethan nodded.

"We're coming to you," Tommy shouted and motioned for Ryan to move forward. "Come on out so we can discuss this. I don't want to hurt anyone if I don't have to."

A tall muscular man dressed in a red flannel jacket and dark blue jeans stepped into the light carrying a small silver pistol in his right hand. He had disheveled red hair and a burly cherry red beard. Taking a few long strides, he glanced over the barrels of death aimed at his head.

"Who are you, mister?" Tommy said, holding the rifle steady in his hands.

"Put the gun down, son," the man said as he maneuvered past the cave entrance and took a step closer toward Tommy and Ryan.

Feeling suddenly cold, Ryan lowered the barrel a few inches and planted his feet in the dirt. "Who are you, and what are you doing down here?" he said as his finger trembled slightly on the trigger. He hoped no one noticed, especially the man pointing the silver-handled pistol at Tommy.

"I can ask you all the same question."

"If you must know sir," said Tommy. "My friends and I were scouting some deer when we stumbled upon this place and found this old mine. We followed it here hoping it would lead us somewhere else, but it stopped at a dead end."

"How about you," Ryan said. "What brings you down in this coal mine?"

The stranger smiled and lowered his gun to the soil. "I'm a deputy marshal for the railroad, and you guys and gals were spotted trespassing on my property." Looking anxious, he glanced toward the puddle. "Give me a minute to look around, and then you kids can follow me out of here."

Following Tommy's lead, he angled the barrel toward the floor.

Behind him, Sage growled and continued to try and break free of Josie's grasp.

Like Sage, Ryan couldn't shake the feeling that this man was lying. He had a hard time believing someone would call the railroad on a group of people trespassing inside of property that, according to Alyssa, was owned by the historical society. "What did you say your name was again?"

"Deputy Stephens," he said with a confident tone of voice, despite a distrustful look deep in his icy blue eyes. Smiling, he took another step forward.

As the man inched closer, Ryan eyeballed the pistol and felt suddenly skeptical. He glanced quickly at Tommy but decided to follow his own instincts instead. "That's far enough," he said and pointed his rifle at him.

"Whoa there, son. You might want to rethink your actions," he said and stopped dead in his tracks. He glared at Ryan and glanced down at his hand as if contemplating a quick draw but deciding against it.

"What are you doing, Ryan?" Tommy said. "He's a cop." He glanced back and looked at Ethan and the girls and then slowly raised the rifle at the deputy's chest. "He's right, mister. We'll lower these guns back down once you show us some credentials."

"You kids are asking for trouble."

He seemed calm, like a man who's been in a tight spot before. The arrogant smirk on his lips reinforced Ryan's belief that he was lying.

"You better be right about this," Tommy said. "Pointing guns at a lawman might fetch us a bit more trouble than I really need right now."

Ignoring Tommy's rant, he stayed focused on the phony cop. "Toss your wallet over here," he said and held the gun as steady as his nervous hands would allow. Despite anxiety igniting his heartbeat, he felt adrenaline surge through his veins. The resentment he felt toward his friends slipped away as he watched irritation fill the stranger's eyes.

"You're robbing me?"

"Not robbing you," he said and felt more confident by the second. "I just want to have a look at your credentials, if you catch my drift."

Like an animal ensnared in a trap, he looked anxious.

"Go get his wallet. Ethan," he shouted. "I'd really like to see if this clown is really who he claims to be."

"Are you crazy, dude? I'm not going anywhere near that guy with that gun in his hand," he said through a sarcastic chuckle. "I've never been shot before, and I plan on keeping it that way, if you catch my drift."

"Drop the gun, mister and move away. Toss your badge over here so my friend can get your identification."

"What if I don't?"

"You'll be on the market for a new head to sit on your shoulders."

After a quick glance at his hand, he looked up and stared at Ryan with two hateful eyes. A second later, he dropped the pistol. It pinged onto the dirt as he took three steps to the left.

"Ryan, are you sure about this?" Alyssa said. "What if you're wrong?"

"I'm one hundred percent sure," he said with the barrel less than five feet from the man's head, "if this guy is a deputy marshal, I'm the next president of the United States."

"But what if you're wrong, Ryan?"

"Alyssa, listen to me—"

A man dressed in blue sweats stepped through the opening. "Yeah, Ryan, what if you're wrong?" he said with a black-handled pistol pointed at Ryan's chest.

Grinding his foot into the dirt to settle his nerves, he steadied the barrel but felt his confidence slip away. He knew he was right about the big man claiming to be a railroad deputy, but the other man's appearance took him by surprise.

"Drop it, Ryan, and maybe I won't blow a hole through your ugly freaking face," he said and walked slowly toward the red-haired man. He looked as confident as a road scholar in the midst of a kindergarten placement test.

"You better do what he says, Ryan, or you'll be feeding the filthy rats for the next few weeks," Mr. Stephens said. A smug grin replaced the caged animal look that had been cemented on his face the past few minutes.

With a nervous twitch, Tommy shifted the barrel at the newcomer as Ryan focused on the bigger man. "Don't think about taking another step, or I'll blow a hole in your ugly face."

"Ethan!" he yelled. "Get his gun."

"Don't do it, Ethan," the man in the sweats shouted. "You'll be pooping out of your stomach, boy."

Ethan stood between Alyssa and Josie and rubbed his palms nervously.

"Dang it, Ethan! Get the gun now." Tommy yelled as hot blood reddened his face.

Ferocious barks echoed through the area as Sage fought to break free from Josie's grasp.

Despite the distraction, Ryan stayed focused on the burly bearded man as Josie struggled with the collar.

With evil intent, Mr. Stephens stared at Sage. "Christopher," he said and began a bloodcurdling laugh. "Kill the dog, and shoot the girl in the leg."

From behind, he heard Ethan scramble for the gun as a thunderous explosion shook dust from the ceiling and showered the area with gritty black soot. Startled, he squeezed the trigger and closed his eyes as phantom sirens wailed through his ears. Feeling disoriented, he opened his eyes as the man claiming to be a deputy collapsed on the ground with blood soaking through a hole in his side. Beside him, Tommy groaned and fell to the floor as his rifle twirled backward through the air like a lopsided boomerang and landed a few feet from the pond. Suddenly nauseated, he dropped to his knees and vomited partially digested peanut butter down the front of his shirt and watched Ethan spin around with the dead man's pistol in his hand and swing it up through the air like a monkey fumbling a banana. Closing his eyes a second to ease his vertigo, he heard footsteps shuffle toward him as the rifle slipped through his fingers.

"You're dead, man!" a voice shouted from above.

Swallowing down chunks of tainted peanut butter, he opened his eyes as the faint sound of a dog barking filled his ringing ears. Christopher towered over Tommy with the gun inches from his forehead. Sick and on the verge of passing out, he reached for the rifle as another thunderous boom exploded through the cavern.

Ethan shouted as Sage continued to bark.

Christopher grimaced as the gun dropped from his fingers and spiraled to the ground. With an excruciating groan, he dropped to his knees and reached for the gun as blood dripped from the corner of his mouth and gathered in a maroon pool in the dirt. He glared into Ryan's eyes a brief second and fell forward in the bloody dirt. His body twitched and then went limp.

Beside him, Tommy moaned in agony.

Feeling on the verge of vomiting again, he crawled to his knees as a middle-aged man with short brown hair hurried toward Tommy and lowered a pistol to his side. Behind him, an older man and a woman with long dirty blond hair stepped through the entrance and stood behind the gunman. After holstering his pistol, the man whispered something to his friends and then knelt beside Tommy.

With fear in his eyes, Ethan kept the gun on the stranger.

"Put the gun down, boy," he said calmly while examining Tommy.

Ethan dropped the gun as if it were a metal plate pulled from a hot oven. It bounced off his foot and onto the ground. He stepped back toward Josie and stared as the man and woman stood behind their friend.

From his knees, the gunman glimpsed up at the older couple. "I think they're both dead," he said and pointed at Ryan. "That kid shot him up pretty good."

The older man gave Ryan a crooked smile as Sage's barking faded in the background.

"What are you doing here?" Josie shouted.

Feeling more confused than ever, he crawled to his feet and hobbled to where Tommy lay on the ground, squirming in pain from a gunshot wound in his shoulder. Seconds later, Ethan and Alyssa stood beside him.

"Can you help him?" Alyssa said.

"The bullet tore through his shoulder," he said and removed his lightweight jacket. He wrapped it tightly around the wound and glanced at Alyssa. "Don't worry, that'll slow the bleeding."

Josie circled around Ethan and stood a few feet from the woman. "I asked you a question."

After pulling the knot tight, the man stood up and stepped between them. "My name's Shawn Preston, and I think I can shed a little light on what just happened."

Groaning, Tommy opened his eyes. "I knew you were involved you in this," he said and struggled to sit upright. "After all these years, I knew you had something to do with my brother's disappearance."

With a tear-streaked face, Alyssa rushed to Tommy's side.

Ryan knelt beside her and helped Tommy to his feet. "This is getting too weird, mister," he said and struggled not laugh. "I could have gotten lost anywhere in the country, but I managed to do it here and get caught up in one of the most unbelievable scenarios that anyone could imagine. What exactly is going on?"

"Before you judge us, you need to listen to what we have to say."

"I've already tried listening to you, but you acted all innocent. I knew you were lying," he shouted with rage in his eyes. "You were supposed to be his friend, and you betrayed him."

Ryan slid his shoulder under Tommy's arm to help keep him balanced. "They may have just saved our lives. I think they earned the right for us to hear them out."

"This is Jennifer," Shawn said and pointed at the blonde-haired woman.

"Jennifer Anthony," Josie said rudely.

"Yes, the same Jennifer that was forced to lie about what happened to her two best friends." He pointed to the burly man. "That man forced her to lie by threatening to murder her family if she ever spoke the truth about what happened." He stared at Josie with a compassionate smile. "She had no choice but to keep quiet."

"What about you, Shawn?" Tommy half shouted. "You were my brother's best friend."

"Two of those things attacked us just before we made it to the trails. They took your brother and the other guys and left me with the burden of knowing my parents would be murdered in front of me if I ever said a word."

"You should have told someone!"

"Do you really think anyone would have believed me when I said that two fairytale creatures lead by a madman carried my friends away? They would have locked me up while that idiot over there slaughtered my parents." He sighed, glanced back at Jennifer, and then turned his eyes to Tommy. "Imagine being a young boy, or a little girl in Jennifer's case, and being assured that if you told the truth, everyone you cared about would be murdered in front of you."

Looking defeated, Tommy glanced at the ground.

"I believed that back then, and I believe it now," Shawn said, lowering his voice. "I think whoever Gregory Stephens is working for will go after our families once he figures out what happened here."

"Me too," Jennifer said and looked sadly at the man beside her. "Kelly and I have two children. They're grown and live out of state, but I really believe they can get to them, and I think they will."

"So what do we do now?" Ethan said, pulling Josie gently toward him.

Shawn's comforting green eyes stared at Ethan. "I think we should take the fight to them. I've never been in their world, but maybe it's about time somebody besides Gregory Stephens goes through that portal."

"Do you know how to get there?" Ryan said, glancing around the large area. "We searched this place three times already."

Shawn smiled. "Yeah, well, it's in this room."

"Why don't we just destroy it?" he said. "It seems to me that would be a whole lot safer."

"No way, we can't do that!" Ethan shouted. "At least I can't."

"If we go after them, more people will die."

"There are people inside we need to try and help," Shawn said and smiled at Ethan as if reassuring him. "Good thought though, it's one I've thought about for a lot of years."

He shrugged at Ethan and grinned. "Sorry, man. I wasn't thinking straight there for a minute. We'll get her back. I promise."

"Don't make promises you can't keep, dude."

"How do you want to do this?" Ryan asked Shawn. Despite just saving their lives, Shawn seemed to be knowledgeable regarding their adversaries, and he already proved he could be trusted. Ryan liked the way he handled himself in a tight spot.

"First things first, get Tommy out of here and to the hospital. Tell them you found him along the trail where he was shot and left for dead." He looked at the older couple sternly. "Can you do that?"

"Yeah," they said simultaneously.

"We all know how the police tend to overlook certain things in this town."

The taste of vomit lingered in the back of his throat. "Kind of makes you wonder how far their influence goes in this town."

Nodding, Shawn looked at Tommy. "Think you can make the walk back?"

"Yeah, we may need to stop a few times along the way, but I'll manage."

"After you get him to the hospital, go back to your house and get in my glove compartment. I have an old green notepad inside that has a code written in black marker with Emergency written above the number."

"Okay," Kelly said while taking his wife's shaking hand.

"In the trunk of my car is a black case. The code is the combination to the case. Listen, guys, I want someone to bring it back down here."

"What is it?"

"Some pretty powerful fireworks." A smile crept across his face. "I'm going to blast their gateway into our town out of existence."

"I thought we weren't gonna destroy the portal, you said that—"

"Relax, kid, we're going inside first. We're going to do everything we can to find our people and bring them back home."

Ethan sighed as tears filled his eyes.

"Now where was I?" Shawn said, gesturing toward the Bissells. "Oh yeah, after you get the case from my trunk, I need someone to bring it back down here. All the person has to do is leave it there." He pointed to the corner opposite the pool of water.

"Sounds like you thought about this," Ryan said. He was excited yet a little frightened at the same time. He felt relieved to have a hotshot detective as an ally.

"Like I said, it was an idea I tossed around my head a few times. Until I met you kids, I was afraid to try it. I imagined anyone they dragged through there would be trapped forever if I blew it into a million pieces. Going inside has always been on my mind but was something I never thought I'd do until I realized that was what you guys had planned."

"So who are they?" Alyssa said, looking with disgust at the dead men.

"The red-haired man is Gregory Stephens," he said with no emotion. "I guess you could say he was their number 1 man. The other guy is someone I've only met today. His name is Christopher."

"They were going to kill you," Kelly said.

"And probably us as well," Jennifer agreed.

Josie gestured toward the bodies. "What are you going to do with them?"

"For now, we do nothing."

"But—"

"But nothing, if you knew what kind of monster that man really was," he said. "Trust me, young lady, you wouldn't care what happened to him."

"They're still human beings—"

"All right, Shawn," Ethan interrupted. "I guess it's you, me, and Ryan."

"No way," Josie said, wrenching her hand free and grabbed the front of his jacket. "You're not going in there without me and Sage."

Ethan sighed and gently removed her hands from his collar. "I think the three of us could get in there and sneak around a lot easier. Besides, you might get hurt or worse." He closed his eyes a few seconds and then latched on to her hands. "I couldn't live with myself if something happened to you."

"It's not your decision. You said fate brought us together, and you were right about that. If we stay together, then I think we can do this." She kissed his lips. "If we separate, our chances of succeeding falter."

"Then let fate guide us," he said reluctantly.

"And protect us," Ryan added.

"Lyssa," Ethan said, taking a step backward.

"Yeah," she whispered.

"I want you to go with them and help Tommy the best you can."

She nodded and then kissed him on the cheek. "I always believed in you, Ethan," she said through subdued weeping. "I never once thought that you could have harmed her in anyway. I know you loved her."

"Thank you," he said. He leaned forward, kissed her forehead, and shuffled backward to where Josie held onto Sage's collar. The dog looked miserable, like a bigger dog just stole his favorite bone as Alyssa helped Kelly lead Tommy through the opening.

Jennifer squeezed Shawn's hand and pulled him gently toward her. "Try to find my friends," she said with her mouth inches from his ear.

"I'll do my best."

"I trust you," she said and let go of his hand. With a halfhearted smile, she turned and chased after the others.

"Jennifer," Shawn shouted.

She turned around as the smile melted from her face.

"Don't forget about Andre," he said and raced toward the puddle. Reaching down, he grabbed Christopher's gun from the dirt and hurried back across the room. He held out his hand reluctantly, glanced at Kelly who stood under the opening and handed her the pistol. "Take care of him."

"We will."

"He'll kill you if he suspects anything is up."

"Don't worry. We'll take care of it."

"Have whoever comes back here bring the gun and throw it into the water."

"Okay," she said and disappeared through the opening.

"Take care of him," he shouted at the empty space. "He's dangerous and won't think twice about shooting you."

47

Shaken by what happened minutes earlier, Ethan glanced back and forth between the two dead men and felt a knot tighten deep in his stomach. Over the years he has lived with regret over both Lauren's disappearance and his mother's suicide, but watching a dead man's blood seep into the glistening black soil left him feeling guiltier than he had ever felt before. According to Shawn Preston, Gregory Stephens was a wicked man who bullied and murdered for the sheer pleasure of it, but the man was dead because of him. Ryan shot the bullet that ultimately ended his life, but because of his obsessive addiction, the man would never see the light of day again. Worse yet, it could just as easily be one of his friends lying motionless on the ground.

That could be Josie laying there.

On the verge of tears, he turned back toward the others and hoped nobody else had to die for his selfish crusade. Spotting Tommy's rifle a few feet from the pond, he hurried past Ryan, Josie, and Sage and scooped it up from the loose black earth. He sighed deeply and then ran a finger along the barrel with a feeling of uncertainty in his heart. As much as he wanted to protect his friends from whatever snatched Lauren, he distrusted his courage.

Shawn circled around the bodies, brushed Ethan's sleeve as he hurried by, and stopped at the water's edge. He crinkled his nose and glanced up. "That stuff sure does stink," he said and swept his fingers through the rancid water.

Ethan lowered his rifle and smiled. "It smells like raw sewage."

"More like rotten eggs," Josie said and rested her hand on his shoulder.

Shawn stared at the water like a man trying to see his reflection. A repulsing grimace stretched across his face as he unfastened his bloodstained button-down shirt and took three steps into the water.

"Dude, please tell me we're not going swimming."

Tossing the shirt aside, Shawn chuckled.

Ethan frowned as the knot in his gut tightened. Imagining the diseases he would probably be stricken with upon jumping into the obviously contaminated water, he gagged and stared at the half-naked man with disgust. He thought of Lauren. If discovering the truth about her meant diving headfirst into the nastiest pool of water he has ever seen, he planned on doing it without question.

"One thing about where we're going," Shawn said, motioning them forward. "According to big red over there, time is different there than it is here. I'm not sure exactly how, but I assure you it is."

"What's that mean?" Josie asked.

"It means we should try to get in and out as quickly as possible. We don't want to stay in that world any longer than we have to." Shawn took a deep breath, waved goodbye, and then dove into the rippling water.

"Holy crap," he said and dropped to his knees on the edge of the pond. "Did you guys see that?"

Josie stared at the water with wide-open eyes.

Frowning, Ryan squeezed both hands on his rifle and staggered waist-high into the water. "See you guys on the other side," he said and fell forward and disappeared from sight.

"I don't think I can do that," he said, climbing to his feet.

"You don't have much of a choice."

Seconds later, he watched in awe as Josie and Sage disappeared into the pond.

He stood alone in the darkness and felt suddenly vulnerable. The bodies of Gregory Stephens and the man he called Christopher rested eternally on the ground ten feet behind him. For a second, he felt sorry for the two dead men but realized they would have killed him in cold blood if not for Ryan, Shawn, and Tommy. As a disturbing fear of the dark spread through him, he waded into the surprisingly warm water and dove headfirst with both eyes shut tight.

48

Gregory's muscular thighs vibrated numbness into his bones as water splashed in the distance and faded into nothingness. For the first time since meeting Cornelius all those years ago, he felt weak and vulnerable. Thankfully, Preston and those troublesome meddlers bought his act of playing dead. With the taste of his own blood strong in the back of his throat, he gritted his teeth and inched forward toward the pool of magic.

Hatred drove him forward.

Despite the agony crippling his mind and weakening his body, he heard the sound of his own laughter vibrating against the earthen walls. For the first time in his life, he underestimated an opponent. Some kid named Ryan managed to get the better of him. He thought of the two girls and felt his desire for violence lessen the physical pain. At the moment, he hated them more than he hated Shawn Preston.

Lust clouded his judgment, giving the boy the advantage.

His head buzzed with excitement as the puddle came into sight. Closing his eyes, he thought of the pretty red-haired girl with the loudmouthed dog and inched closer to his salvation. Instead of using her as a pleasure doll, he planned to strangle her with his own two hands after making her watch the dog die a slow and miserable death.

The stench of the healing portal drifted through his nostrils as hope flickered through his mind. He reached forward and felt the soothing water flow between his fingers and breathed a sigh of relief. As pain swelled in his gut and rippled through every bone in his body, he bit down on his lower lip and rolled into the puddle.

49

With Alyssa's help, Tommy managed to keep pace with the Bissells. They lumbered through the tunnel for what seemed like hours before finally seeing the wooden ladder leading to the basement. Kelly climbed the rungs, shoved the slab from the opening, and then disappeared from sight. Enduring what felt like hot cinders blazing through his shoulder, he climbed the ladder, rolled a few feet from the opening, and waited for the girls. Moments later, he followed the others to the stairs where Kelly told them a man named Andre was more than likely waiting for Gregory Stephens to return.

"Go hide," Kelly whispered. "I'll get rid of him."

Grabbing Alyssa's hand, he nodded and hurried into a dark corner behind a pile of rubbish as Jennifer shined the light toward the top of the stairs.

"Andre, you still up there?" Kelly shouted.

"I'm here," a deep voice said from above. "Where's Mr. Stephens and the others?"

"He wants us to meet him in the tunnel so we can get our stories straight. They're still down there disposing of the bodies."

Massaging his shoulder, Tommy felt numb inside as a husky man trotted to the bottom of the steps and followed the Bissells into the hallway. A few minutes later, he heard a gunshot ring out through the hall.

Alyssa winced and pressed her face into his chest.

Trying to appear courageous, he pulled her tight with his good arm and kissed the top of her head. As her body trembled against his chest, he felt compassion stir inside of him.

Ten minutes later, Kelly appeared in the doorway. "Okay, guys, come out."

Twenty miles later, as they pulled in the hospital parking lot, he climbed from the van and glanced from Jennifer to Kelly. "So what happens now?"

Alyssa leaned forward from the backseat. "I'm going back down there."

"Don't worry, we'll take care of her," Kelly said and drove away.

Tommy stood in the parking lot and watched them disappear over a hill. Despite the agony torturing his shoulder, he stood a few minutes longer and felt apprehensive about Alyssa going back inside.

PART IV

ANOTHER WORLD

50

With Ethan's eyes shut tight, he squeezed his nose with hopes of blocking out the rotten stench and fell into what felt like soft mud. The darkness was discomforting. The fear of seeing what lurked in the water was too much to overcome. After stumbling around in what felt like cool mist rising off a mountain lake, he pushed the fear aside, opened his eyes, and looked around the wondrous fog-like world. Transparent bluish mist filled every ounce of space around him.

In the distance, light shimmered around a dark blue silhouette.

Holding his breath, he stepped forward toward the comforting light as something slithered past his leg. Feeling grossed out by the slimy thing's skin against his, he panicked and opened his mouth. Sweet sugary mist rushed through his lungs and numbed his brain. Within seconds, he lost track of reality. His mind drifted to another time and place as he pushed forward and struggled to hold onto consciousness. With a spinning head, he closed his eyes and concentrated on the lighted silhouette.

Deep in his mind, a bald man with beady black eyes grinned.

He cringed, hoping to block out the memory of Devon Whitfield, but as more of the wonderful mist filled his lungs, he slipped into a dark night at the Peaceful Lady Mental Hospital. Unfortunately, it was the same evening Devon unfolded his horrific tale of the day his parents were brutally murdered by a mischievous demon from hell.

They were murdered, he said, *and I saw every detail.*

The scenes flowed through his mind as if it happened to him and not Devon. It felt real, like it was happening at the moment.

Devon wakes in a dim bedroom to the sounds of muffled moaning and screaming. He's terrified. His bed is warm, yet even at the age of seven, he knows once outside the safe haven of his bed, it will be cold—bitter cold. Paralysis freezes his body as he cowers in his one sanctuary, listening to the eerie noises echoing through the house.

Where were his parents? Why weren't they protecting him from whatever could be responsible for the hideous moaning?

He can't endure the moans anymore. "Mommy," he shouts.

Silence answers his cry.

The waiting constricts his mind. He throws the blanket over his head, hoping it will ward off both the creepy moans and his disturbed frame of mind. The blanket fails on both attempts; the moans echo louder through the halls, and his fear rises into his throat.

His grasp on reality begins to slip away. They had to be coming for him, after all, he was their only child, and they love him. "Mommy," he shouts louder than before. "Please tell me where you are."

Instead, echoing groans eclipse his heartbeat.

Suddenly, his paralysis breaks, and he summons the courage to leave the sanctuary of his bed. His legs shake like swaying willows fluttering in a windstorm as he leaves the bedroom and creeps along the hall toward the violent groans and moans.

"Mommy," he whispers and turns right at the spiraled staircase.

The moans grow louder with every step he takes. Still at the age when kids believe in ghosts, he knows that something evil is responsible for the terrible noises amplifying his heartbeat. Four steps from the bottom, and he expects to see a ghost floating from the dark with a wicked grin twisting its transparent face. Instead, the creepy noises become louder.

Wood creaks under his weight, adding to his fear.

Two steps from the bottom, a strident shriek rings out through the hall.

Fear escalates as he feels the paralysis numb his body once again. Trapped in personal oblivion, he takes another step.

On the last wooden plank, he loses control. Hot urine soaks the front of his pajama pants. Fortunately, sheer terror takes precedence over his shame. After all, he is only seven years old and on the verge of losing his mind. On two wobbling legs, he staggers through the hall until the cellar door comes into sight. He pauses briefly, takes a deep breath, and continues forward to his parent's office door, where muffled noise seeps out from under the crack. As he reaches for the knob, the moans go silent. With five trembling fingers squeezing the knob, his body freezes as his heartbeat pounds inside his head.

Letting go, he takes two steps back.

As if returning from a brief intermission, the discordant tunes pick up where they left off. More afraid of the silence, his fear subsides. He reaches out, grazes the cold metal with trembling fingers, and pushes gently. With a quiet squeal, the door eases open.

His jaw hits the floor.

On the floor, his parents clutch and grope at each other. From behind, his dad thrusts violently into his mother's backside. Though Devon doesn't understand, their actions make him nervous. He cringes as his mother howls upon every forceful push. Humiliation replaces fear as indecision hampers his mind. Instantly, he stands inside the doorway and feels ashamed of his wet pajamas.

With an eerie grunt, his father shoves his mom to the floor and crawls on top of her.

With brief hesitation, he steps backward and hopes to sneak out without them being aware anyone was ever there. He tiptoes into the hallway and is seconds away from pulling the door shut, ending the uncomfortable scene when he glimpses a black stone in a shiny ring sparkling on his father's desk. His parent's groans fade as his eyes focus on the jewelry. Despite the terror trembling through his body, he desires to hold it in the palm of his hand and feel the cool metal and caress it as his fingers gingerly stroke the shining black stone resting brilliantly on the crest.

He tiptoes across the floor and grabs the ring from the desk.

Wear me, *a voice commands.*

Unsure if he imagined the strange voice, he concentrates on the stone.

Wear me, it says again. *Free me of this prison, Devon. Set me free.*

Oblivious of everything else happening around him, he takes the object from his sweaty palm and smiles. Instinct screams to disobey the voice inside the shimmering black stone, but he pushes it aside and slides the ring around the tip of his finger. Intense heat burns his bone as it slides down along his finger. He tries to pull it free, but the ring's power guides his actions. Grey smoke pours from the stone, stinging his throat and nose. Ebony skin shimmers through the haze and grins at Devon with wide scarlet eyes. Relieved to be free of the prison, it stretches two hairy arms into the air, slices long, sharp fingernails through the thick ceiling, and grins.

"Free at last," *the beast hisses, exposing rows of razor-sharp teeth covered in greenish-black slime.*

Enduring its rancid breath, he cringes.

"A deed worthy of a wish you have done."

Confused, he nods.

Draped in a light blue robe and a golden crown atop its humanlike head, it glances at the distraction across the room and steps toward him. "Grant you a wish if you agree I will."

Taking a step back, he nods again.

Anger paints its face red as Devon stands speechless. Two pointed horns spiral from its head above two hairy ears. It appears slightly irked by his silence. "Speak now to me or suffer the consequences."

"I don't know what you want."

"Released me from my prison inside the stone you did." *A leathery forked tongue slithers from two thin leathery black lips and hisses between every spoken syllable. "Agree you must, and I shall leave to return when you call for your wish."*

Devon scratches his head. "I get a wish?"

Chuckling, it nods.

"And if I don't agree."

"Make your world my home and cause death and destruction I will."

Confident it speaks the truth, he asks, "Will you come back when I'm ready for my wish?"

"Held to my word I am, human boy," the beast says. "Don't agree, and forced to dwell forever in your world I will be."

"Okay, please go away. I agree."

"When you want, speak my name you will, and I'll return to pay what I owe I shall."

Feeling cold tears drip down his face. "I don't know your name."

"Call my name only one time. Do you understand?"

Devon nodded.

"Call my name twice, and die a painful death you will. Revenge I will take upon you and all those you love. Life in your world will be harsh if you fail to heed what I tell you."

"Please just tell me your name."

A shriek of outrage escapes the creature's lips.

Multiple chills tickle his spine, leaving his body numb and cold.

"Do you agree to only speak my name once?"

"Yes!"

"Say it you must, or I cannot go free," it hisses. "Do you agree?"

"Yes, I agree to call your name only one time."

"Conclude my business with them I must before we complete the deal."

Fearing the worst, Devon glimpses his parents. Like savage animals, they remain oblivious to anything but tearing at each other's bodies.

Pulling a glowing sapphire sword from a dark blue scabbard, it grins at Devon while slicing through his parents like a hot knife through warm butter. Within seconds, an unidentifiable bloody mess covers the floor. Wiping blood from the sword, it chuckles and speaks a strange language that Devon has never heard before. Seconds later, the magic sword disappears.

Through tears, he screams. "I know my wish right now!"

An expression of hate crinkles its black warty face. Wiping blood from its gown, it advances toward Devon.

The boy cowers as it towers over him. "What did I say wrong?"

"Trapped in the stone that held me are their souls. Impossible to save them it is." Sarcasm glimmers through its wide open eyes. "Choose wisely what you ask for you should. Otherworldly interferences can be a dangerous and powerful manifestation not to take lightly they are."

Cringing beneath evil, he weeps for the loss of his parents.

The beast crouches, whispers in Devon's ear, and vanishes into thin air. Though sickened by his parents bloodied bodies five feet to his right, he sighs, hoping to never gaze upon those eyes again. That malevolent grin would keep him lying awake in a cold sweat on many nights in the dark halls of the Peaceful Lady.

Ethan opened his eyes as blue light filled his vision.

He thought about Devon Whitfield's glum tale as he reached for the shimmering exit. Thirty years had passed by since that evening. Despite being condemned to a mental institution for the remainder of his days, the wish he earned by setting the demon free has never been used. Devon told Ethan that a life behind lonely walls was better than gazing into those eyes of death again.

51

With a troubled heart, Jennifer sat alone on the front porch and thought about the consequences of going against Gregory's monsters. Fortunately, the man lay dead deep under Gastons Gorge and could never hurt anybody again. She thought of her amazing husband who stood by her side all these years. He left a short while ago with Alyssa. She needed a shower, a change of clothes, and a ride to her apartment. Their plan was to take the explosives back to the underground mine and wait for Shawn and the others to return. Part of her felt skeptical about breaking the promise that protected her children, but she finally had a chance to right the wrong committed all those years ago. Despite danger to her family, she decided to join the side of good for the first time in her life. Never again would she turn her back on the people of this town.

Why did you drag Colleen in there? It was your idea to chase after Jessica, not hers.

Throughout the years, Colleen's terrified face haunted her thoughts. On nights when sleep was hard to come by, she would lie in bed and pray for redemption for that one day. Finally, after meeting the kids in the old mine shaft, her prayers were on the verge of being answered.

Rising from the porch step, she descended the concrete stairs, walked across the street, and stared at Shawn's car. Though chilly air whipped through the treetops, her trembling hands dripped with warm sweat. The package in the trunk made her nervous. She dreaded the thought of touching it, but after a moment's hesitation, she strolled around the back of the car toward the passenger side door.

She opened the door and crawled inside.

After a quick glance, she popped open the glove box and saw the green notepad wedged inside a small stack of papers. She eased it free as if it were highly sensitive. Flipping it opened, she saw the numbers 1-0-4-7-1 written in black marker across the top, just as Shawn had said they would be. Closing the notepad, she abandoned the inside of the car, walked to the driver's door, and pulled a small metal latch opening the trunk. Wasting no time, she grabbed the black case from the trunk, glanced nervously around the neighborhood, and slammed it shut.

Hurrying across the street, she stared at the darkening sky and sighed deeply. In less than an hour, all traces of light would be gone. They would be underneath the town, but the thought of a black winter sky frightened her as much as the creatures that threatened her way of life. She walked to the porch and went inside the house to wait for her husband and Alyssa. Though eager for this nightmare to end, she was in no hurry to get started. Eying the case, she prepared mentally for the undesirable journey ahead. Apprehension tickled her skin as car doors slammed outside of her house.

Seconds later, footfalls shuffled across the wooden porch.

52

Ethan emerged in the middle of the greenest forest his eyes have ever gazed upon. Despite nearly choking on the portal's misty vapor, he felt wonderful, like energetic blood pumped through his veins. As he stood on lush grass gazing through acres of mountainous massive trees, every ache and pain endured the past few hours dripped away. He had a feeling the swirling mist might be responsible for his youthful jubilance.

Five feet from the water's edge, Shawn knelt beside a three-foot-tall mushroom, slowly catching his breath. He climbed from the ground, stepped back from the bright yellow fungus, drew his pistol from the holster, and eyed the strange environment with a look of fascination in his eyes. His gun hand trembled as water splashed violently in the pond beside him.

With Tommy's rifle clutched in his hands, Ethan twisted backward as Josie and Ryan emerged from the rippling water and gasped hard for breath. They climbed halfway up a small embankment on the far side and slipped on the loose back dirt. Grimacing, Ryan fell to his back, pulled his pant leg to his knee, and rubbed a bright red swollen ankle. Ethan sat the rifle on the ground and sprinted around the pond. After struggling to help Josie along the slight upslope, he grabbed Ryan by the arm and jerked him into the grass. Concerned about his friend's injury, he helped him across the embankment and onto a wide path carved through the forest.

Josie sat a few feet away, breathing heavy and staring at their strange new environment.

From behind, water rippled as Sage leaped from the pool with a strange translucent object in his mouth. It resembled an eel, nearly two feet long with small serrated teeth protruding from a cavernous jaw. He carried it past him and Ryan and dropped it on the thriving grass beside his master.

Thick bluish mist seeped out from the puncture wounds.

Ryan rubbed his leg in obvious pain. "That thing bit me," he shouted and pointed at Sage's object. "It attacked Josie and took a bite out of me."

His eyes darted to Josie.

"I'm fine," she said, pointing at Ryan. "He kept it from away from me."

Relieved, he grabbed a long branch from the ground and hurried to the water. Oddly fascinated, he jammed the stick into the water until his knuckles rested inches from the surface. Expecting blue slime to be dripping from the wood, he pulled it slowly out of the water. Instead, blue vapor rose from the wood and disappeared into the air. He tossed the stick aside, grabbed the rifle, and rejoined his friends. "What the crap is that thing?"

The creature's flesh blistered and smoked.

He watched with sick fascination as it sizzled like fresh fish on a hot grill. It bubbled a few minutes more and then evaporated, leaving behind a sour aroma.

"Ew," Josie said and inched backward.

Still rubbing his ankle, Ryan scowled. "I guess it can't live outside of that water."

"Dude, that's probably a good thing," he said and glanced through the forest, wondering what strange things might be hiding in the trees and watching their every move. The trees resembled the giant redwoods out in California, only twice as tall. Even the smallest ones towered several hundred feet above the greenest landscape he had ever seen. A dark overcast sky loomed high above the gaps. Though it was October, it felt like early summer. He had a strong feeling that winter had long ago vanished from this strange land. As a slight breeze filled his nose with flowery fragrance, he thought of a fairy tale from his childhood.

"God this place is beautiful," Josie said. "But something seems off."

With a buzzing head, he spun around and eyed the group. "Does anyone else feel like they just climbed the beanstalk to the forest of giganticness?"

Shawn stood, scratching the stubble on his chin. "I know what you mean, kid," he said, looking in awe of his surroundings. "I hope we don't stumble across anything big and nasty."

Thinking Shawn was reading his mind, he chuckled as Josie tended to Ryan's ankle. Sage stood beside him, panting and waging his tail. Though fascinated by the dog's calm demeanor, he couldn't shake the thought of climbing a giant beanstalk.

"Can you walk?" asked Shawn.

"Yeah," Ryan said, crawling off the ground. "That darn thing really latched onto my leg."

Josie ran her hands across her shoulders and looked strangely confused. "How does everyone else feel?"

"I feel like a kid," Ethan said, still feeling captivated by the forest. Warm air shimmered through the gaps in the treetops, scenting the trail with a mixture of fresh-cut grass and blooming flowers.

"I actually feel great," said Shawn, "I'm just not sure how long we were inside that mist."

Ryan glimpsed over his shoulder at the puddle. "To me it seemed like an eternity. I had a heck of a time concentrating for some reason."

"It felt different to me," Ethan said and thought about Devon. "It just seemed like we were in there forever because we were crossing into someplace else—a very cool someplace else I must say."

Ryan glanced at the group with a curious expression on his face. "I don't know why, but it feels a lot later now than it did in the cave."

Josie grabbed Sage's collar. "I think we all experienced different things inside."

Ryan glanced at Josie. "It was like I was back at the graveyard we buried Molly in, except it didn't really feel like a dream."

"Yeah, I know what you mean," Ethan said, "I couldn't keep my mind focused on anything real, only memories I'd rather forget."

Only they were someone else's memories.

"I think we need to get moving," Shawn said. "I feel like a sitting duck along this path."

Josie took a deep breath and grabbed Ryan's arm. "I feel the same way."

"Seriously, I can walk. That bite hurt big-time, but it's starting to feel better." Ryan said defensively. "You guys don't have to worry about me slowing us down."

"Let's go then," Shawn said.

"You lead, dude, and we'll follow you through the emerald forest." Ethan grinned through laughter. "I just wish there was a yellow brick road to guide our way to the wizard."

"You're a trip," Shawn said and started walking along the dirt path.

53

By the time Tommy snuck out of the hospital with his shoulder in a sling, the sun had already set in a starless sky. He caught a ride back into town with a guy he knew from the local bar. As he regurgitated the lie about being shot along the bike trail earlier in the day, they made a left on Barrow Street and sped through town. He felt relieved when the man pulled alongside the road by his house and stopped the car. After a halfhearted thank you and good-bye, he unlocked the door and hurried through the front door and out of the cold evening air.

He thought about the others.

Feeling anxious, he hurried up the stairs and took off the light green hospital gown, being careful not to nudge his shoulder. After a quick shower and change of clothes, he gathered every remaining shell and pulled his brother's old double-barrel shotgun from the cabinet. Back on the first floor, he made a quick stop in the kitchen and grabbed a candy bar from the cupboard and a bottle of Coke from the refrigerator. After gobbling the chocolate in two bites, he swallowed a mouthful of soda and hurried through the door with one destination in mind.

A stroll in the crisp air might ease his mind.

He walked along the road's edge a few blocks, hurried across the shadowy street, and glanced back at the only home he's ever known and hoped to see it again. He took a deep breath and marched along Mountain View Road with thoughts of rescuing the others, especially Alyssa Thorpe.

At the top of Beanery Hill, his heartbeat pounded hard through his chest.

Deep Earth Hotel towered above the tall pines at the bottom of the hill. He breathed deep and then took a step forward.

54

Shawn walked a few feet beside him, holding the pistol at his side. Concentration chiseled his rugged face. He looked cool, calm, and collected, like a man accustomed to staying poised in a dangerous situation. Ethan thought years of police training paid off as Shawn led them through this strange forest. As capable as Tommy was at taking charge and guiding the expedition, Shawn Preston seemed more of a natural leader.

Armed with the rifle, he glanced nervously through the forest. Unlike Shawn, he felt overwhelmed by the thought of firing the weapon. He wanted no part of pulling the trigger but had little choice as they would more than likely encounter something dangerous before the day ended. When the time came to react, he hoped there would be no hesitation. To keep Josie safe, he felt confident there would be none.

Thinking of her, he glimpsed back.

A few feet behind, she hurried along the trail. As usual, Sage trotted guardedly alongside his master. Despite gating into another world, she seemed to be coping with the situation rather well. Ryan limped along behind her, bringing up the rear, clutching the rifle with determination masking the fear in his eyes. He looked different from the man he helped rescue a few days back. After the episode in the mine shaft, Ryan had tasted death. Though he threw up his lunch after blowing a hole in the man masquerading as a marshal, Ryan found the strength to endure. If called on step up and protect them, Ethan knew his friend wouldn't hesitate. He felt somewhat at ease knowing Shawn and Ryan had their backs. Besides, Ryan possessed good intuition. Never in a million years would he have taken Gregory Stephens for a fake. Thankfully, he didn't have to.

Turning frontward, he spotted a clearing up ahead.

Despite being in capable company, one thing weighed heavy on his mind. Did they have enough ammunition to stay alive in this world? Ryan carried a few clips in his worn backpack, but was it enough to insure their survival? Though Sage tore the monster up pretty good the other day, he couldn't help but wonder if their bullets would have the same effect.

After all, bullets don't kill vampires.

He pushed the thought aside as Shawn holstered his pistol and took a seat on a tree stump just inside the clearing. His eyes scanned the forest, "I think Ryan can use a little break," he said, stretching his arms and legs as if massaging a cramp. "Besides, I'm not completely sure what we're up against here."

Eying a boulder a few feet from Shawn, Ryan hobbled across the clearing and fell gently onto the hard stone surface. "I thought you got a good look at them the day they took your buddies."

A few inches off the trail, Josie dropped down in the thick grass beside her dog, stretched out on her back, and stared at the sky.

"Not that day," he said and glanced up with sorrowful eyes. "But I saw a few of them years later with Gregory Stephens. Those things on their faces still give me nightmares."

Ryan looked wide-eyed at Shawn. "Oh my god," he said. "They were like octopus tentacles. I remember now."

"Only octopuses have eight tentacles, and those things have four."

Ryan grinned. "When I first saw it, I thought it looked like a man except for its head and hands. It was on me so fast I barely saw beyond the hood."

"Do you remember now?" asked Josie.

"Barely," Ryan said, "I must have blocked it from my memory."

Ethan stared at Ryan and chuckled. He tried to hold it back but couldn't help himself.

"I know it sounds crazy, but I'm telling you guys, that's exactly what it looked like."

"Dude, I'm sorry," he said, "I'm not laughing at you, I just laugh at stuff like that to help me deal with it."

"It's cool," he said. "In that split second before it attacked me, I remember being drawn to its eyes."

"Yeah," Shawn said, "If we come across any of them, try not to make eye contact."

"What do you mean *if?*" Josie said. "I thought that was the point of coming here, to try and wipe them out."

"No, that's not why at all. The point of coming here is to try and find our people and get them back home."

"Amen!" Ethan said. He liked the thought of rescuing Lauren and Tommy's brother without fighting manlike octopus beasts.

She leered at him.

Feeling humiliated, he glanced away.

"Sorry," he said, "I just think we're better off avoiding them at all costs. I mean, those things scare the crap out of me."

"Yeah," Ryan said and winked at Josie, "but what are our odds of rescuing any of these people without stumbling across one or two of those things."

Ethan frowned. "Probably not good."

"At least we have protection," Shawn said, fondling the holster at his side. "I just hope our weapons are effective against them."

"And if they're not?" she asked.

"I don't know, Josie. I guess we make a new plan."

"What if they come back later?"

Shawn grinned. "That's why we're going to blast that portal from existence."

"What if they create a new portal?"

"Then we do whatever the heck is necessary to get out of here," he said irritably. "Listen to me. I don't know exactly what to do. Coming in here sounded like the right thing back in the cave. I feel I owe it to those poor people to come through and take at least one stab at rescuing them."

"Me too," Ethan said and rose from the grass. "I've carried a ton of guilt and grief over my sister throughout the years. Is it my fault she was taken by those things? I don't know, but I have a chance to find out if Lauren is still alive, and I don't plan on passing it up."

Deep in the forest, strange birds chirped a pleasant song, easing his mind.

"If she's here, and I honestly believe she is, I'm not going home unless she's with me."

"Me either!" Ryan said, "If it weren't for you guys, I'd be one of those people hoping to be rescued."

"Thanks, dude," he said and grabbed his rifle from the grass. "I'm glad you came to Gastons Gorge."

Ryan blushed.

Shawn climbed to his feet and stood beside him. "Let's follow this path and hope it leads us to where we need to go."

Ethan nodded. "Works for me."

"Sure, it's as good a plan as any," Josie said.

Ryan grabbed the rifle from the boulder. "What happens if things go wrong and we get separated—or worse?"

"And if are guns are useless?" Ethan added.

Shawn frowned. "If things get out of hand, find the path and beat feet back through the portal. Wait as long as you deem necessary, but if it looks like no one else is going to make it through, blow it to pieces with the dynamite Jennifer and Kelly will have already left in the cavern."

"What kind of plan is that?" Ethan shouted.

"Relax, kid," Shawn said, "it's just a last resort. I don't want to leave anyone behind, but once we make our move, those things are going to be highly ticked off."

"He's right," Josie said with a halfhearted grin. "If we attack them, and if they're as clever as we think, they'll probably cross over and go after our families."

"We can't let that happen," Ethan said and wrapped his arm around her shoulder. "Everything I love is either standing right here or trapped wherever those creatures are, but I'd rather die myself than let them have free reign over our town."

Josie blushed and glanced away.

He cared deeply for her and thought the feeling was mutual. As he admired her elegant beauty and fearless charisma, he suddenly realized he was prepared to die if it meant protecting her.

55

They made it back to the hotel as the sun dipped below the western horizon. Armed with flashlights, a wheelbarrow, and the guns they took off Gregory Stephens and his goon a few hours earlier, they made their way through the basement to the secret door. As Kelly descended the ladder into the mine tunnel, he saw the body of Andre, the man he shot a few hours earlier, slumped against the lowest few rungs of the ladder. With a queasy stomach, he shoved the man aside.

He backed up a few feet and shouted up to his wife. "Throw down the wheelbarrow!"

"You clear?"

"Yeah, let it fall."

A few seconds later, he watched the bulky contraption bounce off the dirt floor and come to halt on its side. Struggling to breathe through heavy dust, he turned it upright so the front wheel straddled the ground. He pushed it aside and helped the women down the ladder.

After a minor struggle, Andre's body laid in the wheelbarrow. They planned to push the body through the old mine and dump it into the portal along with Christopher and Gregory Stephens. Unfortunately, two hundred pounds of dead weight in a wobbly wheelbarrow maneuvering through the loose dirt is like guiding a sleigh through sand.

Kelly dropped the handles. "Well crap on me," he said and grinned at his wife.

The women chuckled.

"Even though we had no choice but to kill this man," he said. "I don't find anything funny about this situation."

"Sorry."

"Me too," Alyssa said, feeling embarrassed. "I don't know what got into me. Sorry, Kelly."

"Apology accepted." He gritted his teeth and lifted the wooden handles.

"Can I help you push?" Alyssa asked and reached for the handle.

Dripping with sweat, he let go of the handles. The wheelbarrow teetered as the body slumped to one side. "I guess," he said and steadied the cargo with a trembling hand. "But pushing a dead man around leaves a horrible feeling in your belly."

"You had no choice," his wife said.

He scowled.

"If you didn't shoot him, he would have killed Alyssa and Tommy without a minute's hesitation."

"Your wife's right," she said, taking his hand. "You saved me and Tommy and perhaps even yourselves. Once he realized Gregory and the other man were dead, he would have killed you guys too."

"I know you're right." His eyes blinked shut a few seconds. "Nonetheless, I still took another person's life no matter how you try and justify it."

"All right then," Alyssa said, "think of it this way. If they manage to succeed wherever they went, then you helped save anyone they bring back."

He smiled. "Let's see if we can push this thing any easier than I did on my own."

He and Alyssa each grabbed a handle and pushed the wheelbarrow through the dirt. Though heavy and awkward, they kept it balanced enough to keep Andre from spilling out over the side.

"This could take a while."

Alyssa giggled. "I think I just saw a couple of snails laughing at us."

Kelly grinned as his wife smiled.

56

Though the past few days had worn him down, Ethan walked through the fairytale forest feeling rejuvenated. He thought the bluish mist had something to do with his newfound vigor. Except for a few minor aches cramping the back of his legs, he felt like a youthful boy during the energetic years of adolescence. Just as his body experienced youth, his mind buzzed with tranquility. Despite a high chance of dying in this strange world, he felt peculiarly invincible.

Looking around at his friends, he wondered if they felt it too.

Shawn walked a few feet in front of him, tramping on branches strewn about the path. From behind, familiar footfalls pounded the dirt. He felt at ease knowing they still walked behind him. At least for the moment, nothing threatened their safety.

Up ahead, the forest came to an end at a vertical cliff.

Hundreds of feet below, a valley of dark vegetation stretched across a rolling field to another vertical hillside in the distance. Shawn took a deep breath and pointed across the distance. "I have a feeling that what we're looking for is over there."

"Maybe," Ryan said, pointing below into the high vegetation. "I just wish we didn't have to go through there."

Ethan sighed and surveyed the landscape. If high weeds and thorny shrubbery stood in the way of finding Lauren, he was willing to go through it, even if he had to go alone.

Josie stared wide-eyed at the greenery. "Wonder what's in there?"

"My guess," Ryan said, "really bad things."

With her hands on her hips, she said, "Can we can go around?"

"Nah," Shawn said, "I think we'd be walking a lot farther than we'd want to."

With a throbbing heart, Ethan thought of Lauren. Remembering all those years of being locked up in mental institutions feeling sorry for himself, he felt a single tear drop from his eye. He could almost feel her presence. Inside, he felt peace for the first time since the day she disappeared.

Wow, dude, maybe you can share your equally unbelievable tale with Devon. If anyone would believe it, it would be him.

"Let's get going," Shawn said. "If there's anything to worry about, we're gonna find out really soon."

Chiseled into the hillside, a winding trail ended a few feet from the weeds. After a quick glance over his shoulder, he took a deep breath and chased after the others. Sometime later, he stood at the base of the field and stared at the strange expressions on each of his friends faces. No one wanted to go inside.

Though a warm breeze rustled the weeds, his skin felt chilled.

57

The long walk to the room with the magical portal was proving to be difficult. Alyssa and Kelly struggled with the wheelbarrow as Jennifer walked along with a flashlight in one hand and a pistol in the other. Frustration buzzed through Alyssa's head as the awkward wheelbarrow dug deeper in the soil.

"Take another break," Kelly said, wiping sweat from his brow.

With enthusiasm, she let go of the handle and felt the burn in her forearms diminish. They had already taken five breaks since entering the mine. As much as they wanted to get the dynamite back to the portal, short breaks were a necessity.

Grimacing, she rubbed her sore shoulder. "This is a lot tougher than I thought it would be."

"If only I was a few years younger," Kelly said with a halfhearted smile. "I was in tip-top shape in my younger days."

Jennifer chuckled.

"And you find what funny, my dear?"

"Me?" she said, pointing to herself. "I don't find any humor in this."

Alyssa smiled as the couple flirted with each other. She didn't mind. The break felt good on her sore bones. Her arms and legs ached from laboring with the lopsided wheelbarrow. She doubted they would be able to finish pushing it to the portal room unless a miracle happened. She wanted to leave the body in the tunnel but wasn't going to suggest the idea despite thinking that the Bissells would agree.

"Well, my dear. I certainly find no humor here."

Jennifer threw her arms around his shoulders and squeezed. "Sweetie," she said, "I'm just smiling because I love you so much."

Grinning, he pulled away, and after a second's hesitation, he leaned forward and kissed her lips.

Mild embarrassment painted Alyssa's cheeks a light red.

She smiled at the older couple and envied their relationship. She hoped one day that there would be someone in her life that loved her that much and vice versa. For most of her teenage life, she spent every ounce of energy focusing on her studies. Now, as she watched the older couple, she envied what they have.

"I love you too," Kelly said after a brief silence.

His wife smiled. "I know you do."

Breathing deep, Alyssa lumbered toward the far end of the tunnel and sat down on the dirt ground. With her back resting against the wall, feeling began filtering back through her numb legs. For the moment, the dirty ground felt as comfortable as the sofa in her living room. As she watched the older couple join her on the ground, she mulled over the past few days. As crazy as everything had been with secret underground tunnels, bloodthirsty maniacs, and monsters from another dimension, she was happy to be a part of it. Loss of life always left her feeling sad, but the red-haired man and his two sidekicks made the choice that ultimately ended their lives. Though she wanted no one else to die, she knew those men acted out of free will.

An image of Ryan's face flashed through her mind.

He might be the exception.

She thought he felt obligated to aid Ethan in his quest because it was Ethan and Sage that saved his life.

Yeah, he probably felt obligated, but he would have helped them regardless.

Thinking of Ryan kept her motivated.

Her mind shifted, and sadness drifted through her like a rubber tube on a lazy river. She thought of the others lost in that other world. A hollow feeling rumbled through her stomach. Their chances of suffering a painful death at the hands of those monsters were probably pretty great. She closed her eyes and felt an emptiness fill her heart.

Beside her, Jennifer and Kelly mumbled words she couldn't hear.

She wondered how they dealt with such regret and sorrow for all those years, especially Jennifer. She doubted her sanity would have held up if she were forced to walk one day in the woman's shoes. Lauren's memory weighed heavy enough on her mind. She was nine the last time Alyssa saw her. That was over nine years ago. What terrible things happened to her? If she were still alive, Alyssa would help Ethan make her life normal again. Though it happened a long time ago, she missed Lauren as much at this moment as she did the day it happened. And like Ethan, she felt a sense of responsibility. After all, a best friend would have kept her from going on that walk.

I should have done something.

"Are you okay?" a soft voice whispered.

Alyssa opened her eyes and put an end to the haunted memories.

Jennifer stroked her hair like a concerned mother cuddling a child. "Are you holding up all right?"

"Sort of," she said, "I just keep thinking of my friends being trapped on the other side of that gate." Jennifer reminded her of a sweet grandmother. She liked the woman more and more as they trudged deeper through the coalmine.

"They're in good hands with Shawn. He's a hardened police officer and, not to mention, highly intelligent. He'll keep them safe."

"Can I ask you something?"

"Anything," Jennifer said, still stroking her hair.

"How did you manage to stay sane knowing what you knew for all those years?"

"I met Kelly, and he helped me deal with it." She reached for her husband's hand.

He took it and stroked her fingers.

"Before that," Alyssa said, "When you were a girl."

"Before I met Kelly, I was an emotional nightmare. I was afraid of my own shadow because of what that man and his freaks did to me and my friends. Most nights, I would just sit and cry for hours in my bed and wish they took me instead of Colleen. That was always my wish until I met Kelly."

Tears dripped down her face.

"Through Gregory, they told me if I ever told anyone they existed, they would kill everyone I love and will ever love in my life. I believed that then, and I still do believe it." She glanced at Kelly and looked back at her. "If we fail, everyone I love and everyone you love will probably die."

Alyssa sighed. "Wow."

"Makes you feel all alone," Jennifer said with haunted eyes. "I've been feeling that way for a really long time."

Saddened by the older woman's eyes, she closed her eyes.

"Hopefully, with luck," Jennifer said, "Shawn and your friends will make things right."

"I hope so."

"Believe it."

"I believe," Kelly said and pulled his frail body off the ground. "I have no choice but to believe."

Minutes later, Alyssa and Kelly pushed the wheelbarrow through the tunnel once more.

58

Ethan stared into the maze of lush vegetation and took a deep breath. "Seriously, guys, do we really have to go through there?"

"I don't think we have a choice," Shawn said with his pistol drawn. After glancing over the group, he turned and disappeared through the weeds.

Ethan laughed nervously. "I do believe he intends on using that thing."

Ryan cracked a grin and followed after Shawn.

"Here goes nothing," Josie said and chased after Ryan with Sage trotting a few feet behind. The dog glanced back toward him, tilted his head with skepticism, and then chased after his master.

Standing alone at the base of the rock face, Ethan squinted into the blinding sunlight and glimpsed what appeared to be a figure standing atop the cliff. Deep in the furrows of his imaginative mind, he could see four ebony tentacles swaying in a gusty breeze. Against better judgment, he ran into the strange field.

"Wait for me!" he shouted, squishing through hunks of soft unidentifiable plants that smelled like rotted potatoes. Ten-foot thorn bushes and giant cactus-like plants hampered his movement. Ducking under sharp thorns and whisking pesky insects from his face, he stomped through the gargantuan maze searching for the others. Mosquitoes the size of hummingbirds buzzed his head and attempted to feed on any skin not protected by clothing. Trying to ignore the insects, he swatted shrubbery from his face and picked up his pace.

Unbelievable, dude, you're lost in the world's biggest maze.

Sudden fear of being alone wobbled his legs. "Ryan," he whispered and swatted at a mosquito buzzing by his face.

Instead of his friend's calming voice, thousands of unknown insects answered his cry with a rhythmic song.

Great going, moron, he thought and raised the rifle toward the vegetation in front of him. *How in God's green earth could I be lost?*

Dropping to his knees, he searched the ground for footprints. The dry and dusty earth combined with decaying plants revealed nothing. Not one footprint or pawprint guided the way. Fortunately, he saw no monster prints etched in the soil either. He crawled to his feet, and he squeezed the rifle harder in his hands. Being alone in this world frightened him beyond belief, but the weapon's security eased the tension enough to remain focused and level-headed.

Randomly guessing a direction, he sprinted forward.

After a long gallop through the lush field, he heard or saw no signs of the others. With nervous hands, he aimed the rifle at the weeds, swinging his hands back and forth at every little noise. Except for biting bugs and jagged leaves, he sensed nothing threatening at the moment. Hopefully, things would stay that way.

As more time passed without incident, his nerves grew steadier. "Is anyone there?" he whispered as an uncomfortable silence lingered across the field. Over head, a graying sky darkened the land. He cringed as the thought of night blanketing this strange world while he continued searching for his friends made him shiver. He wanted to scream out their names, but the thought of what else might be lurking in the shadows frightened him more than being alone. He fought an urge to scream and picked up his pace, hoping to make it out of the field before sunset.

The sun dipped deeper into the sky, leaving silver beams from a pale moon to guide his way. He thought of Devon standing alone in the dark house and screaming out for his mom and dad. He must have felt the same way Ethan felt when he stood on the stairway of his parent's home soaking his pants with hot urine. Although he had no intention of wetting his trousers, he realized night had just begun.

He thought of Devon's demon.

If he knew its name, he might summon it and use the wish. He wanted to be out this place in a bad way.

Luckily for you, dimwit, Devon kept the name a secret.

He kept his feet moving forward while clinging to any hope of stumbling out of the ominous maze.

59

After breathing in breath after breath of the swirling mist, Gregory collapsed into the spongy bottom of the magic portal, closed his eyes, and welcomed the numbing needles vibrating the deep wound torturing his side. Despite a weakened mind from considerable blood loss, he remembered the healing qualities of the extraordinary vapor hovering between two very different worlds. After a monumental struggle from the far end of the cavern to the portal left his body exhausted, he could only lay still and hope the magic was powerful enough to restore his dying body. For the first time in his long life, he had been fatally injured.

Before he could react, the boy named Ryan blew a hole through his side.

Gregory took him for a coward. Unfortunately, his usually unflawed judgment failed him. For nearly a century, he had been disposing of meddlers who had the misfortune of discovering this town's little dark secret. On every occasion, his judgment proved to be accurate. As icy anguish rippled through every muscle in his body, he realized that overconfidence and an insatiable need for lust might have been his Achilles' heel.

A silvery shape swooshed through the mist above and chased any thoughts of weakness from his mind.

Seconds later, something slippery brushed by his arm, nibbled at his flesh, and then fluttered away. With his eyes closed, he balled up on the soft ground and prayed for it to leave him be. Despite hatred toward Ryan, Shawn Preston, the red-haired girl, and her mangy dog slowly energizing his mind, he felt too weak to fight off an enemy.

As thoughts of murdering Preston and his new friends controlled his mind, he slipped into unconsciousness. Wonderful dreams of stabbing the German shepherd belonging to Josie McShay over and over with the hollowed pipe that he used on the cat nearly a century earlier occupied his sleep.

60

Ahead of him, Josie and Sage squished through the spoiled vegetation trying to keep pace with Shawn. Ryan stayed close, keeping the tip of barrel an inch off the ground for precautionary reasons. He already killed one man today. Though killing the man helped save their lives back in the cavern, he felt more than a touch of regret. Regardless of his feelings, he intended for history not to repeat itself. He felt a lot more relaxed with the weapon aimed at the dirt.

The last few streaks of red and silver faded in the sky as they busted through the heavy brush and stood in a field of knee-high green grass with a few dozen massive willow trees spaced systematically across the wide open space. He followed Shawn, Josie, and Sage twenty feet into the field and flopped backward into the soft grass. Instantly, the feeling returned to his legs and feet. Unfortunately, unless a different way to return to the portal was discovered, they would have to journey through that mess a second time.

A few feet away, Shawn fell to his knees and gasped for breath.

Josie stretched out on the grass and gazed at the sky, looking at peace with the world.

Sitting on the warm ground petting Sage, he took a few deep breaths and eyed the towering weeds for Ethan. He sat a few seconds, amazed by how much better his ankle felt when the hairs suddenly stood up on his arms. Climbing to his knee, he stared at Josie. "When's the last time you saw Ethan?"

"Walking through that stuff," she said and pointed to the field they just came through. "At least I think I remember seeing him. I thought he was right behind me."

With nervous blood, he jumped off the ground and sprinted to the weeds. He stared at the area where they exited a few moments earlier and then glanced at the sky. The brilliant colors seemed to have been ripped from the heavens by some malevolent force and replaced by moonlit darkness. "Ethan," he screamed. "Can you hear me?"

Instantly, Josie was on her feet, rushing to his side with Sage a few inches behind.

Reacting to their sudden panic, Shawn jumped up off the ground, hurried to the edge of the grass next to where he and Josie stood, and stared wide-eyed into the weeds.

A disconcerting hush fell on his ears. "Ethan," he shouted again. "Come on, man, answer me."

"Ethan, where are you?" Josie said. Her screams echoed through the weeds and faded into the distance.

Instinctively, Ryan stepped forward and glanced back at Josie and Shawn. "What do we do?" he said fighting an urge to run off through the bug-infested field and look for his friend.

"We wait," said Shawn.

Ryan wanted to grab him and shake the sense back into his brain. "What do you mean we wait?"

"Shawn," Josie said, "we just can't sit here and wait. What if he's in trouble and needs our help?"

Shawn pointed at the field with a stern stare. "If the three of us go running through that maze in a panic looking for him, then eventually, we'll all be lost out there."

Ryan felt sickened by his words but knew them to be true.

With an infuriated scowl, Josie threw her hands to her hips. "Someone has to go find him."

Taking her hand, he squeezed gently and pulled her to the edge of the grass as tears filled her eyes. He felt like the world's biggest coward as guilt poured into his heart. If the situation was reversed, Ethan would never sit on his backside while we were trapped alone in the darkness.

"As soon as we hear—" Shawn said.

"I'll get him, Josie." Ryan interrupted.

Shawn sighed. "Seriously, Ryan, we shouldn't split up. It's isn't the best option right now."

"You're right, but if it were me out there, he wouldn't hesitate to come get me."

"You sure you wanna do this?"

"No, but I'm doing it anyway." He smiled at Josie and ran back into the grotesque weeds.

"Ryan," Shawn yelled. "Wait up a minute."

"Yeah?"

"If you get lost, fire a shot. We'll fire one back to guide you."

"Good deal, my friend," he said and ran into darkness.

61

Weeds rustled behind him.

Contemplating his next move, Ethan whirled around and felt relieved to see nothing but the usual jagged shrubbery. He stood still and prayed whatever stirred the leaves would pass without noticing him. Expecting the worst, he swallowed hard as his hands trembled so violently he nearly lost their grip on the rifle. While taking a deep breath, his finger slid over the trigger as this world's chirping crickets fell suddenly silent.

Silence ruled the moonlit weeds.

Get it together, dude. There *ain't nothing out here but your own crazy imagination.*

Walking backward, he focused straight ahead. His finger trembled against the cool metal. Holding the rifle eased his mind but tightened his nerves. Sliding his finger from the trigger, he thought of an old friend named Johnny Slocomb. A few months before Lauren's disappearance, Johnny's dad let him tag along on a clay pigeon shoot. Out of the few dozen pulled for him, he missed every target but one. Chilled sweat dripped from his hair and tickled his nose.

Plants rustled in the field in front of him and then went silent.

He swung the rifle up, ready to squeeze the trigger. Sweat soaked his hair as tension heightened his terror. Eying the area, he knew without a doubt that the noise was real. Whatever lurked in the darkness either slithered by wanting to avoid confrontation or was waiting for the perfect opportunity to jump out and attack.

Either way, he backpedaled faster, feeling like a scared mouse being stalked by a clever cat.

Unlike the mouse, he thought, *I got a big gun.*

After a few minutes of silence, he turned and ran deeper in the weeds with a burning need to get as far away from the disturbance as possible. Hope of escaping grew greater with every long stride. Confidence buzzed through his head as his legs feverishly pounded the ground. He was too close to finding Lauren to give into fear created by phantom noises in a dark field.

Minutes later, his legs slowed due to a lack of breath.

Suddenly, a mortifying thought entered his mind. He wanted to disbelieve it, but there was no way of knowing. *Dude, you're going the wrong way.* He stopped and squinted through the shadows, but his eyes failed to penetrate the darkness. Confidence seeped away like a pinhole deflating a bicycle tire. He felt discouraged as he stood bewildered and without a plan.

"Think, dude," he whispered. "What would Shawn or Tommy or even Ryan do in this situation?"

He chuckled.

"I'm losing my mind," he said and laughed silently until tears clouded his vision.

Standing in darkness with an adrenaline headache, he thought of a plan. Grinning, he raised the barrel toward the heavens, intending to make some noise. Ryan and the others would hear the explosion and then know his position. He was desperate and out of options. With his finger seconds away from jerking back the trigger, he saw movement ten feet in front of where he stood.

A shadow rose from the weeds and rushed him.

Adrenaline chased the terror from his brain.

He knew what it was before it was close enough to see. It attacked Ryan in the woods and stole his sister nine years earlier. Without a second thought, he squeezed the trigger and felt needles numbing his finger. Hot pain exploded through his arm as the stock crashed against his shoulder. With both eyes shut tight, he planted both feet on the ground and managed to stay upright.

It shrieked in agony.

Direct hit, he thought and opened his eyes.

Confidence turned to terror instantly.

Despite eating a bullet from point blank range, it rushed toward him. An earsplitting shriek of rage escaped its mouth.

Holding the rifle toward the ground with an expression of disbelief stretching his face, he stood his ground and pulled the trigger. Squeezing hard, he aimed the barrel at the beast, intending to fill it with more deadly metal. He cringed as air discharged through the hollow barrel. The weapon slipped through his fingers and squished into the sludge. Staring into the eyes of the beast, he dropped to his knees and felt the ground for the rifle.

From five feet away, it lashed out with two black withered hands.

During the course of the day, he had been under the influence of hope. He believed Lauren was waiting for him to rescue her. When they discovered the portal leading to this world, he knew without a doubt that the dream would be realized despite what he had to do to make it happen. Now, as the monster reared back to finish him off, he hoped the others would find Lauren and take her back home. Although he wouldn't be there to look after her, he knew Alyssa would take care of her.

Taking a deep breath, his fingers slid through slimy weeds and felt the smooth wood tickle his fingers. With new hope, he grabbed the handle and slung it over his shoulder and saw the monster in all its glory as it leaped through the air a foot from his face. Just as Shawn and Ryan described, four tentacles danced from the center of a grotesque humanlike head. They were magnificent, shimmering against silver beams of moonlight. In the center of the tentacles inch-long yellowish-brown teeth snapped like bear traps in a circular mouth.

The beast's rancid breath churned his stomach.

For a second, he stared into its eyes but quickly glanced away. He remembered what Shawn said about becoming a prisoner to its captivating gaze. Hoping for the best, he swung the rifle with every ounce of adrenaline surging through his body. His fingers felt numb as the weapon thudded against the things flesh and bone.

Strident shrieks echoed through the field.

Off-balanced, he tumbled backward through the dirt and clutched the weapon with stinging fingers. Impulsively, he rolled right and grimaced in pain as his shoulder dug into something hard in ground. Rolling over, he felt a burning pain explode through the middle of his back as razor-sharp claws dug into his flesh. With watery eyes, he swung the weapon wildly across his body and felt a sickening thud.

Howling in rage, it stumbled backward, tumbled on its back, and squished into the mud.

A need to live eclipsed his terror. With poise, he scurried from the dirt, leaned over the foul creature, and slammed the butt end of Tommy Carver's rifle into its chest and throat repeatedly. Hot adrenaline pumped through his veins, igniting his confidence like gasoline thrown on an open blaze.

"Die," he screamed as green blood bubbled from its wounds.

After its twitching body went limp, he rolled slowly off its chest and laid flat on the ground. A faint smile flickered across his lips as he slowly regained his breath. He noticed the stars seemed different in this world. They were brighter yet significantly smaller. He thought this strange world benefited from a lack of human existence and felt a touch of envy. Feeling lucky to have survived the vicious attack, he groaned in pain as adrenaline deserted his body. He stared at the heavens a few minutes more and then climbed from the ground, feeling slightly dizzy.

He reached for the weapon.

Despite being soaked in slimy vegetation and even slimier monster blood, he grabbed the gun from the ground and breathed a sigh of relief. Though the weapon felt disgusting in his hand, he had no plans of leaving it behind. Enduring the burning agony in his back, he hobbled through the field, hoping to find his friends and felt thankful to be alive.

From behind, the monster shrieked.

Whirling around, he saw it standing in front of him with blazing red eyes. He wanted to run, but his legs lacked the strength. Unable to break its gaze, he felt suddenly strange, like something foreign controlled his thoughts. He tried to shut his eyes and block out the feeling but stood and watched as it limped closer instead.

Feeling weak, he lifted the gun, ready to strike.

Shedding the black robe, the beast squatted a few inches from the dirt and leaped high into the air.

Feeling defeated, he closed his eyes and swung for the fences as a thunderous boom exploded through his ears, followed by a sickening weighty thump. Stunned, he opened his eyes and watched in amazement as it squirmed on the ground, spraying blood over his pant legs and boots. Behind the beast, Ryan Laville stood in the weeds, holding the Remington Model Seven with an outlandish smirk on his face. Gray smoke rolled from the barrel and drifted to the sky. Later, when he would regurgitate the story about this night, the black smoke would seem surreal, but he saw it as sure as he beat the monster with the butt end of Tommy's rifle.

He dropped to knees and stared at his friend. "Is it dead?"

Ryan sighed and reloaded the weapon. With a grin, he unloaded another round into its face, scattering brains covered in thick green slime across the shrubbery.

He stood speechless.

"Now it's dead," Ryan said, lowering the rifle.

"Do you think so?"

"Come on, let's go," Ryan said and jerked him from the ground and hurried back the way he came.

"Wait up," Ethan shouted. "I was going the wrong freaking way."

Ryan stopped. "Really?"

"Yeah, now just get me out of this field."

As Ethan followed his friend, he wondered how many more of those things lived in this world.

62

Josie knelt on the edge of the grass, hoping to see Ryan come busting through the high weeds with Ethan. Afraid Sage might run after them, she held his collar tight and thought about her feelings for Ethan. Since first becoming acquainted with him the other day, she had been aware of the chemistry going on between them; though, until this moment, she didn't realize she loved him. He made her feel like a beautiful woman instead of the timid chubby little girl she fought so hard to escape. The thought of losing the only person who ever made her feel beautiful left a hollow ache in her belly.

Shawn stood behind her, gently massaging her shoulder. "How are you holding up?"

"I just don't understand what happened."

He pointed to the field. "That's some pretty thick stuff out there. I can see how we got separated."

"I guess."

"I know it's hard, but I wouldn't worry too much. Ryan's a pretty smart young man. He'll bring him back."

She wiped the tears from her itching eyes. "I hope you're right."

"I'm going to take a quick walk."

"A walk? Where?"

"I want to have a look around and see what's over by that cliff we saw earlier."

"Why not wait till they get back?"

"Josie, listen to me," he said with patience. "If I know what we're up against, our odds of getting out of this crazy mess get a little better."

In silence, she frowned.

"Stay here with your dog, and I'll be back in a few minutes."

Her eyes opened wide. "You better come back for me."

He kissed her forehead and smiled. "Not for a million dollars would I abandon you."

"Please hurry."

"I will," he said and then dashed into the darkness.

After Shawn disappeared, she scrutinized the field with tear-soaked eyes. She stared into the darkness for what felt like an eternity, wondering if she would ever see either of them again.

Minutes later, a blast rumbled through the darkness, disrupting her thoughts.

She looked to the black sky for thunder but saw bright stars sparkling above an incandescent yellow moon. With her fingers stroking Sage's fur, she felt forsaken sitting alone on the grass. Even more than a few seconds ago, she missed Ethan. Staring up with big brown eyes, Sage panted and wagged his tail, reminding her that he would never abandon her. From the day her dad brought him home almost three years ago, his heart belonged to her and hers to him.

Sage jumped from the ground and barked at the field behind her. With teeth bared, his tail and ears pointed to the sky as every hair stood up on his back. Spinning backward, she crawled to her knees and latched on to his collar.

Her heart pounded with apprehension.

Staring into the field, Sage growled and struggled to break free.

"Who's there?" she shouted with her fingers gripping tight to keep their hold.

A figure emerged from the darkness and ran straight at her.

Feeling strength abandon her body, she screamed.

"Josie," Shawn shouted, "it's me, Shawn."

Her stomach rose into her throat as the panicky fear subsided. Feeling instantly relieved, she hugged him until her body quit shaking.

"Sorry," he whispered, breathing heavy. "We need to get out of here and find someplace to hide until Ryan and Ethan get back."

"What happened? You've been gone a while, at least twenty minutes."

"I found the cliff. It's not far from here. There's an entrance at the base of it. A few of those monsters came out and are heading this way."

"How close are they?"

"Pretty close," he said and grabbed her hand. "Come on, we can hide in those willow trees."

With Sage at her side, she jogged a few steps behind Shawn as another booming blast rumbled from somewhere in the weeds behind her. Past the lowest branches of an enormous weeping willow just beyond a circular clearing, she tumbled into a high patch of windswept grass and glared back through the landscape. "Was that thunder?" she said over the sound of her pounding chest.

Shawn slid a sweaty hand over her mouth. "Quiet," he whispered. "That sounded like a shotgun blast."

"Was it Ryan?"

"Yeah, I think so," he said and pointed at the grass to her left. "Unfortunately, I can't shoot back right now."

Turning to look, she saw two hulking figures walking leisurely through the grass as if they were out for an evening stroll and enjoying the sights. Marching in perfect cadence, they looked strangely magnificent silhouetted against a breathtaking landscape as they disappeared into the foliage with moonlight sparkling against their malevolent black robes.

Shawn crawled onto his knees, drew his pistol, and squinted through the dark.

"What now?" she said and let go of Sage's collar.

"We wait for them."

"Is that what we should do? We told him to fire his shotgun if he needed us."

"We can't do that right now," he said. "Those things will be on us in a matter of seconds."

"But we should try and help them."

"Josie, relax."

"Sorry," she said, wiping tears from her cheek with the back of her hand.

"Sorry for what?"

"For making things harder. I just wish they were here."

"Considering our situation, you have nothing to apologize for."

"So what do we do now?"

"Stay out of sight till we can think of a plan."

Frowning, she laid flat in the grass and closed her eyes. Though she felt helpless, she knew he was right. Firing warning shots and running blindly through an enormous field of high weeds would guarantee no one made it out of this strange world. Though she hated it, waiting for Ethan and Ryan felt like the safest plan.

63

Struggling to hold the flashlight, Tommy hobbled down the stairs to the basement. With his good arm, he aimed the shotgun at the hallway in case anyone else who might have a part in this mess waited in the basement. Despite the beam flickering off the walls, the cellar seemed a lot darker than when he searched it with the others. He hurried through the hallway and glimpsed the concrete slab a few inches from the opening.

You're too late. They got the jump on you.

Hampered by the sling, he dropped to his knees, lowered the rifle into the hole, and let it go, half expecting it to fire. Relieved, he tossed the flashlight into the hole and slid his feet onto the top rung. Staying balanced with his good arm, he maneuvered down the ladder and into the coal tunnel with surprising agility. Kneeling on the dirt, he breathed a sigh of relief and gathered his belongings. Except for gritty dirt on the surfaces, both the flashlight and pistol looked undamaged.

He shined the light off the wall and across the floor.

Numerous footprints littered the ground. Discouraged by an inability to distinguish between old and fresh, he glanced up toward the opening and decided to leave it uncovered.

Who'd be stupid enough to come down here?

With a pounding heart, he walked toward the portal.

64

Ethan broke through the brush and stood in awe in an endless field of knee-high grass. Scanning the area for the others, he bent over and grabbed his knees, hoping for a quick break. Behind him, weeds rustled as Ryan emerged with a mischievough grin on his lips and the rifle dangling in his hand. More than any time since meeting him, Ethan appreciated the bigger man's friendship. He hoped to stay friends long after returning home from this crazy adventure.

He chuckled. "Dude, guess what?"

"I don't know, man."

"We're even."

Ryan frowned. "What do you mean we're even?"

"I saved your sorry behind a few days ago with a little help from Josie's dog," he said as Ryan stopped beside him. "Consider your debt to me paid."

"Oh, really."

"We're all good, my friend. After you square up with Sage, you can go back to being a New Yorker."

"Real funny," Ryan said and surveyed the acres of grass stretching into the dim landscape. "Where in the world are they?"

Ethan squinted through the dark and felt the smile evaporate from his lips. Except for the illusion of an occasional shadow caused by the moonlight reflecting through the willow trees, he saw nothing. Seeing no signs of Josie and Sage left him with a nervous feeling in his gut. Though she was stuck somewhere in the vast darkness with those things lurking about, he breathed easier knowing that Shawn was protecting her.

"They were right here when I left to find you. I guess something must have scared them off."

"Maybe we should wait and see if they come back."

"Maybe. Crap, man, I don't know."

"Then let's go find them."

"Man, I hate this. What if we run off and they come back looking for us?"

"Or maybe they were chased off by those things and need our help."

"Maybe," Ryan said with a dubious expression. "I think if they were attacked, Shawn would have fired a few rounds. We'd have heard the gunfire. Even out there we would have heard something."

"Not if it happened at the same time as our little fiasco."

He nodded and seemed to be considering the possibility that Ethan was right. "Improbable, but considering how this day has been going, I guess anything's possible."

With surprising patience, he waited for Ryan's decision. He felt like a sitting duck out in the open but decided to go with whatever plan Ryan came up with. After all, when the crap hit the fan, Ryan stepped up and took charge back in the cavern and out in the weeds.

"All right, let's go," Ryan said and then jogged toward the far end of the grass.

Sometime later, they stood in front of giant crack in the granite. He remembered Shawn's words about time being different in this world. Since first emerging from the water hole, he found it a difficult task to judge how long they've been roaming around in this strange world. Though he would never ask, he wondered if Ryan noticed it too. They had enough to deal with without having to worry about his paranoid thoughts concerning time and space.

Ryan rubbed his finger nervously on his lip. "Man, that's one big opening."

"Let me guess," he said, "we're going in there."

"We can turn back like two cowards and go home."

Wiping sweat with his sleeve, he chuckled. "No, dude, we can't," he said as serious as he knew how to be. "Lauren and all of the other people those things abducted from home and God knows where else may be in there somewhere in need of our help."

"Then I guess we are going inside."

"So be it."

"Ethan," Josie's voice drifted through his ears.

Feeling relieved, he whirled around and saw her running toward them with Sage leading the way. Shawn walked behind with his pistol drawn, guarding their backs.

Her arms squeezed his back as muffled weeping filled his ears. On the verge of tears, he held on to her with his free arm until his back could take no more. Ignoring his stinging shoulder, he broke her embrace and kissed her lips. His head buzzed as her tongue danced slowly across his.

Moments later, she pulled away. A smile lit her elegant face.

"Where'd you guys take off to?" Ryan said.

Grasping both knees, Shawn glanced up. "Those things chased us off a while back."

"Where'd they go?"

"Into that mosquito-infested field," Josie said. "We had to hide."

"Because of how dark it is out here, we thought you guys were a couple of those things. We were pretty sure of it until a few minutes ago when the moonlight lit up the area."

"We killed one out in that field," Ryan said. "Looks like our guns are pretty effective against them."

"That thing took a beating though," Ethan said, still buzzing from Josie's kiss. "They are hard to kill.

"That's not a problem, Ethan, as long as they can be killed," Shawn said and tapped Ryan's shoulder. "Sorry about leaving you high and dry. We heard the gunshots, but those things had us in a tight spot."

"Understandable. Besides if you guys came after us, you'd probably still be running around in there."

"More than likely."

"Guys," Josie said, pointing at the opening. "I think we'd better get moving before more of those things come out and we lose the only advantage I think we'll ever have."

"She's right, let's get going," Shawn said and led the charge into the earth.

Guarding their backs, Ethan turned back and glimpsed over the moonlit field. Taking a few steps in reverse, he took a deep breath. What they were doing was psychotic and possibly deadly. The thought of his friends dying for his cause left him feeling regretful, but it was too late to turn back. They were deep in the heart of evil. The emotional roller coaster he seemed to be riding the last few hours was now steam rolling on a downhill slope. His heart pounded as he stepped through the large opening carved into the earth.

Shawn walked out in front, waving his pistol at the darkness. Despite the chance of being discovered at any second, he looked comfortable. Ethan was thankful to have someone with his police training on their side. As crazy as the events of the last several hours have been, he knew without a doubt that meeting Shawn and the older couple near the portal would prove to be critical to their survival. A few feet behind Shawn, Ryan walked with his head up and his rifle down. Despite the man's easygoing nature, he had no doubt about his friend's courage.

Hopefully, they won't have to worry about yours.

He brought up the rear, keeping Josie in his sights at all times. She walked beside her dog, drawing sloppy figure eights on the cavern walls with the wide beam from the flashlight.

As he followed close behind holding his own rifle inches from the ground, he made a vow to protect her no matter what the circumstances. He would gladly sacrifice his life to keep both Josie and his sister safe.

With any luck, it won't come to that.

Twenty yards from the entrance, the passage sloped deeper into the earth.

As they descended into the tunnel, a faint sound of water dripping echoed from somewhere below. He felt suddenly thirsty as hazy dust hovered through the light reflecting off the wall. The narrow passage twisted deeper into the darkness, which casted doubts on the confidence he felt a few minutes ago.

65

Gregory woke from blissful dreams of rape, torture, and murder.

Despite the agony twisting through every muscle in his body, he felt giddy with delight. With the dream still fresh in his memory, he took a deep breath of the moist mist, dug his heels into the squishy ground, and grunted violently to his knees. With a little more energy after the nap, he crawled toward a dark blue silhouette a hundred feet in the distance.

For what felt like hours, he lumbered toward the exit.

Despite the magical mist slowly regenerating his body, he felt deprived of the strength needed to finish the grueling journey. Halfway to the exit, he collapsed into the soft sand and cursed silently. He rolled over and gazed at the ocean of blue vapor. Later, he would finish the short crawl to his master Cornelius's world. For now, he closed his eyes in desperate need of a little more sleep.

66

Her arms grew numb from the weight of Andre's dead body flopping back and forth across the wheelbarrow. She had no idea how far they pushed the lopsided hunk of junk through the cavern, but it seemed like miles. Kelly seemed to be faring a little better, but his breath grew heavier by the second. Sweat dripped from his damp red hair and stained his collar a dirty yellow.

Imagine how I look, Alyssa thought as the wheel caught a rut and dug into coal dust.

Feeling frustrated, she fought an urge to scream.

Ignoring the slight ache in her arms, she leaned forward and pushed with every ounce of strength remaining in her slender body. The wheelbarrow wobbled, and Andre nearly toppled over the side, but the wheel broke free of the rut. She wanted a break but was too proud to call for it, even if it meant collapsing to her knees in the dirt. At least she wouldn't go out appearing weak.

Her thoughts went to the others as she pushed through the pain. Hopefully they were all right. A part of her wanted to make the journey to the other world with them, but for the most part, she was relieved Ethan told her to stay. Besides, Tommy needed her more at that moment.

Too bad he wasn't here to help push.

For a few minutes, the wheel rode along smooth dirt, easing the pressure in her arms.

Despite encumbrance of the wheelbarrow, she was glad they all came back down together. She drew strength from the older couple. Regardless of the terrible things that they've had to endure the past several decades, the Bissells seemed to be decent people. They inspired her to keep moving regardless of the unbelievable strain her body endured.

She nearly tripped over a bulky rock jutting from the soft dirt as her left foot scraped across the top of it. She caught her balance but lost her grip on the handle. Her right arm crashed against the rusted metal.

"Goddang, that hurts!" she shouted while hopping up and down on the dirt, cradling her arm.

Kelly dropped the handle and took a step toward her. Andre slid slightly as the wheelbarrow plummeted but stopped dead on the upper rim. "Ouch," Kelly said, looking concerned. "That looks pretty bad."

Fighting tears of pain, she bit her lip and swallowed what little saliva was left in her mouth.

Jennifer hurried to her, shining the light over the wound. "Are you okay, dear?"

"Yeah, but, Jesus, it hurts!"

"Let's rest up a bit," Kelly said and limped to the side of the cavern.

Grimacing, she watched him drop into the dirt.

"It doesn't look broken, sweetie."

"Yeah, I banged it, but it'll be all right. I just need a few minutes."

"If you can't continue pushing," Kelly said, "we can just leave him right here. If Shawn manages to set off the dynamite down here, I really don't think it's going to matter all that much anyway."

Jennifer nodded. "Yeah, this whole place will be under a few tons of earth."

She leered at the older woman. "And what if doesn't happen?"

"Then I guess it really don't matter if someone finds the bodies or not."

"I guess not," Kelly shouted.

Holding her elbow, she staggered past the dead man, fell backward into the dirt beside Kelly, and leaned against the chilled wall. She was afraid to think about what would happen if Ethan and the others failed to make it back. With thoughts of the others being stuck in another world going through her mind, she massaged her sore arm, leaned against the wall, and closed her eyes.

67

The downsloped path spiraled hundreds of yards deeper into the musty earth before opening into a colossal hexagonal room. Corroded granite walls rose thirty feet to an arched ceiling with a narrow crack twisting through the center. Water dripped from the crevice, trickled from hundreds of moss-ridden stalactites, and formed a stagnant black pool in the center of the room. Ethan crinkled his nose as the beam from Josie's flashlight danced slowly up the wall, shimmered across the ceiling and stopped in the center of the black pond.

Shawn circled to the right along the edge of the water. "Stick to the side," he whispered and moved closer to the wall. "Maybe we should kill the light as well."

"Why?" Josie said, holding the light steady on the water. "Don't we need to see where we're going?"

"I don't want them to see us. We don't have a clue how many of those things are roaming around in this place. If we get ourselves trapped in here, I doubt our three guns are going to be enough to get us back out."

"I don't know if that's a good idea," Ethan said. "I don't like the idea of running around in here in the dark. It freaks me out a bit. And to tell you the truth, I'm not really in the mood for another swim right now."

"I hear you, Ethan, but if we stay close to the wall, we should be fine. Besides, if anything tries to sneak up on us, Sage will bark."

Ryan grabbed his shoulder. "He's right, man. If they don't know we're here, we have a better chance of finding your sister and getting out of here."

"All right, but move slowly and stay close. I'm in no hurry to get separated again."

Shawn nodded. "Good plan, dude," he said, looking at Ethan with a smug grin. "Kill the light, Josie."

With a nervous sigh, Josie flicked the switch.

His heart pounded as darkness filled the large room. Thirsty, hungry, and sick and tired of being afraid, he walked along the wall hoping to avoid falling in the disgusting black water and a confrontation with the strange creatures. Sometime later, aided by dim light that filtered through the crack high above, his eyes adjusted enough to make out shadowy forms walking a few feet in front of him.

Relax, moron, it's just your friends' shadows.

Beyond the sooty pond on the opposite end of the hundred-foot-wide cavern, two small passageways veered off deeper into the earth in separate directions. Stunned and disgusted, he glanced back and forth between both corridors. "So, what you think? Eenie-meanie-miney-moe or maybe just your customary coin flip?"

Shawn took a knee and searched the ground for footprints.

"We take both," Ryan said.

"Both," he half shouted. "Are you out of you freaking mind, dude?"

"We don't have a choice, man. We can cover more ground if we split up."

Suddenly, every horror movie he ever saw flashed through his mind like an ultimate preview. The characters who die the most painful and violent deaths always have one thing in common: they split up to cover more ground. Unlike his clever plan to split up back in the basement, Ryan's plan was the single worst idea he has ever heard.

Shawn rose from his knees. "Ryan is right," he whispered. "We have to split up, or we'll be down here forever."

Throwing his arms up in disgust, he said, "Imagine that, Shawn thinks we should split up as well."

"Keep it down before they hear us."

After a harsh leer at Shawn, he shrugged with the realization that his opinion fell on deaf ears.

"Settle down, kid," Shawn said, staring at the passage to his right. "She'll be safe with me."

"No way! If we're splitting up, Josie comes with me."

"That's not happening," Shawn said calmly.

"Ethan, you need to think real hard about this," Ryan said stepping in front of Shawn with a worried look in his eyes. "He can protect her a lot better than you or me."

"I don't care. She's coming with me."

Shawn took his free hand and placed it on his shoulder. "I promise you, kid. I'll keep her safe."

"No."

"Come on, man, he's dealt with more dangerous situations than we have," Ryan shouted. "She has a better chance of making it out of here with Shawn."

Tears gathered in the corners of his eyes. "They took Lauren. There is no way I'm letting them take Josie too."

"Hey, man, that wasn't your fault," Ryan said. "You were twelve years old."

"I left her alone, and they took her. It was my fault."

Sighing, Ryan stared into his eyes. "It wasn't your fault. You were just a scared little kid."

Tears dripped from his eyes as he remembered that day a little over nine years ago. He was afraid of losing someone else he loved—first Lauren and then his mother. He couldn't lose Josie too.

Nudging Ryan to the side, Josie smiled. "I love you," Josie said and kissed his cheek. "But I need you to be strong."

Her lips tingled against his skin.

She caressed his cheeks with her slender fingers. "I need you to pull it together right now."

She kissed his mouth tenderly. Her salty tears gathered on his lips and teased his tongue.

"You need to go with Ryan. He needs you more than I do right now." She backed away with a genuine smile that enhanced her beauty. "I'll be in good hands with Shawn. He's more than capable of keeping me safe."

"Okay, Josie, I'll do it. I don't like it, but I'll do it."

She kissed him again. "Besides, if we get into any serious trouble, I have Sage at my side."

Despite feeling like an emotional wreck, he smiled. "I love you too."

She hugged him a brief second and then followed Shawn down the passageway.

68

Alyssa's eyes opened wide. She felt invigorated as the aching bone in her right arm dulled to a minor throb. At first, she thought the previous few days had all been a very strange dream, but upon waking up underneath Gastons Gorge in a long abandoned coal mine where she and Kelly Bissell were toting a dead body and a case of dynamite, she cast doubt on that theory.

Speaking of the Bissells, where the heck are they?

She climbed off the dusty floor and eyeballed the tunnel. "Where are you guys?" she shouted, wiping loose black soot from the back of her jeans. She wondered why they left her sleeping all alone in this place. *Perhaps they took a quick walk ahead and will be back soon,* she thought. As the seconds ticked by, she grew nervous as the realization of being alone suddenly went from a probability to an absolute definite.

"Jennifer," she shouted. "Where are you guys? Please don't leave me here all alone."

Silence drifted through the empty space.

Why would they leave me here? Why in the world wouldn't they have woken me up when they left?

She felt befuddled and forsaken.

Was I wrong about the old couple? Maybe they weren't decent people after all.

She hurried toward the secret door leading back to the basement, wanting to be standing under bright sunlight. Though not thrilled about wandering through the old building in the dark, she dreaded being underground where one of those monsters could carry her away even more. She froze as a different thought flashed through her mind.

What if they didn't abandon me? Was it possible they were in trouble and in need of my help?

She felt more confused than ever. Two options stared her in the face: get as far away from this place as fast as possible or stay and search for the Bissell's. She preferred the first option but couldn't live with it.

No, if they needed help and I ran away like a coward, I could never forgive myself.

She whirled backward and stared in the direction of the portal. "Hope you know what you're doing," she whispered and hurried deeper into the mine.

Minutes later, a form shimmered through the dust, stopping her dead in her tracks.

A small child dressed in a loose white nightgown dragged two filthy feet through the dirt ten feet in front of her. Trembling, she took a few steps backward with an eerie tingle in her arms and a knot tightening in her chest. As the child drew to within a few feet, Alyssa saw a young pale-faced girl with an eerie scowl on two chapped pink lips. Long, tousled blonde hair dangled above two sea green blinking eyes. Her skin felt chilled to the bone. Alyssa wanted to run and escape the girl's captivating gaze, but terror rendered her legs two useless stumps.

"Do you need some help?" she said over her own chattering teeth.

The girl said nothing and continued to drag her feet forward.

"Are you lost down here? I can help you get back home."

The girl giggled.

Hairs rose on the back of her neck as goose bumps broke out along her arms. Mischievousness loomed in the girl's ghastly laughter.

Oh my god, it can't be!

Realization shattered the hypnotic enchantment. She screamed as blood gushed through her heart and freed her legs from their paralytic state. Terrified of turning her back to her childhood friend, she staggered backward, hoping not to tumble into the dirt.

Lauren giggled. "Where are you going, friend?"

"You're not really here! You died a long time ago!"

Suddenly, her sea-green eyes turned a dark shade of scarlet as she closed the gap to within a few feet. "They want you too, Alyssa. You're gonna join me now." Her grin widened and two sharp fangs jutted from her decayed mouth.

Alyssa's heart dropped into the pit of her queasy stomach. "What do you want from me?"

Lauren inched closer, licking the fangs with a narrow, withered tongue.

"Your brother is looking for you," Alyssa screamed. "He's over there right now trying to find you."

"My brother's dead."

"No, Lauren!" She screamed and dug her heels in the loose dirt and whirled in the direction of the basement. "He's very much alive."

Childish laughter echoed off the walls.

She lowered her head and sprinted through the passage, hoping to find the Bissells. She closed her eyes and waited for Lauren's laughter to stop.

Minutes later, comforting silence filled the suddenly dark space.

69

With his hand trembling against the rifle, Ethan followed Ryan through a twisting corridor with thoughts of Josie encumbering his mind. Grey shadows danced along black granite, stretched across a damp ceiling and merged into a glob of darkness above. With faltering nerves, his feet crunched into soft, coarse dirt for what felt like miles until a dimly lit opening came into view. Up ahead, Ryan stopped five feet from the opening, ran his finger vertically across his lips, and then waved him closer.

Muffled grunts struck fear in his mind.

Looking anxious, Ryan glanced at his gun. "You ready for this?"

In a million years. I could never be ready for this.

Deep down he wanted to turn back and run as far from the horrible grunting sounds as possible. Terror ran cold through his veins. Beyond a shadow of a doubt, something dangerous waited in the next room, ready to wreak agony on them both. Instead, he took a deep breath of dusty air and smiled. "I'm as ready as I'll ever be," he said, aware of what was on the line if his courage took a nosedive.

"Good, stay close behind me."

Unlike him, Ryan appeared perfectly calm considering their current predicament. If even the slightest bit of fear ran through him, his eyes covered it well. His friend's take-charge attitude and cool demeanor was impressive. In bleak situations, some people rise to the top and assume the leadership role they were born to become while others—like him—got through by conforming to those leaders. He was accepting of his role. It has allowed him to make it this far without going stark raving mad, although the majority of the doctors who treated him would more than likely disagree.

"Sir, yes sir," he said.

Ignoring his sarcasm, Ryan's expression stiffened as he threw the barrel out in front of his chest and tiptoed through the opening.

Turning the corner, he stared in disbelief as the rifle slipped through his fingers and clanked onto the floor. On the far end of a long narrow room, a large wolflike beast snarled and stared with large yellow eyes swollen to the size of silver half-dollars. In a rage, it rose onto two hind muscular legs, howling and snorting, baring sharp yellow fangs protruding from a mangled mouth. Patches of thick matted fur blew in a phantom wind across its massive underbelly. With catlike agility, it dropped to all fours, scraped its front paw backward through thick dirt like an angry bull, and charged with two protracted ears raised toward a shallow ceiling above. The beast weaved and waved, spraying dirt high in the air behind it as it closed the gap to five feet in a blink of an eye.

With his eyes focused on the charging monster, Ethan scraped his fingers blindly through dirt, groping for the rifle. He cringed, squinting his eyes shut as it leaped high into the air with a brutish grunt.

A thunderous boom exploded through the room.

Temporally deafened from the loud boom, he rolled to the side with his eyes wide open. He stared in awe as a thick ebony sludge sprayed from the beast's underbelly, soaking the ground three feet from where he knelt. With rage chiseled into its hellish face, the beast balanced, wobbled forward, and then collapsed four inches from his outstretched hand with a sickening thump. The fine hair on the back of his neck rose instantly as Ryan pulled another clip from his front pocket, reloaded the rifle and pumped another round of lead into the squirming freak of nature.

Seconds later, the atrocious grunts ceased.

From his knees, Ethan watched with enthrallment as life seeped from the wolf creature's shuddering body. With a soft grumble, its dull yellow eyes dripped dark blue tears and then blinked shut. Certain that at any moment it would transform into a regular man, he grabbed his rifle off the ground, crawled to his feet, and took a few steps back.

Ryan stood beside him with sweat beading on his forehead. "Don't worry, man, that thing is deader than heck."

"What the crap is it?"

'Kind of looks like a werewolf."

He chuckled. "Yeah, I was thinking the same thing."

'Werewolves aside, let's get going."

With a queasy stomach, his eyes focused on the long hallway. A spacious rectangular cage lined the left wall. In the far corner of the cell, an aged man leaned against the bars, staring at the wall with a blank expression on his face. He appeared to be oblivious to reality. Beside him, two decaying bales of hay served as makeshift mattresses. Scattered through the reeking earth, maggots squirmed through moist clumps of what looked like piles of human waste. Roaches the size of small kittens feasting on the maggots hissed their displeasure at the sound of approaching footsteps and then scurried into the shadows. Along the far wall, clumps of brown jelly oozed through a pile of eroding bones.

Ryan opened the gate, tiptoed across the floor, doing his best to avoid the maggots, and examined the beaten-down man dressed in tattered leather rags. Feeling for a pulse, he looked up at Ethan while trying to hold his breath. "Stay alert, we were kind of loud."

"Kind of loud," he said. "I think everything in this place heard us." He pointed the rifle at a narrow passage opposite to the one they came through. "We don't have time for this, Ryan."

"Wait a minute. This guy needs our help."

"Is he alive?"

"Yeah, he has a pulse, but something bruised him up pretty good," he said, loosening the strap on his backpack and tossing it on the floor below his feet. With two shaking hands, he rummaged through the inside.

"What are you doing, dude? Let's get the crap out of here!"

"I have some jerky left. He can use it more than we can."

With an impatient scowl, he watched Ryan drop a piece of beef jerky into the old man's withered hand and gently squeeze his fingers around it. Seconds later, as the broken man nibbled on the dried meat, Ryan pulled a bottle of water from his pack, unscrewed the plastic cap, and balanced it on the ground between the man's shivering legs. He chuckled as Ryan played an awkward game of charades in an attempt to persuade the old man to eat and drink.

"Dude, come on!"

"Give me one more second."

He shrugged in frustration.

"Can you talk?" Ryan said, raising the jerky to his lips.

"Dude, he's beyond talking. Can we please get out of this room before we get the same treatment he got?"

Gathering his pack, Ryan stared at the old man with a strange look of fascination and compassion on his face.

"Eat you," the man mumbled. "They gonna eat you all up."

Ethan trembled upon hearing the man's twitchy voice.

"Stay put, old-timer," Ryan said, ignoring his rant. "We'll be back in a bit."

70

Jennifer towered over her with both hands on her shoulders, shaking her from a horrible nightmare. "Oh my god," she said. "That dream felt so real."

Jennifer ran her fingers through her hair. "That's all it was, dear, just a dream."

"How long was I out?" she asked, still trembling.

"Fifteen minutes," Jennifer said, "give or take a few minutes."

"I guess we're ready to get going."

"Take your time, Kelly will be right back."

She glanced through the tunnel and saw no signs of Kelly.

"We thought we heard something moving around deeper in the corridor a few minutes ago. He went to have a closer look."

With the dream a distant memory, she climbed from the ground. "How long has he been gone?"

"Only a few moments. Like I said, we heard something moving around about the same time you started rousing in your sleep."

Her chest pounded. Perhaps the remnants of the nightmare left her a bit paranoid, but she couldn't shake the eerie feeling that something was wrong. Andre was slumped in the center of the wheelbarrow like a sack of concrete. As grueling as pushing his body along the coal mine floor was, she would feel a lot better if Kelly were standing beside her ready to begin the arduous task of reuniting him with Gregory Stephens and Christopher. She stared through the darkness with a glimmer of hope.

In silence, Jennifer crouched above her, holding her hand.

71

Tommy stopped and glanced over his shoulder.

Andre, the man Kelly Bissell shot earlier in the day, was gone. Kelly said he dumped the body at the bottom of the ladder. Upon shining the light across the ground and along the walls, a mental image of Andre hobbling through the tunnel and searching for Gregory Stephens flashed through his mind.

Maybe the old man only wounded him, Tommy thought. *After all, Kelly was an old-timer and not used to handling firearms.*

Clenching tighter onto his gun, he hobbled forward. Because of his aching left shoulder and the flashlight clenched in his left hand, he was having a hard time keeping the rifle drawn. If something attacked from the dark, he would have to drop the light, steady the barrel, and shoot into the blackness hoping to hit the target.

On the ground, a three-inch groove zigzagged through the dirt.

Dropping to his knees, he inspected the strange marking. Suddenly, it made sense. The Bissells were inside the mine.

They must be taking his body back to the pond.

Grimacing, he climbed from the ground and continued on. Energized by the sudden realization, he broke into a brisk jog, hoping to catch up with the Bissells. Minutes later, he picked up the pace as gunfire boomed deeper in the tunnel.

PART V

Enigmatic Descent

72

With his eye on the passageway, Ethan stroked the cool metal trigger with a sore finger. He was in no hurry to squeeze it. It had been well over ten minutes since Ryan fired the shots killing the wolf creature. He was growing more anxious by the second, expecting to see a horde of monsters rushing from the dark. Hearing the insane man ramble over the past few minutes depleted the little bit of courage he had left. Though he felt sorry for the babbling lunatic, he was willing to leave him behind, at least for the time being. If things went well, they could swing by and pick him up on the way out.

"Ryan, dang it, let's go."

Rising to his feet, Ryan took the rifle from the ground and stared at the man with a somber scowl on his face. Stepping back, he wiped dirt from the backpack, slid it over his shoulder, glimpsed back at the rambling man, and hurried through the cell door where Ethan waited in the corridor. With a look of uncertainty, he slammed the door and engaged the latch.

The old man glanced up, swallowed a mouthful of jerky, and continued chanting about monsters eating them up.

"We'll come back for you," Ryan said and turned toward Ethan. He patted his shoulder on the way by and then disappeared around the corner.

After a last glance around, Ethan followed his friend.

A few hundred feet past the room where the old man chewed on jerky between disturbing rants, he stared at a wooden ladder similar to the one leading into the coal tunnel. It rose ten feet from the ground and ended at a closed trapdoor in the ceiling.

"Jesus, dude, ladders and secret doors are starting to rub me the wrong way."

"Just be ready."

Horrible thoughts plagued his mind. "We don't know what's waiting up there."

"Just be ready," Ryan said again with an impatient glare.

"Oh, I'm ready."

Reaching for the ladder, Ryan handed him the rifle and grabbed hold of the dirty wood.

"Dude," he whispered.

Raising a finger slowly to his mouth, Ryan climbed the ladder and lifted the flimsy lid a few inches off the ground.

Fearing the slightest noise might alert anything above to their presence, he stood motionless, enduring the sound of his own pounding heart. Sweat moistened his palms, loosening his grip on the rifles as loose dirt drifted through the opening and sprinkled the top of his head.

"See anything?" he whispered and dared a quick peek back through the narrow passageway.

Ryan glanced down, shook his head, and then disappeared into the space above. The door thudded shut above him.

"Dude," he whispered.

Boards creaked above his head, which he guessed was Ryan rummaging around. With uneasy nerves, he focused on the trapdoor, praying it would pop back open with Ryan's face staring down at him.

Suddenly, the creaking noises above ceased.

His heart pounded harder.

The silence felt more distressing than the sound of creaking boards. He nearly screamed but thought better of it. Over the last twenty minutes or so, luck seemed to be smiling upon them. Despite Ryan's trigger-happy finger and the mumbling lunatic back through the passageway, they remained unnoticed by the monsters.

With a drawn-out squeal, the door slid open.

From above, Ryan laid flat on his stomach with his arm dangling in the air, reaching for the rifles.

Sighing, he handed Ryan the guns one at a time and then raced up the ladder with a strong desire to be out of the gloomy passageway.

"Eat you up," the lunatic shouted from the prison room as he closed the door.

Shaking his head in disbelief, he slammed the lid over the hole as an overbearing smell of rotten meat burned his nostrils. Beside him, both weapons sat on a dusty floor. Ryan crouched on his knees a few inches from the guns, covering a cough with two sweaty hands. With watering eyes, he pointed toward the back of the room with every ounce of color drained from his once tanned face.

"What is it?" he said and gathered his rifle from the floor. Between the horror-stricken expression wrinkling his friend's face and the overbearing smell of spoiled roadkill, he had no desire to turn around.

After another bout of coughing, Ryan threw up chewed clumps of jerky on the floor boards.

With a queasy stomach, Ethan whirled around.

Instantly, all strength drained from his body. The rifle slid through his sweat-stained fingertips and smacked onto the wooden floor with a soft thump. Dropping to his knees, he tasted sour jerky rising in his throat

"Oh my god!" he shouted and stared in horror at the gruesome sight. Shackled to the wall with two dirt-encrusted chains, a partially devoured naked man stared lifelessly at him. Chunks of rotted flesh, obviously cut from the rancid man, lay in heaps near his bloated yellow feet. Blood seeped from puncture wounds in his chest, dripped down his gored stomach, trickled down between his legs, and formed a small puddle of slimy burgundy on the floor. Deep gashes sliced through what was left of a ripped open chest, and red streaks were carved into an unidentifiable face.

From behind, Ryan continued to dry heave.

"His freaking eyes are gone," he said. "They stole his eyes, and something happened to his brains."

Above, two black voids where eyes once glimpsed the world and bits and pieces of gooey flesh clung to an exposed skull. He thought about everything the unfortunate man must have endured—the pain he must have suffered as his attacker ripped away his flesh and eyes. How it must have been incredibly slow and agonizing. Finally able to look away, he coughed up a mouthful of thick saliva and staggered back across the floor.

Wiping his mouth, Ryan crawled from his knees. "Yeah, something happened to his brains, all right. They ate them!"

Trying not to breathe, he stared at the horrendous scene. Thick dried blood stained the floor below two deserted sets of shackles on both sides of the devoured man. "This must be some kind of torture room."

"I don't know what it is," Ryan said, "but this is bad."

Hopes of finding Lauren slipped away as he wondered if she had met the same fate. Feeling nauseous, he staggered backward and struggled to keep down the sandwich from earlier. Finding it difficult to stay balanced, he closed his eyes and felt a hand slide under his shoulder. After an epigrammatic struggle, he stood at the far side of the room gazing into the empty voids where the man's eyes once saw the world.

"You okay?" Ryan said and let go of his arm.

"Whatever they did to this poor guy, they've done before."

"No doubt," Ryan said, glancing around the area. "But unless we want to end up suffering the same fate, we need to get out of here."

Except for the carnage, the room was otherwise deserted.

Moonlight filtered through two dirty windows, revealing a door in the center of a barren wall. After a silent jaunt through the dusty room, he stood in front of the door wondering what waited for them outside.

"Are you all right, man?"

With a disingenuous smile, he shrugged.

Ryan walked to the window and pressed his face against the filthy glass. After a few seconds, he motioned for Ethan to join him.

Twenty feet across a grass field a large wooden shack caught his attention. He thought it looked like the workmanship of adolescent boys fashioning a cabin from wood they stole off scrap piles. The building looked decrepit, like it would collapse in a minor windstorm.

Ryan tapped the glass and pointed at the field. "Look, man, check it out."

Two small huts sat on both sides of the large building. Beyond the shacks, knee-high grass stretched into the darkness. Curious, Ethan hurried to the other window and cupped his hands around his face, squinting into the moonlit grass. Half a dozen small shacks were scattered through the field. He pushed away from the glass and stared at Ryan. "It looks like some kind of run-down village."

"This feels wrong."

"Yeah, I know. I feel the same way." His mind drifted to Josie. He wondered how she was holding up. Hopefully, they didn't find anything as gruesome as the scene he and Ryan stumbled upon.

Ryan backed slowly across the floor and joined him a few feet from the exit.

"Those freaks of nature are pure evil. I came here to find Lauren, and I pray she's alive. Regardless of whether or not I find her, we're gonna wipe every last one of those things off the face of this earth."

"Yeah, but how many are there?"

"Does it matter?"

"If we're outnumbered by—"

"After seeing this, I guess it might be possible Lauren's dead."

"You don't know that."

"No, I don't, but regardless." His eyes focused on his friend. "The five of us need to make sure those things never cross over into our world again."

"That's the plan," Ryan said."

"So help me God, if my sister's dead." He pointed to the partially devoured man with newfound adrenaline. "I'm gonna avenge her and every other unlucky son of a gun they did that to."

"Come on. Let's go check out that town," Ryan said and walked out through the door.

He turned away from the corpse dangling from the shackles. With a heavy heart, he pushed through the flimsy door and chased Ryan through the shadowy grass with revenge on his troubled mind.

73

At least ten minutes passed since she was shaken from the most terrifying and realistic dream she had ever endured. Jennifer stood to her left in the center of the passage, peering into the darkness. Andre's dead and beaten-up carcass was slumped against the side of the rusted wheelbarrow a few feet from where they stood. Turning, she cupped her hands around her eyes and peered into the darkened path, still trembling from the dream. The vampire version of her best friend left her spooked. She thought of Ethan and prayed the dream wasn't a premonition of things to come. Nine years at the mercy of those things is a long time for anyone, let alone a scared child. Hopefully, if he found her alive, humanity still thrived inside her.

A shape materialized out of the darkness.

Kelly Bissell sprinted toward them with the flashlight in one hand and the pistol he stole from Andre swinging wildly in the other. "Run!" he shouted with horror-filled eyes. With no color left in his cheeks, he waved the gun and continued to shout.

Without hesitating, she turned, sidestepped the wheelbarrow, and sprinted back in the direction of the secret door. After a few lengthy strides, she heard a loud thud followed by Jennifer screaming in pain. On trembling legs, she stopped running and peeked over her shoulder.

Kelly stood over his wife, glancing nervously back through the tunnel.

Wriggling on the ground, Jennifer rubbed her right ankle with a look of agony twisting her face as the pistol she took from Christopher spun across the dirt and came to a sudden halt against wall.

Alyssa cringed as the look on Kelly's face chilled her skin. She sprinted across the tunnel, leaped both the corpse and the overturned wheelbarrow, and dove for the gun. From somewhere in the darkness, she could hear cumbersome footsteps crunching through dirt, growing louder by the second. She grabbed the pistol with a trembling hand, whirled to her knees, and glanced across the tunnel at the Bissells.

Dragging his wife through the dirt with one hand, Kelly shined the beam through the darkness and shrieked in horror and as two hulking monsters obscured by hooded black robes rushed at them.

Suddenly paralyzed with an astringent anxiety, she stood helplessly as the monsters she had been hearing about all day but never really believed existed until this moment bore down on the couple.

Abandoning the idea to lift his wife off the ground, Kelly climbed to his feet and raised the pistol with both hands at the monsters. He squeezed the trigger and tumbled backward as an earsplitting explosion shook loose dirt from the walls.

Unable to hear anything except the dull throb vibrating through her temples, she closed her eyes and fell back against the wall, squeezing the gun so hard it stung her fingers. The raucous buzzing blocked out the sound of Jennifer's braying screams.

Seconds later, a second explosion shook the cavern walls, followed by a muffled shriek.

Breathless, she opened her eyes.

From his knees, Kelly rolled to his right, avoiding the swinging hand of a tumbling monster by less than an inch. It staggered a few feet before collapsing onto the ground a foot from where she leaned against the wall temporarily paralyzed and partially deaf.

Blood spayed from a hole in its throat, painting her face a dark green. Spitting the spicy liquid from her mouth, she fought back an urge to vomit as her stomach grumbled with disgust.

Kelly screamed, breaking her paralytic state.

The other monster heaved Kelly over its head and slammed him into the ceiling. His gun flew across the cavern as the creature hurled him into the wall. With a crackling thump, he crumbled to the ground like a sack of potatoes and lay motionless with both eyes shut tight.

"Kelly," Jennifer screamed and scrambled to her knees in obvious pain. Using every ounce of strength in her left leg, she scooted backward toward her husband's pistol.

Disregarding the older woman, the monster scurried to the right, focusing on her. She tried to look away, but its flaming red eyes held her gaze. With one last unsuccessful attempt to break free from the creature's captivating stare, she heard a strange voice whisper orders inside her head.

Kill the woman.

Against her will, she rose to her feet and stood toe to toe with the beast.

Get her before she kills you.

Raising the gun, she stared at Jennifer, who was crawling on her hands and knees and reaching for the pistol Kelly used to shot the dead monster on the ground. As much as she didn't want to hurt the old woman, she extended her arm with the gun in her hand. Both the dwindling buzz in her ears and the soothing voice in her head left her feeling disoriented. Seconds later, with the monster breathing heavy in her ear, she kicked Kelly's gun from Jennifer's grasp.

"Alyssa, no!" Jennifer screamed with terror alive in her eyes.

Alyssa fingered the trigger, unsure of her intentions. The voice ordered her to kill the woman, but something felt wrong about it. *Why would Jennifer Bissell want to kill me?* Despite the calming voice assuring her she did, it made no sense.

Kill her now!

She gritted her teeth and pushed harder on the metal trigger. She didn't want to shoot the woman, but she had to. *The voice is right,* she thought. *If I don't kill her, I'll be lying dead in this dark coal mine.* She lowered the gun toward Jennifer's head with intentions of obeying the voice. Hesitating, she blinked her eyes. Tears dripped down her face as she felt the cool metal on the front side of her finger. "I'm so sorry," she whispered and closed her eyes.

"Fight the voice, Alyssa!" Jennifer screamed. "I'm your friend."

A deafening blast boomed through the mine, adding to the steady buzz tormenting her head. The voice abandoned her mind. Instead, she heard a heavy thud followed by the sound of clicking metal. Expecting a bloodied Jennifer Bissell on the dirt below her feet, she opened her eyes and jerked her finger from the trigger.

Licking the tears from her quivering lips, Jennifer crawled from the dirt, hobbled to her husband, and collapsed onto his chest.

Confused, Alyssa spun backward and sighed as Tommy Carver walked through the mine, stood beside her, and handed her a long narrow flashlight. With hate in his eyes, he reloaded the shotgun. He grinned, stood over the dying creature, and nudged the hood away from its face with the tip of the barrel. In shock, she jumped back. Four long black tentacles danced from a nightmarish mouth filled with circular rows of long sharp fangs. Shockingly enthralled, she watched as Tommy turned his head and squeezed the trigger. Green slime sprayed across the cavern floor and soaked her jeans. He reloaded, jammed the barrel in its gut, and fired again.

Gagging, she dropped to her knees, stripped off her blood-soaked jacket covered in monster brains, and flung it aside. Seconds later, she dropped the pistol on the ground and hurried to aid Jennifer.

74

With thoughts of Ethan running through her terrified mind, Josie followed Shawn through the semidark passageway and thanked God for giving her Sage. *Perhaps Ethan was right.* She should have stayed behind with Alyssa and the others and left the dangerous expedition for the three men. *Too late now,* she thought and followed a few steps behind Shawn as he led her deeper into the unknown. Sage trotted beside her, sparking just enough courage to keep her going.

Rounding a bend, she saw a light shinning a few hundred feet in the distance. At first she thought one of the creatures was walking toward them, but as they continued along the passageway, she saw a dimly lit room ahead in the dark tunnel. As they stepped within a few feet, a faint smell of fertilizer lingered in the air. With every step, the stench of manure grew stronger. After a few minutes, they stood just outside an open cavern.

A frail woman with long straggly gray hair dressed in a worn leather hide stood with her back toward the opening. She carried a crude watering can in her left hand and poured reddish water into a trough filled with a variety of multicolored mushrooms. Black, brown, gray, yellow, green, and dark red mushrooms lined the odorous room. Though they varied in size, each one radiated a faint fluorescent light. Thick florescent slime dripped from the fungus and oozed into the odorous trough.

"There must be thousands of them."

Shawn slid his free hand over her mouth, which blocked out the unbearable smell.

Unaware she was no longer alone, the woman continued watering the strange fungus.

"Stay here a minute," he whispered. "Try and keep a hold of your dog."

He tiptoed across the room making sure not to come in contact with the grotesque mushrooms and snuck up behind the woman without being seen.

75

After a brisk search, the small shacks glistening under yellow moonlight appeared deserted. Every hut looked identical to the next—empty rooms and dirt floors. It was as if whoever erected the buildings wanted to paint an illusion of a quiet little town. The thought of these monsters ambushing weary travelers and shackling them to the walls within where they intended to devour their flesh left Ethan's stomach feeling nauseous as they finished searching the last of the small huts.

He shuddered at the reality.

While searching the small cabins, he couldn't shake the feeling of being watched. Afraid of escalating Ryan to the same paranoid frame of mind, he kept the notion to himself. As they crept between the shoddy buildings doing their best to hide within the shadows, the feeling of being watched grew more intense. Hurrying around the side of the larger building, he glanced back across the grassy field. Seeing nothing but shadows dancing in the moonlight, he followed Ryan to a closed door blocking the entrance. A warm breeze rustled the high grass beyond as Ryan nudged open the door and slipped inside.

After one last peek across the landscape, he joined his friend inside. As with every other building in the village, the large room stood empty. No pictures hung on the walls. No furniture cluttered the area. There was no table to eat at or any chairs to sit upon.

"Everything looks the same," he said, "except the floors. Those smaller ones have dirt floors."

Ryan brought his foot down hard on the floor as if testing the strength of the wood it was made with. "And this shack has wooden floorboards."

"Yeah, it's kind of weird."

"I don't get it," Ryan said with a worried frown. "We must have missed something somewhere."

"It might help if we knew what we were looking for."

Looking exhausted, Ryan leaned the rifle against the wall, slid the backpack off his shoulder, dropped it to the floor, and plopped down beside it. With a look of disgust on his dirty face, he pulled a bottle of water from the pack and tossed it across the room.

"Thanks," Ethan said and twisted the lid off. Thirsty, tired, and suffering from the burning pain in his back and shoulder, he mimicked Ryan and took a seat on the uneven wooden floor. After a long swallow, he sat the open bottle beside the rifle and leaned back against the wall and thought of Josie and Lauren.

After guzzling half a bottle in one gulp, Ryan pulled a bag of jerky from the pack and motioned at Ethan. "Want some?" he said, extending his hand.

"After seeing what happened to that poor man back in that room, I don't think I'm ever gonna eat again."

A less-than-genuine smile broke out across Ryan's face as he chewed on the food. He admired his friend's strength. They were as different as opposite sides of a coin. Ryan kept his feelings bottled up while he put his emotions out there for all to see regardless of the embarrassment it caused him at times. He genuinely liked the man. Though they had a few minor disagreements from time to time, Ryan seemed to understand him. Most people don't receive his sarcastic humor so well, but Ryan took it for what it was.

"Man, I'm tired of this place."

Ethan attempted to smile, but his minor aches and pains disallowed it. Adding to the already existing soreness in his shoulder and back, a mild throb twitched through the front of his head. He felt like crying and actually thought he was going to. "So now what are we going to do?" he asked.

"I guess we go back and try and find the others."

The hard floor felt good on his bones. Despite inches of thick brown dust covering the wood, Ethan felt relaxed. He wanted to shut his eyes and catch a few minutes of much-needed sleep, but the thought of Josie wondering about somewhere among the flesh-eating creatures brought him back to reality. They had to get moving soon. Finding Josie and Shawn and hopefully rescuing anyone lucky enough to be alive in this godforsaken place seemed like the most important thing in the world. "Good plan, dude," he said and closed his eyes. "Just give me a few minutes and then we can go."

"We need to go right now."

Ethan opened his eyes. "Yeah, I know."

Struggling slightly, Ryan climbed to his feet and grabbed the backpack from the dusty floor. He slid the strap over his shoulder, grabbed the rifle from the wall, and stared at the plastic water bottle. With a halfhearted grin, he kicked it across the vacant room. It spiraled through the air, ricocheted off the wall, and whirled across the floor with a hollow creak. "He shoots and scores," he said through muffled laughter. "Come on, man, let's go find Josie, Shawn, and Sage. Hopefully they're all right."

Ethan wanted to sit right here against the dry wooden wall and catch a few hours of sleep, but Ryan was right. They had to go find the others and get back home before they ended up shackled from the ceiling in that shack of death. The thought of being devoured alive sparked the energy needed to get his arms and legs moving.

"All right," he said and reached for the water. He nudged the top of the open bottle with his hand and watched as it wobbled clumsily on the floor. For a moment, he thought it was going to stay balanced as it teetered back and forth, but as he reached out, the bottle tipped over and spilled water on the dusty floor.

Ryan laughed. "Real smooth move."

He reached for the bottle, intending to throw it at his friend but noticed the puddle shrinking on the floorboards.

"Ryan!"

"Sorry, man, but that was comical."

He pointed to the water on the floor. "Look at this."

The smug grin on Ryan's face disappeared as he dropped to his knees and examined the floor. "There's something underneath us," he said and pointed at the dwindling puddle. "Look there. The water is disappearing through the cracks in the floorboards."

"Nothing gets by you, Mr. Einstein."

Ignoring his remarks, Ryan stood motionless and listened to the water dripping through the floorboards. He squatted as if trying to get a better look between the boards, but years of dust and dirt buildup blocked the view.

Ethan jumped to his feet. He could feel the energy rushing through his muscles and bones. The burning pain numbed as he grabbed the rifle and surveyed the large room. A few feet from where he spilled the bottle of water he found what he was looking for. A large piece of plywood nearly four feet wide pulled easily from the floor, revealing a wooden ladder leading into a corridor with faint fluorescent lights radiating from the ground below.

Handing him the rifle, Ryan slid a leg over the opening and descended the wooden ladder. At the bottom, he sniffed the air with a sickened expression on his face and reached for their weapons. "Let me get out of the way," he said. "Then come down and try to slide the piece of wood back over the hole."

Looking down, Ethan grinned. "Leaving it open might be a better way to go," he said. "I mean, just in case we need to come back through here. After all, dude, we are strolling into the lion's den, so to speak."

"Whatever, man, that's fine."

On the opposite side of the main door, an eerie sound of something sharp scraping through wood caught his attention. With his eyes focused on the door, he climbed onto the top wooden rung and crept down three creaky steps. The door slammed against the wall, creating a mushroom cloud of dust throughout the room. Standing in the open doorway, a black-robed creature shrieked in disgust. Though its hood concealed the strange features of the one he encountered in the weed field a few hours ago, the beast's menacing eyes glared at him coldly. Despite killing one earlier in the weeds, he felt helpless, like prey being stalked by a superior predator. In its hand, a primitive-looking sling with a large blue stone set in the middle of two gummy strings escalated his fear.

Glaring at the beast, he held onto the top rung and couldn't move.

Taking a long stride, the creature jerked back the gummy bands, held for what seemed like an eternity, and then let go. With lightening speed, the blue stone whirled through the air and thudded against the top of his forehead. Dizzy and a bit befuddled, he lost his hold on the wooden rung and plunged to the ground below, missing Ryan by a few inches.

For a few seconds, fluorescent lights swirled around him, and then his world turned black.

76

Sage remained quiet as she held onto his collar. The dog was obedient and intelligent, almost as if he knew the entirety of Shawn's plan. Her raspy breathing and the steady drumbeat pounding her chest were the only noises she heard as Shawn tiptoed closer toward the woman without her sensing anything was wrong.

Focusing on watering the freakish fungus, the old woman hummed an eerie tune she had never heard before.

Sneaking behind her, he thrust his left hand over her mouth and wrapped his right arm around her chest, knocking the watering can to the wet ground. She kicked her legs and flailed her arms, but he overpowered her with ease. He jerked her backward across the cavern toward where Josie held tight onto the dog's collar. Her legs thrashed wildly at her attacker, but he kept to the side, managing to stay out of harm's way. Josie suspected this wasn't the first time the cop was forced to subdue a perpetrator.

Backpedaling, he pulled the woman into the corridor past Josie and Sage. Her eyes were wild with terror, and her legs continued to kick as he pulled her on by. Releasing the collar, Josie jumped back, missing a wild swinging arm by inches. With an outstretched hand in the dirt, she chased Shawn around the corner.

He lowered her gently to the ground. "Take it easy, we're here to help you get out of here."

Responding to his soft voice, she stopped kicking but continued squirming in an attempt to break free from his overpowering grip. After a few minutes of struggling, she seemed defeated. Her body went limp, but he continued to hold onto her waist with his hand covering her mouth.

"If I let go," he said, "you won't scream."

Josie doubted the woman was in her right mind, considering all the unimaginable horrors that must have happened to her in this strange underground labyrinth. Her skin looked whitish-gray, giving the impression the woman hasn't seen the light of day in a very long time. Standing behind them with Sage by her side watching this sad scene play out, Josie felt a strange sense of guilt.

The woman stared at her captor with terrified eyes and shook her head nervously.

"Who are you?" Shawn said, sliding his hand slowly from her mouth.

She remained silent.

Either she didn't know her name or had no plans on telling them. The look in her pale green eyes was all Josie needed to see. The battered looking woman didn't trust them. Judging by her raggedy appearance and the eccentric look in her eyes, Josie guessed this woman didn't have much reason to trust anyone.

"We're not going to hurt you."

She looked at Shawn with reproachful eyes, waved him aside and knelt in front of the woman. It was obvious the she was frightened. They needed a different approach. Gently, she pulled long strands of matted gray hair away from her dirt streaked face and smiled. "My name is Josie," she said, "and this is Shawn."

Her silence continued, but at least she didn't scream.

"We're from a place called Gastons Gorge."

She stared at Josie with a bewildered scowl.

She thought the mention of her town sparked something in the woman despite her continuous silence.

"What's your name?" Shawn asked and knelt beside them.

"Colleen," she mumbled. "My name is Colleen."

"Do you live here?"

She shook her head no.

"Where do you live?"

"In the town you said," she said, struggling with the words.

Josie glanced at Shawn, and for the first time since arriving in this world, she felt hopeful. "Are there any other people here beside you?"

Tears dripped from her eyes, trickled down her cheeks, and gathered on the front of her decayed blackish-yellow teeth between two withered gray lips.

"Can you take us to them?" Shawn said. He let go of her waist and eased her from the ground.

She nodded and pointed back toward the mushroom passage. "That way," she said and walked forward.

On the opposite side of the watering room, two passageways broke away from the main tunnel. Fluorescent fungus lined the walls of both.

Josie stepped in front of Colleen, impeding her movement. "What are these mushrooms for?"

"Eat them."

Stepping aside, she felt sickened and wondered what nasty creatures would eat the foul-smelling and grotesque-looking fungi.

Colleen limped through the room, ignoring both the mushrooms and the tipped-over watering can, and followed the right passageway. She led them a hundred yards along an upslope-twisting corridor to a heavy wooden door. She pointed at the door and stepped aside.

"Grab your dog and stand back," Shawn said.

As ordered, she bent forward, grabbed Sage by the collar, and inched a few steps backward.

Shawn shoved the door open and hurried inside with his pistol drawn.

Letting go of Sage, Josie eyed the room. "My god," she said and felt suddenly queasy.

Caged people stared at them with desperate eyes. They were malnourished but otherwise seemed no different than Colleen. All the women dressed in the same attire as Colleen while the men wore leather hides around their waists barely covering their private areas. A younger woman leaned against the wall of the closest cell. She wore a fearful expression that made Josie wonder if their presence spooked her. To her right, a young man knelt beside the prison gate looking through the bars with a fascinating look of disbelief on his face. Unlike the others, he seemed alert and healthy. Beyond them, an elderly woman laid on her side with a disinteresting look on her fatigued face. An odorous residue smeared both the dirty leather rags draped over her body and her tangled long blackish-gray hair. She seemed oblivious to their present situation; like a kid without a care in the world. A few feet from her, slumped against the wall, an older man with long dirty brown hair gawked at the woman with tears dripping from his wrinkled leathery cheeks. A young girl that looked in her middle to late teens peered out from the next cell. She looked oblivious to reality. Her long blonde hair was tangled and knotted up at the ends. Her blue eyes seemed somehow familiar. Curled up against the granite wall, a few feet from the girl, a young man lay with his eyes shut. He looked skeletal and seconds away from death.

She wasn't sure if he was alive or dead or somewhere in between.

An older man in his late forties watched alertly from the next prison. Hope filled his brown eyes as he attempted to get to his feet, but he fell back to the floor. After a brief struggle, he stood clutching the bars and watched Shawn's every move. Behind him, a middle-aged woman leaned against the back wall staring at the man in front of her. In the last cell, a man sat against the back wall with a strange smile on his face. In his left hand, he squeezed what looked like a dead rat. Brown streaks ran the length of his long face. He looked completely out of his mind.

The muscular man in the first prison cell wiggled his right arm through the gate and reached toward Shawn. "Help us," he said. "The wood's sturdy, but I think both of us can break it."

Without hesitating, Shawn thrust the pistol into Josie's hand. "Take this and watch the door. If any of those things try to come through it, blow their godless heads from their godless shoulders."

With reluctance, she closed her hand around the gun and sprinted toward the door. She slammed it shut, took a few steps backward, and aimed the weapon with two shaking hands at the closed door. She hated holding the gun, but if one of those monsters came through the door, she wouldn't hesitate to pull the trigger.

"Stand back," Shawn said. He stood in front of the cell, turned toward Josie with his back facing the alert man, and slammed the heel of his boot into the gate.

The wood shook and splintered.

Grimacing, he slammed his boot into the gate a second time. A wide splinter cracked along the length of the door.

"Can I help?" the man said and stepped closer to Shawn.

"Stand back," Shawn said irritably.

After a deep breath, he reared back his leg high into the air and rammed it backward, shattering the cracked wood into hundred pieces. Pushing the boards aside, he helped the man crawl through the open area.

"Thank you," the man said, extending his dirty hand toward Shawn. "The name's Alistair."

"Shawn," he said, shaking his hand. "The girl's Josie, and her dog's name is Sage. We're here to get you people back home."

"Come on, Shawn," Josie shouted. "Let's do this before those things figure out we're here."

"Can you help me?" he said and glanced at Alistair while moving toward the next prison cell.

Alistair nodded and followed Shawn's lead.

Five minutes later, the two men broke through the next four gates, freeing their occupants. Except for the skeletal man and the guy clutching the rat, the prisoners gathered in front of the door.

Shawn eyed Alistair. "What's your story? You seem pretty lively compared to them."

"I've only been here a few days," he said. "My cousin and I were on our way home from a work detail in the old mines near Willow Creek. It was getting late, and we were looking for a place to camp for the night when we stumbled across this village. It looked empty, so we figured it was as good a place as any to get a good night's sleep."

"Where's your cousin?"

"I don't know, a couple of those things took us by surprise in the middle of the night and brought me here. I haven't seen him since."

"I haven't seen any village, but we have two others with us," Shawn said. "With luck, they might have come across your cousin."

"Come on, Shawn, we need to get moving," Josie said. "We still have to find Ethan and Ryan."

He shot her a condescending glare, grabbed the weapon from her hand, and turned back to Alistair. "Can you help him," he said, pointing to the man still slumped against the wall, "I'm going to lead us out of this sickening place."

"No problem," he said and hurried to the cell. With ease, he pulled the man from the ground, gripped his waist, and led him out of the prison.

"Let's go," Shawn said and hurried through the door.

77

Curled up against the wall, Kelly stirred and moaned through a shudder.

His breathing was soft, but he was alive. After checking his pulse, Tommy hurried across the cavern, dropped to one knee, and examined the creature lying motionless with sickish green blood bubbling from a deep hole in its chest. Keeping his distance, he poked at the wound with the tip of the shotgun a half a dozen times, nodded, and then climbed to his feet.

"Now what?" Alyssa said, holding the flashlight.

Grimacing, he took three long strides backward and fired another round into the hood covering its nightmare face. After reloading, he sat the shotgun gently on the ground and limped to the wheelbarrow, pulled the front end over Andre's battered corpse, and spun it around toward Kelly Bissell.

"What are you doing?" she said.

Ignoring her, he pushed the wheelbarrow to the side of the cavern where Jennifer sat beside her husband with tears dripping down her face. She stared a second as Tommy approached and then collapsed across Kelly's chest.

"Alyssa, come here and help me get him inside."

"What are you doing?" she said again, irritated by his arrogant demeanor.

"He can't walk, and we have to get these explosives back to the portal before our friends get back."

"Shouldn't we get him to a hospital? He looks pretty bad."

"If we take him to a hospital," he said sarcastically. "Who's going to carry these explosives through this dark coal mine?"

"I will."

"And what if you run into anymore of these nightmarish freaks?" he said, letting go of the wheelbarrow and pointing at the creature. "Tell me, what would you do?"

She was appalled, but he was right. If she continued on alone and happened across more of those creatures, she wouldn't stand a fighting chance. Besides, the leftover remnants from the realistic nightmare she had about Lauren still haunted her memory. Despite her need to seek medical attention for Kelly, she had no plans on traveling through the dark passageway alone. "Then Jennifer and I can finish this."

"Do you really think she's capable of carrying him back through the mine, up the ladder, through the hotel, and to the hospital?"

She stared with judgmental eyes. Kelly needed to get to a hospital, or he would more than likely die within the hour.

"Listen, Alyssa, I'm not trying to sound coldhearted, but if they're fortunate enough to make it back from wherever they went to, then they deserve for us to have delivered this package."

"He'll die, Tommy."

"If that portal isn't destroyed, those things can keep plucking people off our streets for whatever purposes they use them for. Even if they don't make it back, we have to make sure those things can never come back through."

"He's right," Jennifer said, rubbing the tears from her eyes. "I owe it to Colleen and Jessica to make sure those things never hurt anyone else." After kissing her husband's cheek, she climbed to her feet and wiped the dust from her slacks and shirt. "We've stood by for way too long and did nothing while Gregory and those things ruined people's lives. Kelly could never live with the guilt if we abandon those kids."

Touched by Jennifer's sincerity, Alyssa decided to give up the argument. Seconds later, they had Kelly in the wheelbarrow. With a groan, he curled up in the center, breathing shallow but steady.

"Take the shotgun," Tommy said. "It's loaded and ready to use."

"No, I don't—"

"Take it! I can't push Kelly and handle the gun."

Reluctantly, she took it from his hand. The thought of shooting anything made her cringe. Even if those things were hideous creatures gated from another world.

He glanced at Jennifer with an outstretched hand. "Let me see that pistol."

Without hesitation, she handed it to him.

He slid open the chamber, examined it for a moment, and then snapped it shut. "Here, take it. There are three shots left. Try not to waste them."

She grabbed it from his open palm with surprisingly quick hands.

"Where's the other gun?" he said. "The one Kelly had."

Jennifer shrugged.

Alyssa pointed toward her ruined jacket lying on the ground three feet from the dead monster. "It's over there by that thing."

After retrieving the pistol, he checked the chamber and smiled. Obviously content, he tucked it into the back of his jeans, took hold of the handles, and pushed the wheelbarrow through the cavern.

78

Startled by sudden noise above, Ryan jumped backward, slipped on a patch of slimy mushrooms, and toppled forward onto his knees as Ethan thudded hard onto the ground two inches from his feet. Above, heavy footfalls scurried toward the opening above him. Instinctively, he tossed both rifles backward, grabbed on to Ethan's pant legs, and jerked him away from the ladder with intentions of putting as much space between them and whatever was coming at them from above. Dropping his friend's feet, he grabbed the smaller rifle from another patch of mushrooms just as black meaty toes landed on the top rung. With nervous hands, he hoisted the gun toward the ladder and waited for it to touch bottom in hopes of getting an accurate shot.

Its long black robes swooshed like a banner in gusty breeze as it descended.

He slid his finger over the trigger and waited to see the monster's face. With eyes wide with fearful excitement, he squeezed hard and felt the hard wooden rifle slam into his shoulder and grimaced as fire exploded from the barrel. Gritty dirt shook loose from the walls and ceiling as the creature shrieked with rage. Feeling suddenly confident, he squinted through the thick dusty air and watched the beast tumble from the ladder. It staggered two steps backward, regained its balance, and flung the hood away from its grotesque face with a powerful backhand. With a maddening howl, it charged him. It lashed violently at the air with a face full of fleshy, bone-breaking tentacles as it closed the gap with surprising speed. He pulled hard on the trigger and winced as long clawed fingernails emerged from the creatures sleeve and missed his face by inches. The walls shook around him as tentacles whipped through the air from its disfigured face. Shrieking and wailing, the beast reached for its face, wobbled sideways, and collapsed into the soil, showering Ethan's chest and face with dark green sludge.

Gasping hard for breath, he felt the rifle slip through his sweaty fingers and land on the ground beside his friend.

The monster flailed about the ground a few seconds and then went limp.

With a pounding heart, he dropped to his knees and shoved the weighty beast to the side of the wall and away from his friend. Feeling mildly nauseous, he crawled over to the unconscious boy, slid of his backpack, and fumbled around inside for another clip. A second later, he found what he was looking for. He jammed the clip into the chamber and placed the rifle on the ground within arm's reach in case of an emergency. Crawling to his knees, he opened the next-to-last remaining bottle of water, took a small drink, and poured half a bottle on Ethan's face.

"Wake up," he whispered, hoping not to draw anymore unwanted attention, though he was pretty sure the gunshots accomplished that.

Ethan groaned.

Ryan slapped him gently across the side of the cheek. "Come on, man, I need you to get up."

Ethan opened his eyes and sat up. With a bizarre expression, he stared with a dazed look on his face. "Dude, what the heck happened?" he said and rubbed the top of his head. "Everything's spinning."

"We need to get moving," Ryan said and jumped to his feet, "I blasted off two rounds killing that thing. Any chance we had of sneaking around in here unnoticed is probably gone by the wayside."

"Yeah," Ethan said, struggling to his feet, "help me up."

After a few minutes, he grabbed his knees and glanced down at the floor. "Dude, are those mushrooms?"

"Yep, the ugliest darn mushrooms I've ever seen."

"Great," he said and fell back on his knees. With the same perplexed grin, he felt along the moist ground.

Bewildered, Ryan watched his friend. "What exactly are you doing?"

Ethan crawled from the floor with a goofy expression on his face. "I found it," he said, holding up a diamond-shaped blue rock.

"What the crap is that thing?"

"Beats me, but that thing clobbered me with it."

Shaking his head, he opened the pack and pulled out the last four clips. After tucking one in each of his front pockets, he handed two to Ethan. After fastening the pack, he grabbed the other rifle off the ground, gave it to Ethan, and walked along the corridor as quietly as possible.

Ethan walked a few steps behind.

79

He walked with urgency through the corridor toward the area where they first encountered Colleen with the small band of misfortunates hobbling a few steps behind. Except for Alistair, the wretched-looking band of prisoners reeked of body odor and human waste and other sour smells Shawn didn't want to think about. Fortunately, as they hiked farther from the prison room, the mushroom's odor overpowered the stench of death. Glancing back, he was glad to see the wooden door at the far end of the passage growing smaller in the distance. Despite keeping a clear head, he had a feeling that room would be forever etched into his memory.

Wondering if there were any other people trapped in this underground chaos, he thought of his childhood friends. *Could any one of those men be Johnny, Zach, or Bill?* he thought and peeked back one more time. After glancing over each of their faces, he turned around and felt at a loss. *It's been too long to tell,* he thought. *The time for sorting out names is later. Right now, I need to get these people out of here.*

He hurried through the hallway, past the overturned watering can, and ducked around the corner into the narrow passage leading back to the large room with the stalactites and pool of black water. He peered back to make sure all heads were accounted for when a loud bang exploded from somewhere in the distance and vibrated the dust off the walls. He stopped immediately and stood quietly, glancing between Josie and Alistair. "That sounded like gunfire. Did you guys hear—"

Another boom exploded in the distance.

Stepping between Josie and Alistair, he kept his back to the prisoners. "Unless someone else is gallivanting around in these catacombs, which I'm pretty sure isn't the case, I know who is firing those guns."

Josie's eyes widened.

"Josie, keep going," he whispered. "I think our boys may be in need of some rescuing."

She stared at him with pleading eyes.

He grabbed her shoulder. "Get these people through this passageway, and then haul butt back where we split up earlier, I'll get Ethan and Ryan, and we'll meet you back there."

"Shawn, don't let anything happen to him."

"Trust me, I won't." He spun backward and looked at Colleen. "What's down the other tunnel?"

With terror-filled eyes, she stared but said nothing.

Her expression made him nervous. Either she didn't know or was too frightened to tell him the truth. With time wasting, he bit his lower lip in an attempt to ease his irritation with her. "Colleen," he said patiently. "I need to know what's down that other passageway."

"That's where they take the children," one of the men said. "They feed on the children."

Suddenly, he felt disgust rumble through his stomach. The thought of children being slaughtered fueled an inner rage deep inside. Fighting emotion, he thought of all the years he did nothing to help these people and felt a sudden need to fall on the ground and beg for forgiveness. He fought the urge and turned toward the other passageway.

"Be careful, Josie, I'll meet you where we split up earlier."

Without hesitation, he spun around, sprinted through the mushroom-lined corridor, and followed the other passage, expecting to see evil around each and every corner. Though anger complicated his mind, he owed it to everyone that those creatures ever brought here to stay focused, especially the three boys he watched them attack in the woods twenty-five years earlier.

80

Josie struggled with her current predicament. She felt a need to chase after Shawn and help rescue Ethan and Ryan, but leaving these people alone meant being recaptured by the monsters—or worse. She took a deep breath and looked over the faces of the freed prisoners and felt compassion as they looked helpless and afraid.

She stared at Alistair. "Can you help me get them out of here?"

"What do you want me to do?"

"Keep in the rear and make sure everyone follows me," she said and started along the passage. "Let's get these people out of this place."

Sage trotted beside her.

Keeping a slow and steady pace, she pondered Ethan's lifelong dilemma.

With luck, one of those younger girls will be Lauren.

81

Ryan nudged the door with the barrel of the rifle, hoping to ease it open with as little noise as possible. After a few agonizing inches, the faint squeak of the creaking door left him feeling paranoid. *Dang it, man, you're gonna give us away.* Envisioning a flesh-eating creature galloping across the room toward the jarred door with teeth chomping at the air, he changed his mind and kicked it with force against the inside wall.

Dirt drizzled from the wall above the door.

As he stepped inside, a strong stench of death overpowered him. The rifle slipped through his fingers and thudded against moist black soil. He thought the mushrooms in the hallway smelled sweeter than freshly cut roses compared to the stink lingering in this room. Reaching down, he grabbed the rifle from the dirt and noticed a circular stone well in the center of the room.

Ethan stood beside him with an outstretched hand. "Holy crap, dude, what happened in here?"

Ignoring Ethan's words, he tiptoed toward the well, swatting hundreds of buzzing flies from his face. His eyes were wide with horror, and his stomach grumbled with disgust. Partially devoured corpses lay scattered among hundreds of slimy mushrooms throughout the back of the large room. Pieces of broken bones lay strewn about gooey crimson sludge covered in thousands of squirming worms. Rats the size of fat alley cats gorged on both decomposed flesh and fly larva, adding to the horrific smell. Beyond the grotesque scene, a large bloodstained door towered between two empty man-sized prison cells built into the back wall. A few feet away on the right wall, a second door looked like the less dangerous option.

Strength dripped from his legs, and he felt nauseated.

Dropping to his knees, he took a deep breath and used the rifle as a balancing stick. His head buzzed as the room twirled clockwise and the rifle slid forward, sending him face-first into the moist soil. Images of terrified children screaming in pain as monsters gnawed upon their flesh terrorized his mind as he slipped further into oblivion.

"Dude, are you okay?"

Gnats and flies swarmed about Ryan's face, looking for any opening. His stomach churned at the thought of swallowing the flying pests as he took in another deep breath of the tainted air. He closed his eyes and tried to block out the grotesque carnage, hoping to regain enough strength to crawl back to his knees. Despite the stench clouding his wits, he reached for the rifle that lay a few inches away. As his fingers slid across the smooth stock, his eyes popped open and saw Ethan reaching for his hand.

"Come on," Ethan said, jerking him to his feet. "Let's get you back in the hallway and away from this place."

Feeling slightly better, he glanced at the rotted corpses and took a few steps backward, hoping to get out of the room long enough to regain his composure when the smaller door to his right swung open and crashed against the wall.

"Ethan," he said, pointing to the opened door, "something's coming!"

With a wild scowl, Ethan heaved the rifle toward the door and planted his foot in the loose soil. His finger trembled against the trigger, but he trusted his friend's ability.

Unexpectedly, Shawn broke through the doorway, crinkling his nose in disgust as he looked over at the carnage.

"Jesus, dude, I could have shot you!"

"What happened in here?"

"I think it's obvious," Ethan said and lowered his weapon. "We need to get out of here right now. Those things feast on our flesh, and we're smack in the middle of their grotesque buffet."

Still feeling slightly nauseous, Ryan staggered toward Shawn. Though his head cleared a little, he needed to get away from the slaughter to regain his strength.

"We heard shots," Shawn said. "I figured it was the two of you."

With his free hand, Ethan reached forward and wrapped his arm around Ryan's waist, helping him toward where Shawn stood in the doorway. "Ryan killed another one of those things a few minutes earlier back through that hallway," he said, struggling with the weight. "Just when I thought we were even, he saved my sorry behind again."

"Awesome, Ryan, but we best be getting out of here right now."

In agreement, he grabbed hold of the door and balanced between Shawn and Ethan. "Where's Josie?" he said, having a difficult time catching his breath due to the stench. The mixture of decomposed flesh and foul mushrooms proved too much to endure.

"She's leading some people we found back to that room with the black water."

Ethan's eyes widened. "Was there a girl?"

Shawn smiled. "Yeah, there is a girl," he said and lowered his pistol. Looking woozy, he grabbed the rifle dangling in Ethan's trembling hand. "I can't say for sure, but it's possible that she may be your sister."

Despite the look of disgust on his face, he smiled.

Ryan thought his friend looked like a death row inmate who received word of a pardon seconds before being executed. Though happiness for Ethan filled his heart, he wanted to get as far away from this place as he possibly could. Spending another second enduring the gut-wrenching stench, and he would lose all sanity. "Can we please go?"

"Absolutely."

Giving Shawn a pleading glance, Ryan heard a loud squeal behind him. He spun around and stared in horror as the door crashed against the far wall. Two hulking nightmares scurried through the opening and raced toward them. Naked leathery black skin shimmered against fluorescent mushroom light, revealing sharp teeth dripping with black saliva. Two sets of crimson eyes stared with hatred as the beasts hurdled carcasses lying on the ground and continued forward.

Shawn looked in shock as he raised his pistol toward the rushing monsters. "Run!" he shouted as a loud crack boomed through the room.

The creature on his left clutched its neck, staggered forward, but managed to stay balanced. With blood painting its fingers green, it growled and snapped its tentacles at the air like four leather whips. With evil intent, it lowered its squid-like face and leapt high into the air with a mind-numbing shriek.

Forgetting his nausea, Ryan steadied his weapon, squeezed, and stared in awe as a deep gash opened across its throat. For an eternal second, it continued toward him with vigorous force and then toppled face-first into a patch of green and red mushrooms. Luminous glitter sparkled through fluorescent light like rainbow mist shimmering under early morning sunshine. Instinctively, his hand disappeared into his pocket, seeking another shell.

"Die," Ethan screamed as more gunfire shook the spacious room.

He stepped forward and nearly lost his balance. Glancing up, he saw blood spraying from an obliterated eye. A green shell case skipped across the ground under Ethan's feet and spun across the room. Seconds before his fingers slithered across the shells in his pocket, another gunshot boomed beside him. Fortunately, the buzzing in his ears drowned out the noise. Speedy tentacles missed his face by inches and then went limp. Ethan shoved him aside as its lifeless body crashed against the wall.

Shawn pointed across the room.

In the doorway, a creature tripped over a piece of bone, caught its balance, and rushed at them. Two more followed behind it. Like the first two, all three wore nothing but black skin and evil eyes of crimson death.

"Let's go!" Shawn screamed.

"Go," Ethan shouted and pushed him through the doorway. "Follow Shawn to the others. I'm gonna lead them away." He slammed the door, leaving Ryan standing on the other side of a closed door and inside another tunnel.

"Ethan, you dumb idiot!" he screamed and chased Shawn through the mushroom-contaminated passageway.

There was no time to argue.

82

Kelly's breathing remained shallow but steady. Alyssa thought he would be all right for a while, but hated the idea of pushing him deeper into the underground passage. She wasn't sure of the severity of his wounds, but Tommy was right. If they didn't deliver the explosives, those things could continue their reign of terror. *I don't want Kelly to die,* she thought. *But how can I live with myself knowing we could destroy their pathway into this world but failed because I argued to save one man's life?* On the verge of tears, she walked beside Tommy and kept a close eye on Kelly.

Up ahead, Jennifer hobbled through the mine, shining the light into the darkness. Her gun hand trembled as soft weeping escaped her lips.

Mentally and physically exhausted, she struggled to keep pace. Though little time passed, it seemed like hours since the altercation. Muscle-wrenching cramps constricted her calves and burning blisters rubbed through the sock into her worn boots. A nagging headache pounded the back of her head as hunger pains twisted deep inside her belly. Tasting the gritty dust lodged in her teeth, she closed her eyes and thought about the peanut butter sandwich she ate hours ago.

Her stomach grumbled.

Hobbling through the dim passage, frustration weighed on her mind. Around each corner, she expected to see the large portal room. Each time, her heart sank into her stomach as the portal room remained out of sight.

Lagging behind, she watched as Tommy struggled through the tunnel.

Pushing that bulky contraption is your problem now, she thought. A faint grimace crossed her lips. *I wished Kelly never brought that stupid thing down here.*

83

Ryan's distressing words played through Ethan's mind over and over again as he slammed the heavy door. *You dumb idiot,* he thought and considered falling to floor and curling up in a ball as six hulking creatures broke through the door and galloped across the room toward him. Shaking like a crooked tree in a windstorm, he gripped the gun tight in his hand, sprinted along the wall, and ducked through the doorway into the corridor, pausing only to yank the door shut with every ounce of strength he could muster.

With an eye on the door, he hurried to the ladder and prayed the door would remain shut a few more seconds. His heart pounded as the ladder came into sight near the luminous mushrooms. He wanted those things to follow him and allow Ryan and Shawn a few extra minutes to get to Josie.

Using the bloody corpse of the monster Ryan slaughtered as a step stool, he leaped onto the wooden rung and scrambled up the crude ladder to the large room above. Out of breath, he stood at the top and pointed the barrel at the opening.

Three, dude, he thought. *You got three shots left.*

Wide-eyed and nervous, he hunched above the opening awaiting the slightest bit of movement as a terrifying thought entered his mind. Though his heart begged for a quick peek at the door he and Ryan walked through earlier, his eyes remained focused on the hole in the floor. *What If more of those things come through the main door?* he thought. *Then my not-so-carefully thought-out plan would be shot to crap.* He felt his heart drop an inch inside his chest. *Screw it*, he thought and glanced at the entrance. Relieved nothing busted through the open door, his eyes refocused on the glowing lights below.

Seconds passed, and nothing reached for the ladder.

What if they chased after Ryan and Shawn?

Normally, avoidance would be a pleasant conclusion to an unbelievable situation, but for the first time in his life, he wanted to be pursued. The survival of his friends depended on whether or not those things chased after him.

Breathing heavy, he concentrated on the wooden rungs.

Chill, dude, he thought. *If nothing comes in the next few seconds, you can beat feet back to that other building and try to cut them off.*

From below, heavy footfalls squished in the earth.

Panic caused his fingers to tremble, but he took a deep breath and steadied the rifle.

Clawed fingers grabbed the wooden ladder as a large knobby head filled his vision. It climbed fast, shrieked with rage, and lunged for his feet with a wide-open mouth. Feeling for the trigger, he leaped into the air as tentacles splintered the wood where his feet stood a split second earlier. Stepping back, he watched as a long black tongue slid from the center of a rounded deathtrap and wiggled across his leg. Sour breath filtered into his nostrils as his finger pulled back on the trigger. Black flesh exploded, spraying liquid brains across the bottom of his already-stained pant legs. Limp tentacles banged of the dusty wood and disappeared into the tunnel below with a hollow clank. Fear drained from his heart as adrenaline coursed through his bones.

Two shots left, he thought, anticipating more action.

After a few seconds of silence, a second set of feet stood near the ladder. With patience, he waited as a second creature grasped the rungs and hurried toward him. With a smile still on his face, he fired. It screamed as a devastating bullet shattered the top of its skull. Blood oozed from a headless neck and sprayed like a fountain, painting his hair a dark green. Twitching like a beheaded chicken, its body fell to the bottom of the ladder and convulsed across the feet of the monster he killed a few seconds ago.

"Come get some," he shouted, wiping the rancid slime from the corner of his mouth. "Come on, you sister-stealing freaks of nature, I got plenty more where that came from!" Comforted by the two clips in the front pocket of his jeans, he stood over the opening, ready to shoot anything that moved.

With confidence, he stood five minutes with the barrel aimed at the tunnel below. Nothing but luminous light filled his vision.

"I don't blame you," he said, feeling like a superhero from a comic book." I'd stay clear of me too." He dropped to his knees, slid the piece of wood over the opening, and sprinted across the floor to the open door. Without glancing back, he stepped into the moonlit night, sprinted across the knee-high grass, and hurried into the building with the devoured man shackled to the wall. Afraid of breaking his spirits, he climbed through the hole and descended the ladder without the slightest peek at the carnage.

Swallowing the bitter taste in his mouth, he raced through the passageway and into the room where the vacuous man knelt on the dirty floor. Brown sludge oozed between his fingers as he chomped on what Ethan hoped was still jerky. The wolf beast laid on the dirty ground, gazing at the ceiling with cold, lifeless eyes. The wolf man's yellow globes of evil were as intimating dead as they were alive.

"Sorry, old timer," he said as he dashed around the dead creature. "Someone's gonna have to come back for you later on."

He glanced back one last time and hurried through the shadowy corridor. Ryan was right. They couldn't leave him in that prison cell to be eaten by the monsters, but at the moment, he had no choice but to leave him.

84

Guided by fluorescent lighting, Ryan chased Shawn through the passageway. His vertigo dwindled to lightheadedness as they ran through wider corridors infested with more of the mushrooms. His thoughts were on Ethan as the high-pitched shrieks grew louder in the distance. Though nightmarish creatures chased after them, he suspected Ethan had his hands full as well. Thanks to his friend's heroics or stupidity—depending on how things turn out—Ryan scrambled through the passage certain they had a sizable head start.

In front of him, Shawn dashed through the wide passageway and ducked into a narrow shadow-filled corridor.

Hindered by the bulky rifle, he lowered gun to his side, pinched the cool steel barrel in his clammy hand, and sprinted blindly through the tunnel. Hoping not to trip on anything lying about the tight passage, he squinted through impenetrable blackness and concentrated on staying balanced.

High tension amplified his heartbeat.

In the distance, darkness blanketed Shawn like a heavy fog.

Terrified of crashing head-first into a hard granite wall, he slowed his pace. Suddenly, he was more afraid of stumbling into the side of the cavern than having to battle the octopus beasts in the darkness. The thought of regaining consciousness shackled against a wall waiting to be gnawed on scared him senseless.

If things turned ugly, a bullet through the head would avoid the unimaginable anguish of being devoured alive.

Feeling for the walls, he hurried forward, doing his best not to surrender to fear. He jogged through the blackness, praying their eyes weren't capable of penetrating the ebony space. He sensed they were gaining ground but kept going without looking back.

Further along the passage, a faint light caught his eye.

He tucked his head and ran toward the light.

Enduring a cramping pain tormenting his side, he took a deep breath and saw figures standing in the distance. He closed his eyes as the pain bit deeper into his gut and vibrated down through his legs. Despite death hot on his heels, he couldn't run much farther.

"Ryan," Josie shouted. "We're over here."

Opening his eyes, he saw Josie, Shawn, Sage, and a small group of unfamiliar faces huddled together on the other side of the sooty pool with frightened expressions on their faces.

"They're coming," he shouted, "run!"

"Get them out of here, Josie," Shawn said. "Get them the heck out of here now! Hide where we hid earlier. In the willows where we saw Ethan and Ryan come out of the weeds."

Looking nervous, she stared past him. "Where is he?"

With guilt, he glanced away.

"Relax, Josie," Shawn said. "He covered our hides and went the other way. He's perfectly fine."

Handing Shawn the flashlight, she turned toward the shabbily dressed people. "Come on, let's go." With a halfhearted smile directed at him, she turned and led the group of people toward the far side of the colossal room and disappeared around a corner.

He bent over, grasping both knees, and struggled to breathe. "Shawn, I'm sorry, but I can't run anymore."

"Then we make a stand."

A tall man stepped between them. "I'm staying too."

After a disapproving look, Shawn handed him the flashlight. "Keep the light on them, Alistair," he said and aimed his pistol. "Give me a good target to shoot at."

As instructed, Alistair flicked the dim light across the cavern wall and into the tunnel.

Hunched over, trying to regain his composure, Ryan eyed the beam of light and dreaded what would soon appear. Though he saw nothing at the moment, he knew they were only seconds away. Feeling the cramp loosening around muscle, he stood up, aimed his own rifle at the lighted space and whispered the Lord's Prayer.

Beside him, Sage growled.

He trembled, knowing exactly what had the dog agitated.

He sensed no fear in the dog's boisterous growls.

Apparently, one battle with the monsters wasn't enough to whet his appetite.

Digging his heels in the dirt, he suddenly felt a smidgen of confidence knowing the German shepherd would be fighting beside them. The feeling faded as a bulky shadow stepped into the weakening beam, rushed straight at him, and leaped high in the air, disappearing from the light's comforting glow. He pulled the trigger, missed by a mile, and staggered backward, avoiding a lightning quick backhand meant for his face by mere inches. Disoriented, he whirled around, steadied his tumbling frame with an outstretched hand, and howled in agony as jagged nails poked through his sweat-soaked shirt and gouged his chest. Hot blood trickled down his stomach and dripped down the front of his jeans.

Gunshots exploded through the cavern.

Seconds later, Shawn shouted victoriously as a monster tumbled into the dirt.

From the darkness, a second monster jumped into the beam, shrieked inhumanly, sank a mouthful of fangs into Shawn's neck and wrapped its tentacles around his head as if trying to squeeze the life out of him. Kicking wildly, he fell backward and landed hard on his back with the beast landing on his chest. Bright light flashed through the dark space, followed by a deafening boom.

A creature stumbled a few feet from him, fell face–first, and thrashed violently on the ground.

"God, that hurts," Shawn said and crawled to his knees. Somehow he managed to hold on to the pistol. Blood seeped from a dozen gashes in his neck and disappeared under a stained collar.

In shock, Ryan stood over the injured monster, squeezed, and blew a hole between its two crimson eyes, splattering blood and chunks of brain over the top of his favorite pair of hiking boots.

"Look out," Alistair shouted, pointing into the cavern.

Whirling sideways, he aimed the rifle as another monster rushed from the darkness and leaped at him. With little time to react, he held the rifle in front of his face in an attempt to block its razor-sharp claws. Avoiding a disfiguring blow to the head, he shoved the weapon forward and stopped a second dexterous swipe. Sidestepping, he felt the wind from its claws whoosh across his throat and then swung the weapon in an attempt to disconnect its head from its shoulders.

With agility, the beast ducked under the blow and tackled him. The rifle spiraled through the darkness.

Doing his best to block the slapdash swings intended for his face, Ryan knew it was only a matter of time before it wore him down. The creature's weight was too heavy to slide out from underneath. Praying for a miracle, he swatted wildly, trying to knock it off his chest as enraged barking filled his buzzing ears.

Sage hung from its back and sunk his teeth into black flesh. Through muffled growls, he clenched down and jerked backward, attempting to pull the irate beast from him.

Shining light on the brutal battle, Alistair planted his bare foot across its face, knocking it off-balance.

Climbing to his knees, Ryan crawled through the dark and groped for the rifle. His heart raced as his fingers slid across the smooth wood. Without hesitating, he swung the barrel at the monster but was afraid to fire. Sage dangled on the back of its neck, holding on by a mouthful of teeth. Following the motion, he hoped to get a clear shot, but hitting Sage seemed too great a possibility to chance.

"Look out," Alistair screamed, trying to hold the light steady, "here comes another one."

Glancing to the right, he saw another monster draped in black robes zigzagging toward him.

With no time to react, he took a deep breath and hoped lady luck had his back. It lunged through the air and crashed into his chest, knocking breath from his burning lungs and feeling from his body. Gasping for air, he watched in horror and felt the sting of its lightning quick tentacles slash through his arm.

Clutching his wound, he cringed as the rifle fell from his grasp.

He watched in strange admiration as the tentacles slithered like four angry snakes around a lamprey-like mouth. With an inhuman hiss, its jagged fangs lunged for his throat. Unable to free his arms, he closed his eyes and waited for the last ounce of pain he would ever feel. He pictured Molly's face and wondered if they would be reunited. As he felt something slimy slither across his throat, a thunderous bang exploded through his already ringing ears. Wet warmth splattered across his face and filled his mouth as the beast thudded onto the soil beside him.

He crawled out from underneath, feeling more confused than ever.

Beside him, Shawn knelt on one knee, clutching his pistol with a severely trembling right hand. He smiled and then dropped the weapon and fell face-first into the ground, clutching his neck. Dark red blood soaked through his shirt.

Rising to his feet, Ryan spotted the rifle a few inches to his right half-buried in the black earth. As the sounds of Sage growling mixed with the horrifying screeching wails of the creature's cries echoed through the darkness, his hand found the cool steel. Turning toward the chaotic sounds of the violent struggle, he aimed the barrel at the beast, hoping for a clear shot.

Holding on by his teeth, Sage swung from the creature's neck.

With a discordant screech, it slid a hand under the dog's collar and flung him through the cavern. Hissing a maddening screech, it whirled around with graceful agility and glared into Ryan's eyes.

From the darkness, Sage yelped twice and then fell silent.

Feeling confident, he stepped forward and squeezed the trigger, intending to dismember the beast's repugnant head from its soon-to-be lifeless body. His jaw dropped as a hollow click vibrated his through his ears. He stood frozen and in disbelief. The trigger didn't budge under the weight of his finger. The impact of it crashing against the ground rendered the rifle temporarily useless.

With hate-filled eyes, the beast charged.

Out of options, he squeezed harder and sighed in disappointment as the trigger remained jammed. Seconds later, a powerful backhand to the cheek knocked his balance astray. Staggering backward, his legs tangled together. He reached out for the monster's arm to keep from hitting the dirt but missed the target by a mile. He fell headfirst onto the gritty ground. Disoriented and out of breath, he covered his face and silently cursed lady luck.

"Die," shouted a voice from above.

Thunder rumbled inside his head as monster blood sprayed through his mouth. Thick blood tasted strong in the back of his dry and sore throat as the beast's weight shifted to his right and collapsed onto the ground.

"Come on, dude," Ethan said with a mischievous grin on his face. "You're always lying around on your back when I need you the most."

Despite feeling like death warmed over, Ryan laughed and took his friend's hand. "Where have you been?" he said and crawled from the dirt.

"I lured them back toward that village we found and killed two more in the room where I spilled the water."

"God, I'm glad you're all right," Ryan said and embraced his friend. "But I think Shawn's hurt pretty bad. We need to get him out of here right now."

Breaking the bear hug, he hurried to Shawn.

Alistair stood beside him with a bleak expression on his face.

Shawn lay curled in a ball, clutching his neck and in obvious pain. Blood dripped between his fingers as the color drained from his skin. His pistol rested on the ground a few feet from his outstretched hand.

Ryan took a knee beside him. "Shawn, can you hear me?"

"Stand back," Alistair said, handing the light to Ryan, "I need a clean rag or a piece of a shirt or something."

He took the light and stepped backward with a feeling of helplessness.

Ethan stripped off his bloodstained jacket, flung it into the darkness, pulled a dark blue sweatshirt over his head, and handed it to Alistair. "I think it should be clean enough."

"It'll work," Alistair said and took it from Ethan's hand.

He tore a piece from the bottom and wrapped it around Shawn's neck. Shawn winced in pain as the man lifted his head and finished the crude dressing. "Hopefully," he said as he tied the knot. "That'll slow the bleeding enough until we can get him help."

"Can you walk?" asked Ethan.

Shawn stared but remained silent.

Ethan glanced at him. "Maybe we should try and carry him out of here."

Unsure of what to do, Ryan shrugged.

"We don't have a choice," Alistair said, already sliding his hand under Shawn's shoulder. "We can't just leave him here for those things to finish him off."

Dropping his rifle, Ethan helped Alistair get Shawn to his feet. After a brief hesitation, they carried him through the dark passageway. Painful moans escaped his mouth, but otherwise, he stayed silent. After a few feet, his eyes squinted shut, and he slipped out of consciousness.

"Dude," Ethan shouted. "Grab the guns off the floor."

Eying the pistol a few feet from where Shawn laid bleeding on the ground a few seconds earlier, Ryan picked it up, engaged the safety, and tucked it into the front of his jeans. Switching his unloaded rifle from his left to right hand, he reached for the Remington Ethan dropped a few seconds earlier. After shining the light one last time throughout the cavern, he shouted. "Where is Sage?"

"One of those things carried him off," Alistair's said. His voice echoed through the cavern.

With anger boiling his blood, Ryan hurried after them.

85

Gregory opened his eyes.

Except for minor aches and pain, he felt invigorated. Like a child in the thralls of youth, he leaped to his feet and treaded through the heavy mist. He stopped inches from the gate and peered back across his shoulder. Feeling discouraged, he had trouble believing such a short walk could take so long.

You were an inch from death's door.

Tired of being stuck between worlds, he walked through the gate.

Sometime later, as he lumbered along the path toward Cornelius's lair, exhaustion fatigued both his body and mind. He walked several more yards along the moonlit path and then stumbled into the woods. Feeling disoriented, he collapsed on a patch of soft grass.

Once again, sleep found him.

86

Praying no more of the creatures would emerge from the overgrowth, Josie led the survivors across the grass toward the willows where she hid with Shawn earlier. A large moon hung high above the hillside, casting faint silhouettes of shimmering trees across the otherwise deserted landscape. Her apprehension dwindled upon approaching the clearing that served as her sanctuary a few hours earlier.

For the first time since meeting Ethan, optimism filled her heart.

She suspected it had been ages since any one of these people felt hope or set foot outside the morbid catacombs. Fortunately for them, Ethan never abandoned his pursuit of rescuing his sister. It was his determination that guided them toward these people who desperately needed rescued.

How many others have those things killed over the years?

Looking back, she stared at each and every broken soul gathered around her and wondered if Lauren was amongst them. With a heavy heart, she looked away, unable to gaze upon their faces a second longer. She dropped to one knee, squinted through the shadowy field, longing to be reunited with Ethan and others.

Sometime later, three figures emerged from the darkness and hurried across the field with soft silver moonlight guiding the way. As they approached, her heart pounded. Ethan and Alistair carried Shawn across the grass. Ryan hobbled a few feet behind, burdened with a rifle in each hand and a flashlight dangling from his fingers.

Though relieved to see her friends, she scrutinized the high grass with skepticism and felt suddenly sick to her stomach.

Sage was nowhere to be seen.

87

Christopher lay dead on the floor.

Tommy pushed the wheelbarrow another ten yards into the portal room, slid his hands under Kelly's back and eased him flat on the black earth a few feet from the magical water. Pulling the pistol from his jeans, he bent over and glanced around the room.

With exhausted bones, Alyssa sat the shotgun on the ground and flopped down beside it. She had no desire to talk to anyone. Her head felt like mush, and her body felt like it recently survived a head on crash with a diesel truck. She watched as Tommy caught his breath, grabbed the black box from the wheelbarrow and carried it toward the portal.

Wiping tears from her reddened eyes, Jennifer sat a few inches from Kelly with her head in his lap. More tears streaked her dirt-stained cheeks as she stroked her husband's ruffled hair.

She felt bad for both the older woman and her nearly dead husband. Unfortunately, there was nothing anyone could for him but wait and hope the others would return soon.

After sitting the box on the bank beside the portal, Tommy hobbled to the wall and took a seat a few feet from her. Still breathing heavy, he leaned against the wall and shut his eyes.

Her heart ached for Kelly.

88

From behind a huge willow tree, Josie jumped out of the darkness and waved her arms above her head.

Startled, Ethan's grip slipped from underneath Shawn's shoulders. With surprising speed, he caught the top of Shawn's collar and squeezed with all his strength and felt a thousand prickly needles explode through his fingertips. He gritted his teeth feeling thankful to have avoided an embarrassing situation and hurried toward his girlfriend.

Her baffled glare struck fear into his already-troubled heart.

She pointed to a patch of grass behind a tall tree. "Sit him down over here," she said with her eyes focusing on the injured man.

After sitting Shawn on to the soft grass, Ethan stepped backward, bent over, and grasped his wobbly knees and noticed the blue rag soaked with blood. *He's lost way too much blood,* he thought. *Getting him back through the portal before he bleeds to death is going to be a serious challenge.* He closed his eyes and prayed for Shawn's soul. *If he dies, I'm partially responsible.*

To his right, a hollow clicking sound caught his attention.

Ryan loaded his weapon and stared at Josie with a look that made Ethan nervous. The flashlight rested in the grass beside his feet as his fingers dislodged the safety.

"What are you doing?" he whispered, feeling the beginnings of a sore throat.

"I'm going back in there."

A few days ago, Ryan looked like a young man eager to find his place in the world. Now, his friend's aged appearance made him wonder just how different time was here. Though they've only been wandering around this strange new world no more than four or five hours, he thought it felt like a few weeks.

It's been a long couple of days.

In silence, he watched Ryan reload the other weapon and then pull Shawn's pistol from the front of his jeans. He opened the chamber, glanced over its contents, and snapped it shut. "There are four shots left in the chamber," he said and extended his arm toward Ethan. "You might need this to get these people back home."

The look in Ryan's eyes troubled him.

He slid the backpack over his shoulder and tossed it below his feet. Covered in blood and guts from the strange creatures, he looked determined. "Here, man, you might need this too," he said and sat the long barreled rifle on the grass a few inches from Ethan's feet.

"I don't want it."

"Take it!"

"What about you?"

He grinned confidently. "I only need this one," he said, raising the smaller rifle a few inches into the night sky. "And besides, after you hand me those clips in your front pockets, I'll have twelve shots left."

"What in the world are you going back in there for?"

Ryan glanced past him and looked toward the clearing under the willow trees. The confident look melted from his face.

Afraid to turn and look, he heard painful wheezing from behind. Ryan's blank expression painted a clear picture of the horrific scene. Even though Shawn deserved his attention, he couldn't turn and face his guilt. He closed his eyes and listened as Shawn took his final breath.

For a few seconds, he stood in silence and felt overwhelmed.

With reluctance, he turned and watched Alistair close Shawn's lifeless eyes with the tips of his fingers. Though guilt filled his soul, deep down he knew Shawn came to this world out of free will.

Tears dripped down his face as he watched the expression on Josie's face.

Though he barely knew Shawn Preston, he treasured what few hours they spent together. Ethan planned to never forget Shawn Preston and the courage he demonstrated on their unbelievable journey.

As the moon hung high in the sky, he dropped to his knees and prayed for forgiveness. Despite Shawn's longtime involvement in their town's best kept secret, he felt partially responsible.

After all, it was you that got the ball rolling.

A gentle hand brushed through his hair.

He glanced up and saw Josie standing beside him with tears dripping down the side of her face. Her long red hair blew gently in the warm air. Sadness filled her eyes and, Ethan guessed, her soul as well. The compassion that poured from her eased the guilt from his heart. Although Shawn's death would weigh him down like a wrought iron anchor digging the ocean floor, he climbed to his feet and gazed deep into her tantalizing eyes.

Her mouth pressed to his lips.

Brackish tears tickled his tongue.

For the moment, he forgot about Shawn lying dead on a patch of blood-soaked grass. He forgot about Ryan and his crazy suicide mission of trudging back into the mouth of the beast. He forgot about the stranger who fought to keep Shawn from slipping into death's eternal embrace. He forgot about the group of people gathered on the grassy field. He forgot about everything except the love he felt for Josie McShay.

After what felt like an eternity, she pulled gently away and ended the passionate kiss he wished could have lasted forever.

Physical pain and mental anguish rushed back into his head like a high-speed locomotive screeching along miles of cold steel rail. Opening his itchy eyes, he watched Josie wiping tears from her own eyes. Inches away, Alistair stood over Shawn's lifeless body and stared at the starless sky. Ryan stood above Shawn with his head hung in silent prayer.

He wondered about God.

Just maybe, he thought. *Different worlds can be gazed upon from the same heaven, and if Shawn's soul floated away from this dark earth toward that heaven, he could steal one last look at the odd lot of people left behind.*

Taking Josie's hand, he turned toward Ryan.

"You never answered my question," he said and rested his palm on Ryan's shoulder. "Why are you going back?"

"Two reasons," he said. "I told that man in the cell that we'd be back for him. I made a promise, and I intend to keep it."

He felt at a loss for words.

Ryan reached up and removed his hand from his shoulder. "Take the other rifle and get these people back home before it's too late. They've endured more than enough hardship in this place."

He shook his head.

"Josie," Ryan said, staring past him.

Wiping her tears on her sleeve, she took a step closer.

"I need you to help Ethan get these people home. Can you do that?"

She nodded.

"I'm going to find Sage."

Her eyes widened, "Is he alive?"

"I don't know, but if he is, I'll find him."

"Thank you," she said and wrapped her arms around his back. "You're an exceptional man, Ryan Laville. It's an honor to have you as my friend."

Returning her embrace, he kissed her forehead. After a few seconds, he slipped from her arms and smiled at Ethan. "This isn't good-bye," he said and started back through the meadow.

"Dude, hold up a second."

Ryan stopped, turned around and gave him a less-than-genuine smile.

He closed his eyes and embraced the tears staining his cheeks. "I'll wait for you at the portal."

"Don't wait too long. If I don't come back, blow it."

"No way, you'll make it back."

"I need to know I can trust you to destroy it."

At a loss for words, he stared at Ryan.

"Can I trust you?"

"Just do your thing and get back."

"Will do," he said. "I'll see you soon."

Josie handed him the flashlight. "You might need this."

"Thanks, Josie."

Alistair stood beside them. "I heard you mention a village earlier. I need to know how to get to it."

"I'll take you," Ryan said, "I'm heading in that direction anyway, but we need to get going."

"I appreciate it."

"I'll see you guys in a bit," Ryan said and led Alistair through the grass toward the cave.

Watching the two men disappear into the darkness, he pondered Ryan's question.

Hopefully, it's a decision I'll never have to make.

Minutes later, he walked hand in hand with Josie back to the clearing under the willow trees.

A blonde-haired girl stared across the moonlit field with a vacant look in her haunted blue eyes. Without a doubt, it was Lauren. In awe, he stared at his long-lost sister with a hundred different emotions pumping into his beating heart. She looked barely older than the last time he saw her, despite disappearing from the face of the earth nine years earlier.

Suddenly, he felt guilty all over again.

"Lauren," he said, still teary-eyed from his good-bye with Ryan. "I don't know if you can hear me, but I'm gonna get you out of this place."

She continued to gaze into the distance, seeming oblivious to his words.

Feeling guilty, he glanced away.

Seriously, dude, did you think she'd jump up and down and be excited to see you?

For nine years, she had been a prisoner at the hands of those monsters, enduring horrible acts he couldn't even imagine. Of course she would be in a state of shock. At the moment, none of that mattered. His concern was getting her and the others back through the portal without running into any more monsters.

"Help me get these people to their feet."

Josie nodded and then approached the prisoners.

Ten minutes later, they walked through the grassy field toward the maze of vegetation.

89

Ryan led the way into the cave with Alistair a few steps behind carrying the flashlight. Guided by the dim beam, they walked cautiously through the downsloping corridor until arriving back where the fatal battle with the monsters occurred.

He stopped and searched the area.

Sage was nowhere to be seen.

"Let's keep moving," he said, feeling disappointed. "The man I told you about isn't far from here."

Keeping to the edge, he led them past the scummy pool to the far end of the room where two narrow corridors came into view. He stayed left, following the shadowy passage to the room where the wolf beast laid dead on the floor. The ragged-looking man was leaning against the wall, clutching an empty bottle of water in his frail hands.

"I know that guy."

"Is he your cousin?"

"Nope, but those things took him from the prison room a few days ago."

"Let's get him out of here," he said and pointed at the far end of the room. "The ladder to the village is around the corner."

"No problem, I can carry him if you can handle the light."

Pleased by his offer, Ryan reached out with his free hand, took the flashlight, and shined it on the old man as Alistair opened the gate and hurried inside.

With a grunt, he hefted the man off the ground and flung him across his shoulder like a sack of grain. Despite being held prisoner for almost a week, he was strong. His take-charge demeanor and upbeat spirit impressed Ryan, considering all the man has suffered through recently.

A few minutes later he climbed the wooden rung through the open hatch and set the rifle on the ground beside him. With a hefty shove from beneath, he grabbed the man under his frail arms and yanked him into the room. Alistair climbed the ladder and crinkled his nose as a horrified expression appeared on his face.

"Yeah," he said. "I should have warned you about this place."

The old man sat on the floor. "Eat up you up," he said over and over.

Ignoring him, he glanced at Alistair and pointed at the devoured man. "Is he your cousin?"

With horrified eyes, Alistair cringed and shook his head. "I don't know who that poor guy is."

"Good deal. Now let's get out of here. I can't take the smell anymore."

Alistair picked the rambling man from the floor and tossed him back over his shoulder.

"Follow me," he said and hurried through the open door. With Alistair lumbering a few steps behind, Ryan stopped at the edge of the grass in front of the large building to catch his breath.

"What is this place?" Alistair asked while easing the old man to the ground.

"I was kind of hoping you could tell me."

"All I know is my cousin and I came by here about a week ago. It seemed like a good place to catch a few winks before finishing the journey back home."

"How far away do you live?"

"My village is about half a day's travel along the road out there," he said and pointed through the blackness past the small huts.

"Can you get him there?"

"Yeah, I guess I can if I take it slow."

"Maybe you should go. You have a tough trip ahead of you."

"What about you?"

"Earlier, Ethan and I found this room similar to what you just saw back there, except a lot worse. I think a lot of pain and death occurred in that room."

A look of disgust twisted Alistair's face. "I was only down there a few days," he said. "A few of the other prisoners were talking about those things feeding on their children. Unbelievable, but that's why they always kept a man in with a woman."

"Are you telling me they breed those people for food?"

"I think that's exactly what they're doing."

"On my god," Ryan said and glanced at the door to the building. "I'm going back down there and finding Josie's dog. If any of those freaks of nature are still alive, I'm gonna end their miserable existence."

"I'm coming with you."

"No way, man, you need to get him back to your village."

Alistair's eyes widened. "I haven't found my cousin. How can I live with myself if he's alive somewhere down there and I don't even attempt to rescue him?"

Ryan handed him the flashlight. "If anything happens to me, get out of there as fast as you can. There's no sense in both of us dying."

Taking the light, Alistair nodded.

"Drag him inside one of the smaller huts for now, and you can get him afterward." Ryan laid the rifle on the ground near the building and helped with the old man. A few minutes later, they entered the open door and stood above the hidden entrance. Monster guts stained the floor around the area. As Alistair shined the light on the passage, they immediately saw the slaughter at the bottom.

90

Tommy appeared calm despite Alyssa's constant nagging obviously striking a nerve. He paced a few steps back and forth across the cavern floor with the shotgun in his good hand, looking like a soldier guarding a secret outpost. The camouflage attire draping his body reinforced the previous comparison of the soldier.

"We have to do something. I don't think he's going to make it much longer," she said, trying to keep her voice low. The thought of Jennifer hearing them argue over whether or not her husband would live or die felt wrong on so many different levels.

Tommy stopped pacing and stood toe-to-toe with her. "I get it, I do," he said. "But if something goes wrong, someone needs to be here to set off the explosives."

Tommy had a legitimate point. They owed it to Ethan and the others to blast the portal into oblivion if they somehow failed, but Kelly deserved more from them too. His pulse grew weaker by the minute, and the color had drained completely from his skin. She knew beyond a doubt that if someone didn't do something very soon, he would probably be dead within the hour.

"You go, I can wait for them."

"We've discussed this, Alyssa," he shouted. "What if one of those things comes up through that puddle? What then, sweetheart? What would you do then?"

"I don't know. I guess I'd shoot it."

"No!"

Her cheeks burned with anger. How could he be so insensitive when a life was on the line? His stubbornness might ultimately be responsible for Kelly dying. She wanted to slap his face with the back of her hand in an attempt to knock some much-needed sense into his brain. Unfortunately, she didn't believe it would do any good. "No what?" she said, doing her best to stay in control. "No, I can't shoot it, or no, I can't stay?"

"Both!"

"Who says you're in charge?"

"No one," he said, appearing more irritated than before. "I'm just telling you that you're not staying down here by yourself. You honestly think I could just carry Kelly out of here and leave you here all alone to die or worse?"

"I'm not going to die."

"That's a chance I'm not willing to take."

"Ew," she said and then walked across the cavern needing to put as much space between the two of them as possible.

She glanced back and was thankful Jennifer didn't notice the commotion between her and Tommy. She took a deep breath and squeezed the pistol tight in her hand. As much as she didn't want to stay down here alone, she would if it meant getting Kelly the medical attention he so desperately needed. If only she could convince Tommy of her sincerity.

Fighting anger, she stood against the wall contemplating another round of arguing when water splashed in the puddle. A large hooded figure emerged and glared at Tommy. Before she could scream, a second figure dashed from the puddle and stood a few feet from the shoreline. Noticing Tommy with his back turned and gazing into the dark corridor, the first monster sprinted in his direction. The other creature raced toward the Bissells.

"Look out!"

With wide-open eyes, he twirled around and aimed the shotgun at the creature. Without hesitating, he squeezed the trigger. "Oh crap!" he screamed as the ammo splattered against the cavern wall to the right of his target.

Fear crinkled his face as it slapped the weapon from his hand.

She ran toward Tommy, raising the pistol, intending to shoot. Despite terror weakening her legs, she hurried across the floor in need of a better shot.

Tommy screamed.

She cringed as its head flung backward, snapping sharp bloodstained teeth at the air like a possessed bear trap. Crimson eyes of death bit into her soul. Pulling the trigger, she watched in sick fascination as a hole the size of a waterlogged baseball opened in the back of its head and covered the cavern wall behind it with blood and guts.

With an agonizing wail, the beast whirled around and sprinted at her.

With eyes squinted, she fired again and watched in sick fascination as it tumbled to the ground, skidded through loose black soil, and went limp a few inches from her backpedaling feet.

"Alyssa!" Tommy screamed through the pain and pointed at the far wall.

Behind her, Jennifer was slumped against the wall with blood trickling from the corners of her mouth. Beside her, the second creature pulled Kelly by the back of the shirt collar, dragging him across the floor toward the portal.

She fired again and watched in disappointment as dirt sprayed through the air a few feet in front of it.

With a demonic screech, it jerked Kelly closer to the portal.

Hoping she had time for one last shot, she closed her eyes and fired. A dull click echoed through her ears, followed by an energetic splash.

Dirty waves rippled across the puddle.

Dropping the gun, she ran to Tommy. Blood dripped from deep gashes carved through his neck. His red-stained fingers massaged his flesh a few inches from the bandaged bullet wound he took earlier. A look of agony contorted his face as he toppled sideways into the dirt. "Check on her," he said and struggled to roll over on his back. Clumped black earth clung to his sweat-soaked neck.

Obeying, she hurried to Jennifer. Blood flowed from a deep gash in her head. Slimy dirt gathered in the wound. No pulse beat in her pale wrist. "She's dead, Tommy, oh my god, she's dead." Tears dripped down the side of her face as her heart beat with anxiety.

Closing his eyes, Tommy lowered his head.

Climbing to her feet, she hurried toward him. "What about Kelly?" she shouted. "What are we gonna do about Kelly?"

"I don't know, I guess I'll go after him."

"You're in no shape, and you know it."

Tommy looked like a bloody mess. The idea of him going through the portal after Kelly sounded absurd. The pain alone would thwart his movement, not to mention his already-ailing shoulder. There was no choice in the matter even if he argued until his death guaranteed her victory.

"He's probably already dead."

"Maybe so, but I can't just leave him."

Despite the painful expression on his dirty face, he frowned. He said nothing, only looked at her as if she were a disobedient dog.

"Give it to me."

"Give you what?"

"The other pistol," she shouted. "The one I used to save your sorry rump is out of ammo."

He smiled and pointed across the room. "Jennifer has it."

With an aching heart, she walked across the room and stood over the dead woman. The silver pistol lay a few inches past her legs. She grabbed it and walked quickly back to Tommy and handed it to him.

"So now what?" he said, taking the gun from her hand.

She was tired of his cynical humor and the lack of respect he showed her. Because the last several hours left them both feeling tired and irritable, she decided to let it slide. She frowned. "See if it's loaded, I don't know how."

He returned her frown with a smile and checked the chamber. "Four shots left." His eyes focused on hers. "Be careful, and for the record, I'm completely against you going through there."

She grabbed the pistol from his hand. "Yeah," she said leaning forward and kissing his cheek. "I know you are."

She turned and hurried toward the puddle. The creature dragging Kelly ran in the pool of water. Disgusted by the thought, she tucked the pistol down the front of her jeans and jumped into the water.

91

Avoiding the carnage at the bottom of the ladder, Ryan led Alistair through the open door and into the slaughter room. The mushrooms lit the way as they walked past the well in the center of the room and approached the bloodstained door in the back wall. Despite the same odorous atrocities still overpowering the area, he felt much calmer than the last time he set foot in the room.

From behind, Alistair gagged on the stench.

He pointed to the bloodstained door. "They came from there," he said. "When we tore off out of here, that door was open."

Alistair steadied the light on the door. "I'll follow you."

He swatted flies from his face, shoved the door, and watched as more dust filled the air as it crashed against a dirt wall. An overpowering stench of death poured through the doorway. "Jesus," he said. "That's god-awful."

From behind, Alistair continued to gag.

Holding his breath, Ryan's stomach churned as his eyes stared in disbelief at an earthen spiral stairway leading deeper into the ground. Hundreds of glowing mushrooms lined the granite walls, lighting the narrow staircase with a soft glow. The mushrooms left him slightly nauseated, but he was thankful for their illumination. "I think we're gonna see what lies at the bottom of that well."

"I don't think I want to."

He stopped and glanced over his shoulder. "Are you good, man?" he said, afraid of turning around on the narrow steps. "If you want to go back, I'll understand."

"Let's just get this over with."

Taking a deep breath, he gagged on a mouthful of tainted air and continued on. After a lengthy descent down the narrow spiraling stairs, he stood in front of a flimsy door and pressed his ear to the wood. Hearing nothing, he pulled away and glanced at Alistair. "Are you ready?"

Alistair frowned and nodded his head reluctantly.

Taking a step back, he kicked the wood and cringed as the door flew inward and banged into the wall. Three robed monsters towered over Sage on the other side of a large room. Immersed in the cat-and-mouse game they played with the irritated dog, they took no notice to Ryan and Alistair.

Ryan sighed with determination.

For the moment, though clearly agitated, Sage seemed uninjured by his tormentors.

"Get up the stairs," he whispered. "If this doesn't go well for me, get your rear end as far away from here as possible." Feeling aggravated by the scene across the room, he watched as the hooded freaks toyed with the roped up German shepherd. He crept forward as Alistair's footfalls ascended the stairs.

Steadying the rifle, he tiptoed closer to Sage, feeling eager to spill more of the monsters' blood.

Sage glanced up with a strident bark, blowing his not-so-well thought-out ambush.

With astounding dexterity, they turned and ran at him, abandoning tormenting the dog for the moment.

Despite nerves shaking his hand, he squeezed the trigger and stared in amazement as the fastest of the three collapsed into the fungus, slid through the dirt, and crashed into the wall with a sickening thud. For a quick second, it twitched on the ground and then went limp. He hoped it was out of commission for good—or at least long enough to take out its two companions.

Twenty yards away, he watched crimson eyes burn with brutish abhorrence as they charged. Their tentacles snapped with furious agility, dislodging the hoods from their grotesque faces. Stepping back, he squeezed hard with clenched teeth. Dirt sprayed to the left as they continued to bear down on him. He had time for one last shot. Trying to stay calm, he blinked his eyes and concentrated.

Make it count, or you're gonna be dinner.

He inhaled deeply as sharp claws swept through the air, missing his face by a few inches. Ducking backward, he fired and felt warm guts spray through his hair, soaking his face and chest. Half-choking on the grotesque liquid, he grinned as a green fountain watered the glowing toadstools under his feet. He took another step backward, barely avoiding a lumbering left clawed hand, and chuckled as the headless monster fell dead on the slimy ground.

Sage continued to bark in the distance.

Caught off-guard, he tried to sidestep the leaping beast but took the full brunt of its knobby head instead. He wheezed as air deserted his lungs and felt the cocky grin disappear from his face. The rifle slipped through his fingers, skidded across loose dirt, and landed on the stairwell as the soft mushrooms cushioned his blow.

From above, it pounced on his chest with a hollow thump.

With horrid breath, its face lunged forward, snapping for his jugular, but sank its fangs into his arm instead. Struggling with its weight, he dug his feet into the dirt and scooted sideways, barely avoiding another painful bite. He kicked with every ounce of energy his exhausted legs could muster but failed to slide out from underneath the heavy weight. Feeling his strength drip away, he gritted his teeth and pushed as another mouthful of saliva dripping fangs targeted his neck.

In the background, Sage's barks steadied his nerves.

He closed his eyes, searching for strength, and kicked wildly for freedom. Instead, agonizing shrieks pained his ears as the beast slapped its tentacles wildly at the air and leaped to its feet.

Rolling to his right, he eyed the scene as breath slowly returned to his lungs. Alistair stumbled backward toward the earthen stairs with the enraged beast closing the gap.

Though still dizzy, he reached into the mushrooms and grabbed the rifle. He swung it easily up in front of him and hurried toward Alistair.

"Hey!" he yelled.

With the barrel inches from its head, the creature spun around with hate-filled eyes. He screamed a war cry as an unexpected swipe opened five shallow gashes across his neck. "Eat this," he screamed and fired the rifle, sending the last bullet through its brain.

Alistair stumbled and fell backward onto the bottom step.

Calmly, he pulled another clip from his pocket and loaded the chamber. After jerking Alistair to his feet, he marched across the room toward Sage, stopped at the first monster he shot and nudged it with his boot. Uncertain if life still beat through its black heart, he pulled the trigger and watched every fang in its circular mouth shatter. With a pounding heart, he dropped the weapon, ran across the room, and untied the loose knot around Sage's neck.

Sage licked his hand.

"Come on, boy, Josie's waiting for us," he said and turned toward the exit.

Across the room, Alistair screamed and pointed at the ceiling.

In the center of a domed ceiling, a silver-haired man draped in dark red robes floated down from the upstairs well. He waved his hands through the air as an evil smirk streaked across his radiant black skin.

Across the room, Alistair backed into the stairwell.

Ryan raced across the floor, dove headfirst into the slimy fungus, and grabbed the rifle as he rolled onto his back and glared at the dark man. "Stay back," he shouted with intentions of opening three holes into the magical floating man.

"You killed my pet's boy," he said, wiggling his fingers. "Plan to pay with your life."

Holding his malevolent dark gaze, Ryan felt numb.

"*Casa par freer tama*," the man mumbled while waving both hands high in the air. Dark haze drifted from his fingertips and swirled like two miniature tornadoes. As both hands swept down through the air, the tornadoes merged into one, gathered speed and exploded into Ryan's chest with breathtaking force.

His bones tightened as ice flowed through his veins. Every muscle in his body froze. He couldn't move as paralysis infested his bones. The silver-haired magician floated toward the ground above him.

Alistair dove through the air, intending to tackle the lanky man, but screamed in pain as an invisible force knocked him backward into the mushrooms.

The magician drew a small red-bladed dagger from inside his robe. "Now you die," he whispered and ran the flat side of blade across Ryan's chest. He turned the knife vertically, intending to plunge it deep into Ryan's heart. Instead, an agonizing grin twisted his once-confident face.

Feeling invisible fingers release his bones, he collapsed onto the ground beside Alistair and watched Sage cling to the man's leg with his teeth. With no hesitation, he grabbed the gun and pulled the trigger. As the bullet exploded from the barrel, the man muttered in a strange language and vanished into thin air.

Sage fell to the ground with a soft whimper.

Alistair stared wide-eyed. "What was that?"

"I'd say he was their leader."

Sage barked in agreement.

"Come on," Ryan said and hurried toward the stairs.

Sage and Alistair followed him back up the spiral staircase, through the large room, and back along the short corridor leading to the village. Once out of the room, Ryan closed the door and took a deep breath of fresh air in hopes of drowning out the sour taste of blood lodged deep in his throat.

"Thanks for saving my butt back there," he said, offering his hand to Alistair.

Alistair shook it. "No, my friend, thank you," he said. "If it weren't for you and your friends, I'd still be their prisoner. I don't even want to think about what kind of things they had in store for me."

"I hope you can get the old man back to your village. I'd help you, but I really need to catch up with the others."

"No worries. I can manage."

"Sorry we couldn't find your cousin."

"I'm going back to my village and finding volunteers to come back here. If there's anyone left alive, we'll find them."

"Good luck to you, my friend."

Alistair handed him the flashlight. "You too," he said and disappeared around the corner.

He drew in a few more deep breaths of fresh air and then led Sage back through the trap door, feeling anxious to be out of this world.

92

A vaporous mist swirled through the air and filled her lungs. Unlike the water she plunged into minutes earlier, the mist hovered around her head as if gravity had abandoned the space. Every ache and pain from the past few hours numbed as she inhaled cavernous breaths of the sugary-sweet blue mist. Energy rushed through her veins as her feet shuffled toward a lighted gateway in the distance.

Reaching for the gateway, Alyssa closed her eyes and ran through.

Opening her eyes, she stood in a shallow pool of the same disgusting water as in the cavern in the largest forest she had ever seen. Warm tropical air felt heavenly on her skin. Every ounce of pain in her body surrendered to the healing qualities of the misty vapor.

Feeling rejuvenated, she splashed through the water and stood on the bank and admired the breathtaking scenery a few seconds. Her eyes glimpsed a dirt path cutting through the massive forest. Dozens of different-sized footprints ran both ways on the trail.

Here goes nothing, she thought and pulled the pistol from her jeans.

Amazed by her sudden adrenaline rush, she ran with both speed and endurance along the path, hoping to catch up to the monster. With the extra weight of dragging a man, she felt confident in her ability.

In the distance, strident shrieks disrupted the peace. The familiar screech filled her heart with rage. The creature she saved

Tommy from made the same noise after it sunk its teeth through his neck. With death on her mind, she hurried around a corner, hoping to catch up in time to save Kelly, and stopped dead in her tracks.

The beast knelt on the grass beside Kelly with its face buried in his throat.

Sudden horror chased away her confidence. She waved the pistol with a shuddering hand at the monster and picked up her pace with intentions of closing the gap. Fearing Kelly might be too far gone to save, she squeezed the trigger. Peebles exploded inches from Kelly's legs but interrupted the monster's feast.

With incredible speed, it jumped off the ground and landed on two muscular feet with eyes of fire burning through her confidence.

Steadying her hand, she stopped running and remembered the mesmerizing gaze. With her confidence dwindling by the second, she closed her eyes and fired. Clamorous bells rang through her ears as a boisterous shriek echoed through the trees. With reluctance, she opened her eyes.

The monster galloped down the path and disappeared around a corner.

Despite warm air gently blowing through her hair, she shivered at the grotesque sight of the man she knew as Kelly Bissell.

93

Anxious to get back to Gastons Gorge, Ethan led the bewildered band along the path. It seemed like hours since last seeing Ryan. After a short rest near the clearing, he led them along the path through the forest toward the magical portal leading into the mineshaft.

How long does one night last here? he thought and glanced at the sky. *It seems we've been gallivanting around this world for days.* A colossal moon loomed high above, lighting the path. He remembered the sun setting not long before battling the monster in the weeds. *That seemed like a lifetime ago,* he thought as every muscle in his body began to ache. Feeling exhausted, he thought of home. More than anything, he wanted to go home and take care of Lauren and Josie.

A loud explosion chased away his pleasant thoughts of home.

"Ethan," Josie shouted, tugging on his hand.

"That sounded close."

"Really close," she said.

Eyeing the path ahead, he readied the weapon, anticipating danger. After everything he witnessed the past few hours, nothing could surprise him. *If flesh-eating octopuses kept human slaves in a parallel universe,* he thought. *Anything was possible.*

A second shot echoed through the forest.

"That's gunfire!" Josie shouted.

"Stay here," he said. "I'm gonna check it out." Waving her back, he jogged cautiously along the path.

A large figure galloped around a corner and stopped on the roads edge at the sight of him.

He aimed the rifle, ready to shoot if he had to.

"It's one of those things," Josie shrieked from behind. "Shoot it!"

Obediently, he pulled the trigger.

Tossing all four tentacles in the air above its head, it howled like a wolf under a full moon as dirt sprayed inches from its feet. Wailing in what he perceived to be anger, it rushed into the woods and vanished in an impenetrable green forest.

"Let's go," he said. "I don't think we'll be seeing that thing anymore."

Despite his words, he walked backward on the side of the grass aiming the barrel where the monster broke into the forest until they rounded the corner. Feeling relieved, he took a deep breath and chased after the group.

"Ethan," Josie shouted. "Come see this."

A lone figure stood on the path with the small pistol in her right hand lowered at the sight of the pathetic-looking caravan. Tears filled her eyes as she extended her left arm in a waving motion.

"Alyssa," Josie shouted.

Behind her, a body lay on the side of the path. As he approached, he saw Kelly Bissell staring lifelessly at the sky with half of his throat ripped out.

94

Ryan emerged from the opening with Sage at his side. He turned the flashlight off, intending to save the batteries for the journey back through the underground mine and into the hotel. Thankful to be alive, he walked through the high grass toward the field of mutant undergrowth. The journey back to the portal would be long, but in a few hours, the nightmare would be over. His thoughts went to Ethan.

Hopefully one of the girls Shawn and Josie rescued was Lauren.

"With any luck," he said to Sage. "Maybe both Tommy and Ethan will have happy endings."

Warm air blowing across the grass steadied his nerves. Taking a deep breath of the fresh air, he felt a sense of tranquility fill his heart as he turned around and took one last look at the opening in the large hillside. "Come on, Sage, let's go home," he said, turning back toward the colossal moon hovering above the nightmarish field.

95

His shoulder throbbed, but the wounds in his neck blazed like wild fire under his skin. His bones throbbed with agonizing pain. Blood boiled hot in his veins. Alyssa had been gone at least a few hours, but the pain had gone from bearable to agonizing in that short time.

You're buzzard meat, he thought as the agony cramped his legs. *Unless they come back soon and plop your rump in that wheelbarrow, you're buzzard meat.* Feeling more exhausted with each passing minute, he dry swallowed and continued to look at the disgusting puddle of water in anticipation of Alyssa's return. Fortunately, he was getting used to the foul stench. Fatigue weighed down his mind, and every muscle in his body felt like razor blades were being scraped across his flesh from the inside.

Poisoned, he thought and grinned. *You were done in with gosh darn monster venom of all things.*

The room darkened as his eyes began to sting. Sharp pains tore through his head and rippled through his entire body. Rather than deal with the agonizing swelling in his eyes a moment longer, he closed them tightly and hoped the pain would pass.

96

Feeling once again rejuvenated from the journey through the mist, Ethan waddled through the pool of water and stared in disbelief at Jennifer's body slumped against the side of the wall with a crushed skull.

Tommy leaned against the opposite wall with his eyes shut.

As the prisoners splashed through the water hole behind him, Ethan felt a low pulse in Tommy's wrist. His breathing was shallow, but life still flowed through his veins. Alyssa warned them about Jennifer, but he expected to see Tommy all wide-eyed and happy to see them.

Josie and Alyssa stood behind him.

With concern in her eyes, Alyssa hurried to Tommy's side and reached for his wrist and then glanced up at Ethan.

"He's alive, but barely," he said. "What happened?"

"It bit into his neck, but he was all right when I left."

Josie knelt beside her, running her hand gently across her back. "Maybe their bites are poisonous."

"I doubt it, Josie, I was bitten a long time ago, just before Ryan finished it off in that weed field."

"Maybe he had a bad reaction," she said, "like an allergy or something."

Ethan felt wonderfully stronger than ever. Despite the length of the coal mine, he thought he could carry Tommy to safety. The walk was long, a few miles at the least, but something had to be done soon, or he would die down here. "I can carry him," he said, turning to look at Alyssa.

She said nothing, only stared peculiarly at the eight people standing near the portal. She appeared lost in thought.

"Alyssa!"

A strange smile rested on her lips. "Look at them," she said. "They're different somehow. That mist made them better."

With curious eyes, he turned and stared. "Holy cow, you're right," he said. "Lauren and the others do seem more alert." He glanced at the water and remembered crossing over earlier in the day. "I felt re-energized after swallowing a few mouthfuls of that stuff." He rubbed his shoulder and smiled. Both my shoulder and back feel great. He felt rejuvenated. "Oh wow," he said and climbed to his feet. "Let's get him in the water and see what happens."

Without waiting for help, he reached under Tommy's shoulders, dragged him across the floor, pulled him into the water hole, and shoved his head under the surface. Smiling at both girls, he dove under the water and held Tommy at the bottom.

Hope you know what you're doing.

After what felt like an eternity, Tommy's eyes opened wide.

Excited, he grabbed the back of his friend's shirt and swam to the surface. Waiting by the edge of the water, Alyssa and Josie pulled Tommy out of the mist.

"How do you feel?" Alyssa said and wrapped her arms around his waist.

Realizing Alyssa's feelings for Tommy ran deeper than just friendship, Ethan smiled, grabbed Josie's hand, and walked across the cavern to where the prisoners stood on the far side of the cavern. Lauren looked beautiful despite the ragged leather hides fastened around her waist. Both her long blonde hair and complexion seemed somewhat rejuvenated after crossing between worlds. Where sores and blemishes stood out like a bad rash a few minutes earlier, smooth clear skin radiated her youthful face.

The mist healed their physical wounds. Hopefully it will heal their mental wounds as well. They probably endured more mental abuse than he could imagine. All your years living in mental institutions was probably like a trip to Disney World in comparison to what these people must have endured. With any luck, the magic mist will speed along their recovery. At least she is home.

"Do you know who I am?"

She stared into his eyes. "You're Ethan, my brother."

He kissed her forehead as tears dripped from his eyes. "Yes, sweetheart, I'm your brother."

"You found me."

"I had some help, but, yes, I finally found you."

After another brief hug, he pulled away and noticed the expressions of disbelief on the faces of the other seven people.

Beside him, Josie wept.

He squeezed her hand gently and smiled. "Is everyone all right?"

Tommy and Alyssa walked across the room and stood beside them. Tommy looked exhausted and mildly bruised but otherwise seemed to be his normal self. A grimace formed on his face as he stared at the men and women.

Too ashamed to hold Tommy's gaze, Ethan dropped his head upon realizing his friend's brother wasn't amongst the survivors.

"You tried," Tommy said and patted his shoulder. "I'll be forever in your debt, kid, I'll never forget what you guys, Ryan, Shawn, and Sage did for me."

"Shawn didn't make it," he said, feeling even more mortified. "He died saving their lives."

"What about Ryan and Sage?"

"We think Sage might have been killed. Ryan went back for him. I guess he felt he owed the dog that much. I don't know where he's at."

Tommy grinned, "I'm sorry, Josie, I know you love Sage," he said with compassion in his voice. "But we have to do what Shawn asked and blow this portal."

"Yeah, we are," he said, "but we're waiting for Ryan."

"Ethan, you can't—"

"No, Tommy, we're waiting."

"Okay, for a little while, then we blow it."

He was right, but he owed it to Ryan not to obliterate his only way back home. They only knew each other a few days, but Ryan had become like a brother to him. How many people would risk their life to help a stranger, especially for something as mind-boggling as what they were forced to endure? *Tommy might be right*, he thought, *but Ryan deserved a little extra time to get back home.*

"All right, Ethan."

"Good," he said, "but I want you, Josie, and Alyssa to get them out of here. I'll wait for Ryan and then destroy it after he comes through."

"Yeah, I don't think so," Tommy said. "I think we'll leave this place together."

Ethan felt angry but decided arguing would prove pointless. Tommy had no right to decide his fate, but Ethan had a funny feeling Josie would want to stay with him. She could be stubborn, and he loved her for that amongst a number of other things.

"Where's the dynamite?"

Tommy pointed toward a black box sitting a few feet from Christopher's body.

He walked past the body, took a knee, and examined the shoebox-sized container Shawn's powerful firecracker arrived in. A thin metal latch fastened the top of the box to its base. Trying to be careful, he unclipped the latch and slid the lid from the top.

"Tommy, come here a minute."

Hurrying across the room, Tommy squatted beside him. "That will work," he said and smiled. "It's a bomb. It has a timer and all."

"Think we can set it?"

"Yeah, I know I can!"

"Then set it."

Tommy flicked a narrow red switch, and a green screen lit up. Seconds later, numerical codes filled the screen. With dexterous fingers, Tommy flipped through Shawn's green notebook and then entered a code on a small black keyboard. He felt like the world's biggest idiot as he watched Tommy work the keys like a professional hacker.

"We can set the timer from one second to four hours," Tommy said and glanced up with a heartfelt smile. "You make the call, buddy."

"Four hours, let's give Ryan as much time as possible."

"Consider it done," he said, running his fingers across the keyboard. After pressing a few buttons, Tommy slid the box closer to the water and closed the lid. He tapped the lid and rose to his feet. With a look of triumph on his face, he walked toward the others.

"What about him?" Ethan said pointing at Christopher.

"What about him?"

"Should we just leave him lying here?"

"Doesn't matter," Tommy said, "in four hours, this place will be buried underneath tons of earth."

"I don't know, Tommy. If anyone finds the body, they'll ask questions."

"Not in this town."

Ethan scowled. "Maybe not. Gastons Gorge has a way of overlooking the details," he said, staring at his reflection in the water. "I have a feeling there might be more people keeping those thing's secret then we think."

"All right, kid, tell me what you're thinking."

"I say we toss him in the water."

Tommy laughed. "Why didn't I think of that?"

"Josie," he said, "I need you a minute."

She hurried across the room with a frolicsome look on her face.

He pointed to Christopher. "Me and Tommy are gonna toss his body in the water. Get them moving," he whispered. "I don't think it's necessary for them to watch us doing that."

"No problem," she said and then hurried toward Alyssa and the others.

Looking around, he saw no sign of Gregory Stephens "Where's the redhead."

"What redhead?"

"You know. The big, burly guy posing as a cop."

Tommy glanced around nervously. "I don't know, kid."

97

Monstrous shadows shimmered across the hillside.

The luminosity of the large moon proved a more than competent coconspirator in his effort to get back home. Unlike earlier in the evening when he tracked down Ethan under an ominous sky, silver moonlight guided him through the field. Hoping to preserve the batteries, he carried the flashlight at his side. It would serve him better in the coalmine.

Emerging from the weeds, they hurried toward the trail carved through the front of the steep cliff. Staying a few feet ahead, he led Sage up the path with hopes of arriving back at the puddle before Ethan and the others destroyed his only way home. As they approached the top, Sage growled.

He reached for the dog's collar but missed.

Sage dashed passed his outstretched arm and disappeared over the summit toward something out of Ryan's line of sight.

Trusting the dog's instincts, he raised the rifle and hurried forward on two exhausted legs. As much as he hated the thought of another painful and bloody battle, he felt ready for anything. Driven by sheer determination, he had no intension of dying in this godforsaken world. Ten minutes later, he stood on a ledge twenty feet from the top of the rock face, expecting another challenge as the dog's clamorous barking echoed from above.

"Sage," he shouted.

As the moon ducked behind a cloud darkening the landscape, a silhouette peered down at him from above a quick second and then disappeared over the edge.

Sage whimpered.

Disregarding the sudden terror that spread through his body, he climbed with the rifle aimed where the silhouette stood and watched him seconds earlier. He was down to the final clip. He had four shots to exterminate whatever evil waited at the top. As he climbed over the top, the moon darted out from behind the clouds, revealing a familiar foe towering above Sage with a sick look of fascination on his face. Feeling his heartbeat rise, he dropped to his knees and pointed the weapon.

Gregory Stephens smiled.

"Get away from him," Ryan shouted.

He took a step forward toward Ryan.

"Stand still or I'll—"

"Or what? You'll shoot me?"

Ryan nodded.

"I think you've done that already, son."

Noticing an object in his hand, Ryan rose to his feet. Being careful not to stumble backward over the edge to certain death, he took a step back.

"How did that work out for you, son?" Gregory said with a bloodcurdling grin etched on his face. "I don't think you're very good at killing."

"Take one more step, and we'll find out."

As the smirk disappeared from his face, Gregory's arm flung forward.

Pain exploded across his forehead. Feeling lightheaded, he focused on Gregory Stephens and fired. As the ammo screamed through the trees behind his adversary, Ryan fell forward on two shaky knees. Though his world spun out of control, he attempted to squeeze off another round. Instead, the rifle slipped from his fingers.

Above him, Gregory kicked the rifle aside.

Ryan grabbed his leg and jerked, hoping to even the playing field. Despite a strong grip, his fingers slipped free as more pain shot through his head.

Menacing laughter rang out from above as the evil man kicked at his face.

Trying not to panic, he threw his arms across his face, hoping to get his bearings. His forearms took the brunt of the redhead's heavy boot. Grimacing, he rolled a few inches away from the vertical cliff as heavy blows continued to punish his arms. He maneuvered backward with hopes of getting to his feet. Instead, Gregory dropped on to his chest and landed blow after blow to his face. With unmatched strength, Gregory leaned forward, pinning his shoulders to the ground with both knees. "Where are your friends?"

Struggling to breath, Ryan said nothing.

With a smile, he balled up his oversized fist, raised it high in the air, and crashed it into Ryan's lips.

Hot blood stung his tongue.

"Where are your friends?"

"Dead," he said as blood trickled down his throat.

A familiar grin widened his lips. "That figures," he said and jerked his hand backward. "I was kind of hoping to have my way with that pretty redhead before Cornelius killed her."

Despite the agony torturing his face, Ryan felt sickened.

"It doesn't matter, son. I'll find other toys to play with. Besides, I'll take pleasure in watching you suffer."

Ryan attempted to wiggle free as Gregory's fist flew forward, but his adversary was too strong. He closed his eyes and waited for the blow.

Instead, Gregory collapsed onto the ground beside him as Sage's aggravated barks reverberated through the night air and disappeared above the treetops.

He jumped to his feet.

Wiping blood from his lip, he saw the rifle to the right of Gregory Stephens. As Sage battled the monster concealed in human flesh, he crept closer to the gun.

Sage whimpered as Gregory climbed to his knees.

Ryan lunged forward and reached for the weapon. Unsure how far away the man was, Ryan grabbed the barrel, spun around and swung the weapon like the Louisville Slugger. His fingers vibrated as the wood collided with the man's flesh and bone.

Gregory winced and stumbled forward. With rage in his eyes, he reached for Ryan.

Twirling the gun, he swung for the fences.

Steel thudded into the madman's shoulder as his hand snagged Ryan's shirt. With an agonizing screech, Gregory wobbled backward and tumbled over the hillside.

Knocked off-balance, Ryan broke free of the man's grip, staggered forward, lost his footing, and slid over the edge and fell to the ledge twenty feet below. Lying on his back, he watched Gregory dangle from the top of the cliff through blurry vision.

After a long struggle, he lost his grip.

Fighting to stay cognizant, he rolled sideways, hoping to avoid a collision with the falling man as he plummeted toward him. Moving too slowly, the fast-falling monstrosity slammed into his side, thudded off the path, and spiraled down the steep cliff.

Sage barked from the top of the hill.

Ryan collapsed on the flat ground, feeling lucky not to be plummeting down the side of the cliff like the madman man splattered on the ground below. Thankful to be alive, he closed his eyes and felt consciousness slip away

98

Minutes after the girls led the others into the coalmine, Ethan noticed the garbage littering the ground where they broke for a quick snack earlier in the day. Distracted by Ryan's unconventional pep talk and Gregory Stephens's sudden appearance, they forgot to clean up their mess.

Grabbing five empty bottles littered amongst crinkled sandwich baggies, he left Tommy and dashed to the far side of the room.

Tommy dropped the dead man's legs. "What are you doing?"

"Getting a refill."

Grinning, he gathered the bottles, splashed through the water, twisted off the lids, and submerged them one by one into the water. After a few seconds, he screwed the lid on the last bottle and ran back to Tommy, who stood by the corpse with a grin on his face.

"Grab his feet," Tommy said.

Obeying, he looked at Tommy. "On the count of three, we toss him in."

Tommy nodded.

"One," he said and swung the dead man's legs.

Tommy mimicked Ethan, staying in sync with his movement. "Two."

They looked like two men gripping opposite ends of a hammock and swinging a friend through the air. The ebb and flow was rhythmic, like a finely choreographed dance recitation that lacked toe-tapping music.

"Three."

They let go simultaneously.

Christopher tumbled through the air and into the water hole with a loud splash. A few seconds later, he sunk like a lead weight into the sea.

"I'll take care of her," Tommy said and stared at Jennifer.

With regret, he stepped aside and watched Tommy lift her from the cavern floor and carry her body to the water's edge. After kissing her forehead, he dropped to his knees, whispered into her ear, and rolled her body into the water with tears dripping from his eyes. After wiping away his tears, he stood up and looked at Ethan. "Let's get going, kid."

Being respectful, Ethan pretended not to notice the man's emotional breakdown. "I'll catch up," he said and walked toward the box. Taking a knee, he reached over and flipped the metal lid up. Something felt wrong. He thought of the man Ryan shot and wondered if he was actually dead. If not, where did he get off to? Seconds later, Gregory Stephens slipped from his mind. He felt hopeful. Ryan still had almost four hours to make it back through the portal.

Thinking of Ryan, he gathered the bottles and chased after the others.

99

Ryan's eyes opened wide.

The moon hung farther away in the night sky. Most of the brightness seemed to have burned away. The once colossal brilliance in the sky was now an unexciting shell of its former self. Unsure of how long he laid on the small ledge, he climbed to his feet. Dizziness swirled through his head, causing mild wavering in his legs. Afraid of slipping over the side, he climbed to his knees and waited for his vertigo to fade.

Sage approached from above. His tongue hung to the side of his mouth as he trotted down the path. After a soft bark, he licked the side of his face.

Ignoring the dog's sour breath, he stroked the top of his head and felt thankful to have met the dog.

With strength returning to his body, he climbed from the ledge and finished the uphill journey. Staying a few feet behind, he followed Sage through the forest, hoping to reach the gateway home before they destroyed it. Looking up, the stars proved the fateful night still continued, but he felt it was on the verge of ending. He wasn't sure how long he lay unconscious on the ledge, but he knew it had been a while.

Feeling exhausted and hungry, he wanted to go home to Gastons Gorge. Since Molly's death, Raging Gap never felt like his home. He could go and visit his parents whenever he had an urge; maybe Ethan, Josie, and Sage could go with him on those visits. Maybe even Lauren, if she was fortunate enough to be among the survivors they saved. For Ethan's sake, he prayed she was reunited with her brother. He thought of Tommy Carver and hoped his brother was rescued as well. He thought of his new friends as he followed Sage through the big woods.

He felt alone.

Ethan and Josie filled his thoughts. If not for them, he would not have escaped the first attack. With a smile, he glanced at Sage. His courage allowed Ethan to catch up with them in the basement. He could never leave them. Gastons Gorge would be the perfect place to start over and forget about the demons that have been haunting him for so long. Molly would be forever etched in his mind. He would always love her, but after the last few days, he felt confident his life could be normal again.

Up ahead, Sage barked.

Clutching the rifle, he sprinted toward Sage despite pain cramping his legs. As he approached, he saw Kelly Bissell dead on the ground with his throat ripped open. He closed his eyes, said a silent prayer, and continued on. Tired of seeing death, he left Kelly behind and prayed no one else suffered the same fate.

As a bloodred sun ascended the eastern sky, he spotted the water hole at the far end of the path. Glorious shades of red and orange hung along the horizon, reminding him of a magnificent painting he once saw in a high school art book. Looking at the beautiful scenery, he couldn't help but smile. Next to Molly, the sunset was the most gorgeous sight his eyes had ever witnessed.

Fighting tears, he stopped beside the portal and took a deep breath.

"Sage, come here, boy."

Obediently, Sage trotted to him.

He grabbed the dog by the collar and jumped into the water with one thought on his mind: returning to Gastons Gorge and assessing the aftermath of their unbelievable journey.

Thick mist filled his lungs and instantly dulled the pain hampering his body.

In the distance, dark blue silhouettes shimmered above the entrance to the coal mine. Feeling anxious to be far from a world where monsters feed on children, he broke into a fast jog. They were almost there, less than twenty feet away, when thunder erupted around him. A bluish wave swept forward and tossed them backward deeper into the unknown. Spinning out of control, he clutched the rifle in his right hand and squeezed tighter onto Sage's collar with his left hand as they rolled into oblivion. Dizziness filled his world as they continued spinning. Holding fast to the dog's collar, he closed his eyes and waited for the tidal wave to disperse.

100

"What are we going to tell them?" Ethan asked, helping the last escapee up through the opening.

Tommy frowned as he looked them over with skeptical eyes. "Jesus, kid, I didn't really think about what would happen afterward."

"Tell them the truth," Alyssa said, stepping forward, "Just tell them the truth."

Ethan laughed, "Seriously, are you crazy?"

"She's right," Josie agreed, "We tell them the truth. They might think we're crazy, but if we all maintain the truth of what happened, they can't do anything to us."

"Besides," Alyssa interrupted, "what possible story could we make up? These people have been missing for years and all at different times. We just can't pop into the police station and tell them we just so happened to find these people in an abandoned coal mine under the Deep Earth Hotel"

Tommy laughed mildly. "There are twelve of us. If we all say the same thing, then what can happen?"

"They'll probably lock me back up in the mental ward."

"Then they lock you up," Josie said, "but they'll have to lock all of us up."

"Then so be it," Ethan said and continued to walk through the hallway. He led them into the large room, up the creaking stairs, through the littered up lobby, and out the door into the bright sunlight. The chilly air felt wonderful on his skin.

101

A dog barked in the darkness.

He opened his eyes and saw the rifle lying on the ground a few feet away. Sitting up, he rubbed his head. Despite feeling slightly groggy, he felt reenergized.

Sage barked once more and then fell silent.

Beside him, a small pool of water bubbled into the ground and disappeared. A hollow pain beat through his heart as the realization of being trapped in this monstrous world suddenly overwhelmed him.

Ethan kept his promise.

With regret, he grabbed the rifle, rose to his feet and eyeballed the area for the dog. "Sage," he shouted and lowered the rifle to his side. Praying he wouldn't have to use it, he followed the path through the forest, scaled the cliff, hurried through the weeds, and sprinted through the cavern to the deserted village.

Sage trotted by his side.

Sometime later, he walked along the road toward Alistair's village, thinking of Ethan and the town of Gastons Gorge.

102

Josie moved in with Ethan to help care for Lauren. A few months later, they married. Alyssa visited every day, spending hours getting reacquainted with her best friend. Over the last few months, Ethan, Josie, and Alyssa taught her to read and write.

No longer afraid of the hotel, Ethan searched the basement and what was left of the old coal mine for Ryan Laville every other day. Though his friend never made it out of the coal mine, he knew deep down that Ryan still lived. As the months passed, the feeling grew stronger. Ryan filled his thoughts and dreams; it became a bizarre obsession he couldn't shake.

Lying in bed, he looked at his wife. "I know he's still alive. I can feel it."

"Stop doing this to yourself," Josie said. "He wouldn't want you to feel guilty."

"Maybe not, but he's trapped there because I didn't wait."

"Ryan made a choice," she said. "He felt he owed it to Sage to go back."

"Josie, he's alive. I can feel it in my bones."

She kissed his lips and rolled over.

"Maybe they both are."

Hours later, while she slept, he laid in bed staring at the ceiling and thought about Ryan Laville.

Just like Lauren, he couldn't shake the feeling that his friend was still alive in that world. The portal was gone, blown into oblivion. If Ryan was still alive, that magic gate was no longer a means to find him.

There's another way, he thought and closed his eyes.

His idea was brilliant, yet dangerous. The chance of death was high, but Ryan was worth the effort. He glanced at his wife and kissed her cheek. Josie and Lauren were two of the three most important people in his life. He loved them both more than anything, but he loved Ryan too, and Ryan deserved to be rescued.

Tomorrow morning, he intended to make the journey to the Peaceful Lady with a bottle of magical mist. Tomorrow, he would visit with his old cellmate and former best friend. Hopefully, he would acquire the most important thing of his lifetime.

Devon Whitfield is owed a wish.

CPSIA information can be obtained at www.ICGtesting.com
Printed in the USA
LVOW10s0356140716

495511LV00010B/134/P